Wildflowers

A Novel

Delores Lowe Friedman

ISBN: 1974638596
ISBN 13: 9781974638598
Library of Congress Control Number: 2017914758
CreateSpace Independent Publishing Platform
North Charleston, South Carolina

*This book is dedicated to my husband, Karl, my cherished
muse, my constant inspiration for almost fifty years,
and the love of my life; and
to my son, Ian, who never ceases to excite and amaze me with
his gifts of a keen intellect, courage, and goodness.
He makes us proud every day.*

ACKNOWLEDGMENTS

Family and friends have encouraged my writing in many ways over the years. My husband, Karl, was the driving force in my beginning as a published author of nonfiction in 1978, when I authored the education column in *Essence* magazine, called Education by Degrees. He was the initial editor of my first book, *Education Handbook for Black Families*, published by Doubleday in 1980. He supported my doctoral studies at Teachers College, Columbia University and my scholarly writings.

From the time we met in 1970, however, when he first read snippets of my jottings, he encouraged my writing fiction, from my poetry to short pieces of poesy, to children's books, and this novel, *Wildflowers*. A talented playwright, he has tirelessly supported my writing, always eager to read what I next wrote. He has read major and minor changes in *Wildflowers* to answer my concerns on the slimmest nuances of meaning.

My son, Ian Friedman, a gifted software engineer, has helped me with software and computer support at any time of the day or night. He has been a bright light in my husband's and my life since he was conceived and born. Most recently, when I lost my way, finding no time for my writing because life got in the way, he said, "From what I hear from friends, you must get out of the house to write. Go out; bring your laptop." He was right, and he is the one who is responsible for my finishing *Wildflowers*. A lifelong friend, Alan Goff, a Buddhist, said when he first saw Ian when he was just a month old, "Let me see what soul chose to come and live with the two of you." I am grateful Ian chose us.

I would also like to acknowledge some friends and family members for reading the book and for their encouragement and support over the years in good times and difficult times. I would like to thank Nancy Mintz, my dear friend, who didn't live to see *Wildflowers* published but who read it and encouraged me to finish it, and her husband Richie Okon for his kindnesses; and my friend Myrna Rivera and her husband, Joe Gonzalez, who have always been there for us, and who have already suggested a fine translator for *Wildflowers* into Spanish.

I would like to thank my beta readers, Rose Ranieri Crosby, my friend from fourth grade, who read *Wildflowers* through three of its iterations; Christine Rose Pollice; Donna Laurin; Barbara Dodick; Iris Plafker; and Katrina Greenswan for reading and for all their feedback. Their reactions lifted me up, and propelled me forward.

I would also like to thank my family—my mother, Louise Lowe, who was a creative spirit in my world; my father, Lloyd Lowe, who always made me think; and my sister, Barbara Lowe for her encouragement, all of whom believed in my writing when I began *Wildflowers* years ago.

Lastly, I want to thank two people who were instrumental in my beginnings as a writer. First, Marcia Gillespie, gave me my start as a professional writer, by granting me the opportunity to do my column, Education by Degrees when she served as Editor-in- Chief at *Essence* magazine. I will be eternally grateful to her and to *Essence* magazine for that beginning. And I would like to thank the person who gave me permission to write fiction, Mrs. Klein, my fourth grade teacher in PS 77 in Brooklyn. She unveiled a library of classics to my class and said, "Now you get to read the good stuff." She handed us journal notebooks and encouraged us to write about the books we read and the passages we loved. She would read our writings and respond—validating the power of our words. She later set us on the task of writing our own fiction. Reading and writing have been my escape, my solace, and my joy ever since. Thank you, Mrs. Klein.

1

CAMILLE

Right after Ruby's death, I started reading the obituaries. I stopped a couple of years later, because it seemed morbid. But in the past few months, I found myself searching through them again, because friends and relatives seemed to die for no good reason.

I never saw anyone I knew personally in the obits after Ruby, but every so often I turned to the section and read through the names, anticipating anyone I might know. Lately, I hadn't even been reading the news. Too depressing. Instead, I poured myself a second cup of coffee, pushed my glasses up on the bridge of my nose, opened the *New York Times*, and immediately turned to the columns titled Deaths. And today Death did not disappoint. It had taken another friend, or rather a memory of a friend.

"Jewel Jamison dead at 64. The founder and head of Onyx Management, America's premiere entertainment agency in black media, died in her penthouse apartment in New York City. The publicist for the agency said there are no surviving relatives. Provisions are being made to continue the agency despite the loss of its founder."

I searched for my cell phone in my pocketbook beneath my keys and a half-eaten bag of pretzels. Three missed calls told me she knew. My voice mail confirmed it.

"Camille, call me" was the first message.

"Camille, you'll never guess who's dead. Give me a call" was the second message.

The third message just said, "Jewel's dead. Call me. Gotta tell you, girl. Call me."

I thought I heard a snicker in her voice. I touched the Call Back button. The phone rang only once. "Camille, hated to leave the message like that…"

"Saundra, I know. I just read it in the *Times*."

"I saw it on this Black Enterprise News show on cable."

"Did they say what she died of?"

"No, but they said she was sick for more than a year. The hospice nurse said that she died alone in her apartment…no visitors in months."

"Just like I said. Remember how she was that last…never mind." I had said too much.

"You didn't listen to me. I kept tryin' to tell you…" She paused, and the silence filled my ear. "When did we…"

"I don't know. I tried…couldn't fix it…" I felt a pang of guilt.

"Those black movies, with the girlfriends' arms wrapped around each other, with some soulful music playing in the background— that's not real."

I didn't know how it had all started. Saundra's comments boxed me in with it. "I don't know." I felt an edge in my voice, and there was a bitter taste in my mouth.

"This is 2012, then…was it twenty years ago that we got back together? Camille, where did the time go?" Saundra muttered something, but I was too trapped in my memories to hear her.

"Time took us in different directions," I said out loud before I could edit myself. "Things were said that couldn't be unsaid." I feared that I was not faultless, and my own regret was hidden in my memories like a timeworn stone.

I tried to piece together my recollections to understand what had gone so wrong between us…when? I recalled that I had reached out to Saundra and to Jewel because of the deep void I felt. I remembered it was the fall of 1992...

> September 8, 1992
> There are no wildflowers in Williamsburg. There were only the occasional dandelions that grew in the cracks of the sidewalks just because they felt like it, and so the children could pick them on their way to school. "You want a wish?" one little girl said as she gave one to me. All of them were gone now. Desperation about surviving permeated the air.

I wrote in my journal the morning of the first day of school that year in my last few moments of solitude. Septembers always made me tense. It was the timing. Beginnings of the ends. The night before, I had put away my writings and my watercolors and mentally given up my whenever-we-want-to time reading to my son, Shawn. I was facing the new school year at PS 31 in the midst of the teeming tenements of Williamsburg, which spilled their contents out into the streets like so much wasted milk.

It was 6:25 a.m., and I was already late. I gulped the last of my coffee down and woke Shawn. It was his first day of kindergarten, so he rushed into the bathroom without being told and came to the table to eat his Cheerios, already carrying his backpack.

"I have my pencils, and my sharpener, and my notebook, and my crayons," he said, dropping it on the floor next to him.

I remember putting him on the school bus at 110th Street and Central Park North. He said, "What do I have for lunch, Ma?" and I said, "Tuna sandwich," and he said, "Yum!" He climbed the stairs of the bus and waved, and the doors closed behind him. I trekked down the stairs into the subway, with its offensive odors stuffing themselves into my nostrils and people pushing past me. I slid my token into the slot, pushed through the turnstile, and rushed to get into the D train as the doors closed. I got out at Fourteenth Street, made my way to the

M train, and finally walked down the stairs from the el to Flushing Avenue.

It was barely eight o'clock, and it was already wet hot. Down on the street, young girls with painted faces sauntered about pushing baby strollers, stretching themselves up to see and to be seen. Old women with sagging cheeks and fingers like fat sausages, weighted down with sacks of food, tugged toddlers along beside them. On the side street near the school, men sat wearing white athletic shirts, slapping dominoes on card tables tilted toward nowhere in particular. Strains of *merengue* and salsa spilled from windows with a booming, garbled rap, creating a cacophony, which intruded into everyone's consciousness. No wildflowers.

When I got in to the school, Ruby Greene, the principal and my dear friend, and Saul Elliot, the other assistant principal, asked me to come into the office. They had a list of eight new students we needed to place. I suggested we place them with the teachers we knew would welcome them and not squawk, at least not for them to hear. Saul called the custodian to ask for additional chairs to be brought up while I went out to the yard to deliver the news to the teachers.

"Ms. Warren, you have got to be kidding me," a wonderful young teacher whispered to me, pointing to the long line of students already in front of her. As I looked into the eyes of the children standing on line talking to their friends, I spotted one little one tapping the child in front of him and then ducking to hide. They always made me laugh. They made fun out of so little. But now, seeing the long line of children twisted me up inside. Budget cuts throughout the city had left us reeling, and there was no end in sight. There was a sense of hanging on by one's fingernails.

It was two thirty when Mrs. Salgano, the school aide, came into the book room, where I was doing inventory and looking for additional books for too many children.

"Sylvia said she needs you in the office right away." The look on her face made me anxious.

"What's the matter?"

"I don't know. She just called me in and said to run and go get you."

I put down the worn reader with its frayed cover, clapped the dust from my hands, and grabbed one of the wet paper towels I had been using to wipe away the grime on the bookshelves. I caught sight of myself in the broken pane of glass in the door leading to the hallway. I was glad I had gotten my hair cut, because my Afro was in place. I frowned at my too-full face. I tucked my blouse into my skirt and walked as fast as I could, trying to catch up with the tiny woman, who always seemed in a hurry.

As a second-year assistant principal, I had been called to the office like that only once before, when Shawn was ill. When that thought came back to me, I held my breath, scared to death. In my mind's eye, I saw him waving good-bye as he got on the school bus this morning. I could not breathe. My mother said I was always fearful because he was a "late-life baby" and my only. I walked as fast as I could.

As I entered the outer office, the secretary, Sylvia, ran out of the principal's office and began talking so fast I could hardly tell what she was saying.

"Ms. Warren, I called 911 twice already. It's Mrs. Greene. She's in there."

I moved past her into the principal's office to find my friend, Ruby, slumped in the chair behind her desk. A small paper cup had overturned on it, and water was seeping into layers of paper with fading ink. I heard Sylvia's raised shrill voice say, "But this is the third time I am calling."

It was strange to see Ruby so crumpled. She was a tall, strapping woman with square shoulders and the same proud, erect bearing that my grandmother had tried to instill in me. "Stand up straight," she'd say.

"Camille?" Ruby tried to summon a smile. "I need to lie down." Her strong, booming, preacher-like voice was now thin and reedy.

Her mahogany-brown skin had lost its reddish cast and now seemed like gray clay that could be pushed and squeezed into any expression one wished. I took her arm and tried to support her back to move her to the sofa while Ruby rested herself against the wooden desk. Then I felt Ruby's weight give way, slipping out of my grip a little at a time, and then tumbling, like one of the huge sacks of rice Ma would buy when I was a girl. I could feel Ruby's body escape from my grasp and hit the floor, elbow, wrist, hand. Once her body rested there, I cradled her head. I wanted to tell her how much I had learned from her.

"Camille, call my son. His number is over there." Her finger lifted and seemed to indicate a direction near her desk, though I wasn't sure where.

"Ruby, don't you worry. We've called for an ambulance, and everything will be fine."

Her eyes flashed, stopping my words of comfort in my mouth and stuffing them down my throat. The fear and anger in Ruby's eyes seemed to squeeze all sound from the room. It was curious how quiet it became at that moment. I had grown accustomed to Ruby's strength. She was like so many of Ma's church-lady friends. She was unflappable. This stare was unnerving. It seemed to say she was outraged at her body for betraying her. It demanded my honesty. I tried to tell her I loved her with my eyes, but despite how I tried, Ruby seemed to slip off to a space far away. The room fell silent.

The paramedics disturbed the calm. They pushed their way into the small space. The tall man took hold of Ruby's wrist while the short, sturdy woman asked me what had happened.

"I have pain here," Ruby said, taking charge for a brief moment and then gasping to take in air. Her eyes rolled back in her head. The two paramedics pushed me out of the way. The man hovered over her and began pounding on her chest, rhythmically bobbing up and down, while the woman darted from one place to another, bringing in a metallic suitcase and then a rolling stretcher.

The female paramedic commanded us to step back out of the way. Her tenor voice pushed me back against the wall. Then there was a mask placed over Ruby's face, and they lifted her up and out. They said something about Woodhull Hospital, and they were gone, leaving a gaping hole in the room.

"Ms. Warren, I didn't know what else to do. I called them three times." The blood pooled itself in Sylvia's pale neck and chest as she shook her head and stared into my eyes as if she were asking for an answer.

I squeezed her hand. "They'll take care of her. Don't worry."

Sylvia looked up at the clock, and shook her head in disbelief. "The hospital is barely around the corner, and it took them twenty-five minutes."

"Sylvia, just ring the first bells for dismissal. I'm going to call Ruby's son."

I went into Ruby's office, behind her desk, and searched for the paper she had spoken of on the bulletin board to the side of her chair. I couldn't use her phone, because it felt wrong, so I went to the outer office to call. Before I could pick up that phone, Claudia Rodriguez came into the office speaking half in English and half in Spanish, dragging her two-year-old grandson behind her. "Qué pasò con la principal? She sick or something?" The elderly woman pushed her hair back and tucked it into the bun at the back of her head. She rested her hands on the center of the partition that separated her from the school officials.

Saul Elliot pushed his way past the woman, threw open the gray swinging door, and turned back to secure it with a latch.

"The ambulance just took Ruby. I think it's her heart," I whispered to Saul. "I just rang the bell for dismissal."

I turned to Claudia and patted her hand. "We don't know anything yet. No sabemos nada, ahora. Mañana de la mañana nosotros esperamos a saber mas, pero…ella esta en el hospital, Woodhull." My Spanish was good. I could tell by the look in Claudia's eyes that she understood me.

"Ay Dios, mio!" she said, shaking her head from side to side as if to say no and then crossing herself. "I will pray for her."

When I turned my attention back to Saul, I could see disapproval written all over his face. He had always bristled when I spoke with the Latino parents in Spanish. He turned on his heel and moved himself into Ruby's office and behind her desk. Saul Elliot was a short, balding man about fifty-five years old who had been an assistant principal at PS 31 for at least ten years. He was sweating profusely from the heat, but he always perspired, even in the winter.

"Weren't you taking care of the book orders, Mrs. Warren?" he said loud enough for everyone in the office to hear.

As usual, I could feel him trying to put me in my place. It was like having ice water thrown in my face. Ruby had told me when I was interning under Saul, just learn what he knows about organizing administrative matters. He hasn't a clue about people. Long after I passed the test for assistant principal, however, he had always pulled rank. Ruby said over a cup of coffee one day, "Two strong black women are too much for this little man to contend with. He can't help it." We both laughed, and somehow Saul seemed much more manageable after that.

"Sylvia, get me the superintendent's private line. Camille," he added in an off-handed way, "everything's under control here. You can go back to whatever you were doing."

"What about Ruby's son? I was about to call Ruby's son when you came in. Ruby needs someone there with her. If he can't come..."

"I will handle this. First things first. Like I said, Sylvia, get me the superintendent's private line."

I could feel my cheeks grow hot. I smoothed my cropped natural hair at the nape of my neck. I tried to squeeze the pain from the muscles at the base of my skull. Now, please don't make me go off on this man, I thought.

"No, no, no, no. No! I told Ruby I would call her son," I said, and I took the phone and dialed the number on the slip of paper I held in my hand.

"Under different circumstances I'd call this insubordination, Ms. Warren," Saul said.

I was so focused on the phone that I didn't even register his comment until after the phone had begun to ring. First I had to talk to Ruby's son. I told him what had happened and where she was. His voice broke, and then there was a click. I had such a sinking feeling in my chest, because I wasn't even sure I had said the right things to him. As I hung up, I saw Saul, who had planted himself in the doorway of Ruby's office. Seeing his sweaty little body taking possession of Ruby's space disgusted me. I tried to think of what to say to him and came up blank and turned to leave the office.

"I'll speak with you about this tomorrow morning," Saul sputtered at me.

His words hit me in the back of the head like small pebbles as I reached the doorway. I stopped. I turned back to face him and said, as slowly and deliberately as I could, "In case you haven't noticed, Saul, we are equals."

Over the next few days, I watched people Ruby didn't know say words about her. I watched them lower her into the ground. I left when they began to shovel dirt on top of her casket. My eyes filled with tears. I missed her deeply. I had let our workaday life interfere until our time together had run out. There had simply not been enough of it.

By the end of the first week, in my grief I cursed time. Then, as the days mourning Ruby's death grew, time seemed an endless chasm. I began an intellectual game, writing about and toying with the notion of it, touching its walls, probing, prodding it, to give myself some sense of it. My inquiry left me with an understanding that suited me and planted an urgency in my chest. It was not a definition of time, but rather a reflection on the nature of it. I knew that time had a way of stretching itself out and folding itself up, and it was hard to know where one was every so often.

Memories flooded in around me. Images from my childhood and college days filled my mind. I realized that while I was focusing on my career, I had lost touch with Saundra and Jewel, whom I had considered my family. I wondered where they were. I felt such loneliness. Then I remembered that that aloneness had begun long before I met them. I remembered feeling it first when I went to live with my grandmother. I called her Ma.

Before I began to write, I felt. I remembered feeling sad that I had lost my mother, that the woman was not where I thought she should be. Then I remembered that it was I who had been misplaced.

I can't say that I remembered that day. I later imagined that I did. It was one of those days that had been recounted to me so often that my memory, the retelling, and my imagination were tangled so tightly together that I could not sort it out. I imagined that spring stopped early in the morning of an April day in 1952 in Bed Stuy. The yellow buds of the forsythia had burst the woody stems the night before, and the faint breaths of green on the tips of the sycamore and maple trees that my grandmother had pointed out and named for me were now choked in the cold. Frost burned the young leaves and threatened to turn them back and make them retreat into darkness. Left was apprehension about newness and becoming. At least that was how I imagined it must have been.

A frigid, gray veil of damp surrounded the row of houses on Hancock Street. Pa's black forty-eight Buick, the pebble-embedded sidewalks, and the brownstone stoops all seemed to weep silently. The wildflowers, which had sprung up each year, finding their way into the small patch of soil against Ma's house, were hiding from the cold. A thick mist hung close to the window like a sad wet kiss above the spot where they once stood.

I was sleeping at Ma's house when the telephone rang. Ma woke me to pee. I could get up on my own. I never wet the bed anymore. I was four years old. But Ma woke me and pulled the potty out from under the bed. I sat drowsily down. She had neatly parted and plaited my hair in rows, which pulled my scalp too tightly. I was tired and waited to go back to bed after I pleased Ma with the golden liquid that seemed to mean so much to her. I did this only for Ma, and only on weekends when Mommy and Daddy went out for their time by themselves.

The old woman's heavy yellow-brown hands lay rested in the droop of her skirt like fat sticks of butter. She did not fuss with my undershirt strap, as she always did, twisting it flat, smoothing it out.

"Camille, honey, listen to Grandma. Your daddy and Eleanor aren't coming back here for you this morning."

It was strange that Ma never called my mother Mommy, or Ellie, the way Daddy did. She always called her Eleanor. I wondered why. I pulled up my panties and fixed the ribbon of elastic 'round my waist.

"Did you hear what I said, Camille? Stop playing with that and listen to me." She shook me.

"Your father is in the hospital, and Eleanor is locked up."

"Don't tell the child all that," Pa said. I didn't know where he was hiding.

"Well, it's true. She almost killed my son."

"You don't know all what happened yet, so hush," he said, trying to pat my head.

"I know my son is half dead, and the cops say that she was driving drunk."

"I said hush about all that in front of this child," he said, cupping his hands over my ears. "Eleanor is going to need our help. She doesn't have anybody else up here."

"Then you help her. I don't have it in me."

I looked at my grandmother's face, focusing on the tiny brown moles around her eyes. I remembered Mommy and Daddy saying they were going to a dance. I pictured them dancing in a big house. My father was swinging my mother around. My mother was giggling and saying, "Johnny, stop." I will go to the dance too, I thought. My father will pick me up and swing me 'round and 'round.

My grandmother was wiping water from her eyes.

"You're gonna stay here with Pa and me."

"Can't I go too, Ma? I want to go too."

"What are you talking about, chile? Didn't you hear what I just told you? My son is almost dead."

"Don't tell her that," Pa said. "Johnny...is in a coma, a deep sleep. Your daddy is sleepin', Camille," Pa said.

Daddy is sleeping. Daddy said that Penny, my dog, was sleeping, but I can't remember where. Grandma held me too tightly. I didn't like it.

"I know how to wake him up, Ma. Don't cry."

Ma stood up and walked into the hallway, disappearing into the shadows. I will wake Daddy up later, when Mommy comes to get me. I will climb into the bed and pull one of the feathers out of his pillow and brush it on his nose and then on his ear.

"Wake up, Daddy," I'll say. And he'll say, "Who is this lovely little lady?" And I'll say, "It's me, Camille."

2

SAUNDRA

"**Y**ou're gonna be sorry for dis, Mami." His black eyes focused on me. "You better not do dis." His words echoed through this place. It was as if he sucked the air out as he left. You'd think it'd be the opposite, but no. His absence and his words took up all the space. I felt as if I could choke.

It was the stench of him I tried to clean away. I came to the spot where he said he found jelly and crumbs before he hit me the last time. I know I didn't leave anything...crumbs here. I used Clorox this time. Strange—even though he wasn't here, my shoulders hunched, afraid that he might walk in at any moment. The odor of the bleach filled the air around me. I tried to rinse it off, but the slippery feeling on my fingers remained along with the smell.

The phone rang, made me jump. Didn't want to answer it. I felt like hiding inside myself. I covered the mouthpiece in case I decided not to speak. There was a voice I thought I knew. I switched the phone to my good ear.

"Yes?"

"Saundra? It's me, Camille."

"Camille? I don't believe it." I felt so alone, and there was a little light. "I was just thinkin' about you the other day." I sat down at the table, leaving the sponge on the counter.

"Cut it out." We both laughed.

I don't know how many times we had said those words. "I'm serious."

"How are you doin', girl?"

"OK, I guess. Tell me about you. What are you doin'? How's the baby?"

"What baby? Shawn's no baby anymore. He's a little man. Five goin' on fifty. He's so smart. Sometimes I wonder who's the parent. I'm fat. Size eighteen. Still tryin' to lose that fat from the baby."

"Yeah, I am too. My baby fat is almost a teenager."

We laughed. It felt good to laugh. I thought I had forgotten how.

"I'm an assistant principal, still in the same place."

"You're an assistant principal? Oh, Camille, how wonderful! It's funny, you calling. You'll never guess who I saw the other day on TV. Jewel."

"You're kidding."

"No, Jewel was on Black News doin' an interview with that woman—you know, the smiling one. I just caught the tail end of it, but she was sayin' that she was opening an office in Chicago."

"Well, go on girl. Jewel always was a go-getter. How'd she look?"

"She looked just a little bit drawn, if you ask me. But hey, I could stand to look a little drawn, shoot."

"Get outta here, Saundra."

We laughed again until the fullness of the sound became strained.

"What's doin' with Santos?" Camille asked.

I was thinking about what to say, where to start. What measure of the past few years should I reconstruct and have to hear it out loud? "I had him arrested a few months ago. He's in Rikers Island… getting out a couple of weeks before Christmas. I'm waiting on my divorce papers. I put in for them a couple years back, but you know…"

"Saundra, are you really doin' it this time?"

"Camille, I had to have him put away. He's not comin' back here."

As the words came out of my mouth, I thought about how ridiculous that statement sounded. I wondered how I would keep him out. Santos was only about five eight, but he was wiry and strong. He had broken the bedroom door down twice. I searched my mind to find why I had waited so long to press charges. All that I remembered was how intriguing his eyes were when I first saw him. He was so handsome. Curly black hair, brown skin the color of caramel. He was at a poetry reading way back then. He had a gaze that could switch from engaging to fierce in an instant. I thought it was romantic. But he had a way of wrapping me up in his anger and trapping me with no escape. My eyes wandered, scanning the kitchen, and I noticed the door to the bedroom and the splintered dent he punched in it just before I called the cops the last time. I have to get that fixed, I thought.

"All I have to say is, it's about time." Camille's voice sounded as if it were in a tunnel. She made me leave the dark thoughts that had closed in around me.

"I have to go get myself a job. I been in this group—you know, for women tryin' to get on their feet. They're helping me. They started me back with my typing. They keep tellin' me I should move." I picked up the mirror I had left on the kitchen table and looked at my face. I was waiting for the bruise by my eye to heal. My skin was too light, and it had stayed purple and then green for so long. I just about looked normal. My curly hair could use some help, but maybe I could look presentable enough for someone to hire me.

"Maybe you should move, Saundra. Was he still beating up on you?"

Hearing Camille say that out loud gave my memories substance. I felt myself choking as if I would vomit. "Camille, I can't talk about him now. I just have to find me a job. Then I can start thinkin' about finding my own place. I called some temp agencies last week. I'm supposed to go to this interview on Monday morning. We'll see. That's why I was thinking about you. I kept sayin' to myself, how many times did Camille try to get me to do this? I should call her."

"Saundra!"

"No, really. Then I see Jewel on the television. I said, let me get on the phone. But then I thought maybe I should wait till I have a job. You know…"

"Why?"

"I just felt…"

"Saundra, we've all been through too much together for you to feel that way. Forget that. I was thinking maybe we could all get together. I mean really see each other you, me, and Jewel. I don't know. Maybe I'm feeling old."

"You think Jewel would be up for it?"

"I don't even know how to get in touch with her anymore, Saundra."

"She probably moved out of that little itty-bitty apartment in the Village. You remember that place?"

"I'm sure she moved into a bigger place down near Sixth Avenue," Camille said.

"I didn't see that apartment." I always knew there were times I was left out. It was my own fault. I was either stoned with Santos or embarrassed by bruises that I wanted to hide from them.

"I bumped into to her down on Eighth Street. I was getting my hair cut back in 1985, maybe '86—yeah, '86, 'cause I was pregnant with Shawn…she had already started the business. As a matter of fact, she said she started the business in that apartment a few years earlier."

"Let's do it," I said before I could stop myself.

"I guess we could get the number for the business from information."

"Don't remember…know what? I'll call the show."

"Saundra, stop!"

"Why not? You know me. Shoot. Camille, I do want to try to get a job first. Just 'cause it would make me feel better."

There was a pause. "I can understand that. You know what? I've been writing again."

"Camille, you were always writing."

"Poetry. But now I have a good number of short stories, and I'm working on some longer pieces. I'm having so much fun creating these characters. They talk, and I write down what they say. I'm thinking of sending my stuff to an agent."

"You still have that poem about me?"

"I don't know. Which one? What did it say?"

"Can't remember all of it, but it was about me, and you know how I used to be sort of out there."

"Flamboyant?"

"That was me. You wrote it when you lived at my house. That poem almost made me cry, 'cause it was like you really were seeing things in me that I couldn't see." I remembered snatches of it. "'Sassy sister'—that's how it started. Remember, Camille? 'Sassy sister, sashay your way down the street. Let the music lift your feet and send your hips this way and thataway.' Something like that. I remember it just sounded like the way I walked."

"That's what would get you in trouble."

"Yeah…it did…well, if you ever find it, I'd like to have a copy. You know, one of those 'where I wases,' like the fat picture you hang on the fridge."

The silence grew.

"So, I'll call and get the number from the TV station, and you'll call Jewel."

"You'll call me back?" Camille said.

"I will. I promise."

When I hung up the phone, I felt that maybe this was what I needed to help me do the things I had said I would do. It was strange how my friends showed up just when I needed them, I thought. It wasn't that I was superstitious, that this came into my mind. I just felt that so much that happened to me was out of my control.

"Sssss…sssssssss…Saundra, Saundra." He hissed like a snake before he whispered my name.

"Sssss. Saundra," he repeated. His voice slid down the steps at me.

I didn't actually hear my name at first. I had to get my key out of the lock of the heavy wood-and-glass door before it closed on my hand. My key was on a string tied around my neck, so that I wouldn't lose it. As I pulled it out of the lock, I had to take care not to hit myself in the chin. My hair was pulled back in two long braids that were tied with navy-blue grosgrain ribbon. One bow now hung in a loose loop, and the other dangled down my back. As I squeezed the large brass doorknob, turning it to push open the door, I could see tiny pink teacup shapes painted just above my fingernails.

"Sssss. Sssssst. Saundra." There it was again, coming from up above me somewhere in the shadows.

"Who is that calling me?" I couldn't see through the darkness. Up at the top of the landing, there was a bulb, but its light only stuck itself against the ceiling. There in the darkness was Mr. Lynch leaning over the banister smiling at me. It was difficult to see his dark face, but I saw his gold tooth shining there in the shadows.

"Your parents aren't home yet. You can stay up at my house."

"Nope. My mother said I have to go in and lock the door."

"Remember, your mother sent you up here to play the number."

"My daddy said not to go nowhere but home too!"

"You gotta remember when your daddy and I went drivin' on Sunday? And we got you somethin', but if you want to see it, you got to come up."

"What is it?"

"Come on up, pretty girl. You'll see."

"What did you say? But suppose my mommy gets mad at me?"

"We just won't tell her, OK? Don't want her to get mad at you for doin' nothin'." His words stank. They fell down on me like dirty bits of bedsheets.

I walked up the stairs. The sound of my footsteps hid in the old maroon carpet and the dirty cloth bits that rested there in the darkness. Then, as I looked into the dark hallway, I turned and began to grab for the banister to go back down.

"I don't see nothin' in...it's dark in there."

"Shhhh. I'll turn on the light for you."

I turned. The light painted the walls yellow. Where the wall ended, there was an enamel dish and a tiny gray kitten sipping milk. The tiny powder puff of fur, with wet paws and whiskers, looked at me, milk dripping from its chin.

"Oh look, a kitty. What's its name?"

"I don't think she got no name. You should give her a name."

"I don't know. What about, um...Fluffy? That's what we'll call her. Fluffy!" I stepped up on the top step and leaned down to pet her.

"That's a good name," Mr. Lynch said, picking up the cat. He took it in the door and down a long hallway.

"Where are you going? I want to see the kitty."

"Putting it down here where you can pet it."

I stood still, feeling that something was wrong. "I have to go home, Mr. Lynch. I'm supposed to go right in after school and lock the door. Mama's gonna be mad at me."

"Don't worry. I won't tell her you were here."

The kitten mewed and yawned, made me laugh. "D'you see that?"

"Would you like for this to be your kitty?"

"Yes."

"Then sit on my lap."

"I don't want to."

"You will if you don't want me to tell your mother."

He squeezed my arm and pulled me up onto his bony legs. I tried to pull my arm away, but I had the kitty in the skirt of my dress. The room was quiet until Mister Lynch started to rock his body. The couch creaked. His breath stank. I tried to turn my head away…to pull away. He held my arms and rubbed his smelly self on me. When I told him to stop, he said, "I think I'll tell your mother you was up here when you shoulda been home." My belly hurt like when I threw up from the cold in my stomach. He was moving faster and then made a sound that scared me. I pulled away from him and ran down the hallway, down the stairs. I pushed the apartment door open and tripped over my book bag.

"Sssssss Saundra," I heard him say again.

"Ssssssss Saundra. You come up tomorrow."

As I closed the door, it squeaked. I locked the bottom lock and tiptoed to reach the chain. I stared at the door with its locks, which were there to keep me safe. I knew that they wouldn't. Something in my child self had been ripped away. I knew it even though I had no words for it. I felt only fear, which I would escape only by daring it to go away.

3

JEWEL

The shorter of the two roses drooped and seemed to nestle its head just under the chin of the taller one. I had bought them on my way into the office just to perk myself up. It was six forty-five in the evening, and Verta had come in almost a half hour before to say that she was heading home. I was exhausted.

My day had begun at two in the morning when Candace, one of my younger and more talented actresses, said she had forgotten the time zone change and called in a snit. When the director called an hour later, telling me to rein the kid in, I was just getting back to sleep. This little twenty-year-old had presumed to tell the director, "Black people wouldn't say these lines." So what? Did she think it was so easy to get a running feature on an evening series?

"Say what they tell you to say. You're not in a position to pick and choose, yet."

"I'm not going to sell out, Ms. Jamison," she said.

Was this little wench suggesting that I was? "You don't remember how it was when they didn't need us at all," I told her. "They don't really need us now. You mess this up for yourself, and you mess it up for any other black actress who comes along behind you, Missy."

I shouldn't have called Gordon at that hour. He must have been sleeping soundly. I just wanted to hear his voice. Stupid me.

It was late. I just needed to know if he had gone home to his wife. I couldn't sleep. I woke him, and he wasn't happy.

"Jewel." Verta startled me. I had thought I was alone. "I just got off the phone with Tonio. He's in New York. He tells me they're not using any of our girls in their new show. He said something about wanting the attention on the fashion, not on the models, and that they were going for the waif look."

"I can't believe this. Their code words make me sick. *The waif look.* If they mean *the little white girl look*, why don't they say it? Is he set in stone on this?"

"It sounded that way to me. I was heading out of the office, and I said to myself we haven't heard from him, and we should have heard last week. I called his assistant, and Tonio picked up. He said he just didn't feel that our girls would fit his designs."

"Black women can't wear his clothes? What the hell do they mean when they say these things, and in such a boldfaced way. I'll call him tomorrow. I just don't have the energy tonight." I thought about where to place my anger, but it wasn't only Tonio. The industry had started a trend away from using models of color. Each designer would frame the decision in artistic terms—the colors he was using, the lines he was creating. It was clear that where there had been three or four women of color on the runways of Milan last year, this year in some shows, there was only one.

"We'll talk tomorrow. We also have to deal with the cost overruns in Chicago," Verta added with a tone of admonition in her voice. She was my alter ego, keeping my spending in line.

"I know, the carpeting. It is gorgeous, Verta. It's an investment." I massaged my temples. Verta's brow was creased. She looked tired too.

"By the way, you've got a bunch of messages," Verta said as she left.

The telephone message slips were clipped to the blotter on the right-hand side of the desk. On the left were two stacks of photos. She had tagged each one with her own notes to consider.

I had to stop myself from reading the tiny slips of paper. I was on automatic, but I needed to get out of there and get some rest. The back of my neck was twisted into knots and kinks so tight that no twisting, stretching, or rubbing gave me relief. *I just need to relax.* I reached into the top right-hand drawer for the Tylenol, but there wasn't any. A bit farther in was my pillbox. I pushed away the white pills and the yellow ones and pulled out a tiny blue tablet. I placed it on the back of my tongue and swallowed. I fingered the first two messages and flicked them aside, deciding not to deal with anything else for the day.

I pushed the two folders marked "Tavern on the Green" into my briefcase. The menu for the cocktail reception had to be finalized. Verta had taken care of the invitations and all the other prearrangements. The celebration in New York had to be in grand style as a prelude to the event in Chicago. If there was any question that I would be an important player, this party would dispel it. It was also an opportunity to showcase my new model, Nadege. And it was a chance to let the designers know that my influence was now fully extended to film and television, a huge bargaining chip.

The sunset, all pink and purple, presented itself and made me sit for a few minutes to take it in. Gordon should be here with me. I shuffled through the messages, glancing at the top two. The sheet on top was a message from George at the Tavern. The second read, "Camille Warren called. Give her a buzz if you can."

"Camille." It was so odd to see that name. I had thought about Camille from time to time over the past few years. Like so many other thoughts that might take too much time away from what I was doing at the moment, I had dismissed them.

As I thought about her, my stomach began to flutter. It was strange, how hearing from someone in your past can place you back in spaces you had so long abandoned. I felt small and insignificant. I remembered how I had first seen Camille. She was hiding behind the draperies in her grandmother's parlor window. Saundra and I were on the stoop playing with her paper dolls, which were in a shoebox. That day, I could swear that Camille smiled at me and then backed away from the window.

I tried to recall when I had spoken to Camille last. When I first started the business? I think it was later. Why is she calling? She probably wants something. As I picked up my briefcase, the stack of photos was set askew. A few fell. This is ridiculous. She may just be calling to touch base. I restacked the pictures. I'll call her from home.

The tension in my neck tightened. I'll just call from here. I'm more comfortable here. I put everything down and sat staring at the telephone. I took a deep breath and dialed the number. The phone rang several times, and then I heard a voice say, "Hello."

"Camille?"

"No!" There was a giggle. "This is not my mother. This is Shawn. Who may I ask is calling, please?"

"Tell her it's Jewel Jamison."

"Mommy, it's Jules Jamison on the phone."

"Jewel?"

The telephone hit the floor.

"Shawn! Jewel? Well, how are you, lady? Long time no talk to."

"What can I say? Things are wonderful. Busy, as usual, but wonderful."

"You've been on my mind for weeks. You and Saundra. I called Saundra a week or so ago, and she said she saw you on Black News. We thought we'd call and say hello and...we...I also wanted to congratulate you. She said you had a new office opening in Chicago."

It felt good that they knew about my business. "That piece was done a few weeks back, and it's been nonstop since then to keep to our timeline. I have a few more interviews to do to publicize this move. We have to get as much mileage out of it as we can. So how are you?"

"Busy too. I'm an AP, an assistant principal. Finished up going to grad school for my state certification in administration a few years ago. Being mommy."

"I heard. He sounds precious. I didn't know you went through with it." It hit me—that was when we last spoke. She didn't respond. I guess she forgot how we had talked about the abortion. I told her that it would be an embarrassment for a teacher to be an unwed mother. But I guess she didn't listen.

"Shawn's five and brilliant."

"I'm sure," I said. "And Saundra?"

"She's hanging in there. Getting a divorce, it seems like. She's temping. I guess she's pulling it together. We're both proud of you. We were just saying how far you've come from Bed Stuy. Anyway, we were thinking about getting together, a sort of a reunion. What do you think?"

I tried to mesh these pieces of my life together, and they just didn't seem to fit. I wondered what Camille meant by her comment. Bed Stuy had been so long ago. It reminded me of so much sadness. I turned the chair around and looked out at the purple sky. I had bought that view. I had selected every item in the office in which I sat. I didn't know from whence the insecure feeling in the pit of my stomach sprang. I decided to move through and past it.

"Sure, why not. I'm still at the office and a bit tired tonight, and I have a couple of important meetings tomorrow morning that may affect my calendar. How about if I give you a call at the end of the week or early next week?"

Camille was silent.

"Jewel, it didn't occur to me that you might be too busy with the new office and all the...you know...things you must be doing to get it ready. Maybe this is a bad time. But I didn't ask you, how's your love life?"

"I'm seeing this wonderful man from Los Angeles and also has an office in Chicago. He's a lawyer—a partner in a firm, entertainment law. He's back and forth."

"He would have to be from the West Coast," Camille said.

"What did you say?"

"It was just a bad joke. I was saying he'd have to be from the West Coast because there aren't any eligible black men in New York. Remember how we'd say that all the time?"

"There aren't any eligible black men, period."

"Don't I know it? Is it serious?"

"We're talking about marriage. I'm planning on June…always wanted to be a June bride. I just have to get the new office established, and then we're finally going to do it." I wanted to tell Camille the truth about Gordon. What felt good about hearing her voice was that she was one of the few people with whom I could be myself. There had been so many nights when I called Camille at two or three o'clock in the morning just to cry. But it had been so long.

"What about you? You seeing anyone?"

"Jewel, please! I don't even remember what it was like to see anyone. I've got no time for anyone other than Shawn and my mother in my life anyway, so…" It was quiet again.

"Camille, I didn't mean to give you the impression that I didn't want to get together. We'll work something out…good to hear your voice. I really mean that. I see your number here on the ID. I'll call you next week. I promise."

When I hung up, for a few minutes I was lost in memories of these friends. The memories went back further than I cared to recall.

"Jessie, wake up! It's burning! The couch is burning. Mama, please wake up." I filled up a dirty pot with water. Not meaning to, I ran and stumbled, spilling the cloudy liquid with pools of red oil and bits of food all over my mother. The water seeped into the cushion, but it was still smoldering.

"You little bitch," Jessie shouted.

I saw her hand, and then I felt my head jerk to the left. I was afraid my head would just spin around, but it didn't. Everything turned upside down after that. Then I heard a metallic sound in the shadows.

"Jessie! You're drunk. You gone and set the house on fire with that stuff you been smokin'."

Daddy'll fix it. Daddy, I can't talk because I can't move my face.

"What'd you do to the kid? Shit!" I saw my father walk past. He looked like a mechanical man held to the ceiling by some magical force. *How can you walk upside down?* He picked up the pot and moved away. He came back, still moving slowly, robot-like. Water cascaded to the floor, creeping under my back, making it feel cold. I watched the smoke billow and stick to the ceiling-floor. My mother was kneeling over me.

"Baby, I'm sorry." She drooled on me. Her spit felt warm.

"That's it, Jessie. I don't know how you expect me to stay here, drink with you, and forget. He's dead," Daddy said.

I was seven, but Jessie would pull me away when the women in the neighborhood would whisper. Mama said to me, it wasn't her fault. If anyone blames me, they are lying. But I heard them. They said Jessie had no business spending her time pushing that big navy-blue baby carriage up and down Tompkins Avenue, wearing her yellow dress and her red dress and her spring green with red and yellow flowers, and her platform shoes that strapped around the ankles. They said she was showing off her tiny waist and big hips, sauntering up and down the street, and tossing her "good" hair this way and that. They say that Red Simpson had had his head turned by her. He didn't know what he was doing when he ran over the carriage with his big old 1952 Pontiac Chieftain. I was in school that day, but they said my baby brother was thrown from his coach and hit his head on the curb. They say that Jessie squeezed him to her chest and tried to stop the blood from rushing from the gaping hole in his head. After the funeral, she didn't want to go out. She took to drinking. It had been more than a year now. Daddy said he was sick of it.

Then there were the men. I saw them, but Jessie said not to say nothing to Daddy. Miss Thorne, who lived next door, told him about them. They would come in and go out before he got home from work. He never saw anyone there, but Daddy said he smelled them on her. *Daddy, don't go. Mama'll be good. I'll be good.*

"I'm taking Jewel to my sister's house. Do the kid a favor and get yourself together."

"Don't you take my baby outta this house," Jessie said, looking at him out of the corner of her eye.

"I don't want my child learning to be a whore from you."

I didn't understand his words, but then I felt a scratchy cloth as Daddy lifted me high into the air. I was wearing only my undershirt, my socks, and my underpants that had a hole in 'em. I held on to his neck as tight as I could. He put me in the back seat of the car. I fell asleep. I woke up, and Daddy was gone.

4

CAMILLE

The phone rang at five or so, Friday evening, while I was making a grilled cheese sandwich for Shawn. I was sure it was my mother seeing if Shawn and I had gotten home all right. "Shawn, it's ready."

"'kay, Mom."

The phone rang a third time. It was a ritual my mother and I would go through. Not much said, but I'd hear whether she needed me to buy anything for her on Saturday. Before I had Shawn, when I got home early, I'd nap until five-thirty or so. But I hadn't had that respite in years. My mother had offered to take him for me for an hour or two on Friday evenings, but even though she was right upstairs, I didn't trust her. For some time, I told myself it was that she was getting old and had grown frail. The truth was that I didn't trust who my mother was. When I looked at my mother, I saw only the self-involved woman who had killed my father and abandoned me. She was the woman who went crazy for no good reason. She was the woman who certainly couldn't be trusted to care for my son when she couldn't care for me.

Since Eleanor came out of the hospital, she never had to go back. She was on medication for her depression, which she took regularly. But I never felt fully at ease with her. I made sure she had food and toiletries, all the necessities. I took over paying her bills, cashing her Social Security checks, did her banking. I made sure she had spending money. I often questioned myself about why I did it. I felt I did it out of love. Not love for her, because I did not feel that I could love this mother. It was out of love for the mother I wished I had.

For her part, Eleanor tried to show me her appreciation. She would tell me stories of how she'd dress us in matching dresses when I was little and comb my hair into drop curls. My father loved to take pictures of us, calling us his lovely ladies. I tried but could not hide my disdain for her frivolous stories. I could tell that she saw it was too late for us to find closeness. So I turned down her offers to take Shawn. She saw him when I dropped off her groceries. She tried to do for herself and call as little attention to herself as she could. It was as if she tried to disappear. I knew she hurt inside for the person she could not become, but I hurt more.

Shawn picked up his sandwich, mouthed "Yum," and licked his lips.

I grabbed the phone.

"I got the job, Camille! I can't tell you how long I've wanted to do this and couldn't. I actually got a job, a real job. I was temping at this place last week and they liked me, and they offered me a permanent job. There's one string. They want me to learn computer, but hey, I have been wanting to learn the computer. They call it word processing, my dear."

"Saundra, you are too funny."

"Hey, I know it's no great shakes. I'll only make three hundred a week to start, but I'll have medical benefits for me and Wanda. You are talking to a United Standard Life employee. What's that commercial? 'Get Met. It pays.' Well, get United Standard Life. It pays me, honey."

We laughed and laughed. It was a catharsis, conceived when we spoke weeks before, that had now burst from our bodies full blown.

"And you haven't heard the best part. I just came in, and in the mail were my divorce papers. I started all this more than a year ago, and it's finally happening. It's like everything is turning around for me."

I hated it when Saundra placed so much stock in things outside herself. I always pointed out that it was what she *did* that mattered. I didn't want to launch into a weary old lecture, so I didn't say anything that would dampen her enjoyment of the moment.

"Did you call Jewel?"

"Yeah, sure, more than a week ago. I didn't call you right away because it didn't sound as if she was really interested. I don't know. It sounded like she was real busy and...from her perspective, maybe she wasn't interested in...I don't know. Anyway, I haven't heard from her."

"You think it was me. Maybe she would have wanted to see you, but not me. In college, she was closer to you."

"Well, you can't blame her for that, Saundra."

"What do you mean?"

"At the very beginning, you weren't very..." I couldn't find the words.

"You mean when we were kids? I know. What can I say? I was a kid. You think I should call her? Wait a minute. You know what? I've been setting up these conference calls up for my boss. We could have ourselves a conference call."

"Saundra, you're too much."

"No seriously, 'cause I was thinking I'd like to have a...maybe a...brunch. I can't afford dinner, but a brunch to celebrate my divorce. There's this great place in Brooklyn I heard them talking about in the office. It's called the Caribe. Owned by black folks. Elegant as hell. And they're supposed to have a beautiful Sunday brunch. And I want to treat."

"Saundra, stop. You just got your job, and you want to spend your money treating us. Are you crazy?"

"Camille, let me do this. I want to."

"You're supposed to be saving money to move. You need money for clothes for work. This is stupid. Certainly Jewel can afford to pay, and I can. Don't be ridiculous."

"I can't explain it. I feel good about you calling me and seeing you guys again. God knows I feel good about getting out from under Santos. And I want to do this. I priced the brunch. It's not outlandish. I know I can do this. Please don't take this pleasure away from me. So, let's call Jewel. Give me her number. I'll tell her about the conference call."

"What time is it? I don't have her home number, but when I spoke to her, it was late and she was still at the office. You want me to call first?"

"No. When I speak to her, I'll at least be sure whether she didn't call because of me."

I dug out the frayed telephone book, leafed through the pages, and found the number next to Jewel's name. I had doubts about whether it was a good idea to call, but I couldn't stop Saundra from trying to set up this celebration. I gave the number to her, hung up the phone, and waited.

I put a pot of water up for tea and then found myself watching the bubbling surface of the liquid. Wondering what was taking so long, I checked on Shawn, who had fallen asleep on the couch. I worried that he would be up in the middle of the night because he had fallen asleep too early, but when I checked the clock, it was already past seven. Then I figured that Saundra couldn't reach her and said she would only call back if she got her.

The phone rang, and I ran to pick it up before it roused Shawn. "AT&T operator. Is this Camille Warren?"

"Yes."

"We have a three-way call to you. Go ahead, Miss."

"Camille, it's me, Saundra, and Jewel is on the line. Say something, Jewel."

"Camille? Do you believe this girl? She tells me she's gonna set up this call."

"Yeah, then she tells me she will do it," Saundra said.

"They're included in my business account," Jewel said.

"But I'm doing the brunch. Now get out your calendars, ladies."

"She's too much," I said. "Jewel, you're the one with the busy schedule. When can you do it? I'm pretty free—just can't leave Shawn with my mom or the sitter for long."

"I defer to you, too. Since I am a full-time employee of United Standard Life, your typical nine-to-five, I do rest up on weekends. But my Sundays are free."

"Saundra, stop."

We all laughed.

"What about the last Sunday in October?" Jewel said once there was a lull. "My event is set up for November, but the publicity is done."

"That's not Halloween, is it? No, it looks good," I said.

"There are three of us on the phone, and Camille talks to herself...looks good to me too," Saundra said and laughed out loud again.

"How about ten o'clock? Is that good?" I asked.

"How about eleven? I like to sleep late on Sundays," suggested Jewel.

"My girl," Saundra said, laughing. "Love it. Just my speed."

We finally settled on eleven thirty, and Saundra gave us the address of the restaurant. You could hear the genuine joy in her voice. Jewel still seemed a bit distant—or maybe it was businesslike. I wasn't sure. There had always been a tension between them, no matter how Saundra tried to dispel it. It had started at the beginning, or what I remembered as the beginning.

It was a hot summer, and Ma kept the windows open to catch a breeze. I could hear the girls playing down on the street. I was about ten and had grown accustomed to watching them by standing back, to the right of the window, where they couldn't see me. Ma made me study all evening, so I hardly got out except to go to school and back. I went to Our Lady of Victory Catholic School, even though we weren't Catholic, because Ma didn't want me in the public school, where all the *ruffians* went. I heard the girls singing.

> This the way you Willoughby, Willoughby, Willoughby,
> This the way you Willoughby all night long.
> Oh jump back, Sally, Sally, Sally,
> Jump back, Sally, all night long.
>
> Oh, struttin' down the alley, alley, alley,
> Struttin' down the alley, all night long.

The tall, yellow-skinned girl with the long wavy hair raised her skirt above her knee. All the girls were lined up facing each other, clapping and squealing as she held one hand on her waist and swished her hips, strutting her way down the space between them. She was the best, the very best. As she got to the end, she said, "OK, now let's play double dutch." She swung herself around to watch the girls, who were all watching her.

"I didn't get my turn," another girl, one they called Queenie, said. She was next to go down the alley. A short, dark-skinned girl they called Jewel sat on the stoop watching. She didn't seem to like the game. Saundra, the tall one, loved the attention, especially when the boys were around. Then she would swish her hips, making them snap from side to side.

I couldn't hear everything she said except, "Jewel, go get your rope, and you can go first, Queenie." The one sitting on the stoop made no move to go, so the taller one said, a little louder, "OK, Jewel will go first 'cause it's her rope, and Queenie, you'll go second, and I'll go third, all right?" The other girls called out "Fourth," "Fifth," and "Sixth."

"Go get my purse in the bedroom, Camille. I want you to go down to the grocery store. I want you to get a piece of codfish for dinner. I just feel like eating some codfish cakes and bakes. I need to soak my salt fish, so…Camille, you hear me? What are you looking at out that window?"

"Yeah, Ma, I'm going. I'm not looking at nothing."

"You're not looking at *anything*, not *nothing*. And it's *yes*, not *yeah* or whatever you said."

I went into my grandmother's room and looked on the bureau. I glanced into the mirror. I hated it when Ma plaited my hair in such small parts. I liked having bangs and no braids, and when she pressed my hair with the hot comb and put a ribbon in it, tied at the top, like Alice in Wonderland, I liked that best of all.

"Girl, what's taking you so long?"

"I don't see it, Ma. I don't know where your old purse is."

"What did…isn't it on the bureau next to my Bible? Don't make me have to come in there and find that purse, Camille."

"No, your Bible isn't here either."

"Oh, I think it's in the kitchen on the table. I took it…I forget now, but…"

"You always forget."

"What'd you say?"

"Nothing. I've got it. I'm going."

"You wait a minute, young lady."

I heard her, but I didn't stop. I ran down the hallway and out the big glass door. There were the girls playing rope on the sidewalk in front of the stoop. The tall, light-skinned one whispered something into the short girl's ear. I walked up to where they were and waited for the rope to stop so I could pass, but they kept turning.

"Hey you! Stuck up! Little Miss Stuck up!" the short one shouted.

"That's not my name."

"Look at her shoes! Do you believe those clodhopper shoes," the taller one chimed in with her hand over her mouth, laughter bursting through her fingers. All the girls looked down at my feet and laughed. I hated those shoes. Ma had taken me way over to East New York and made the man at Julius Grossman Shoe Store give them to me. He said they were good, sturdy shoes that would support my arches. He pulled the strap on the right shoe too tight and then patted my foot, telling me to take a walk around the store to see how they felt. I hated them even more when I read the color on the box: "OX BLOOD."

I looked up, and my eyes met Saundra's. Jewel was not laughing. She looked down at her own feet and pulled her pinky toe in through the hole in her left sneaker. I noticed that Jewel had on a dress like mine. Jewel must have felt my eyes on it. She tried to cover the skirt with her hands. I knew that my grandmother had put that dress and other old things of mine in a box to give to a poor family down the block. I looked at it as I stepped down into the gutter to pass. The tall girl stepped behind the short one. I kept walking, not looking at the girls until I reached the corner. They were laughing, and the tall one was saying that I thought I was better than everyone.

"But she's just a scaredy-cat. Watch," I heard the one they called Jewel say.

I walked faster. There was a whooshing sound behind me, and then a sharp pain in my back. My shoulders flew back, and my hand jerked back to the place where the pain was. I turned around, and there was the short girl with the braided short hair.

"You don't like it? What you gonna do about it?" she taunted.

"Kick her ass," someone said.

"See what I mean? She's scared," she said, turning her head to look at the other girls.

I reached up and clutched Jewel's hair, my fingers digging down to her scalp, and jerked her head back. Her body followed and hit the pavement like a broken puppet. She sat there, stunned. She looked at her hands, and I could see tiny pebbles embedded in her palms. I was scared. I didn't know if the tall girl was going to hit me too. She went over to the other one and helped her up.

"You let her do that to you, Jewel?"

"Leave me alone, Saundra," she said.

She got up and stared at the girls. No one said a word. I turned around and walked down the block. It was quiet behind me. I wanted to turn around and run back to my house, but Ma would yell at me. So I walked to the store thinking about the girl with the short hair without daring to look back.

5

CAMILLE

The sun finally forced its way into my bedroom window. I had been lying there, contemplating the checks I had not written and the manuscript of poetry and short stories on my desk I was supposed to mail. Sunday morning had caught me by surprise again. On Saturday I had taken Shawn to the library and checked out a stack of picture books and two chapter books that he had wanted to read. I had fought my way up and down the narrow aisles of Sloan's, pushing my cart and mechanically picking up and tossing in whole wheat bread, Cocoa Puffs, skim milk, chicken legs, hamburger, and Red Zinger tea. I had taken the laundry downstairs and sat guarding it so that no one would take it out of the dryer before its time.

Shards of light defied the thin drapes and slashed their way into the room, insisting that I take notice. The writer in me studied the way the air segmented into patterns of shimmering patinas, wedged against patches of darkness into which I wished I could escape. The mother in me hoped that the slivers of light would not disturb my son. He lay motionless on the high riser across the room, sunlight kissing his eyelashes and dabbing his tightly curled dark-brown hair with gold. I knew that as soon as he began to stir, I would have to summon the energy to lift my too-heavy body out of bed and tend to his needs. *No rest.* My mother wanted to be that cushion, that support, when I felt too tired to continue, but I tried to keep my child and my worries to myself. I once complained that I was too old for all I had to do to take care of Shawn, saying, "I'm forty-four years old, Ma. I don't have the energy these twenty-year-olds have to run after a baby."

"I told you that before you had him. You can't say I didn't tell you, and I tell you to let me help. An' what did you say? You would make up for youth with love?"

Sorry I said anything. I couldn't stand her I told you sos.

I reached up to pull down the shade behind the drapes, and the crocheted ring flew out of my hand. It went flying up, winding around the rod and smacking itself against the window frame at the top. Shawn sat up in his bed, his eyes still closed and his mouth in a yawn. He shaded his eyes with his fists, frowning and searching for me. He didn't seem to notice the window shade. It was the strip of white light filled with tiny white particles that caught his eye. It hung like a thick curtain, draped about his feet. As he moved, the flecks danced around him, swirling, delighting his imagination, which now endowed the bits of light with life. He wiggled his right foot and laughed out loud as his tiny playmates tickled his fancy, hopping, jumping, and leaping over his toes.

"Shawn, what are you laughing at?"

"Look, Mommy! Watch this!" he said, shaking his foot and sending the tiny white flecks into wild movement once again. He shook with laughter that filled the room like music.

I looked forward to weekends with my son. His innocence was a stark contrast to the complex web of political machinations that were taking place at my school during the week. Since Ruby's death, Saul Elliot was serving as interim principal, assigned by the superintendent. A cadre of the older teachers began to hold meetings after school to talk about how to best show their support of him to the school board. A group of parents had come to me, asking me to apply for the position. I was totally overwhelmed because I did not know that they had taken me seriously in the role of assistant principal, much less principal. I tried to turn them down, but a few of them told me to think about it, and to just not say or do anything to stop the events that they hoped to set in motion behind the scenes.

Saul kept his distance from me at first, and then he brought me into Ruby's office one day and, leaning back in Ruby's chair, approached me with an offer of staying on as his assistant principal. I mused to myself, hearing Ruby's words, "He can't help it." I told him I would think about it and left. It galled me to see him sitting at Ruby's desk.

From then on, he alternated between superfluous kindnesses to me in front of parents to shunning me during the course of my morning administrative duties. He tried to keep afternoon school-based management meetings from me, claiming I must have received memos even though he never sent them. I would find out about district meetings at the last minute. It was stressful.

Shawn climbed under the covers to put his head where his feet had been and shook as hard as he could. Then he scrambled out as fast as he could to catch the tiny flecks in flight as he came out, which caused him to let out a cascade of giggles that tickled like champagne bubbles breaking against your nose.

"Come here, you funny boy, you giggle box."

He ran on tiptoes across the room and climbed into my bed.

"Tickle, tickle," he said, his tiny fingers under my neck.

"Tickle, tickle to you too. You know what? We're going out for breakfast today. What do you think of that?" I was already feeling guilty about leaving him with my mother to go to brunch with Saundra and Jewel. I felt torn because I was looking forward to seeing my friends.

"Can I have pancakes?"

"Sure can."

For the first time since Ruby's death, I tied back the curtain, fully letting the light of this day fill the room. There was a chill despite the bright sunlight. The juxtaposition of warmth on my face and the chill that still permeated the room made me want to write.

I wanted to escape to the scenes, which I could construct, and to the characters, who drew themselves in my mind.

I sent Shawn to wash his face and brush his teeth. I dressed him in a couple of layers of cloth and knit and corduroy. He looked like a short stuffed toy, which made you want to squeeze him, lift him up, and put him on a shelf.

He bounced down the steps out of the house and stamped his feet down the street, bending to pick up red, brown, and gold leaves that had collected on the sidewalk. We stopped at the newsstand on 110th Street and Broadway, picked up the Sunday *Daily News* for the comics for Shawn, and got a new Mead marble notebook for me. We continued up Broadway to the coffee shop. The air was warm inside and smelled of morning coffee. The woman at the register took two menus and showed us to a booth.

"No, we know what we want. One order of pancakes, one order of fried eggs lightly over, one orange juice, and one coffee, please," I said, wiping my fogged glasses as I slid into the booth.

The waitress, a thin woman wearing glasses, scribbled on her pad and said, "Home fries with that?"

"Sure, why not?"

Shawn climbed into the booth and pulled at his scarf while I tugged at his zipper. Between us, we wrestled his jacket, scarf, and hat from his body, and he propped up his face with his fists and sat reading *Peanuts* while I did some jottings describing autumn.

The waitress brought my coffee and Shawn's juice, and then she hurriedly set down a plate of scrambled eggs and toast in front of me and a plate of pancakes in front of Shawn. Noticing the eggs, I called out to the waitress, who was already pushing the swinging doors to the kitchen open.

"That must be mine." A dark-skinned man with silver flecks in his hair and wearing a black turtleneck sweater reached out for the plate I was holding.

"Were the eggs over yours?" he said politely, handing me the plate with his left hand. His smile was warm and his voice was deep, but I didn't really look at him closely because I was too focused on the plates that I didn't want to drop.

We exchanged dishes, saying yes and thank you appropriately. I began scribbling notes in my book.

"Is he your son? How old is he?"

"Are you talking to me?" I asked, a little annoyed at being distracted.

"I just asked how old he is. Is he reading that?"

"Yes. He's five. He's been reading for a couple of years already." I looked at Shawn, who was pouring syrup on his pancakes.

"Shawn, stop. That's too much." As I got the words out, the hinged top on the pitcher opened, pouring the entire contents out all over his plate and the table in front of him. I tried to grab it, and the man stood up, lifted Shawn out of the booth, and put three napkins down, trying to catch the sticky liquid as it slowly moved past the paper and dripped onto the seat and the floor.

"Mommy, he's strong like Colossus."

"I don't know if that's good or bad," the man said, laughing. "There seem to be no more tables. Would you like to join me? It's going to take a little while before they clean this up."

"No, we'll wait." I couldn't help wondering why this man would be giving so much attention to my child. My own heavy body moved slowly as I pulled myself out from behind the table and tried to move my plate and saucer with coffee cup out of the way of the moving golden syrupy pool.

"Why don't you take my table, then? You look like you were busy writing something important."

"Hey, what's the deal?" I said.

"No deal. Just trying to help," he said, carefully putting Shawn down, bending at his knees with his back straight and his shoulders erect.

"Waitress, we've got a spill here," he said in a commanding yet cordial tone, and then he sat down and picked up the folded back section of the *Sunday Times*. His smile disappeared.

"I didn't mean to be rude." I felt foolish as I stood there uncomfortably in the aisle of the coffee shop holding Shawn in front of me.

"No problem," he said, looking up for a second, and then he glanced up again and broke into a smile.

"What are you smiling at?"

"You. Very independent, aren't you?"

"I don't know. Why do you say that?"

"Well, you're standing there letting your food get cold just to remain..." he paused searching for a word.

"Look, I don't know you. I'm not going to sit down with you."

"We can remedy that. My name is Coleman Barnes. Cole. Now will you sit down?"

"Coleman. Where did you get a name like Coleman?"

"My grandfather. Anyway, would you like to sit down?"

I didn't know why I felt so awkward. He was disarming in a way. There was a formality about him that simply caught me off guard. At first I attributed it to his politeness, which seemed a bit excessive. Then I realized it was his manner of being.

"Thank you, but I couldn't." I felt a little suspicious, but Shawn was fidgeting and trying to dip his finger in the syrup.

"Here, you take this booth. I'm almost finished anyway. Could you help us here?" he said, raising his hand and beckoning the waitress again.

"A little accident, sweetie? I'll get you another. A stack!"

"I can't take your table."

"So, would you like to sit? I'll just finish my coffee."

The waitress cleared the table and wiped it with a gray dishcloth. "I'll put in an order for your eggs and get someone to take care of the floor."

"So, what do you do?" the man asked.

"I teach. Well, actually, now I'm an assistant principal." I finally looked right at him. Then, catching his eye, I looked away. His hair was closely cropped. And his arms seemed very muscular.

"I do a little teaching of sorts too. I'm a sergeant major in the marines. I do some training. I used to be a DI, a drill instructor."

"That's...nice," I said, not knowing what else to say.

He finished his eggs and motioned for the waitress. She came in an instant.

"Those pancakes will be right here, sir."

"I'd like another cup of coffee. More for you?"

"Uh...yes." I was trying to fit into this awkward situation. The sound of his deep voice had reached into my belly and stirred something in my center. I had still not really looked directly at this man since I sat down. I was so uncomfortable that I could not get my bite of toast down. I had not been out with anyone since Victor, and that had been more than six years ago, while I was pregnant with Shawn. My life had been swallowed up with teaching, going to school and home, and tending to Shawn. Somehow, since Victor died, almost three years ago, there were no men in whom I was seriously interested.

As I sat there trying to find something intelligent to say, all I thought was, I am so fat. I felt so unattractive that I could barely utter another phrase. I realized that for the last six years, my world had closed in on itself. It was just Shawn, my mother, and me. I really didn't know how to be there, just talking with this man.

"So you're writing assignments of some sort," he said, pointing to the black-and-white notebook I was holding.

"No. My mommy's writing a book," Shawn said with a giggle in his voice as he picked up the syrup to pour it on his pancakes.

"Let me do it for you. Say when." Cole poured the stream of syrup so that it would drip down the sides of the pancakes.

"That's enough!" I answered for Shawn.

"No, I want more, Mom," Shawn said, sounding very much five.

"That's plenty," I said, trying not to become irritated. "I write poetry and short stories. These are just some jottings on autumn."

"A writer."

"I don't know if I'd call myself a writer. I haven't sold anything."

"What does selling your work have to do with it? You write. You're a writer. Are you married?"

"That's a very personal question. My husband died some time ago."

"I'm sorry. So you're accustomed to being independent, aren't you?"

"Yes, I am."

"Mommy. I want some more juice, please."

"Shawn, why don't you finish up."

"You don't like me, do you?"

"What do you mean, like you? I don't even know you."

"Well, I've tried to start a conversation, and your tone is—"

"Look, I'm just not accustomed to sitting with strange men and making small talk. If that offends you, what can I say? Frankly, you're too friendly and a little too nice." I finally looked more closely at him. He had a barrel chest. His jaw was square and set. He seemed so solid and firmly planted.

"Waitress, check please."

"Here you are, sir," she said, smiling at him. She tore the green slip and turned it facedown on the table. He stood up, put his hand in his pocket, and took out his wallet.

"I'm sorry. I don't know what's wrong with me," I said.

"No problem," he said, lifting his newspaper and standing in that same erect way that he sat.

"You really don't have to go. This is your table."

"Hey, enjoy your meal. Bye, young fella."

He walked over to the cashier.

What is wrong with me? I don't even know how to sit and talk to a man anymore. OK, so I wasn't attracted to him. Why couldn't I just talk to him?

"Mommy..."

He was nice enough. Maybe that was it. Why was he being so nice to me?

"Mommy."

Talking to Shawn. What, did he think he could start a conversation and then take me home and crawl into my bed? And what did he mean, "You don't like me?"

"Mommy!" Shawn said, louder now.

"What is it, Shawn?"

"The man—he left his gloves."

"When the waitress comes, I'll give them to her." Gray kid-leather gloves were neatly tucked in behind the sugar rack.

Shawn finished his pancakes and his second glass of juice. He held his sticky hands up, not touching the table. I dipped my napkin into the water glass and wiped them, his upper lip, and his chin, then began to dress him. When the waitress squeezed past Shawn carrying two plates, I asked for the check.

"The gentleman took care of it, honey."

"What?"

"I said the gentleman you were sitting with paid the check."

"Oh, well, these…he left his gloves. He might come back for them."

I stood up and put on my coat, stunned that he had done that. I wrapped my scarf around my neck and reached down for Shawn's hand, somewhat in a daze. I felt embarrassed that I had been so rude. As I turned, I bumped into a sturdy chest. It was him.

"Sorry, I left my gloves," he said, trying to step out of my way.

"I'm sorry for the way I spoke to you."

"That's OK," he said, trying to make a path for me to pass.

"You really didn't have to pay our bill."

"I know."

"Why are you being so nice?"

"Just born that way, I guess," he said, smiling and letting the moment last.

"I gave your gloves to the waitress, but I was hoping that you'd come back…so that I could apologize."

"It's OK. Everyone is entitled to a bad day."

"I've had a bad week or two. A good friend died a few weeks ago."

"Sorry," he said softly.

"Well, anyway, I guess that's why I'm so out of it."

"I never did get your name," he said.

"Camille. Camille Warren."

"My name is Shawn Warren," Shawn interrupted. "I live at…"

"Shawn, shh," I covered Shawn's mouth with my hand. "And yours was Coleman?"

"Cole, please. I'd ask you if you wanted to go for a cup of coffee, but we just had one."

"Thanks for asking." I felt myself blushing.

"Feel like walking off some of that breakfast?" Cole suggested tentatively.

"I don't think so."

"It's a nice day. Maybe walk down to the park?"

"Oh, Mommy, can we go to the park? Please? Please?"

Cole went over to the waitress and got his gloves.

I thought about walking down to the park with this man. There was something protective in his eyes that made me feel safe.

"Well, OK."

He pushed open the door, held it for me, and rested his hand at the small of my back. I walked through, pulling Shawn behind me but feeling changed somehow.

"Uptown or down?" Cole asked. "We could take Shawn into the park up on Riverside Drive, or we could walk over to Central Park."

I chose Central Park so that we would be nearer to my apartment when we were done. We walked across 110th to the park, with Shawn kicking leaves everywhere he found them. We went into the playground, and Cole pushed Shawn on the swings for what seemed like forever. As Shawn's giggles and shouts of "higher" bounced about in the playground, and as he explored the climbing structures, Cole and I followed nearby. We sat and watched and began to talk. I learned that he had two sisters. He had been in the service for twenty-nine years. He was not married. We walked farther downtown and found ourselves at the Museum of Natural History, where we went inside. Then Shawn pointed out the chalk-drawn bowl of spaghetti on the propped-up sandwich board on the sidewalk in front of a restaurant. So we had dinner there. Then we talked about me, and my job as assistant principal and the stress I had been feeling since Ruby died. He was easy to talk to.

The day flew by. When we reached my apartment, it was after eight o'clock in the evening. It had grown dark, and Cole was carrying Shawn, who had fallen asleep in the cab on the way home. Cole said, "I can put him in his bed for you, and I'll go."

I had learned that Cole had a niece and nephew, which probably accounted for his ease with children.

"All right, but the house is a mess. We weren't expecting company." The sight of unmade beds and Shawn's toys on the living room floor embarrassed me.

"No big deal," he said as he laid Shawn down, took off his shoes, and placed them neatly on the floor just under the bed.

"Shawn had a great time today. Thanks for...I had a good time too."

"Glad to hear it. Does that mean I can call you sometime?"

I couldn't help laughing out loud.

"You are so straight. You tickle the hell out of me."

"What do you mean?"

"Oh, I don't know. Just the way you talk."

"Does that mean yes? That I can call, I mean?"

"I guess so."

"This is where I'm supposed to suavely take a piece of paper out of my wallet to write down your number," Cole said, laughing at his own awkwardness. He took down my number, repeating it as I told it to him.

"But wait a minute. I don't leave Shawn at sitters too often, and my mom is not too well."

"We'll take him with us somewhere."

"Are you for real?" I remember pushing my glasses up on the bridge of my nose to get a better look at this man who had walked into my life.

"Yes, ma'am," Cole said. "I'll call."

He opened the door and closed it behind him. I was left with the sense of being in a dream. I wished I were attracted to him. He was a nice guy, the kind of guy whom, when I was younger, I'd consider a great big brother or friend, but not a lover. He was stable, like a father figure. Of course I didn't know my father. My mother killed him. But this guy was protective, as I imagined a father might be. Although Cole was about forty-eight, only a little older than I was, he seemed older in his demeanor. I headed into the bathroom. I caught sight of my image in the mirror. Who am I kidding? I thought. I am not as young as I used to be. He'll probably call, too, I thought, laughing to myself.

It was fall when we moved to St. Albans in Queens. I had made friends with Saundra after the fight with Jewel, but I didn't see the girls anymore after I moved. Pa began to lose his way the first autumn we lived there. He kept looking for his old friends and wondering out loud about Mr. Griffith.

"Griff?" he'd say to no one in particular. "Is Cora keeping you locked up? Come on down. We'll go for a shine." Then he started wetting himself. Ma would scold him and make him change and threaten to put him in a nursing home if he didn't learn to hold his water. But, one night, when I was fifteen, Pa went to sleep and never woke up. Ma grieved but began "putting her things in order." She called her lawyer and had him explain her will to me. I sat there as he told me that the house we lived in was to be mine. Ma also had a piece of land in Barbados that her sister lived on, which was to be mine when my great aunt died. Aunt Elsie had never married, and I had only seen the sepia photograph of her sitting on a piano bench with a sad expression on her face. Ma left her other sister, Lillian, as the executor of her will, because she was her only other living relative and because she said she was the only one she trusted. She lived in Manhattan, and I had only met her a few times. Ma told me where her insurance papers were and showed me the bankbooks. She didn't have much. She told me when to expect her Social Security and when to pay the mortgage and the electric.

The old church ladies would come get Ma and help bathe and dress her for church. I would bathe her during the week, but most of the time Ma would sit in bed with her Bible and her old photo album. She'd tell me stories about how Daddy climbed the fence to Mrs. Weeks's house when he was a boy, and how he looked in his sailor suit when he came back from the Pacific. She told me how she got sick the day Daddy and Eleanor got married. Ma knew it was the cake Eleanor's mother got in the Italian bakery. Ma had offered to make the cake, or have one of the ladies at the church make it. She wanted them to make a Black Cake, a traditional West Indian wedding cake, even though Eleanor was an American girl. But Eleanor's mother insisted on doing things her way. And, of course, the cake made Ma sick. It made Mrs. Weeks and Cora Griffith sick too. They were the only friends Eleanor would let her invite to the wedding.

Ma talked and talked, and I really got to know her in those last two years. Even her old angers were clearer. She laughed when she told stories about how Daddy got into trouble as a boy. She'd laugh and hold herself and then stare off into the room at the air, as if it had substance.

Ma was leaving me little by little. Those times of staring grew longer, and the stories stopped in the middle or would trail off into nothingness almost before they were begun. Ma would say, "I remember when your daddy…" or "You don't remember Mrs. Adams, because she died when you were a baby, but…" She'd stop as if she were seeing the scene happening right there in front of her. Once she focused herself there, she'd rather stay than come back. She would close her eyes and slip off to sleep, enjoying the company of her memories.

It was the day before my seventeenth birthday, and Ma seemed to summon strength from nowhere. She called Mrs. Weeks over to the house, and the two of them spent time with the door to Ma's bedroom closed, talking about something. They insisted that I leave the room. I knew it was something about my birthday, so I left without questioning her. When I tapped on the door to say that I'd like to go out to the library, I heard Ma say, "Good," and then she added, "I have a few errands I'd like you to do. Olive will give you my list." When I went into Ma's bedroom, the shades were up, and the sunlight draped itself across her bed. There was a sparkle in Ma's eyes that I hadn't seen since long before Pa died. She winked at Mrs. Weeks but kept her lips pursed, with an expression on her face that said she was hiding something.

Mrs. Weeks took Ma's black shoes out of the closet and closed the door behind her.

"Winnie said you should go to the fish store and get her some butterfish. Then stop at the grocery and get some corn meal. She wants to make some fish soup with dumplings. And go to the shoe shop and get lifts put on these shoes."

"But Mrs. Weeks, Ma doesn't wear those shoes no more. She hardly ever comes out of her room, much less out of the house. What does she want those shoes fixed for?"

"She doesn't wear those shoes *any*more," Mrs. Weeks corrected, looking at me over the top of her glasses, frowning as she did in Sunday-school class. "Look, girl, I'm telling you what your grand-mother said. And pick me up a few things at the market, please," she added, handing me a slip of paper with a torn edge. I hated Ma's endless lists of errands, which I performed every Saturday. Now Mrs. Weeks was heaping them on me too. I couldn't argue with Mrs. Weeks, though. The years had given her a warm but uncom-promising expression that permitted no questions and no backtalk. She had been my Sunday-school teacher three years in a row, and her stare alone moved me to do whatever she asked. As she turned to head back into the kitchen, I remembered how, when I was a child, I used to think she resembled an overstuffed armchair that stood up, leaned over, and walked. I sucked my teeth and grumbled under my breath, "Old armchair!"

"What did you say, young lady?"

"Nothing."

Ma had not really required much of me in the past few months, and, in a way, I had become accustomed to making my own rules. But Ma wanted some fish, so I grabbed my sweater and pocketbook and went down the steps and out of the house. I took the list and crossed things off as I bought what Ma and Mrs. Weeks wanted. I backtracked to the shoe shop and picked up the shoes. I pushed my key in the lock, turned the doorknob, and called out, "Mrs. Weeks, Ma! I'm home." It was so quiet in the house. I went through the living room and down the hall, tiptoed past Ma's room, and put the three bags down on the kitchen chair. On the table I saw Ma's cherry cake, complete with pink frosting and cherries in a ring around the edge. It made me smile so.

"Ma. It smells delicious." I peeked into her room, and seeing her resting so peacefully, I turned to leave, whispering, "No wonder you're so tired."

On her bent wood coatrack, next to the closet, was a rose-colored organza dress that was absolutely beautiful. "Ma. I'm sorry for waking you, but this dress is lovely. It's perfect." I swung the dress off the rack and twirled 'round with it, holding it close to me as if it were my dancing partner. I hung the dress up and began to smile. My smile grew into a giggle and then into a laugh as I plopped down on Ma's bed and threw my arms around her and pulled her close in order to kiss her cheek. It was cold. Ma was heavy, and her head dropped to the right, as if she were asking why.

It was strange what went through my mind at the moment when I was certain that Ma had left for good. At first I thought, "Get up, Ma. I got your shoes done." Then I felt like I might cry. Sadness filled my belly and began to rise up in my chest, and tears shaded my eyes. It was just then that it all stopped. I grew numb. I felt nothing. Then the thought intruded, "You could have waited till after my birthday." I felt it first as an irritating sensation in my head. I closed my eyes tightly, trying to squeeze it from my consciousness. It would not be pushed away. It ached as it was born. "How come you didn't wait until after my birthday? I am all alone for my birthday." Rage exploded in my brain and ran like a mucky river all over me.

"Tomorrow is my birthday," I bellowed within the walls of my mind. I looked around the room filled with old things—the photograph of my father, Pa's silver brush, Ma's cream-colored doilies—and, disturbing the quiet, I heard my own voice whisper, "They left me here alone. God, I'm all alone."

6

SAUNDRA

The phone rang, and I stared at it in a crazy attempt to figure out who was on the other end. The papers had been served on Santos over a week ago. That day he called when he got them. He told me that he wasn't going to bother me, but he knew that calling me did just that. I had just started packing stuff when he called. I was thinking, funny how much stuff you accumulate in twenty-five years, even when you never have any money.

That day I wasn't thinking, so when the phone rang, I answered it. His voice was flat. He said he was calling to find out when he could pick up his things. "Just reminding you I'm getting out the week before Thanksgiving." Hearing from him while trying to wrap up my memories so unnerved me that I couldn't think straight.

Now, the phone was ringing again. Each ring meant that he could be there in my ear again. The sound was persistent. I tried not to let my fear rule me. Maybe it was Camille. Maybe it was a woman from my group, checking up on me. I picked it up.

"Mami." There was his voice oozing into my consciousness like warm oil poured into my ear. The thick, warm liquid blocked out sound and then ran into my brain.

"I been thinkin' 'bout these papers they give me, Mami. What are you doin'?"

I could not speak. My throat was closed.

"You don' wanna do this to us, Mamita."

"Santos, I can't do this anymore."

"You don't have to do nothin'. I'm getting help for my anger. Trus' me."

"Santos, I gotta go. I am going to my mother's to get Wanda."

"How's my little girl? She miss me? You know you can't do this— take my baby girl."

"*You* can't do this. She's not a baby no more. She's a young lady, and I can't let her see this going on. You can't beat me up and then act like nothing happened. Leave us alone. Tell me, what did you do to her that day?" I covered my mouth to stop my words.

"Nothin', I didn't do nothin'. And I'm gonna make it up to you. You'll see. To both of you."

"Don't! It's too late." The distance between us loosed my lips. "I'm finished."

There was a deafening silence. It went on for more than a couple of minutes. I could only wait. I didn't dare hang up.

I heard him clear his throat. "You know nothing's finished till I tell you it is. You know that, right, Mamita?"

There was another deafening silence that poured into my ear and plugged it. I was alone, with his words surrounding me and tightening themselves around my chest. Then there was a click.

My mother told me that she could move our things into the basement apartment, and I could stay there until I found a new place. She said she would keep Wanda and care for her as long as I didn't let Santos near her. "If you want to go back to that maniac, it's your choice, but you can't take my grandchild back there." My mother had that way of owning everything that I did that was worthwhile. Now she was taking ownership of my child.

My hands shook as I tried to wrap the pictures from the summer. The pictures of Wanda and Santos together made me remember the day I brought her to my mother's. I found Wanda in her room staring at the wall when I came from the grocery. I asked her what was wrong, and she just looked at me with a strange expression in her eyes. As I studied her face, I realized that I knew that expression. It turned my stomach. The silence that passed between us slashed away at my insides. I would have screamed from the pain, but he might have heard. I shook my child, trying to loose the words from inside her mouth, or wherever she had buried them. They would not come free. I covered my mouth with my hand to trap the cry in my chest.

A sick, ugly feeling swept over me like a wave. I whispered to her, "You get dressed," and I got a shopping bag and put her panties, undershirts, and socks into it. Wanda pleaded with her eyes for me to stop. I put the bag in the closet and went to check on him. He was in the kitchen drinking a beer. Trying to sound matter of fact, I said, "You know, I forgot to tell you my mother invited Wanda over for a sleepover. She said somethin' about renting some movie they wanted to see."

"It's too late for you to be goin' over there now, and I'm not takin' you." Santos looked at me with his eyes with no back, the kind that made him seem more like a feral animal than a man.

"It's only seven thirty. Still light out," I said, waving Wanda back into the room when she peeked in. "I'll be back by eight thirty, and we can have the evening to ourselves, and we can get up whenever we want tomorrow," I said entwining my arms around him.

"Nah. I want you both here in this house," he said.

"But I already told my mother yes, Santos. Come on, I've been thinkin' about us bein' together all day long." I held his head against my chest, although the touch of his oily hair made me sick.

He brushed his hair back from his face. He seemed to be studying the label on the bottle of beer, and then he took another long swallow of it and told me, "You don't stop, do you?" He put his hand on my behind and said, "All right."

I went to get the bags and Wanda before he changed his mind and put my finger to my lips, telling her not to talk. When we got to the door, he said something about me being awful anxious to go. Then he grabbed the bag and said, "How much stuff are you taking?" He pushed me across the room, took my arm, and wrenched it behind my back. When I tried to pull away, he took me by the neck and banged my head into the bedroom door. I couldn't figure out how to get away from him.

"Papi, stop," Wanda said, and he slapped her, leaving a crimson pool under the skin on her cheek where his hand had been. I ran to the window and shouted, "He's killing my child! Call the police, please." He pulled me in and punched me in the mouth. The taste of flesh and salt collected in my throat and made it burn.

Leroy, the cop on the second floor, banged on the door and shouted at Santos to leave us alone. He told him the precinct was sending over a squad car. He yelled for him to open the door. When Santos told him to mind his own damned business, Leroy kicked the door open, grabbed him, and put him against the wall. When the cops got there and asked me if I wanted to press charges this time, I was holding on to Wanda and had a bag of ice on my mouth Leroy's wife had given me. I said yes and nodded at the same time.

Now I held on to the table and chair and eased myself down so that I would not fall. I looked around at the kitchen with its dingy walls and table with splintered edges, and I knew I had to get out of there as soon as I could. He wasn't going to leave me alone. He would find me at my mother's place. I began to think of how I could do it. I had saved more than $200 from temping, and I would get a two-week check tomorrow. A woman in my group told me about a building in Queens with a super who might not ask for a whole month's security if he got something under the table. I didn't know how much. Another one told me about a shelter, but I didn't want to go there. I needed to talk to someone so I could think straight and stop shaking.

I dialed Camille's number. The phone rang one short ring, and she picked up.

"Yes, Cole."

"Who's Cole?" I said, more to distract myself than anything else.

"Girl, where have you been? I called your house I don't know how many times..." Camille said.

"I haven't...well..." I did not have words.

"You OK?"

"Yeah, sure." I didn't want to just spill all my fears all over the place. I needed to sort through them and pick the ones I could cope with. "Who is this Cole?"

"You are not going to believe this. I met this man. I'm sitting having...you got time?"

"Sure, just sitting and thinking." I tried to concentrate on Camille's voice, so that it could take me away from the dark place Santos's voice had put me.

"I took Shawn out for breakfast, and he spills his syrup, and this man—he's reading the *Times*—he offers us to sit at his table."

I wanted to tell Camille that I hurt. I could not get the words out. She went on. I tried to catch her words.

"I ended up sitting there, but Saundra, this guy's not my type."

I got lost there in her words. There were too many. "I don't understand what you mean."

"He's sort of muscular. About five ten, and he's built like a football player."

She was babbling. I could not make sense of what she was saying.

"You know the type I always liked were the tall, lean guys. And he just sounded so straight, and it turns out he's in the military. Now really, Saundra, the military."

I lost my patience. "Camille, you haven't had a type since Victor. At least he's got a steady job, more than I can say for some shaky Negroes I know."

"I just didn't feel any spark. But here's the thing: he paid our bill."

No man ever did that for me. I would give anything for a man to just not hurt me.

"So, something he said made me laugh, and we spent the day walking to the park and talking. He's a nice guy."

I began to follow the pictures she was drawing in my mind. "Camille, I don't understand what the problem is. Someone was nice to you." I wished I knew what that felt like.

"I can't make myself feel something for somebody."

"I'm not saying that. I'm just saying that maybe we would have been happier if we had picked one of the guys in college who were good guys, who we used to laugh our heads off at. I always went for these guys who were cool, the bad boys. Look what it got me."

"Anyway, he called me just now and asked me out on Sunday, to take Shawn to the planetarium. So when you called, I thought it was him calling back."

"Camille, did you forget the brunch is on Sunday?"

"He said he'd come down to the restaurant to get me after the brunch and drive me uptown to get Shawn. I mean…do you see what I mean? Too nice. But Shawn would like to go, so I'll go. I just hope he doesn't try anything."

"Why don't you just enjoy this? You know what I would give for just a few minutes with a guy who cared about me. I never had that, ever."

"I'm past my days when I…I'm not going to sleep with him just 'cause he takes me out, with AIDS and everything."

"Sooner or later you're gonna want to…at least he's a nice guy." There was a long silence. "Camille, Santos called here." I couldn't stop the words from escaping my lips and the images from churning about in my mind any longer.

"From jail? Isn't he still supposed to be in jail?"

"He got the divorce papers. He's getting out of Rikers in a couple of weeks."

"What did he say?"

"He says it's not over until he says so. I have to put together a plan to get out of here." I told Camille my thoughts, mostly so that I could hear them out loud myself.

"Hang in there, girl. That's why I don't want you treating us to the brunch. You need your money. And I can give you some if you need."

"Huh?" I heard what she said, but my mind was racing through my options.

"I said, I know you have to save your money to move, and if you need…"

"I don't want to ask you for money, Camille. I am just so happy to have you to talk to. It helps me think straight."

"Well, if you need."

Here I am again, I thought. The one Camille helps, because I can't get my shit together. I tried to choke the tears out of my voice. "Yeah, sure." I hoped I could be brave enough to handle everything I had to do. No matter how hard I tried, my life was…

"Camille, appreciate this man. God knows I never chose the good guys. I gotta go."

"Virginity is like a smoke ring. When it's gone, you're left with ashes and a butt," I laughed as I poked my finger through the last one. "I lost mine in the locker room with Leon last Friday." Camille and I sat on the floor with our feet propped on the bed. I blew smoke rings that floated above my head.

"Really? You did it? How did it feel? Did it hurt a lot?" Camille asked. "You didn't tell me you were going to do it."

I lit another Salem. "I don't tell you everything, you know. And I didn't know I was going to do it just then. Remember last Friday, I told my mother we were going to the library to study."

"I did go to the library to study," Camille said.

"Yeah, well, I met Leon down by the schoolyard, and he starts rappin'. He tells me he's hangin' out with Charlene now. He looked so cute. So I tell him I met this guy at school, just to make him jealous, and he starts askin' me if he's as good as he is. So we're standing on the corner, and he starts kissing me. And then says he's got a key to the school building, and we can go into the locker room. I said, 'You lie,' and he takes out a key. So we go over to the school, and, sure enough, the key works, and we go in."

"Weren't you scared someone would catch you?"

"No, I wasn't scared. It was sort of spooky, but it was sexy. So we go into the locker room. He takes off my bra and stuff, and we did it."

"Did it hurt?"

"A little. Anyway, Leon and the guys, Bullet and Jelly, are supposed to be down on the corner. Come on. Let's go down."

"I really can't. I have some homework to do."

"Figures."

"And I promised your mother I'd cook tonight, so…"

"You know, Camille, you make me look bad when you volunteer like that."

"I just feel I should help. Look, it's really nice of your folks to let me stay here while Aunt Lil is in Barbados. And you better be careful of that guy Jelly."

"Ol' Jelly. Why? He's OK."

"He got suspended from school for being drunk in class. He just seems…I don't know. He's just bad news. Be careful."

I pushed my head out the window, and Leon was standing on the corner smoking a cigarette, laughing and pointing his finger at Jelly. Jelly laughed and then cupped his hand over his crotch. I put on my sandals, lit a cigarette, and walked out onto the street. Ever since Leon and I had done it, my breasts had felt full, and now I could feel the wet heat of the June day drape itself around my hips and backside. I wanted to go talk Leon into going to someplace cool.

"Hi, Leon!"

"Hey, my sweet thing."

"Hey, Jelly, Bullet."

"Where's that friend of yours?" Jelly said. "The one with the glasses. I likes the quiet types."

"Camille? She's home, cooking. Hey, Leon...can't we go somewhere?" I could feel Jelly's eyes on me as I whispered in Leon's ear.

"I got some reefer. Want to go up on the roof at 349?" Jelly said, walking toward the building.

"Yeah. Come on, baby." Leon laced his fingers in mine and pulled me along behind him.

Jelly and Bullet walked ahead of us, whispering, and then Jelly glanced back at me with a funny look in his eye. We all waded through kids playing on the sidewalks. At the apartment building, we had to step around and past a slew of kids playing stoop ball and jumping rope, and one little boy who blocked our path just for the fun of it.

"You can't make me move," sneered the little boy as Jelly lifted his leg and stepped over him.

Leon led the way up the stairs. At the top landing, a few steps above us, was a red, heavy metal door and a strong smell of urine. Jelly pushed past us, in a take-charge attitude, and opened the door. He looked behind it for anyone who might be hiding there. The floor of the roof was covered in tar, which spread underfoot, like soft clay, with each step I took. Jelly dragged around a big wooden beam and propped it against the door to keep it closed. Then he put his hand in his right hip pocket and drew out a small manila envelope. His usual broad gestures now became controlled as he pulled out a thinly rolled cigarette. He lit it and then inhaled deeply, keeping the smoke in his lungs, and then he passed it to Leon.

"Hey, my man," he said, his voice straining as he tried to keep the smoke inside as he spoke. Leon took a drag and handed the joint to Bullet.

"Here you go, Saundra," Jelly said, taking it from Bullet and giving it to me. "Don't you want a hit?"

"Sure do." The few times I had smoked with Leon, I liked how free it made me feel. I took a drag. It burned my throat and made me cough. With each cough, I felt as if my head was expanding. Jelly took a hit and then handed the joint back to Leon, and then he lifted his chin and pointed it toward me to be sure I wasn't missed in the go 'round.

"You want to go somewhere?" I whispered in Leon's ear again. He pulled me around the back of the brick enclosure to the stairwell and into the shadows, which had grown long and violet, casting a purple hue on Leon's dark face. He kissed me deeply. I felt my dungarees loosen at the waist. He kissed me again, and I lost myself in his arms and his lips. He reached for the joint, which was handed to him by Jelly.

"Man, why don't you guys get lost?" Leon said.

"That's my joint, my man," Jelly answered.

Leon put the joint to my lips. I drew again, this time letting the smoke enter my lungs. I looked into Leon's face, and his stare was intense, taking my breath away. I kissed him again and felt his hands on my body. We made out for I don't know for how long. He pulled my blouse out of my pants and rubbed his hands on my butt.

"Take them off," he said.

In the stupor of the smoke and his gaze, all of my inhibitions were stripped away. I pulled my pants down, and, hearing him say "off" again, I did what I was told. He took them out of my hands and flung them down and motioned for me to lie on them while he undid his. Now he was a black silhouette surrounded by the deep violet sky. He put his own body down on mine. At first I was aware of only the muscles and taut flesh of his abdomen. Then I felt him enter. As I held on, I tried to become one with him. He eluded me, asserting his selfhood, slamming into me again and again until he collapsed into me in one final assault. It was so quick.

He rested a few minutes, and I stared into the darkness. My skin was damp and cooling now, but tingling. The pressure of him on my chest and stomach gave me a sensation of heat in my belly. My center was pulled off in too many directions so often that I felt torn inside. Now I had a center.

Leon pushed himself up into a kneeling position. In my mind's eye, I saw him looking at me. Then I heard some whispers off to my right, and I remembered Jelly and Bullet. I had forgotten they were there. I covered my breasts with my hands and reached around for my pants. There were more whispers moving closer.

"She's hot, man," I heard Jelly say in a raspy voice. "She looks like she could use some more. She your woman?"

Leon said nothing. I felt Jelly move on top of me and grab my hand as I tried to reach for my pants.

"Open up," Jelly said in a guttural voice, pinning my hands down beside me. I felt I should struggle or tell him no, but something made me stay still to feel what he was like. He was different from Leon. His chest was bony, like a wooden birdcage turned on its side pressing against me. His arms were long and his hands were rough, and he held my buttocks as he pounded me in jerky movements. Then, as if he were possessed, he began making growling noises like an animal. I would have been afraid had I not been so curious about the sensation of him until, without warning, he simply stopped moving and lifted himself off me. Though my body was numb, my mind was strangely focused. My skin felt cold, and I heard voices over me.

"Go on, Bullet," I heard Jelly say. The sound of his voice made my shoulders hunch, and before my mind actually felt shame, my body did. I contracted and I pulled up my knees to my chest and tried to cover myself with my pants.

"Naw, man," I heard Bullet whisper.

"You pussy, Bullet."

Then I felt two stubby hands pull my heels straight out. As I stared at the darkness, a heavy weight pinned me to the ground. A scream was trapped inside my chest. I knew no one would help me. I was alone, and I could not stop them. I had no real thoughts, just a sickness that rose in my stomach and got stuck in my throat. I wanted to cover my face, but my hands were pinned under the bulk of him, and I remembered trying to stay absolutely still, waiting for it to be over. It was a feeling from so long ago.

I had done it again. I had let it happen again, I thought. I must like it. How did I do this again? I was the nasty little girl who had let this happen again.

For an instant I felt that I must be dying, because I was sure I could not draw a breath. My body was now dead. I could see nothing in the blackness that enveloped me. All was still, save the droplet of water and salt that drew a line from the corner of my eye down my temple and rested itself in my ear.

I heard their footsteps in the tar, and the door squeaked open and then shut. My face broke, and I held myself as I listened to the sound of sobs trapped in my chest.

A glass wall came down between Camille and me after that. Words passed back and forth, but I was sealed in behind the wall, and Camille couldn't touch me. Camille ended up living at my house for three weeks. I spent most of the time in the house, because the boys were all talking about what Leon and the others had done to me. Camille denied it whenever she heard it, telling the girls what liars Jelly and Leon were. But whenever we did go out, there were whispers and snickers. Camille would tell me that the pain would end and that I would feel clean again, but I bathed myself in my tears and peered through the glass wall at Camille as if to say, "You'll see. It's not over."

Then something changed. I felt it. Camille said she saw it too. She said that I looked as if there was a small smirk painted on my lips. I said maybe it was simply the way the light played on my face. I looked in the mirror. She was right. It was an expression that made it appear as if I was saying, "I don't care." But as I looked more closely, it was more like "I can't care anymore."

Several days passed. Camille was working as a counselor at the church day camp. The girls in the neighborhood still whispered behind my back. I challenged them with an expression that had now changed to a sneer. A gulf now separated me and the others and the wall.

It was that summer that I began to wear the brightest yellows and oranges and reds. It was then that I perfected my walk. I sauntered down the street tossing my wavy, long brown-black hair in the hot, sticky summer air. I knew that my walk enticed men to stretch and crane their necks into the most peculiar positions just to gain a glimpse of me.

7

JEWEL

"Who am I kidding? I don't want to go to this brunch." *And why won't Gordon call me back? His damned secretaries wouldn't even tell me whether he was in LA or Chicago.* "I know if he is in LA, his wife is going try to sink her fangs into him and get the kids to guilt-trip him." I took a gulp of my coffee, but as soon as it went down, I knew it was a mistake. *Variety, Show Business* and the *Sunday Times* in pieces all around me in bed, and I didn't remember reading a thing. I moved the tray over to the other side of the bed and opened my night table to get my Mylanta.

"Why did I agree to this? I don't feel like seeing Camille and Saundra right now." I am talking to myself out loud again. And what is their agenda anyway?

It was nine thirty-five. I caught sight of a photo of Gordon and me on the night table. It was the night we met at the music awards. God, he was gorgeous. His skin all coppery, and there was a bluish cast to his jaw where the shadow of his beard was. He had just a few silver strands in his temples, and he was impeccable in that silk tux. *Gordon, you make me so hot! Why don't you call me back?* That night I knew, as soon as I saw him that he was going to be my husband. Of course, I didn't know about his wife then. Later that night at the bar, he mentioned his divorce. Then, of course, I was certain. It was fated, my meeting him there. Perfect timing. After he made love to me that night, that was it. Done deal.

What was I thinking, making plans to go out on a Sunday morning? I put some cottage cheese on a piece of melba toast, took a bite, and brushed the crumbs from my fingertips. Instinctively, I reached for the phone to call Gordon. My hands were trembling. I put the phone down. I wish he wouldn't do this to me. He knows how upsetting it is when he doesn't call me back. I carried the tray into the kitchen, took the almost-empty bottle of white wine out of the refrigerator, and poured it into a glass. "I'll just have a spritzer to help my mood," I said, unscrewing the club soda and topping it off.

I caught sight of myself in the mirror in the foyer. I wonder if Camille and Saundra have kept their bodies in as good shape as I have. Probably not Camille; she always had a weight problem. Saundra is probably still beautiful in a "yellow skinned," "good hair" kind of a way. She always had that hourglass figure, big hips, big boobs. I don't work out enough, but I am still size six, and my stomach is flat as a pancake. The more I think about it, the more I want to see them—better yet, I want them to see me. Seeing them at this point in my life would mean that it was all connected. My life so often seems like scenes in a play in which I perform, but I always feel so lost. But now my business is growing, and I am planning a June wedding, although Gordon doesn't know about it yet. Men are so naïve. Everything is coming together.

I stood at the counter and ate the last bit of my Melba toast and finished off my wine. I walked into the bathroom, grabbed the bouffant shower cap, and looked into the mirror. The facial I got Friday night at the salon didn't help. The dark circles and puffiness under my eyes were still there with the lines in my brow, even though I had been using my best night creams. As I was about to step into the shower, I thought I might not hear the phone if Gordon called. I have to call him first. I grabbed my robe, ran into the living room, and sat in my big armchair.

I reached for the phone. It rang. Startled me. He was calling, finally. "Hi, Gordon," I said, swallowing my hurt.

"Jewel, it's me, Verta. I just wanted to give you a heads-up. There's a prob...Nadege is sick."

"But isn't she in Rio?"

"Exactly."

"Can't she see a doctor? Tell *Vogue* to send us the bill."

"No, she's throwing up, chills—really sick. I have Toya to fill in, and if she can't do it, Justine as a backup. I have June working on the airline tickets. You have that brunch engagement today, right?"

"I do, but I can cancel it...actually, I want to cancel it."

"No, you should get out. Jewel, you need to...I have this covered."

"I need to what?"

"Focus on something other than the office, and..."

"And...and, what?"

"Jewel, I know you don't want to hear this, but between opening the Chicago office and Gordon, you seem almost frantic sometimes. You had June call him about ten times this week."

"June is exaggerating. I am sure it wasn't that many calls."

"Look, you need to focus on something else. Seeing old friends might be a good thing. I just wanted to let you know about this. I've got this covered. I'll buzz you later."

There was a click. You don't know, Verta. Seeing old friends. Every time I think about them, I remember things I want to forget—Hancock Street and my mother. So many ghosts back there.

I scanned my living room. I had asked the designer to give me pristine, and we decided on white on white. I wanted the antithesis of Bed Stuy and the muck I remembered being my home when I was little. But the light from the terrace and the large picture windows reflected off the white sofas and the armchairs. This room is too white, I thought. I feel suffocated by all this white. Verta has to get the designer to come in and tell me what to do here. *My mind is wandering.* I checked the time. "So it's nine fifty-five here; it's eight fifty-five there. It's not too early to call, but I'll wait till nine o'clock his time, and I'll just say I forgot the time difference. Then I can take my shower, do my makeup, and call a cab, and I will get there at just about eleven forty or so. I don't want to get there first and have to wait for them anyway."

The phone rang again. "So what happened, Verta? Do you want me to do some handholding with the photographer?"

"Jewel? It's me, Camille."

"Oh, Camille, I'm in the midst of something with the office."

There was a long pause.

"Well, I just wanted to touch base with you before the brunch... today. You are coming, right?"

"Frankly, all morning I've been thinking about calling you. I just don't know. I've got this thing with a model in Rio. I think this was just a bad time to schedule this. Here I am going on and on. Why were you calling?"

"Well, if you aren't coming, it doesn't matter," she said, and then she was silent.

"I didn't say I wasn't coming. I have to see if I can work out this issue. I've got a lot on my mind."

"I am sorry."

That's what pissed me off about her. She always sounded like she cared.

"Jewel, I was just calling because Saundra was saying that she wanted to treat us to the brunch, and she just got a steady job. I know she's trying to get a new apartment to get away from her husband, who—"

"Camille, net it out for me. What's going on?"

"I was wondering if the two of us could just insist on picking up the check."

"Sure. Look, I'll just pick it up." That's it. They want me to pick up the check. "I don't know if I'm coming, though."

"I wasn't asking you to pick it up. We can split it. I just didn't want Saundra—"

"Whatever. Look, Camille, seeing you and Saundra...this is the worst time for me. I'll see...if I can come, I will be there. If not..."

There was that quiet again. Camille always had a way of inserting her silences into conversations and making me feel guilty.

"Jewel, we were really looking forward to seeing you. But...I'll explain it...if you don't come, to Saundra. And maybe some other time...when things are less..."

"This is my world, Camille. It's always hectic. Look, I will try to see you later."

When I hung up the phone, I felt so bollixed up. My stomach was in a knot. In college it had been the same thing. I was the one with the apartment. Where did they come? My place. They thought it was so great, me having my own place. I would have given anything to be living at home with my parents like Saundra, or have an aunt like Camille's aunt who gave a shit about me. I am not going. Every time I think about them, I am this little dark-skinned black girl with no home.

Instinctively, I reached for the phone, to call Gordon. I dialed. And once it started to ring, I hung up. Verta is right. I shouldn't be calling him. He should be calling me. Maybe she's right about getting out. I have to get out of here. At the very least, Camille and Saundra will be a distraction.

I walked into the bathroom and took off my robe. I looked at my body in the full-length mirror. I was still hot. My breasts were still firm and my best asset. I stepped into the shower. My coconut vanilla shower gel filled the room with sweetness. I began to lather myself up. Thinking about Gordon made me feel excited. I remembered the first time we made love in the shower. He pushed me up against the cool tiles and then turned me around, and I had to grip the faucet to keep my balance. *You're not going to screw with my mind, Gordon.* I let the water rinse me off and then turned the cold water on to regain my senses. *Stay on track, Jewel.*

I took the brush and scrubbed my back and the heels of my feet. I scrubbed my elbows to get off any dead skin. I used the loofa, and it was beginning to burn. Women with light skin, like Saundra—they don't know how much easier it is on them. I have to be so careful of my appearance, of everything.

I scrubbed my face with the glycolic cleanser, just to renew it. I shut off the water, stepped out, and closed the door to see my reflection again. The water glistened on my breasts. Gordon's wife would pay big bucks for tits like these. She's a saggy, fat mess.

I decided to give myself a quick facelift by snatching my hair back and up into a topknot. John, my hairdresser, had given me a full, soft style, letting my hair brush my shoulders, good for tossing about. But I needed to get rid of the drooping flesh above my eyes and the lines that creased my forehead. I sat down to moisturize from head to toe. *Can't be ashy.* "What does one wear to a brunch in Brooklyn?" I hadn't been back to Brooklyn in years. It wasn't that I was avoiding it. There was just no one there that I wanted to remember.

Understated, accomplished, ease, no glitz, I thought. Armani, of course! I stepped into my closet and pulled out my café au lait–colored Armani suit. I had an ivory-colored blouse that contrasted beautifully with my chocolate-brown complexion. My open-toed sandals showed off my pedicure. As I selected each piece, I held it up in front of me, to study it in the full-length mirror, and then draped it carefully on the bed.

It was ten thirty-five, fifteen minutes behind my schedule. *Maybe Gordon didn't call me back because...something happened to him.*

The phone rang four times. *Where is he?* I glanced over at the clock, which gave me the time in New York, Chicago, LA, and Paris simultaneously. It was a cute little gadget I had gotten for myself for Christmas, after we started seeing each other. I wonder if he's in LA. When I noticed that it was a little after seven thirty there, my hands began to shake so hard I almost dropped the phone. At the same time, I heard him say "Yes" in a tired, husky voice. I was certain I had awakened him from a deep sleep. I could hang up, but once I heard his voice, I needed to talk to him.

"Gordon, did I wake you? I didn't realize you were in LA. I had a really bad week, and when I didn't hear back from you, I got worried."

"Jewel?" he said in a hushed tone. "Was it you on the phone before?"

"No, before? No. I did call your office this week. Did your secretary—I think it was Janice—did she give you my messages?"

"Yeah, I got them, all of them. I was in Boston. Jewel, you can't expect me to drop everything to call you all the time." His voice was raspy, as if he was trying to whisper. "Look, it's barely seven thirty here."

"Why didn't you tell me you were going to be in Boston? Maybe I could have come up...I just needed to hear your voice. Are you coming to New York for the reception?"

"What reception?"

"What reception! Gordon, my reception at Tavern on the Green."

"When is it?"

"Didn't you get the invite? I can't believe those girls could screw up like that. It's November twentieth."

"I'll see what I can do. Look, I'm half asleep."

"I'm sorry, Gordon. I love you. If you can't get here, it's OK. I'll be seeing you the week before Christmas. I've arranged to be in Chicago from December fifteenth through the fifteenth of January."

"Jewel," he said, "I told you, don't make plans for me. I also told you not to count on me for Christmas. I'm with my kids on Christmas." He seemed to raise his voice and then muffle the phone.

"I know you have the kids. I thought maybe we could both do something with them."

"Jewel, this is a bad time for them. Cut it...I told you not to do this already..."

I heard a woman's voice in the background. I asked him, "Who's there? Is someone there with you, Gordon?"

"What do you mean? No. Well, yes. Look, I told you I can't talk. I gotta go."

The click pounded my eardrum. *Why did you do that?* I drew in air, conscious of the breaths filling my chest. *I needed to talk to you.* I closed my eyelids and rested my fingertips just above my hairline so as not to mar my makeup. *That's OK. I didn't want to spend Christmas with kids, anyway.* I concentrated on the tears, which were forming just behind my eyelids, to make them stay where they were. *I will not cry.* I was very good at this. *We will spend New Year's together. No need for tears.* I had been able to stop myself from crying occasionally when I was a child and when I was living with my aunt and uncle. I had perfected my ability to stop my tears working for my first boss, who would humiliate me in front of clients. *That bitch wants to see me cry.* Owning my own business made me develop this ability into an art form. *I could probably let the tears fall, begin to roll, and have them turn back and recede at will if I want to.*

I grabbed my purse, walked back into the kitchen, ran the water, took out a glass, and filled it. I dug my pillbox out of my bag and took out a small white pill. *Just for the edge.*

Back in the bedroom, I surveyed my outfit. Perfect. I slipped the blouse over my head, stepped into the slacks, and slipped into the heeled sandals. I painted my lips, blushed my cheeks and nose, and then put on my jacket. I didn't feel finished. On the right side of the closet, on the wall where I had pegs and cubbies built in, I pulled out a honey-colored scarf sprayed with wisps of aquamarine. I threw it over my shoulder and watched how it billowed and then rested naturally in place. Done, I thought. Drop-dead gorgeous. *Such a waste! I should be going out with a man.*

The forgotten tears draped themselves over my mind, making me feel melancholy. The sadness lay just beneath my consciousness. It made me mad. It produced an edge in my voice that sliced through everything I said. I could tell because of the way the cab driver looked back at me when I told him the address.

"Ma'am, I was here on time, and waiting, and you came down almost twenty minutes—"

"I know when I came down," I said. I didn't need him telling me anything. So I will be there a little late. Camille and Saundra will wait. It will be great making my entrance. I can't wait to see them see me, I thought.

I bet you it was his wife's voice I heard. She is such a conniving bitch. But he should know that by now. Gordon needs to get it together. I have set the date for a June wedding, and he is messing with my timeline.

"I'm going to have you out of here so fast your head will spin," my aunt said. I remembered the sick mix of guilt and shame I felt as I walked to my room. It had happened in an instant. I hadn't thought about the consequences when I did it. It was spontaneous, and it felt like a kind of thrill at first. I was in the shower and felt that wonderful tingling chill when I turned off the warm water and the cool air kissed my breasts. I caught sight of my image in the mirror and wondered if I was correct in the fleeting thought that maybe I was beautiful. My skin was dark and my hair short, and my only really positive attributes were my large breasts and small waist. But with the beads of shower water resting on my skin and the light playing on the droplets, yes, I thought maybe I *was* beautiful.

I could hear my uncle in the living room, yelling at the Knicks on the television. He yelled out to my aunt, "Janice, is there any more beer in the fridge?"

"I'll get it," I yelled out. I wrapped the towel around myself, tucked the corner of it in covering my breast, and walked into the kitchen. I took out a bottle of Pabst Blue Ribbon beer, dug into the drawer for the bottle opener, and brought it to the living room. I felt my uncle's eyes on me before I saw them.

"You better go put on some clothes, girl," he said, as he seemed unable to stop his eyes from traveling the length of me.

It had only been a split second after I heard my aunt say, "I think there is some still left" when she entered the room.

I was struck by the power of my towel-wrapped body. My aunt literally took a step backward at the sight of me. She began to speak, and her voice seemed to get blocked in her throat. Her eyes flashed from me to her husband and then back.

"What in the hell are you doing? I told my brother the apple doesn't fall far from the tree. You are a whore, just like your mother." She had finally said it, and it was no surprise. I had felt as if they thought there was something dirty about me from the start. From the moment I entered this house, I felt sullied as if they wished they could scrub me with a brush each night. Instead, my aunt would bathe me, brush my hair and plait it, and make me kneel and pray each night that God should help me be a good girl. That prayer now popped into my mind, and made so much more sense after my aunt finally said what she had been thinking all this time.

"You must think you are the woman in this house. You think you are going to parade yourself around in my house in front of my husband? You better go and get yourself some clothes right quick. I am not going to have this going on in my house," she said, flinging her words at me as I left the room.

"Give me the phone. I am calling my brother. This ungrateful bitch is not going to continue this behavior in my house," she shouted so I could hear her.

She came to my room and flung open the door with the phone in her hand, the long, snakelike coiled cord stretching from the living room. "I'm going to have you out of here so fast your head will spin."

I would have felt something if I had had the time. But what struck me was that my aunt knew my father's number. I had asked to speak to my father many times, and my aunt had always said she couldn't reach him. I had stopped asking on my eleventh birthday, because it was such a disappointment. Each time I asked, it was something else. He did not have a phone, or had moved, or could not be found. I wrote him some letters and gave them to my aunt. She said they came back, but I never saw them.

But now my aunt was calling him, as I watched. "James, you better come take this girl out my house. What did I tell you about the apple not falling far from the tree? She is a whore, just like her mother."

He must have said something, because she listened and then fired off a comment. "I told you how she keeps walking around in a bra and panties when I told her that that wasn't appropriate in front of her uncle. Well, today she goes walking in front of him in a towel. Naked and a towel."

She listened and then said, "Where did she get that from? She doesn't see me walking around exhibiting myself. I told you, she has it in her blood. I can't deal with this anymore. You come get her." She hung up the phone.

The house was silent for a long while after that. I tried to talk to her, but it was as if I were invisible. She walked past me as if I weren't there. I had no one to talk to, no real friends at school. So I began to look at myself each morning for signs that my aunt was right. Was I a whore? I knew I wanted to feel that my uncle felt I was pretty. I did deliberately walk in front of him. I wanted him to look at me. I loved the stares of the boys at school. When I would leave home, I would hike up my skirts to show my thighs. I would put on brightly colored lipstick and black pencil to outline my eyes while looking at my reflection in the windows along the avenue on the way to the bus. By the time I got to the stop, I had transformed my appearance to attract the attention that I needed.

Was there something in my blood? I wondered at the details of what my mother had done. My aunt and uncle never told me why I was living with them. They shielded me from the events that had led up to my being brought to them and I couldn't remember. I knew that my father had taken me from my mother. I knew that my aunt always told me that the colors I chose were too bright, and my blouses shouldn't be so revealing. Now it was out in the open. My aunt had finally said what she had wanted to say. The full shame of my mother was mine.

Over the next two weeks, my injured feelings were mixed with the anticipation of seeing my father. I wondered when he would come for me. I ironed my favorite blouses and slacks each day, thinking that it might be the day that he would come for me. Exactly two weeks passed. It was a Saturday morning, and I was cleaning the kitchen counters and emptying the crumbs from the toaster when my aunt came into the room and said, "Your father is here in New York, and he wants to see you. He will be here in about an hour."

I felt good that my aunt actually looked at me, and I began to say I was sorry, but she put up her hand as if to block my words from reaching her. I finished cleaning the counter and the kitchen table, and then I ran to the bathroom to wash my face and shower off the perspiration I felt in the creases of my underarms.

I could not think straight. I put on a white blouse I liked and buttoned it demurely. I picked out my Afro, then put on a touch of makeup. I looked at my face and thought, I hope he thinks I'm pretty. I pulled a pair of black slacks on and tucked in the blouse. As I was looking for a belt, I heard the bell ring and heard voices in the foyer. I ran to my dresser and opened the top drawer to pull out the certificate that said I was in the honor society in school. I wanted to show my father that despite what my aunt said about me, I was a good girl.

I heard conversation in the living room between my aunt, my uncle, and my father, but I couldn't make out the words they said. When my father entered my room, I tried to embrace him, but his stare stopped me in my tracks. He stared at my breasts and my hips and looked at my face. He looked so much older than I remembered. "Daddy, I don't know what they told you, but I—"

And then it came. It was a barrage of anger spewed at me that seemed stored up for years. "You write me these letters asking for the truth of why I left your mother. I took you out of that house because your mother was drinking and bringing men into my house and whoring herself. I sent you here so that you could be raised the right way, but you are throwing that all away. Look at you wearing makeup, tight clothes, and now exhibiting yourself half naked in front of my sister's husband. I am washing my hands of you."

I remembered wanting to say they had gotten it all wrong. "Daddy," I was going to say, "that's not what happened." But the look in his eyes and the way his eyes swept over my breasts and my hips stopped the words in my mouth, choking them back into my throat. I wanted to take a shower to clean the stares off, yet I felt that somehow he knew the truth. I did want my uncle to see my naked body. I had fantasized about him looking at me for a long time. I did want my father to think me beautiful.

"Your aunt has had enough. You are going to be eighteen," my father said. "We're going to get you into some kind of a group home. Maybe they can do a better job than we have. I have the money from your mother's insurance put aside for you for college."

It was done. My things were packed, and I was in the home in less than three weeks. I begged them not to send me, but I could see that my aunt wouldn't budge. My father was gone and once again could not be reached.

When I arrived at the group home, the kids looked like a group of misfits. One girl had dyed black hair and was wearing gloves with the fingers cut off and dungarees with frayed bottoms and holes in the knees. Another girl had wild hair that seemed as if it hadn't been combed in days. There was a black boy, Juan. Juan was the only name I recalled from the names thrown out by the social worker, a woman who seemed to want to be upbeat and cheery even though none of us felt that way. She showed me to my room. I shared it with the girl with the leather cut-off gloves.

The girl tried to tell me which side of the closet was hers. "The lounge is down the hall," she said as she left the room. I looked around the room, with its Formica furniture and worn, stained carpet. My eyes surveyed the confined space and scanned from the door to the desk to the dirty window looking out on an alleyway, and back to the beds. I could smell the institutional odor of the room and became lightheaded and nauseated. I had no one to protect me. I was on my own. That was when I realized that my aunt was right all those days ago. My head did spin.

8

SAUNDRA

Why did I plan this brunch? What's wrong with me? I don't think before I do things. It always gets me in trouble. I peeked in the window before I opened the door to the restaurant. It looked fine.

"You going in?" A woman asked, holding the door for me.

"Yes...thanks."

"Welcome to Caribe," the hostess said.

"I have, um...reservations for three. Farrell."

"Right this way. Dennis, your waiter, will be right with you. Here's the brunch cocktail menu."

I was early. I wanted to be sure everything was perfect, though I didn't know what I would do if it wasn't. It looked really beautiful. There were freshly cut, colorful daisies in vases on each table. The peach-colored cloth napkins stood up with their points pointed out like little bird wings. There were couples and people in small groups chatting with each other. The place had a good vibe, I thought. I just hope they like it.

I started to read the menu but was distracted by my thoughts. I wondered if I could make a real place for myself at this table. Camille and Jewel had both done so much with their lives. All I credited myself with was having Wanda and finally divorcing a husband who beat me. I felt my shoulders turning inward and some-how remembered the things my support group had said.

"Straighten them shoulders. This ain't your fault." Franny, a skinny little white girl who had run away from her husband to New York from South Carolina, told me that the first day.

Devora, a brown-skinned, heavyset mother of four, said to me, "Don't you let that man make you think you are less than you are."

The group leader made me write down a list of attributes and put it up on the mirror in the bathroom, on the refrigerator, and on the door leading out of the apartment. "I'm strong and enthu-siastic and funny and loyal and attractive, and I'm good inside." Mentally reciting their words, trying to make myself really believe them again, didn't work this time.

A hand rested on my shoulder. I heard a soothing voice. "Sandy? You seemed so deep in thought, I didn't want to startle you."

"Camille? God, it's good to see you." Before I could think, I was throwing my arms around Camille's neck. She held me round the waist and rocked me from side to side.

"I missed you," she said.

"Me too."

She took my face in her hands. "Look at you. You look terrific. You're not fat. You're still so beautiful," she said, and she seemed to mean it.

"Size fourteen, but who cares."

"For me, try eighteen, twenty, but you're right. It's good to see you. This is a nice place."

"I told you I'd hook it up."

"Jewel's not here?"

"Not yet. You think she's going to show up?"

"I don't know. I actually called her earlier."

"Why?" I tried to read Camille's expression.

"No reason, really. Just to touch base."

"So, she's not coming?"

"I couldn't tell. She was telling me all the trouble she's having with a model...this is a bad time. I wasn't going to tell you until later, but she might not show."

I couldn't speak at first. Camille could tell that this was going to make me cry. "She probably isn't coming because of me. Let's face it, I'm not really in her league, or whatever you call it."

"Saundra, don't do that to yourself. This is a beautiful place you found. Let's call the waiter and get the menu." Camille dug out a packet of tissues and handed them to me.

"It is a nice place, isn't it?" I wiped the tears from my cheeks and my eyes.

"It's only eleven forty," Camille said. "She might still come."

"True. So tell me about this man."

"There's nothing to tell. The one thing that bothers me in all this is how just being in a man's presence seemed to make me so uncomfortable. I must've really cut myself off."

I sensed that what Camille said was true. Her movements were seemingly unaware of her body in its sensuality. She had never worn much makeup, but now the little that she wore seemed to have been applied to seem presentable, like when my mother would say, "I have to put on some powder to take this shine off my face."

"So, we get to meet this man later?" I asked.

"A man in New York? What man? Don't tell me they're talking about men already," Jewel said.

"Jewel, figures you'd come just about now." I stood up and stepped back to look at her. "Somebody's not fat. Don't you hate her? You look fabulous." I hugged her, and Camille held her hand until we were done and then embraced her, saying, "It's been too long. I wasn't sure you'd come."

"I told you I'd try. Let's not do the let's-see-how-long-has-it-been thing. Saundra, this is a lovely little place."

As she made that comment, a piano began to play soft strains of jazz in the background. It seemed to gently weave its way about.

The waiter, a tall, dark-skinned young man with a twinkle in his eye, brought us menus. "May I suggest a mimosa to start?"

"That's just perfect! Don't you think?" Jewel said, attracting the young man's attention with the enthusiasm of her answer.

Camille whispered, "What's a mimosa?"

"It's delicious. Trust me," Jewel said.

"I remember the people at the office mentioned that they had these great mimosas. Guess it's a drink," I whispered.

"Brilliant me. I thought they were just flowers," Camille said.

"I'll have one. Come on, girls," Jewel said.

"I'm game. Come on, Camille."

"Sure. This seems like déjà vu. Except here, Jewel is taking the lead on the drinks. Remember that day in the Village?" Camille said.

"That's right. It was the first time we met. Met again, that is."

Jewel looked up at the waiter, who was waiting quietly, and caught his gaze. "I think this handsome gentleman has something to tell us."

The young man seemed to enjoy her comment and asked if we had been there before. When we said no, he explained that it was a buffet and that we should step into the next room and note that there were Belgian waffles to the right and omelets being made to the far left. Scrambled eggs, sausages, and bacon were in the center. "We also have some dishes from the Caribbean, codfish cakes, crab cakes, and other seafood. Fresh fruit, including mango, papaya, and pineapple, and coconut bread, banana bread, and pastries are to the left. Take a look around. Help yourself."

"So you were talking about men. He was cute, wasn't he?" Jewel whispered.

"He was a little young, but cute as sin. Still can't take your eyes off the tall, dark, lean ones," I said. I couldn't help but laugh. "By the way, Camille met a man."

"I take it you mean recently. Describe him to us," Jewel said.

"You're going to get to see him later today. He's picking her up, honey."

"I don't know if I even like this man," Camille said.

"What does he do?" Jewel asked.

"I don't know. He's in the military. I don't really want to talk about him."

"Ladies," the waiter said, placing the mimosas in front of us, "enjoy."

"Thank you very much," I said, "and since this party is about divorce, I propose a toast to me."

"Saundra, you are too crazy." Camille laughed.

"Here's to me and my divorce and new beginnings."

"Absolutely. And to Jewel's new venture." Camille raised her glass to me and then to Jewel.

"And to Camille's new man," I said and giggled.

"This is delicious, but it tastes as though it's spiked."

"Of course it is—with champagne," Jewel said to Camille, seemingly amazed that she didn't know that.

"You're kidding," Camille said.

"No, why?"

"It's eleven o'clock in the morning."

"Eleven forty-something. Almost twelve. Camille, where have you been?" Jewel said.

"I think I would like some Belgian waffles. I wonder if they have fresh strawberries," Camille said, shaking her head and changing the subject.

We went into the next room, which was down a step, where there was an artistic display of dishes. I took a plate and was starting to serve myself some of the codfish cakes when I felt as if someone was looking at me. I turned to see the pianist, who seemed to smile and nod slightly at me. Reflexively, I smiled back and then commented to myself, not another musician, and I looked around to find Camille. Something drew my eyes back to him again, and as I squinted to try to see him better, I noticed that he looked like

Lester. I hadn't seen him in more than twenty years, so I wasn't certain. I went over and looked more closely and mouthed, "Lester?" He nodded, and I pointed to where our table was.

I grabbed a plate and took some eggs and fish cakes. My mind was taken up with memories of the last time he and I had spoken. I was trying to recall what had happened why I had lost touch with him. "You're never going to guess who I just saw. You probably won't even remember him." I tried to remind Camille and Jewel of the brief time that I was involved with Les as we worked our way down the buffet table.

"Les. 'Member that guy who I told you about, who lived in the Village, that I dropped acid with years and years ago? He's the piano player here."

Camille stretched herself up to look in his direction as we sat down with our plates. "I think I recall that. It was when I was still involved with Derrick. I don't remember you saying he was white."

"I think I was still on and off with Eric. He's white? I don't remember that either," Jewel said, stretching herself up to see him.

"I don't remember that being important one way or another. He was cool. He let me stay at his place when my parents put me out. I even called him later that week when you wouldn't let me in." I probably shouldn't have said that to Jewel, but she didn't even seem to have a clue as to what I was talking about. Better not to bring it up.

"I see a lot of that in my field, and very often it seems as if it's done to make a point, or to be noticed," Jewel said, as if she was holding court.

"A lot of what?" Camille asked.

"Interracial dating. Some of the men in the industry love to be seen with a black model on their arm. I'm always curious what that statement actually means. And let's not even talk about our men thinking that white women are some gift."

"Well, he was a good guy. That's what I remember. We were both a little crazy, but he never hurt me," I said more to myself than to my friends.

"So how've you been?" Camille asked, looking at Jewel. "You look terrific."

"I guess I shouldn't complain. I'm a little tired. This running back and forth takes a toll. A business like mine is like a baby. You can't leave a lot to other people. They aren't going to watch it like you will. I've got a very good assistant who keeps close tabs on everything here when I'm in Chicago. I have to establish a real presence there, and that will take time and money. And the truth is, I'm tired."

"You don't look it," Camille said.

I didn't agree. Her makeup, hair, and clothes were beautiful, but her eyes did look tired.

"I'm in love with a guy who is a lawyer, a partner in a firm in Chicago and LA. I'm just waiting for him to tell me if the beginning or the end of June is best for the wedding. I'm holding two days at a hotel here in New York, and then who knows."

"Jewel, you're getting married? You're not thinking of giving up your business, are you?" Camille asked.

"Girl, you make sure you hold on to something of your own. Don't make the same mistake I made."

Jewel's eyes dismissed my comment. It was stupid of me to have compared myself to her.

"No, of course I'm not giving up the business. But I'd like to have more time to myself."

"I can understand that. I'm just trying to decide if I'm going to apply for the principalship at my school."

"You didn't tell me. Camille, do it. It's what you've been working for."

"I don't know. I already see how time consuming it would be. People are calling me in the evening. They want me to attend all the school board meetings. It seems there are some people who want to hold the position a whole year for me until I can take it."

"I think you would make a wonderful principal. You care about kids. You can communicate with parents," I said.

"No, it's not that. I *can* do it, but I don't know if I *want* to. Every time I step into that arena, it feels like I lose who I am. I have Shawn to think about."

"You have that private school to think about too," I said. "Wouldn't you make a lot more money as a principal?"

"I know, and because of the private school, I haven't saved a penny for college. That's why I didn't just dismiss the idea."

"You should think about it long and hard before you do it," Jewel said.

I tried to stop Jewel from talking with a look, but it didn't work.

"People don't realize what's involved in running things," she said.

"Jewel's right about this. There's a lot involved, and I...I don't know. I think I'd rather just spend time with my son and write."

"Well, I think you can do it," I said. I don't know why Jewel was so discouraging.

"Saundra, it would mean politicking and glad-handing, and someone is coming over to talk to you," Camille whispered, leaning down to sip her drink.

"Sandy, right?" Lester said, nodding the way musicians do, seeming to be listening to some rhythm of life in their heads.

I did the introductions, and, feeling the quiet at the table, I stood up and moved to the bar with him.

"So, how have you been? Jeez, it's been a long time." Talking to him was like having one foot in the present and one in a flashback of my life. It had been so long ago. He still had long hair, and I saw a few streaks of silver. But his face, especially his aquamarine eyes, still had the playful, warm expression that had attracted me way back then.

"Yeah, it has. You're as beautiful as I remember you."

I couldn't help blushing. Nobody had said anything nice like that to me in a long time. "I can't believe you even recognized me or remembered me."

"Sure I did. I waited for you to call me back for a while."

I was just trying to remember what happened. I had a vague memory of what he said, but all I remembered for sure was the mess with my parents. I was supposed to call him. I thought I did. I couldn't remember. "What can I say? It was a long, long time ago. My life was in complete upheaval back then."

His eyes seemed to take in my pain. "I remember. Anyway, then I got drafted, went to 'Nam. Came back and finished college, and now I teach music and play gigs on the weekend. What about you?"

"I got married. I have a daughter."

He nodded again, listening, not saying anything.

"But I am here today, celebrating my divorce."

"Well, you are still as beautiful as ever. I said that before, didn't I? I didn't mean to take you away from your friends so long, though."

I was in a state of disbelief that he remembered me at all, or that he had waited for me to call back. Those days were so chaotic for me. I didn't know what else to say, so I changed the subject. "You play beautifully, by the way."

"Thanks, but this is the easy-listening version…met the owner at another gig. What I really like to play is a little more progressive. But gotta pay the bills."

"Don't I know it!"

"Can I call you sometime? Maybe you can come to a gig and hear my real stuff," he said, nodding again.

"Sure, I guess." I was caught off guard by his asking, but I gave him my number, and he handed me his card. Though I never expected to hear from him, it felt good to think that anyone would take an interest in me. As I walked back to the table, I noticed a guy standing in front of the restaurant and leaning on the fender of a long dark blue car. He was kind of clean cut, and I wondered if it was Camille's guy.

"Boy, does that bring back memories. I met him a few weeks after you met Eric," I said, turning to Jewel. "And Camille, that was the year you almost got kicked out of school...the demonstrations and the petition for a black studies class."

"Eric. I wonder what ever happened to him," Jewel mused.

"Camille, were you still on and off with Derrick?" I asked. After I said it, I realized I shouldn't have asked that.

"Who remembers? I was always on and off with Derrick, high school and college."

I looked at Jewel. She looked back at me. She knew why I was looking at her, but I didn't say anything. She looked at Camille, and the table got quiet. I filled the silence. "The codfish cakes and banana bread were delicious here, right?"

"The food was great," Camille said.

"And I can't believe I ran into Les. He's such a sweetheart."

"Saundra, you just got out of a mess."

Jewel still had a way of making me feel stupid.

"I don't think you ever actually saw Shawn," Camille said, fishing her wallet out of her purse. I could tell that she was trying to change the subject.

"Camille, I never asked you, who's his father? Did we know him?" Jewel asked.

"Victor, but he was not involved with him at all."

"I thought you broke up...actually, he broke it off, didn't he?" Jewel added.

"Sort of, yes. We broke up years back and then met up again about seven years ago. But he passed away a couple of years after... you know, Shawn's so smart. He's reading everything he can get his hands on, and he's just in kindergarten."

"Oh, Camille, he's such a little man. Cute as can be," I said, taking the pictures from Jewel, who stared at them without saying a word. "By the way, I got this temp job last week, and they asked for me to come back. They liked me."

"What kind of work are you doing?" Jewel asked.

"Did you bring pictures of Wanda?" Camille said.

"Receptionist and office stuff…I do…looking for them now. Just so glad they really liked me."

"She's beautiful, Saundra." Camille was smiling ear to ear. "She looks like you when you were her age."

"She's a lot smarter than me."

"She is lovely," Jewel said, handing the photo back to me.

Just as I was putting the pictures of Wanda back in my bag, I remembered. "Camille, what kind of car does your friend have? There was this guy sitting outside the restaurant on a long, midnight-blue automobile. Good-looking man, I might add."

"Saundra, stop. What time is it?" Camille blushed, shaking her head.

"Twelve twenty-five. The man is on time. Even a little early. He's been down there since I was over there talking to Les."

"I'm not ready to go. You see what I mean about this man."

"Go bring him in, Camille, and introduce him," Jewel suggested, raising her hand to get the attention of the waiter and pointing to her glass.

Camille stood up to try to see out onto the street, and when the waiter noticed her movement, he quickly went to the bar and brought the check, saying, "Your drink is on the way."

"Don't hurry off…" Jewel said, staring into the young man's eyes. "Anybody ever tell you, you should consider modeling?"

"No ma'am."

"Lose the ma'am. I'm Jewel Jamison. Are you familiar with Onyx Management?"

The young man looked confused.

"Here's my card. If you're interested, I could help you turn those good looks into a career in modeling, maybe even film. What's your name?"

"Dennis. Dennis Howell."

"Well, we can change that. I mean, come up with something a bit more suited to…give me a call, and we'll chat. By the way, can you call me a cab? I need to go into Manhattan."

When he left, I looked at Camille, and she looked at me. We couldn't tell if Jewel's comment was business or pleasure. I laughed. I started to reach for the check, and Camille pulled it away, saying, "Jewel and I discussed it and decided we cannot let you do this. Jewel and I will split this two ways. It's our treat. Happy divorce, and happy new beginning."

"Of course that's what we said. As a matter of fact, it's on me. This was great fun. You do take American Express," she said, smiling at the dimpled waiter one more time.

Camille excused herself, telling us she just wanted to tell Cole to wait. I told her we could talk another time if she wanted to leave right away. She insisted on coming back to say real good-byes and seemed a bit irritated that he was there so early.

"So, Saundra, what are your plans?"

"Well, just got this job as a receptionist. Just taking one step at a time. Hoping to move soon—"

"That's good." She cut me off. "Never bite off more than you can chew."

I felt so small in that moment, but I looked, up and there was Camille walking toward us. I stretched up to see the man, and he was standing at the doorway talking to the hostess.

"Camille, didn't you invite him over?" I asked.

"No, I just felt it was a little pushy of him to ask to come in. You see what I mean. Something about him irritates me."

"Get over it. Do you see how he's built? Mmmm. Mm. Mm. Mm. Girl, what is wrong with you? That hostess is about to come out of her skirt, her hip is so cocked to the side trying to keep his attention."

Jewel hadn't said a word. I noticed how she had looked at the man from head to toe. Cole looked in our direction, and I kicked Camille under the table. "You call that man over and introduce him. This is not like you," I said under my breath.

Camille raised her hand, beckoning Cole to the table. He was wearing a beautiful navy-blue wool blazer and a cream-colored turtleneck sweater. His upper arms bulged slightly as he unbuttoned his jacket and walked toward us. He was attractive with a strong square jaw.

"Coleman Barnes, these are my friends, Saundra Benitez…"

"Saundra Farrell," I corrected, smiling and looking approvingly at Camille.

"And this is—"

"Jewel Jamison," Jewel announced, putting her hand out as if it should be kissed.

Cole shook her hand and looked around the table at me, nodding and saying nice to meet you. He looked at Camille for guidance as to what to do next.

"Cole, I'll be out in a minute. I have to stop at the ladies' room."

"Camille, I have to go too," I said, walking after her.

"Why don't you sit down and keep me company, Mr. Barnes?" Jewel asked, gesturing for him to sit down adjacent to her before he could leave.

"Camille, what is wrong with you?" I whispered as we walked to the ladies' room and were out of earshot.

"Nothing. I just don't like him. There's no chemistry. He's not my type."

"Camille, this is a good-looking man, very good looking. What is your problem?" I said, pushing the door to the bathroom open a little too forcefully.

"I don't know. What is he doing trying to take me out? Frankly, I…I don't trust the guy. I keep wondering, what is he up to?"

"What do you mean, what is he up to?"

"I don't know."

"Camille, you go out. If he's up to something, as you put it, you'll figure it out. But why can't you just go out? What's wrong?"

"Saundra, leave me alone. I have Shawn to think about. I don't have men come and go in my house," she said, going into the stall.

"We're not talking about men here. We're talking about one man in how long?" I said through the door, insisting on being listened to.

"Forget it. I can't explain it. I just feel I don't know why he asked me out in the first place."

"He must like you."

"Right, that's what I mean. Look at me, Saundra," Camille said, pushing the door to the stall open and walking over to the sink. "I'm overweight. I can't imagine any man in his right mind asking me out. Can you?"

"How can you say that? Your face is as beautiful as when we were in college. You've put on weight, but hey, you know only dogs like bones. You are beautiful, Camille. When did you forget that? Now you get out there before Jewel snaps him up."

When we approached the table, Jewel seemed to be engrossed in conversation with Cole. She had her hand propping up her chin, staring into his eyes. Cole seemed to be leaning back away from her, and he looked relieved once he saw Camille approaching the table. "Camille, did this man tell you about all the places in the world he has been? I was just going to ask if he knew about Shawn."

I wondered what Jewel's motivations were for that comment.

"I met Shawn. He's a wonderful little guy," Cole said, seeming to study Jewel's expression more closely. Then he turned his attention to Camille.

Camille looked down at Jewel. "I'm so glad we finally did this. I hope we don't let so much time go by again."

Cole stood up, politely adding, "No rush, Camille."

"No, I've got to get home for Shawn."

Jewel stood up to embrace her and then glanced at Cole and said, "We won't let so much time go by. As a matter of fact, I was thinking you guys might enjoy this. Would you like to come to the cocktail party I'm having at the Tavern on the Green next month? It's a celebration of the Chicago office opening. It should be fun. Lots of models, actors, editors, designers. I'll send you both invitations. Bring dates, of course." She sparkled looking at Cole.

Camille hugged me and kissed my cheek and whispered in my ear, "We'll talk."

When, Camille and Cole left, I told Jewel I wanted to say good-bye to Les. As I got up, he had begun to play again, so I just waved.

The waiter brought over Jewel's credit card. He seemed cautious. "So you'll call me, and I can set up an appointment to talk, have some head shots done. Why don't you give me your number. That way, if anything specific comes up for your type, I can call you."

"I'll think about it, ma'am."

Her eyes flashed.

"I mean Ms. J…" He searched the air for her name.

"Jamison," Jewel said, put off by his stumble. "We will work on your memory too when you call." She laughed and turned her attention to me. "He doesn't realize the opportunity he was just given."

"I think he was just nervous…or maybe modeling isn't his…"

"He's waiting tables. Please. Is this his thing? Trust me, he will call me tomorrow."

The young man doubled back and slipped a folded up napkin into Jewel's hand. "Ms. Jamison, your cab is here. Let me get the door for you."

Jewel turned to me. "You see what I mean," she said, raising her eyebrows, indicating his attention to her. "I'll have my secretary send you an invite to my affair, and tell Camille to bring that handsome guy, Cole." She started to leave but came back and gave me a double cheek kiss that seemed more meant for the air than for me. I saw the young man hand her something. She smiled and then stepped out to the street.

I looked over at Les, who seemed to be heavy into his music. His eyes were closed, and his face registered each stroke of the piano as if the music lived in his mind. I glanced around the restaurant before I left. Some of the brunch items were being cleared and others brought in their place. The day was nothing like I had planned.

I struggled with the sense of rivalry I felt toward these friends, even though I was certainly no competition for them in any way. It was nothing that they did that I could put my finger on. I couldn't believe that this feeling still existed after so many years. I always seemed to need to stretch higher and seek out more sun than they got. I couldn't help it. It was something in our friendship that was so instinctive that I could not root it out. It had started when we met Jewel again in college. One night years ago, Camille said, maybe it was something in our *woman-ness* that drew us all together again. We would spend so much time talking about the boys who we loved and who didn't love us back, I thought maybe it was something in our femininity too, our openness, the spaces we needed filling. I know that I always felt an emptiness back then, so maybe we met because of something that was not.

We met in the spring of '67. Camille was in her junior year. I had dropped so many courses that I don't know what year they said I was in. It was Friday, and I always met Camille in the cafeteria on Friday afternoon after my last class. Sometimes I didn't even go to class, but I always met Camille, no matter what. We had been good friends since her family started dying on her at the end of high school.

The cafeteria was darkened slightly on Friday, to discourage students from hanging around. We still sat around drinking coffee, some students playing cards until we went out into the weekend. Lately, since her Aunt Lil had gotten ill and was in the hospital, Camille didn't want to go home. She stayed with me and shared my room, keeping it better than I did. I was thinking about dropping out since I couldn't focus. I had just met Santos, who wrote angry poetry and played the Latin drums. He only went to classes when it suited him. I said I'd meet Camille in the cafeteria around four.

Camille was staring into a textbook and then looking up, as if she were trying to memorize something. Her 'fro was like a halo that framed her face. I had helped her color her hair, so it was a reddish-brown color that complemented her cinnamon complexion. But I always felt as if she was hiding behind her big glasses.

"I see my girl is buried in the books as usual," I said. I realized I was speaking too loudly when a few guys looked up from their game of cards. I brushed my hair out of my eyes to give them a better look. It was now a mane of red-brown waves and curls that framed my face. Now that I had some attention, I pursed my lips, which I had painted a strawberry color.

"Close that book, Camille. It's Friday," I said, looking around to see if there was anybody left in the cafeteria I knew. A dark-skinned boy across the room and two white boys behind Camille all watched as I plopped my big shoulder bag on top of the table in front of her. I couldn't help smiling at how easy it was to capture their attention. I didn't know why I so enjoyed their stares, but I did.

"Camille, I need a cigarette. You got any?"

She pulled out a half-empty pack of Salems and handed them to me, so I drew one out, lit it, and exhaled the smoke. I stretched myself up in the chair to see if the dark-skinned guy was still watching. He smiled at me, and I tossed my head and brushed my hair back.

"Saundra, you are a trip."

"Come on, Camille. Close that book, and let's head out."

"It wouldn't hurt you to break open the books. Don't you have a midterm in history on Monday?"

"It's Friday. You hear of any parties?"

"There's a poetry reading downtown at NYU," Camille said off-handedly.

"Nope. Santos might be there. He's too possessive." I threw my head back, looking in the direction of the young man in the corner, who had now gone. "Where are the men, Camille? I need to meet some interesting men."

Camille laughed. Her tone hushed, and she whispered, "Saundra, don't turn around now, but in a few minutes, I want you to look at this girl. Doesn't she look like that girl who used to live on our block?"

"What girl?" I turned around, and her face looked so familiar. "Who is she? Wait a minute. That's the bitch who hit you," I said. "But you kicked her ass."

"Saundra! You were on her side, the way I remember it."

"I was an instigator back then. She didn't have to listen." I laughed.

"The poor girl probably thinks we're...I'm going to go over and tell her we're not laughing *at* her," Camille said.

"Let her sweat, Camille," I said playfully.

"No, don't be mean. Hi! Did you used to live on Hancock Street in Brooklyn?"

"Yes," she said tentatively.

"You lived with your aunt, right?"

"Yes," Jewel answered, nervously looking at me.

"OK. OK," I said, moving over to her table. "Cut the crap. You hit Camille, and she knocked you down. I wasn't laughing at you just now. I was laughing at myself. My name is Saundra Farrell. I'm the one who said hit her. This is Camille, Camille Warren. And you are...Jewel, right?"

"Saundra, shhh! People are looking at us," Camille said.

"Yes, Jewel Jamison."

"Those two white boys? They're looking at me, girls."

"Saundra, stop!"

"It's true. They've been watching me since I came in. Now girls, it's Friday night. Are we going out to party and find some men, or what?" I picked up my bag and threw it over my shoulder. Sometimes there was such a loneliness inside me. I needed to fill it. This was one of those times. I think I saw some of that in Jewel too. "Jewel, you want to come out with us?"

"Where are you going?" Camille asked.

"Don't know…the Village…maybe the Limelight? Have a hamburger or some chili, and a drink. I could use a drink. Ever been to the Limelight? Their food is good. Want to come, Jewel?"

"Sure, I guess so. Why not?"

"So, ladies, should I pick up these two white boys and let them pay?" I whispered. I made myself laugh.

"Don't believe her. She gets like this on Fridays," Camille said to Jewel.

"Don't believe me? Watch!" I sauntered over to the table, where the boys looked down into their books.

I looked back at Camille, who was putting her books in her bag, trying not to laugh. I heard her say, "Saundra, we're leaving."

The boys looked up when I got to the table. I said something I knew would get a rise. Then I turned and sashayed back to the table where Camille and Jewel were waiting.

"Saundra, what did you say to that boy?"

"Oh, nothing. I just said he looked familiar. I wondered if he was the nude model in my art class."

"You didn't." Jewel laughed.

"Knowing Saundra, she did."

I shook my hair back and laughed out loud.

"Did you see that white boy's face turn red? They really do turn red. Red, red."

"Saundra, stop!" Camille said.

We took the subway downtown. It was crowded, so we had to stand and were separated, but we exchanged glances and smiles. I eyed every attractive man within ten feet of us, and then I'd catch Jewel's eye, or Camille's eye, and raise my eyebrows as if to say, "What do you think?"

We got out at Bleeker Street station and walked upstairs into the warm evening air.

"How is your grandmother?" Jewel asked.

"She died about three years ago," Camille said.

"I'm sorry."

"She was sixty-eight, and she missed my grandfather."

"Your grandfather was great, right Jewel? He'd be outside that shoeshine parlor for hours—you know, with the other men. But every time we'd pass by, he'd say, 'I have a granddaughter just your age.' He'd say it every time he saw us." I laughed.

"And remember, Jewel, he'd give us kids a nickel—for ice cream, he said. But ice cream cost a dime. He was so funny."

"Yeah, I remember we'd get penny candy and have one of our parties. We'd sit on the stoop and have a party with a five-cent bag of potato chips," Jewel said.

"Which we'd break up into crumbs so it seemed like more," I said.

"And remember, we'd get some pennies from our banks and get a string of licorice, 'cause your aunt never gave you any money, Jewel." She didn't say anything, so I went on. "And some buttons— 'member buttons? And two Kits, chocolate and banana, and a stick of Kool-Aid, which used to get our hands all red. And I would put it on our lips pretending to be wearing lipstick." The images of that time in my life filled in around me. In so many ways, those days were the best of my life. They were before I felt self-conscious and afraid that people could see the real me.

"I remember I'd watch you. My grandmother didn't want me out."

I don't know what it was, but after Camille said that, we all were quiet as we walked across the street. I felt sure it was as if we all had opened up the past, and it had dark corners and sad places that we had left walled up so long.

"Not too many people in the Limelight." Only one couple sat on the street in the open café, drinking a pitcher of sangria with orange slices trying to reach the top.

"No men. You want to go over to the Ninth Circle?" I wanted to flirt, and there were just no men there.

"No, let's have something to eat. I haven't had anything all day," Camille said.

"OK! OK! But then we head to Washington Square or the Ninth Circle to find some men."

As we entered the bar, I sat near the outdoor tables where I could see out onto the street.

"Drinks?" the waitress asked as she put the menus down in front of us. She was dressed in a black leotard and a short black skirt. She stared out onto the street, holding her pad and pencil poised to write but seeming not to care whether she did.

"Give me a sloe gin fizz. I'll order my food later," I said.

"I don't," Jewel said, and then she continued. "And I don't know."

"Am I the only one eating? I'll have a hamburger, and just a hamburger," Camille said. "Maybe a rum and Coke later."

"Camille doesn't drink much."

"Not on an empty stomach."

"I'll have a rum and Coke too," Jewel said.

"Do you have a boyfriend?" I asked Jewel.

"No...not right now."

"Hmmm."

"You'd be better off thinking about passing English," Camille said.

"Camille is waiting for her prince in shining armor. While I wait for him, I sure the hell hope a Mr. Hot drops by."

Jewel laughed.

"I work and go to school, and I haven't met anybody in college I want to..."

"Tell me about it. There are absolutely no men. Half of them are in Vietnam. You remember Billy," I said. "His mother said he went to 'Nam about a month ago. Bullet got drafted, and Robert did too, and Leon signed himself in. Couldn't happen to a nicer group of guys."

"Saundra!" Camille said.

"Well, it's true. Leon was a shit. Anyway, like I was saying, there are no men."

The waitress brought the drinks. Jewel sipped her rum and Coke. Camille asked for water and for the waitress to bring her drink too.

I sipped some of my drink. "The bartender here must love me." I looked to see if he was looking this way. Not catching his eye, I turned back to Jewel. "Where do you live now? Still with your uncle and aunt? Someone said they put you out..." I stopped midsentence, realizing how this was coming out.

"I've got an apartment up on Broadway and Ninety-Ninth Street."

"You're kidding." I laughed. "Do you believe this, Camille? She's got her own place, and we're living at home."

"I'm saving up, but it's so expensive," Camille said. "Until I can get a job..."

"You're lucky..." I paused. "And no boyfriend."

"No. I don't know how lucky I am. It gets lonely sometimes."

"Well, if you ever want company, give us a call. Right, Camille? We'd love some privacy from my folks. If I had a pad, boy, I'd have parties all weekend long."

"Saundra, that's why you don't have an apartment. You wouldn't know how to act," Camille said.

"Oh my goodness gracious. Do you see what I see?" Three guys were walking down Seventh Avenue. One was tall and slender and fair-skinned. The one next to him was a little shorter and lean, but muscular. The third one was taller than the one in the middle, and he was bulkier and had a thick neck. They were talking to one another and looking up at the sign above the windows.

"Camille, what do you think?"

"I think you ought to stop."

"I can get them for us. Speak now. Oh shit, they're looking in here. Should I say something? Yes or no."

"Girl, would you cut it out?" Camille said. "They're not looking in here."

Jewel took a big sip from her rum and Coke. "They look cute to me."

I took out a cigarette and lit it. "So what do you say, girls? Should I snag 'em?"

"I'm game," Jewel said.

The tall, light-skinned guy caught sight of me and winked. I winked back. He was incredibly cute. He was wearing black jeans and a navy-blue T-shirt. His arms had long, lean muscles like a swimmer. He grabbed the arm of his buddy and motioned into the bar.

"Good evening, ladies," the light-skinned guy said, looking straight at me.

"Good evening, boys," I said.

Looking down at the books between Jewel and me, one of them said, "CCNY?"

"This is Darrell, in town from Howard. I'm Steve. They call me Scat, NYU. And this is Gene, in from Grambling."

"Hi. This is Camille, and Jewel, and my name is Saundra."

"You ladies staying awhile? Can we buy you a round of drinks?" Scat said, gesturing for the waitress.

"No, thanks," Camille said as he ordered.

"Sure, I'll have another," Jewel said.

"I wouldn't mind," I said, staring into Steve's eyes. "God. Are your eyes brown and green?" I said dreamily.

"Yes. A round of drinks for the ladies, I'll take a Seven and Seven. You, bro?"

"Scotch on the rocks," Darrell said.

"I'll take a gin and tonic," Gene said.

"When did you start drinking gin and tonic, man?" Scat said.

"This year. Coach drinks them. So I tried 'em." Gene's speech was thick and slow.

Gene pointed to the glass and said to the waitress, "Don't let this little lady wait on her drink."

"What team are you on?" I asked Gene, but keeping the focus of my attention on Steve and looking to Camille and Jewel to pick up their ends of the conversation.

"Huh? Football," Gene said, tensing his arm, which flexed his biceps.

Jewel drained her glass and put it down next to Gene's hand. "Boy, your hand is big. Look," she said, placing her hand in his.

Jewel was a girl after my heart. I wished Camille would say something, anything.

"He's a receiver. He's got to have good hands," Steve said, drawing out the phrase and putting his arm around me. Gene, growing more at ease with the attention, smiled broadly at the compliment.

"Are your feet big too? What size shoe do you wear?"

"Twelve," Gene said, blushing.

"Can I see?"

Gene pulled his chair back and moved his foot next to hers.

"Oh, my! Camille, look!"

The waitress brought the tray of drinks and took the empty glasses away. Jewel reached for the drink and took a big sip.

I looked at Camille. I wanted to ask her if she saw what I saw. Jewel seemed tipsy. Scat had put his arm around my shoulder, and his touch was turning me on. It always made me feel fuller and more powerful when I knew a man wanted me. I liked the control.

"Jewel, the hamburgers here are terrific. Why don't you have some of mine?" Camille said.

"Yeah. Miss, could you bring me a burger, rare, with a side of fries?" Gene asked.

"Make that two," said Darrell.

"Three," said Steve.

"How tall are you?" asked Jewel, and she took a bite from Camille's hamburger.

"What's with your friend? Is she taking a survey or something?" Scat asked, somewhat annoyed.

"I think she's just a little drunk."

"How much did she have?" Scat asked.

"Just the one, and now this."

"You're kidding."

"No. I think that's why my friend's trying to get her to eat something."

"Hey, she's a big girl."

"I guess."

"What year are you in?" Darrell asked, trying to make conversation with Camille.

"End of my junior year."

"What's your major?"

"I've got a double major. Biology and education."

"What are you going to do when you get out?"

"You mean when I grow up?" Camille laughed. "Teach. What's your major?"

"Journalism."

"What's your major, Scat? I'm just curious," I said. I really didn't care because he majored in gorgeous.

"What do you think?"

"Well, the obvious choice is music."

"No, prelaw."

"He got the name Scat," Darrell said, "because in his debate class and on the team, the guy opens his mouth, and you never know what the hell is going to come out. He's damn good. He may be prepared with one argument, and three others come to him. He's deadly."

Scat whispered in my ear, "You want to come up to my dorm room? I could get rid of my roommate."

"Why should I want to?"

"I might have something you want."

"I think I have something *you* want."

"I wouldn't deny it. So, shall we go?"

"How can I just abandon my friends like this?" His warm breath on my neck made me almost come out of my skin.

"Everybody here is an adult. I think they can all take care of themselves."

"I have to talk to Camille first. Camille, I'm going to the ladies' room," I said, indicating with my eyes that I wanted her to follow.

"Jewel, why don't you take a walk with us," Camille said.

I looked over and saw her take another sip of her drink and then lean her head on Gene's shoulder.

"I don't feel so well," Jewel said as she tried to stand. Camille supported her on her right, and I grabbed her left arm.

"Is she all right?" Gene asked.

"She's fine. I think that drink just hit her," I said.

"Darrell, could you put some ice into a napkin for me?" asked Camille. "I'm just going to get her into the bathroom."

Camille and I guided Jewel, sat her on one of the bowls, and put ice at the base of her neck and across her forehead.

"Camille, I was going to tell you that I wanted to split with Steve. He lives in NYU's dorm."

"You sure?"

"Sure, I'm sure." I got a paper towel to wipe Jewel's brow.

"Remember what your father said—you know, about you staying out late."

"Don't worry about him."

"When you're not there he questions me, and it's hard for me to lie to him."

"Just say you don't know where I am, which is the truth. She sure can't hold her liquor."

"I'll see you whenever, but help me get her out to the table first. This guy Darrell's kind of nice. Too bad he goes to Howard. I wish Derrick would just call and stop jerking me around like he does."

"Howard's not far. It's about three hours to DC, isn't it? And I think you should stop waiting around on Derrick."

"I don't feel right, Camille. My head is spinning," Jewel said.

"Let me get her outside. I have to get some coffee in her...sober her up...and...I don't know, see if I can get her home."

"Jewel, can you walk?" I asked. I hoped she wasn't going to be sick and mess everything up.

"Think so."

"Let's get back to the table. Can you handle it, Camille? I mean getting her straight. You really going to take her home?"

"I just don't want that guy to take advantage of her. She doesn't know what the hell she's doing."

The bar was fuller now. As we arrived at the table, Camille asked Darrell to order some coffee.

"Well?" Scat whispered.

His warm breath caressed my neck, making me want his lips. "Shit. Let's go. Camille, I'll see you later."

"I want to put my head down," Jewel whined, trying to push away the dishes in front of her.

Seeing the crowded table, Gene said, "Why don't you put your head on my shoulder?" He sat up and cradled her with her head resting on his arm, bracing her against him.

Steve stood up, took his wallet from his back pocket, pulled out a ten, and threw it on the table. "Dig you later." He drew me to him as he pushed the chairs out of our path.

"Glad to get out of there."

"Me too," I said.

"You smoke?"

"Yes."

"I have a friend who lives near the dorm, who can hook us up. Can't smoke in the dorm, though."

"That's cool."

His arm, which was resting on my back now, tightened around my waist, and he pulled me closer. The sensation that went through me at that moment was so strange. At first I felt so hot to have him clutch me and hold on to me. My insides had an anchor. We walked up Seventh Avenue and then turned down Bleeker Street. I began to think about Jewel and how drunk she was. At the very next moment, I was petrified. I didn't know where we were going. Maybe

Camille was right. Maybe I shouldn't just go off like this. The two sensations twisted me up.

"You know, I think I better get back to my friends."

"What's the matter?"

"Nothing. My friend is drunk, and Camille was trying to get her home."

"I'm sure Gene will help."

"I know he will help her, all right."

"You're a real tease, aren't you?"

"Look, I'm getting back."

Scat's eyes flashed. He turned and walked in the opposite direction. He was right, I did love to tease, but I didn't want to leave Camille in a lurch. She wouldn't leave me. I didn't know Jewel that well, but there was something about her that made me feel we were kindred spirits.

I walked back to the Limelight and saw Camille and Gene, on either side of Jewel, walking to a taxi stand across from the Limelight. Darrell was stopping the traffic.

"Camille, wait for me." I ran around to the other side of the taxi and got in. The guys looked kind of helpless after we closed the cab door.

"Jewel, what is your address?" Camille spoke loudly, trying to get Jewel's attention. I dug in her pouch-like pocketbook looking for her wallet.

"I live at Ninety-Ninth and Amsterdam."

"Ninety-Ninth and Amsterdam," the driver repeated and dropped the metal flag that started the meter.

"Yes," Jewel said.

"What happened with Steve?" Camille asked me.

"Nothing. He's pissed. I figured you needed help. She's a mess, isn't she?"

Jewel rested her head on my shoulder and held on to Camille's hand.

"I really like you guys," she said, closing her eyes.

Camille couldn't keep from smiling, and I laughed out loud.

"I wonder if she's going to remember any of this," Camille said.

"Probably not. She's swacked."

It was then that it began, as the cab wound its way up the West Side. We were a threesome. Jewel and Camille would meet after class. I would show up after tutoring. We'd sit and talk in the cafeteria for hours. We'd speak about our childhoods, the men who were and weren't in our lives, and our hopes and dreams.

As we talked, we shared secrets we would share with no one else. One day Camille said, "We were like three beautiful wildflowers. Opening slowly petal by petal, each exposing her delicate center…" I can't remember the rest, but I think that was how she put it. I didn't know about that so much. Camille was the poet. I just felt it was good not to be so alone.

9

CAMILLE

Cole was quiet as we drove uptown to get Shawn. He was pre-occupied with something, but I didn't want to engage him in conversation. I was mentally going over bits and pieces of the morning as it had unfolded. Being in Jewel's presence had made me feel totally inadequate. I felt as if I could just shrink away and disappear. Once in that mind-set, I could not find my way out. I wished that Cole would get me home and let me off, so that I could be by myself.

Somehow Saundra entered my thoughts, and I could hear her admonishing me, you better get out of the bathroom before Jewel takes that man. The way she said it made me want to smile every time I rediscovered it in my mind. It made me look at Cole. I tried to identify what it was about him that made me so uncomfortable. I sensed that what bothered me was that I couldn't figure out what he saw in me. This brought me back to that sickly sadness that seemed to rise up in my chest. It had been so long since I had even thought of being with a man. I had buried the thought away and could not find its resting place.

As I looked at his smoothly shaven cheek, I noticed the muscle at the base of his jaw pulsating. "Cole, is something bothering you? You've barely said one word since we left the restaurant."

"Nah. It's probably nothing. These are good friends of yours?" He glanced away from the road and looked at me.

"I haven't seen them in ages, but they're my best friends." My mind wandered a bit. "Why?"

"Nothing. I forget their names, but the shorter one—I just got a funny feeling from her."

"Jewel. Was she rude or something? She is sort of assertive."

"No, she wasn't hostile or anything, kind of the opposite. It just put me off. I wouldn't have mentioned it except that I thought you might have a clue as to what was going on. Never mind."

"What do you mean?" I could not cull out of Cole's comments anything that had meaning for me. "Are you sure you feel like going through with this date, Cole? It is after one o'clock," I said, looking down at the tissue that I had twisted beyond recognition. "I'm just feeling terrible. I went there, and I was talking about something good, that people in my school want me to apply for the position of principal. By the end of the conversation, I felt incompetent. Incapable. You name it. I don't feel like good company. And if you really want to know, I can't figure out what you are doing here. You were sitting with Jewel. Why didn't you just say bye, and go home with her?" The words just vomited out.

Cole just looked at me. His expression was an enigma. He was silent for a long time.

"It's too bad you can't see yourself as others see you."

"All I know is Jewel looks just like when we were in college, and I've gained weight, I've aged...I..."

"You know something? I'm away a lot doing training, and when I'd come in to town, and I'd be buying a paper, or picking up a few things at the Korean grocer, there you'd be, usually with Shawn. I noticed how your eyes seemed to make anyone around you smile." And after a long pause, he said, "You compare yourself to your friend? She looks like...she's...let's just say she seems as if she is always calculating."

"That's probably just her business head. I was looking forward to seeing her. I was so proud of everything she's doing. Somehow I felt so inferior in her presence." The sadness filled my chest. I missed her.

"I don't know what happened there this morning to make you feel bad, but I'm willing to bet it wasn't you. It was your friend."

"She didn't do anything, really. It's me. Anyway, you hardly know her."

We pulled up in front of the house, and Shawn was peering out of our apartment window, bouncing up and down, pointing at us and waving.

"Do you want to stay down here until you feel a little better?"

"Are you kidding? Look at Shawn. He's about to climb out the window, he's so excited."

As we got to the apartment, I could hear him. "They're here. They're coming in right now. Come on, Grandma." He started to unlock the door.

"Shawn, don't you touch that lock. You let Grandma do it. Haven't I told you…"

"Sorry, Mommy. Hurry up, Grandma!"

The energy bubbled over in the child.

"Shawn, relax. I'm coming. Your mother has her key," Ellie said.

As she opened the door and we stepped into the apartment, Shawn brushed past me and leaped up into Cole's arms.

"I was waiting for you. I saw you coming. Are we really going to see the solar system? Saturn. I can't wait to see Saturn."

The child almost toppled Cole over backward a bit till he caught his balance.

"How're you doin', little guy?"

Shawn's reaction threw me off guard.

"Shawn, calm down. Mama, this is Mr. Coleman Barnes."

"Cole, please," he said, shaking her hand with the one hand that was free.

Ellie smiled at Cole and tugged at her housedress, setting the waist straight. "Shawn, give Grandma some sugar to take upstairs with her. Did you have a good time with your friends, Cammy?" she added, moving toward the door.

"I guess. Strange seeing them again." I could tell that my mother was disappearing, as she usually did. I couldn't help feeling responsible for that, and it made me feel guilty. "You don't have to go, Mama." Seeing her continue on to the door, I followed.

"Cammy, I think this man is taken by you," she whispered in my ear.

I drew myself back to look at her. It was odd to have her as a confidant.

Shawn leaped up on his grandmother, which made her droop under his weight, but she smiled and drew his head into the crook of her neck with her hand.

"See ya, Grandma," Shawn yelled excitedly and a little too loudly as she left.

"Shawn, get your jacket. Cole, I'm sorry Shawn is so hyper. I've never seen him behave this way." I worried about how attached Shawn seemed to become to Cole in such a short time. He was so hungry for Cole's attention.

"It's nothing. He's just excited. Don't worry. He's fine."

We drove down Broadway, and Shawn talked nonstop, telling Cole about his school; his best friend, Jordan; his teacher; his grandma; MacDonald's—anything that came into his mind.

When we got to the planetarium, Shawn held hands with Cole and me, skipping and jumping and trying to lift his feet in the air, loving being between us. I might have scolded him, but his laughter was like music. I was sure this would be the last time I'd go out with Cole. I felt out of sorts around him.

After we went to almost all the exhibits and saw the show, Cole got Shawn a book about planets and a box of rocks with a magnifying glass. Then he took us out to dinner at an Italian restaurant downtown in Little Italy. By the time we drove uptown, Shawn had fallen asleep. Cole lifted him out of the car and carried him into the apartment. I turned on the lights along the way into the bedroom.

Cole had been terrific with Shawn, letting him ride on his shoulders and holding his hand. I hadn't known how much he'd taken in about boys and fathers, but it was as if Shawn wanted to fill in five years of male affection in this one day.

"He's a great little guy."

"I'll do that," I said, reclaiming my son, who had given himself up to this man. I took off Shawn's jacket, scarf, and pants. He kept curling up after each piece of clothing came off. His chin would wrinkle when he was bothered, and then his face became peaceful when he turned over, grabbed his pillow, and pushed it between his legs.

"Do you want a cup of coffee before you head home? You know, I don't even know where you live." I wanted the opportunity to show my gratitude to Cole, but also to let him know that there was no future for us. I didn't dare let myself feel anything.

"I live on 110th, but up by Riverside Drive."

"That's right, you said you didn't live far from here."

"I'll take a cup."

"Cole, you do realize we are complete opposites?"

"You know what they say about opposites." Cole had a playful gleam in his eye.

"First of all, I can't get over the fact that you're in the military. I abhor war. It bothers me that you recruit young boys to go and fight in wars."

"There are lots of reasons people go in to the military, Camille."

"No, I mean it. I can't quite relate to this military thing. Do you know I demonstrated against the war at my college fifteen—no, it's more like…damn…more than twenty years ago—because of the war in Vietnam. And now that I have a son, the last thing I want is for him to think that war is glamorous or something to aspire to."

"A lot of people didn't understand that war. I was there, and I didn't understand it."

"I bet you weren't even drafted."

"No, I signed myself in. Camille, do you really want to end this evening talking about Vietnam?"

"I don't believe in war and killing, and I don't want Shawn to be exposed to it. And I think this is all wrong."

"What's wrong?"

"This. My going out with you." I put the saucer down on the table too hard. The kitchen became silent. Cole didn't say anything. He just stared at the table. I felt relieved. I had to stop this anyway, better now, before feelings were toyed with and hurt. Something about his being there annoyed me. It wasn't anything he did or said. It was his presence. I feared that somehow during the past five years, I had closed the space around me that might have included a man. I had secured that space. There was room for occasional fantasies, thoughts about the possibilities of a man, but no room for a real man to poke his head around and knock about in my world.

"I thought we had a good time today, Camille."

"I did, but we're wrong for each other. You're a nice guy, and I don't want…look, we are just wrong for each other. That's all." I put a napkin on the table and took a spoon out of the drawer.

There was another long silence, and then Cole said, "I think you're wrong."

"What did you say?" I was not quite sure I had heard him correctly.

"I said, I think you're wrong," he repeated.

He was so calmly steadfast, and what he said was so pure that it made me laugh. I sat down in the chair adjacent to his and laughed a huge belly laugh.

Cole smiled and shrugged his big shoulders. "Are we having that coffee you offered me?"

"Don't you get angry?" I taunted. "I thought sure you were angry just then, and what did you say? 'You're wrong.'"

"Oh, I can get angry, but I don't let myself do it too often."

"Controlled, are you?"

"No, just disciplined. Self-disciplined."

"You see? You're not my type. I hate discipline." I laughed at the ridiculousness of my own statement. I don't remember when I last laughed with a man. It felt so good, having Cole sit at my kitchen table, that for a few minutes, I just stared at him. His hands were thick and large. His chest was wide and muscular and outlined itself against his cream-white turtleneck sweater. His arms bulged in his jacket as he crossed them across his chest. His dark eyes seemed to contain so much more than he shared. His jaw was strong; though earlier he had been clean-shaven, now he seemed to have grown dark with a five-o'clock shadow. There was a peaceful, almost content, look in his face. When our eyes met, his gaze seemed to look too deeply. It was as if he peered into my soul. I wanted him to hold me, just to know what it would feel like. I needed to remember the feeling of a man's arms around me. I wanted to remember that calm. That I wasn't attracted to Cole didn't matter now. The sound of the coffee dripping into the pot stopped. I poured it and placed the cup in front of him.

It was ironic that after all this time, a man should come and care to be with me, and he should be so unlike anyone I could love. There was something about him I liked, though, like an older brother. I had always heard about the baby my mother had miscarried just before she became pregnant with me. He was sort of the phantom big brother who had a presence in my family when I was little. Ma used to say, "I would have had a grandson just a little older than you." Ellie talked about him too, as if he were real. So I always felt cheated of this brother who was there, and not there, for me. That was how I felt toward Cole. He was like the straightlaced, protective older brother. But he was a man, and perhaps I could feel something more if he would just touch me.

"Sugar?"

He shook his head no.

"Milk?" I asked, taking out the container and placing it on the table. He opened and sniffed it.

I laughed. "Cole, do you think I would give you sour milk?"

He smiled and shrugged. "Habit, from living alone."

"Cole, you should know...I don't think I feel the same way about you that..."

"I know. Couldn't miss that." There was a longing in his eyes that I hated. I don't know what he read in my eyes, but he pushed the coffee cup away and said, "Maybe I'd better go."

"You don't have to go," I said, meaning it. The house felt full and warm with him there.

"Camille," Cole said, and he paused to clear his throat. "Never mind."

"No, say what you were going to say."

"I don't know. It's like you didn't give it...me...a chance." His brow furrowed, and he took a sip of the coffee. "It's like you...I can't explain it."

"Cole, I think you're being very nice to Shawn and to me, and I like you, but..."

"But..." Cole said, pushing me to finish the thought.

"But I don't know." I wanted to rest my head against his chest. I wished I could rest my mind. "Can we be friends?" I had never said that to a guy before. I could see hurt flash across his brow. He stood up, shook his head, laughed briefly, and then said, "It's OK. I get it."

I stood up, and for some reason my mind and body moved off in separate directions. I kissed him gently on the lips. I had wanted to touch his soft turtleneck and let my fingers explore the landscape of his chest. He pulled me in to him, and I could feel him breathing, and my hands enjoyed themselves stroking his back and seeking out the newness of him. But as my body began what I could only think of as an awakening, my mind drew away. I needed to protect myself from being too close, and I had to start before I lost myself in sensation.

He caressed my cheek with his right hand and ran his left hand down the center of my back slowly. Having tasted his mouth, I wanted to taste him again, and I wanted him to climb inside so that I might know him intimately.

"Cole, we can go into the living room. But we'll have to be quiet," I said, letting my body please itself. So much time had passed since Victor, it was as if my need to feel overwhelmed me.

He followed me in, tiptoed over to the bedroom door, and silently pulled it shut. His sense of responsibility made me smile. We sat on the couch, and he put his arm around my shoulders, lifted my chin, and kissed me again, parting my lips with his tongue. I was surprised that he was an artful kisser. We kissed, and I stroked his chest. I was lost in the sensations of him. He smelled clean, as if he had just stepped out the shower. I wanted to breathe him in. He began to stroke my chest, near my cleavage, and I felt so excited, I stopped him. "It's been a long…I don't have…we're living in different times."

"Don't worry. I have protection, if you're worried about…"

It was strange. Somehow, I hadn't thought that Cole would have carried condoms. I was put off for just a minute, but as he kissed me again, I felt myself succumb to his touch. It had been too long. I tugged at one of the sofa pillows, saying, "This opens out, but…"

"I've got it." He pulled out the bed and reflexively smoothed the sheet in a brisk hand movement reminiscent of soldiers in boot-camp movies. I felt a giggle seeping through my lips. They tingled with the lasting sense of him. Cole pulled off his turtleneck, exposing a pristine white undershirt and powerful muscular arms. His skin was taut from his waist to his well-developed chest. Before I could catch my breath and look away, he removed the shirt, and his barrel chest twitched and flexed as he neatly put his shirts on the arm of the chair. He took my hand and lifted it, opening the palm to his mouth, and kissed its center. I had to look at him to recognize him as the one who had so deftly made me forget my fears. I kissed him, letting him inside my head.

"I need you to touch me," I said, not knowing the words would escape my lips.

We were sitting next to each other on the bed. It would have been awkward, except that he was so gentle. He unbuttoned my blouse and let it hang open at the shoulders, and I took it off. He stroked my cheek again with the back of his hand. Then he let his fingers stroke my neck and shoulders like a sculptor feeling his statue, making certain that his fingertips felt all that he had intended.

Wanting to feel him against my skin with nothing interfering, I unhooked my bra and let it fall. I stood up, unbuttoned my slacks, and tugged at them, and he helped peel them down over my hips. I felt self-conscious. I had not stood naked with a man in years. My sagging stomach, having never grown tight again after the birth of my son, embarrassed me. I bit my upper lip. My cheeks grew hot.

I think Cole could feel me withdraw from him. "Camille," he whispered, "come back. Don't worry. I will protect you." He gently sat me down on the bed, and I pulled the second sheet to cover my legs and up over my breasts. I turned my back to him and stared at the darkness around the lamp. I was petrified. Then he draped himself over me and held me, gently at first, and then more tightly. I was shivering, and he warmed me by rubbing my arms with his large, strong hands. I imagined his hands would be rough, but they were not. They were smooth and well manicured. Wherever he touched me, he seemed to care to stay there and know me better. He made me love the feel of him. I wanted to take him in and let him stay with me. He stopped and turned away. I heard the crackling sound of the wrapper. Then he went to where I guided him, and I could feel my body giving way. He took me so gently, I accepted him, enjoying him. The openness and the fullness surprised me until I felt a scream ready to leap from my lips.

He covered my mouth with his. It was then that I felt that he was climbing into my mind. He frightened me. He touched me too deeply. I felt my belly open. He seemed to tear away at something. He pushed things aside, and my mind felt like a gaping hole. I resented the intrusion. He had gone past pleasure and pain, to that empty space that is private and alone.

"You leave me alone," I said, tears bursting from my eyes and flowing down my cheeks. "You leave me alone."

I pushed him out of me. I tried to cover myself and close the space. It was as if my insides were exposed and I had to shut myself up. He had seeped into the tiniest interstices of my being and touched places no one should have known existed.

He knew he had been there.

"Camille, what's wrong?" he said, kissing my forehead and cheeks and tasting my tears.

"I just want," I breathed, "for you to leave me alone." I pulled away from him and turned my back and drew my knees to my chest, trying to protect what little of myself I could find that was still untouched.

"Camille, don't pull away from me. I won't hurt you. I swear." He kissed the back of my neck and tried to wrap himself around me and held me so gently that my body rested in his embrace. As I lay there as still as I could, a calm washed over my body, bathing and soothing even the center of me. It felt safe in him. I had never felt that kind of safe before. It was warm and soft and easy. It was scary, this safe place, so new. I'd have to walk around in it and explore it before I could know it well enough to just be. For now, I would rest there and hope that it was real enough to know, and maybe to love.

We lay there until sleep took me and enveloped me. The cool darkness dispersed itself into a film of violet and charcoal blue.

"Camille," he whispered.

I was startled.

"Shhh, it's OK. It's me."

"Cole, what are you doing?"

"Just sitting here waiting for you to awaken, enjoying watching you sleep."

He was fully clothed and sitting in a chair he had brought from the kitchen.

"Watching me sleep?" I rubbed my eyes.

"Just waiting. I didn't want for Shawn to…I wanted to just say…"

"What time is it?"

"It must be about six o'clock by now."

"I don't get it. Why are you still here?"

He didn't say anything.

"Shawn is not accustomed to seeing men here. I think you better go before he wakes up."

"That's why…never mind. I just thought I'd wake you to tell you I was leaving."

"OK. So now I know you're going, so you can go." I didn't know why I said what I did and in the way that I did. I knew I wanted him to leave. I felt exposed by him.

He did not argue. He stood up, carried the chair to the kitchen, and left without uttering another word.

I felt an engulfing void spread around me. This man had come and made a place for himself in my house, and now he had left a space. I would have to fill it up.

"Your mother is living here in New York," Lil began, seemingly for no reason. "I heard it from a woman from Hancock Street that she's living in Harlem somewhere."

The words sort of swirled around my head like bubbles, light and delicate. They floated up and away and popped with no sound, leaving only tiny droplets of moisture hanging in the air, which disappeared instantaneously. As they left without a trace, I had the sensation that they did not exist. In fact, I was sure that my imagination had created these bubble thoughts. I continued putting away the laundry, the washcloths and dishtowels, and then I picked up Aunt Lil's beige slip with its tattered lace bodice and carried it into the bedroom.

"Camille, did you hear me…hear what I said?" Aunt Lil said, trying to capture my attention from its dallying place.

"Yes, Aunt Lil?" I asked, looking back at her.

"I said Cece said she saw your mother, and she's living here in New York now."

This time the words sat there in the now-dense air, and I could not escape them. Ma never talked much about my mother except to say she had gotten what she deserved for killing her son. They put her away was all she said. My aunt told me that she knew she had gotten out of jail for vehicular manslaughter, but someone told her that she wasn't right since she had gotten out. No one knew where she was for a long time. Then someone heard that she was in the hospital for a while. Aunt Lil had always said that my mother wasn't near as bad as Ma made her out to be. She had written to Lil a few times since I came to her. Lil showed me a note she had sent with a money order for a hundred dollars:

> *Dear Lil,*
> *This is for Camille. Thank you.*
> *Ellie*

When I read it, it hurt that she never asked how I was. The only way I dealt with thoughts of my mother was to place her so far away that somehow she did not exist. She was like a dot in a painting of a crowd. A dot that was indistinguishable from any of the other dots.

"Cammy? Do you want to see her? You can call her work. I got her work number."

"I don't think so."

"I think you should call her." Aunt Lil went on without taking notice of what I had said—or, having taken notice, setting it aside.

"I know it was hard for you," she said, "but she did what she could. She paid her dues for the accident. Your mother is better now, from what they tell me, but she was very sick. And frankly, my sister didn't help the situation the way she treated her."

"I don't want to talk about her," I said, trying to get away from these words, which now seemed to surround and squeeze me.

"You only have one mother, you know."

"I said, I don't want to hear about her. I'm going out."

"No, you're not. You sit right down, right now. Sit down, Camille!"

Aunt Lil's voice had a high-pitched timbre, and when she got angry, she sounded shrill, like a small bird. It was a strange sound coming from such a large woman. I wanted to swat her away, but I sat dutifully and listened to the woman who had bathed away the hurt when Ma died.

"Camille, you're eighteen years old. It's time you start seeing your parents like you were an adult, not an angry, scared little child."

"I'm not."

"Every time I talk about them, you find something to do, like you don't hear me. I know my sister made everything out to be your mother's fault, but Johnny was to blame too. He was the one who always drove. That night he was too drunk to drive. That's why Ellie had to. She was just trying to get them home. It was an accident. And my sister made her out to be a criminal. She didn't have to press no charges, but she did. She did it out of spite."

"I've heard all this before. I don't need to hear it again. I also know what Ma said."

"Just shush. My sister never wanted Johnny to get married. You hear me. Never. No girl was good enough for him. She wanted to keep him there with her. Thank God your father was a man of his own mind. He fell in love with your mother, and he married her. When the accident happened, my sister used it to punish your mother and to take you away from her, because she couldn't have Johnny back. That's the truth. I'm not saying she didn't love you— she loved you more than her own life—but she didn't have to steal you away from your mother. Your mother sent money for you. She tried to see you, and my sister wouldn't let her. My sister wanted you for herself. Well, my sister is dead now, and the least you could do is try to contact your mother. Here is the number."

"What for?" I searched Lil's eyes for answers or sympathy, or that comfortable expression.

"Camille, I put my sister in the ground more than two years ago. I waited all this time because I didn't want you to think I was talking bad about her. But this has gone on long enough. Your mother is here. My sister made her suffer enough. She is still keeping your mother from you, even from her grave. Call her." The old woman set her jaw.

"What am I going to say to her?"

"You could say, 'I'm Camille. How are you? Aunt Lil just got your number.'"

"I don't think I can do it."

"Girl, here is the number. You call your mother."

I felt trapped there with my fears. "Are you going to force me to call her?"

"No, I can't force you to do anything. You're a grown woman. You take this number and do what you want. But remember this. Your mother is not a young woman."

I heard my aunt's words echo in my mind. I had no mental picture of the woman called Eleanor. Aunt Lil had some old photographs of her, but the way Ma described her, I never wanted to see them. I sat there alone with thoughts of a woman with no face whose body had grown old. Time had always been measured differently for me. When I went to live with Ma, time was that space when I first knew I was alone. When I came to live with Lil, although Lil was always there when she wasn't working, I became aware that the aloneness was inside myself. Now time was shifted to include this old woman with no face. It was somehow ticking away my mother's life. I couldn't escape her. Aunt Lil had planted her in the midst of my world. No matter how painful it was, I would have to look directly into the mysterious mask that was her face and see the woman who was my mother.

After work at the college bookstore, on Thursday night, I went over to Saundra's house. I needed to talk about this ghost-mother who haunted me.

"My mother's here in New York. She's living in Harlem." I blurted it out.

"You're kidding! How did you find out?"

"Lil heard from a friend of hers from Hancock Street."

"D'you know where she is?"

"I have the phone number of her job. She's there every day but Sunday and Monday."

"Are you going to call her?"

"I don't know."

"I think you should."

"Why? After all this time…"

"Because she's your mother. Look, the hardest thing I had to look at was that my father and mother are just people. They are not gonna save me from anything. Hey, but they're my parents."

"But my mother has never been there for me, and I told you she killed my father."

"Camille, I think your grandmother said that just because she didn't like your mother."

"My aunt said that I shouldn't believe everything my grand-mother said, but…"

"And didn't you say she sent money to your aunt for you?"

"Yes, but—"

"That was being there. You should call her."

"What would I say to her?"

"You'll know."

"I'm scared."

A truncated laugh escaped Saundra's lips. "You think I'm not?" Saundra said, and then she stared off out the window, at the openness.

When I woke up Saturday morning, there was a photo of my mother on the night table next to the clock. Lil had put it there. At first, I wasn't sure what it was, and I had to put my glasses on to see it clearly. It was a black-and-white picture of my mom and me when I was about a year old. I could just about stand, but she was holding me, and my foot was curled in.

She was smiling and resting her face next to mine. Somehow, though we were both smiling, it made me feel like crying. I had been thinking about what Saundra had said for two days. I walked into the kitchen and put up the kettle for tea. I stared at the torn slip of paper that was still on the table from the week before. My mother's number was written in Aunt Lil's handwriting, and under it, "Tues.—Sat., 9 to 5." I didn't know what this workplace was, and even if she was still there or not. I didn't want to think about it too much and lose my courage, so I just dialed. The phone rang once, then again, and I decided that she was not there and began to hang up. There was a lot of noise on the other end, and a man answered. I didn't make out what he said.

I asked, "Can I speak to Eleanor Warren, please?"

"Get Ellie to pick up," he shouted. I heard a loud rumbling sound like machines, and then someone yelled, "Ellie, pick up!"

"Hello." Her voice was soft and a little weak.

"This is Camille."

My mother was silent. She must have carried the phone into a less busy place. I heard her swallow, as if she was choking back her words or tears, and then she said, "I have waited"—she paused and swallowed again—"to hear your voice."

"Aunt Lil asked me to call." There was some kind of noise behind her, and then I could hear her footsteps. She seemed to be moving, and then the room grew quiet.

"I am just happy to hear your voice."

I let the silence grow. I didn't know whether it was because I didn't know what to say or that I did not want to make it easy for this mother who had left me alone for so long.

"How are you? I heard you're in college and so smart."

I felt that her voice sounded familiar, as if I might have known her. I said nothing.

"I would love to see you," she said. Her voice seemed strained.

I was silent. I couldn't believe that this was how it was. She was telling me she wanted to see me. How could she say that so freely after all this time?

"Maybe we could just meet for lunch. I have something for you."

I did not feel anything but a tightness in my chest. I wanted to yell and scream at her. You want to see me after all these years. You want to see me. If I could just scream my hurt. It was as if I had locked up my heart for so long, I feared that it might loose itself of its fastening without my permission and run wild.

I don't remember what else we said, but I know we made plans to meet in Manhattan at a place near her job, a factory in the garment district.

By the time the day arrived, my mother had taken up most of my thoughts. The more I tried to squeeze her image from her mind, the more she intruded. I awoke early on Saturday and lay in my bed, contemplating my meeting with her. I had unearthed another old photograph of her from Aunt Lil's box of pictures, which was in the bottom dresser drawer, earlier that week. Her face was beautiful. As I lay on my bed in the cool morning light, the image of my mother's face haunted my consciousness. Almost every thought was of her. When I chose my dress, a red-and-blue print, one of the last dresses my grandmother had made, I thought, "I wonder whether she will like it." As I put on my makeup, which was always just a touch, and put back on my glasses, I thought, "I'm too plain." I patted my 'fro into place and looked into the mirror. I found myself longing for my mother to think I had turned out all right. "She won't like me," I thought as I left the house.

By the time I caught the subway to Manhattan, I was panicked. I was certain that my mother hadn't wanted to meet me at all. I was sure she wouldn't show up. She had not talked much about herself on the telephone. She had only said she had something for me. As the train pulled into the Thirty-Fourth Street station, I was convinced that this apparition from my past would not gain substance. And it was probably best.

As I got to the top of the stairs, a man almost toppled me over in his haste to run down to the station. Seventh Avenue was crowded with lunchtime shoppers and garment workers pushing rolling racks of clothing. I looked around behind me, pushed my glasses up on the bridge of my nose, and peered across the street. I walked up Seventh Avenue to Thirty-Seventh Street and then continued, squinting at the signs that ran across the tops of the storefronts. There it was—Dubrow's Cafeteria. My mother had told me to meet her there.

Now my heart was pounding. I felt my breathing become shallow. I could not draw in a deep breath. I wished I could take off my glasses, but I could not see a thing without them. I felt awkward standing there in front of the cafeteria. It was so obvious that I was waiting for someone. If she did not come, it would be difficult to walk away. I felt as if I were onstage waiting for the play to begin and the other actors had left me there to face the audience alone. Perspiration beaded my upper lip. I curled the paperback book I had carried to read on the train but had never opened. There were so many people pushing past me and around me. I cupped my hand against the window to shade the light, so that I could see inside the cafeteria, although I did not know why. I was certain that my mother had said she would meet me outside.

"Camille?" came a voice, a bit thin and tentative. Despite the gentle sound of it, I jumped. It was a reaction to my anticipation, which made me as tense as a taut string.

"I didn't mean to scare you."

Time has made her eyes sad and her cheeks hollowed, I thought, comparing the vision of her to the image in my mind from the photograph.

"Yes."

"I'm your mother." She looked as if pain had painted itself around her, and curled her shoulders with the weight of it. There was a pause. It would have been awkward had it continued too long. Then she said, "Are you hungry? We can go in. They make great sandwiches in here." She pushed the revolving door and let me step in before her. I put one foot in front of the other, but I felt numb. The sound of the street went away as I entered. Inside, the sounds of dishes and people talking echoed around me, but all I could think about was her.

She came in behind me, and then I felt her stop. When I looked back, she was taking tickets from a machine. There were lots of people seated at tables talking and eating, men in clusters of four or six. Women had packages and shopping bags from Macy's and Gimbels.

"We just have to stop over here and get trays," she said, gesturing with the hand holding the tickets. "You never ate here before?"

"No." I didn't want to look straight at her. I didn't want to stare. I could tell that her back looked tired. She was no longer the woman in the photo.

"Any kind of sandwich or salad you could want. Have anything you want. There's soup over here," she said, seeming to try to fill in the silence between us.

I peeked through the glass at the trays of salad stuffs. The menus on the walls were all a blur. All I wanted to do was to sit and listen to her and look at her. I wanted to find out who this mother person was. I wanted to hear her side. I wanted to let the sound of her voice fill up my ears.

"Do you know what you would like?"

"Yes, tuna salad on toast. Rye toast with tomato, please," I said, now becoming aware of the man behind the counter who was waiting, listening to my order.

"To drink?"

"Tea."

My mother got herself a cup of coffee and began to take hot water and a tea bag for me. She moved up on line and paid the cashier, and I followed her to an empty table close to the wall. It was quieter there. Now that we were sitting and I could look at her, I didn't dare.

"Your face hasn't changed a bit. You have the same face you had as a child." Her voice was thin, weak, and not at all what I expected.

I could feel her looking at me. I felt self-conscious.

"Aren't you hungry?"

The sandwich was piled high with salad, and I knew that it would squeeze out and I would drop it, and I wasn't really hungry, anyway. I simply wanted to look at my mother. I wondered if I looked at all like her. When I lifted my eyes, they met hers. I felt I knew her—not the photograph from the box, but her. That woman. A flood of memories swirled 'round me. Bits and pieces of memories. Holding hands, and wearing look-alike dresses in a green-and-white print with yellow piping round the neck. A whipped creamy thing that was sweet that she would buy at what I thought must be a bakery. Sitting on her lap as she made twists in my hair. Tears filled my eyes, and I looked down, and they spilled out. "Why didn't you ever come back for me?"

There was a long silence. I searched for answers in her face. There was a pained expression there. She looked away, not directly at me. My question was so sudden that it stunned her. I wanted her to explain a lifetime of decisions to me. "Didn't you ever want to see me, see what I looked like?" I cried, tears bathing my cheeks.

"I did see you. I used to watch you at your school," she said before she could stop herself.

"What do you mean?"

"That school up on Brooklyn Street."

"Brooklyn Avenue," I corrected.

"Yes," she said, staring off. "Your grandma used to put red barrettes in your hair, and one day you wore a little red sweater and cardigan."

I remembered that sweater set.

"Camille, it wouldn't have worked. It just couldn't."

The resignation in her voice was complete. She had no reservations. She seemed sure her choices were irrevocable. Her eyes told me she was resigned to the twists and turns of her life, as if they had been predetermined. She seemed sorry she had caused me this suffering.

"Camille, when your father was in the hospital, I almost went crazy. I couldn't get any sleep because I would just try to will him to wake up and come back to us. Then he didn't, and I knew it was my fault. I couldn't tell you what I had done. I knew you would ask me. You were so smart. I didn't know how to tell you what I had done."

"But why didn't you ever come back?"

"Your grandmother wanted you. She had the wherewithal to take care of you. I didn't."

"I want to get out of here," I said, wiping my cheek with the back of my hand. As I moved past faces made grotesque by the tears that sheeted my eyes, I felt a hand on my shoulder. It was such a gentle touch that I slowed my gait.

"Camille, don't go. I have something for you. Please."

I turned and looked into my mother's eyes, and before I could think about what I was doing, from deep within me came the words. "I missed you. But this is too hard. How do I erase fifteen years of you not being there? Birthdays, Christmases, Thanksgivings—it was me, by myself. I lost my family because of you."

"I am so sorry. I know you hurt." She reached out and pulled me to her.

I don't know why I let her. My mother's embrace swallowed me up. People brushed by. Time was filled up with her. I did not let it move for as long as I could. But then the ache of the loss of all that time gone, burned with her touch. I pulled away as hard as I could. "I can't stay here. I gotta go."

"Camille, please…I have something…"

10

JEWEL

"**O**h my Gawd!" Prim and proper Greta, my bookkeeper, fanned herself with a yellow legal pad as she stared transfixed by the photo of Mr. January. He held a red towel around his neck so that his biceps framed his chiseled chest and sculpted six-pack. I had selected his red Speedo swimsuit and remembered how he actually blushed when he came out of the dressing room for the shoot.

Verta had the calendar photos displayed as I had asked, to get some feedback on the calendar from the women in the office. The first six months faced one side of the conference table, and the last six the other side. Each page revealed a large photo of a different model wearing a swimsuit, with a smaller snapshot inset in a tux. The bathing suit photographs were shot at a pool and at the beach. The men's skin glistened with suntan oil and droplets of water. I had overseen the shoots, so I knew they were super sexy. Looking at them brought back the same excitement I had felt while posing them. The men ranged from a deep-dark, delicious chocolate complexion to a green-eyed, fair-skinned café au lait. Every hue any woman might imagine. As I stood in the doorway, the women didn't even notice me.

"Do we get to go home early today? Jesus," June asked. "Greta, come on down and take a look at my namesake. Let me just wrap him up and take him home." She laughed and blew a kiss to the photo of the mahogany-skinned Mr. June.

"Don't hold back, ladies," Verta said with a laugh.

"These guys are on fire! Great idea to have them in swimsuits *and* tuxes. Greta, come look at Mr. August," June said. I had hired June as my receptionist because of her air of refinement. It was a joy watching her lick her lips as she studied the photo of Mr. August.

"Just give me Mr. January for, say, until March. What is he packing in this swimsuit?" Christina said. The secretary, who was in her forties, had backtracked twice to Mr. January and nudged Greta. "I don't know if I can look at him quite the same way the next time he comes into the office."

"Will I be able to get one?" the intern, Joy, asked tentatively, pushing her glasses up on her nose.

"I think he prefers older women," Christina said and laughed.

"So I take it you like our calendar," I said, entering the conference room fully.

"Wait till the folks from *Essence* see it," Verta said.

"I was keeping it under wraps until next week at the Tavern on the Green event. It will be part of the press packet."

This was my first calendar using my male models. I finally had enough male talent to be able to put together a book that included models and actors to showcase. Observing the reactions, I began thinking about ways to mass market it. I made a note to myself to call my friend in advertising at *Essence* to discuss some kind of quickie promotion. I was sure that it was too late for an article in their January book. Had I more faith in my own judgment, I would have done this sooner.

"Maybe we can get an article and an ad in the February issue for Valentine's Day. I'll call Jonelle later. Back to work, ladies," I said. "Verta, can you give me the list of RSVPs. I just want to see who's coming and who's sending a rep. And what's the total we have so far?" I really wanted to see if Gordon had called. Those models' bare skin made me hot for him. It would be so great to have him to go home with that night.

"Looks like seventy-two, so far."

"That's all?"

"Don't worry. We're still doing follow-up calling. Christina, did you finish calling the design houses? After that, start working on the magazine folk, and beauty product people, and ask who they're sending. Then we have the movie and TV casting agents to call back." Verta shooed the women out of the conference room.

"Jewel, you know the folks in fashion. They just show up. Too busy for a call. And we're new to some of the casting offices you invited. They might show just to find out who we are and why we're throwing this shindig."

Verta was probably right, as usual, but I had a lot invested in this party. We were showcasing thirty-five models and actors at the event. I needed to make the expenses involved in opening the new office pay off.

"We sent out almost two hundred invitations. I ordered food for one hundred fifty…" I talked as I walked into my office. "Just bring me the list."

As I thought about the photos again, I couldn't help reacting to the portraits of the male form I had collected there. Last year, when I was out to lunch with a beauty editor from *Vogue* magazine, she joked about my "stable" and asked if I ever went "riding" after hours. She was usually stuffy, but with two martinis under her belt, she didn't care what she said. I was always careful, because you never know how much they're storing up to use against you. So I laughed and told her that was not my style. I was more like a good den mother. "The boys are always polite and deferential," I said. I wanted to be sure the squeaky-clean image of the agency was untarnished.

"Pity," she said, and I filed the conversation away.

"Here, Jewel," Verta said, handing me the list. "Checkmarks indicate they are coming. The question marks, they have someone getting back to us with a rep. The plusses, they're bringing someone."

"We should be calling the ones with the question marks, not waiting on them." I skimmed the list, and Gordon's name had no check. I scanned down farther, and Camille's name had none either. I backtracked up the list, and Saundra's name was also a no-show. "Are you kidding me? They haven't RSVP'd." I circled all three.

"We'll call them by the end of the day."

"I'm just worried about Gordon. He hadn't gotten his invite when I called him last week. Ask June to call Mr. Ellis's office for me." I felt warm and started to pour a glass of water, and the pitcher was empty. "There's nothing in here, Verta. Is the air conditioning turned off in here?"

"Jewel, it's November. It's been off for a month already. I'll get some water."

"Did she say she would have June call Gordon? I didn't hear her say that." All that beautiful bare skin!

The intercom buzzed. "His secretary said he was out of town," June said and hung up.

Is she being cheeky with me? Where the hell is he all the time? And who was with him the other day? His wife, I'm sure of it. Maybe if I was busy when he called. I could be busy. Maybe that's it. I'm just too available.

The waiter from the brunch popped into my mind. "Whatever happened to that kid?" Shit. I am talking to myself again. I buzzed Verta. "Verta, did a kid…his name, I forget, Derrick? No, Dennis…" God, where did that name come from? I remember Derrick. Hmm.

"Howell?"

"That's it."

"He called. I told him to come in tomorrow around ten, though this is such a bad time. You want me to cancel him till after the Tavern on the Green?"

"No, leave that…I'll see him. Call him and make it around four instead." I do that every time. Always there when they need me. OK, Gordon.

"Switch it at this late hour? Suppose he has other plans?"

"Just say my schedule has changed. Oh, and have June make me dinner reservations for two at the Right Bank for six thirty tomorrow evening."

"Jewel, why don't you go home and get some rest."

"I'm bothering you, Verta? I'm just so edgy." The annoyance in her voice was obvious.

"We only have until five to do the calling."

She was right. From the moment I started thinking about Gordon, I had lost my focus. "OK, bring me the list of the designers. I'll call them myself from home."

"Jewel, we have it covered. We'd have to explain who we have special contacts with."

"You're right. I'll leave it to you."

"You know the press packets have to be assembled, and the bags should be filled."

"That's scheduled for Friday…we get the calendars on Thursday."

I was exasperating Verta. I was wound up so tight I felt I would pop. I put on my jacket, turned up the collar, and took the elevator down. Out on the street, the air was brisk. I decided to walk home, up Broadway from Forty-Fourth Street to Seventy-Second Street. It wasn't even four thirty, and it was dark and the sky was a slate gray. My feet pounded the pavement. At Columbus Circle, I turned up Central Park West. The trees were almost bare, and it made me furious. I hadn't seen Gordon once this fall.

"Not a good day, huh?" The doorman, John, a short, balding, mustachioed man in his fifties, noticed my mood. He checked his stand. "No packages. Have a good evening."

I tried to smile. It took too much effort. In the apartment, the plant I had bought a few days ago to give the place some life was already drooping. "Guess you're setting a new record for dying in this place."

I opened the blinds, but there was not enough light to brighten the space. So I went to each of the glass tables and turned on all the lamps. I could not rest. I poured myself a glass of white wine, and I ran a bath to relax. I climbed in and sat for I'm not sure how long, but the scents of my bathwater began to remind me of Gordon, and I couldn't breathe.

I threw on my robe and went into the kitchen and searched the refrigerator. Only a small piece of Brie, a stale baguette, and some olives were left from days before. I put the baguette in the microwave and softened it a bit. I tore off a piece and spread a sliver of the Brie on it. I was so famished, I ate it all, finished off the glass of wine, and poured another.

All the while, images of Gordon raced through my mind. I wanted to call him at home and tell him how angry he was making me by ignoring me this way. Verta says, "Mr. Howell is coming in tomorrow…" That's OK, Gordon. I'm going to be busy too. "Cute smile, and good bone structure in his face…perfect for print ads."

I tidied up the kitchen, threw away the wine bottle, and chilled another. I put away my clothes, tossed my suit into the dry-cleaning bag, and put my makeup that was strewn in the bathroom and bedroom away.

I looked at the clock—too late to call the boy. Not professional, I thought. My head began to throb. I felt trapped. I need to connect, to talk to someone. It was black outside.

My address book with his number is in my bag. *I need someone to want me.* The napkin he wrote his number on is in my book. Where is it? I can't call him—am I crazy? But I need to talk to someone. I turned the pages, searching for someone to call, and found Camille's name, as I had done so many times in the past. I dialed.

"Camille? Did I wake you? I didn't think that you'd be asleep already."

"Jewel?"

"I was here working, and it occurred to me that I didn't know if you got the invitation yet. Are you planning to come to the reception?" I needed to keep Camille on the phone.

"I got it. I guess I just didn't call yet, but what time is it?"

"November sixteenth at six thirty."

"No, I meant what time is it now. Never mind. It sounds OK, but can I call you tomorrow after I ask my mom about babysitting? I'm half asleep."

"Call the office tomorrow and ask for Christina. Sunday was wonderful, wasn't it Camille? It brought back so many memories."

"Me too."

It felt like old times talking to Camille like this, calling to talk late at night. I needed to keep the conversation moving. I couldn't let her go. I needed her.

"Camille, I know this is going to seem like it's coming from left field, but I've been thinking, since Sunday, about you saying you wanted to be a principal. One thing that would maybe perk you up is a makeover. Why don't you come in and let me treat you to a facial and makeup makeover. Maybe do your hair in some new style, a perm or something asymmetrical."

There was silence on the line.

"We could go shopping together."

"Jewel, I don't think I'm the makeover type. You know I'm not into a lot of makeup, and I don't want my hair permed."

"What about a little color? Just getting rid of the grays will… Camille, I think it will give you the lift you need to dive into battle. You know if you look successful, you feel successful."

"Jewel, you sound like some…women's magazine."

"Camille, when I saw you Sunday, I was worried."

"Worried about what?"

"Well, you just didn't look like the person I remember. I didn't want to say anything in front of Saundra, but I was truly concerned for you. You just don't look like you can handle the added stress of a job with more responsibility and the fight to get it…sorry."

"I'll think about it."

For me, Camille was a reminder of the time that had passed. I saw time as a formidable foe, which I had to outwit and physically oppose every day of my life. In my field, with its emphasis on youth and appearance, I never rested. I had to look the part of a successful businesswoman in the industry even when I was in my little apartment in the Village. Back then I only represented three girls, whom I had stolen away from the witch I worked for after college. I remembered spending my last dollars on getting my hair done even though I had no food. I had been waiting for checks and had a meeting at the bank where my proposal for a loan to cover my accounts was being decided. No question but that my hair and makeup were more important than food.

"Camille, you have to take care of yourself. Even when I work a twelve-hour day, I make time to work out. I know we're obsessed with youth and health in my field, but I'm always thinking about being fit. I've got to be sure my models are tip top—"

"It's late, Jewel. I'm too tired for a pep talk. I've got to be up at five thirty."

"Just offering a little advice. I knew I'd say the wrong thing. Good old, direct me." I needed to repair the damage. I didn't want to be left alone. "Camille, don't hang up."

There was silence.

"I didn't call about that. Don't even know how I started in on that. I don't know what I'm going to do. I'm in love with this wonderful man, and I think I'm going to fall apart."

"Jewel, you're not going to fall apart over some man. That doesn't make any sense."

"He is wonderful, and we are perfect together. I just don't know if he realizes it. He's in the middle of a divorce, and I think he's a little confused." I couldn't think straight. "Maybe I'm imagining things. I know he can't spend all his time focused on me. He has a successful law firm. The divorce is a big deal. He's a wonderful father, so he takes the kids on the weekends."

"When did you speak to him last?"

"I called right before the brunch. He hadn't returned my calls the week before."

"What did he say?"

"I couldn't make heads or tails of it…got the feeling that I was annoying him. He did this before…" I remembered the month after we met, Gordon said he needed some breathing space, so I backed off. I didn't call for two weeks. At some point, I sent him a rose, and he called. He had plans to come back to New York, and when he did, we spent the most beautiful weekend together. He was supposed to leave Sunday morning, but I persuaded him to take the redeye. He said I was just what he needed at that point in his life. Then I didn't hear from him for three weeks.

"Maybe he's just not right for you, or the timing is wrong, or…"

"Camille, I can't go through this again."

"He's not the last man on earth. Don't do this to yourself."

"Camille, you know there are no men. There were no men when we were in college, and there are minus no men now."

"Why don't you just take a break? Don't try to make anything happen. Relax."

"I'm almost forty-five years old. I've never been married. I thought Gordon was the one. I was counting on it. I can't do this again."

"There are other men, Jewel."

"They're all so young. That boy at the restaurant—he asked me for my number. I told him that he had a good face for modeling. He's coming to see me, but he's young. Gordon should know how attractive I am to these young kids, boys nineteen, twenty, twenty-one."

"Is that what you want?"

"I want Gordon to want me. I don't know how I mess it up all the time. You know this is not the first time. This has been happening to me since Eric. I can't go through this again. I just don't seem to be able to make anything last with anyone."

"Jewel, I've come to realize that it is not so terrible if I never marry. My life is what it is."

"But you just met that man…what's his name?"

"Cole? I'm not sure what his story is. But I'm resigned to my life. It's OK. When I think about Shawn, it's much better than OK."

"You don't understand. I thought you'd understand." I couldn't think straight. I was closed into a tiny box with my thoughts of being alone. There was silence on the line.

"Jewel, you're a successful woman. You have a business with offices in two cities. You have models and actors all counting on you for their livelihoods. You can't go off the deep end over some man who can't get his act together."

"You're right. I'm going to call him and make him tell me where he sees this relationship going. He owes me that…just don't want to pressure him. He's going through a lot right now."

"That's not what I—"

"From the first minute I saw him, I knew we were meant to be together. Why doesn't he know it too? I'm going to tell him. You are coming next week, Camille?"

Leaving this man was too difficult for me. It always seemed to be the same. It had been the same with Eric at the very beginning.

It was the summer of 1967, and Saundra persuaded me to have a party at my place before summer classes got too heavy. She helped me clean up the apartment and make the punch. Camille made a pot of her chili and some dip. I couldn't believe how many people came, even though we had just started mentioning it a week before. There was only one red bulb glowing dimly in the corner of the living room. Smoke filled all available space and contacted everyone in the room. A curtain of hot, damp air draped the open window. Coconut incense sweetened the cloud. Percy Sledge was singing "When a Man Loves a Woman," and hips and thighs moved just enough to tantalize. I was sitting on a pillow in the corner near the window, hoping for a breeze, when a body sat down next to me. A deep voice moved gently into my consciousness.

"You have a beautiful body, you know that? I've been watching you for about an hour now." The deep baritone voice bathed me in sound.

I looked to my left and saw a deep, dark smile and a cleft chin. *Oh, this man is so cute.*

"You have a delicious smile too."

"You're very sure of yourself, aren't you?"

"I'm sure of what I like."

The sound of his voice washed over my body like a summer shower.

"What's your name?"

"Jewel."

"Perfect. Absolutely perfect."

My thoughts were jumbled. I had this big smile on my face, and I couldn't take my eyes off him. I was always much more coy and able to manipulate situations with men. I felt defenseless.

"What's your name?" I tried to take control of the conversation.

"Eric," he said confidently. He glanced at the dance floor, indicating he'd like to move in that direction. No words were said. He stood up, put his hand out, and lifted me to my feet. He rested his arms on my shoulders, still gazing into my eyes. I blushed and averted his gaze and rested my head against his cheek. I felt his pelvis slide against my stomach. He felt good.

"Do you know your body feels as lovely as it looks?" he whispered in my ear.

"You're embarrassing me. I don't know what to say to all this. You have to admit it's not the average rap."

"It's not a rap. A rap implies insincerity." He kissed my neck lightly and closed his arms around me.

"I don't know what to say." I was accustomed to teasing men and making them jump through hoops.

"Then don't say anything." Before I could say no, his lips covered mine. He tasted so sweet. I did not hear the music stop, but Eric led me back to the pillow and sat down next to me.

"You have cute little hands. Someone said this is your party… your place?"

"Yeah, yes."

"You work? What do you do?" He dug a pack of Marlboro cigarettes from his pocket and squeezed up a few cigarettes, offering one to me.

"No, no thanks. I'm a student. I go to CCNY. I work part time." I felt around behind my pillow till I located my Newports and took one out, and before I could find my matches, he lit it.

"This is a nice place. You share this with friends?"

"No. Well, my mother died and left me a little money. My uncle and aunt raised me." I didn't want to tell him I had gotten the money from insurance as a death benefit for my mother. "I've got to be careful, but I'm OK. Why am I telling you all of this?"

"I guess you wanted to."

"Are you a student?"

"Yes, Columbia, prelaw." Eric held the cigarette upright, balancing the ash, and looked around for an ashtray.

"Someone must've taken mine…more in the kitchen." Hating to leave for even a moment, I made my way through the crowd. I thought I sensed his presence behind me but didn't dare turn to look. I hated disappointment. I tiptoed and reached up into the closet for the ashtray, and his large, dark hand moved over mine and took it out. It startled me and turned me on, feeling him behind me, but I tried not to show it.

"Where can we have a little privacy?"

"What do you mean?" I asked, knowing full well what he meant, but I couldn't make it easy for him. He had already taken away most of my defenses. They had been stripped off so gently that I hadn't noticed. I felt naked but warm.

"I mean let's go into the bedroom, where it's quiet and we can talk."

"Talk. That's a cute line. You must think I'm—"

"I think you're lovely, and I'd like to get to know you better."

I felt lost. None of this conversation was what I was used to. Words never failed me, but with Eric, words did not come. I stumbled, and he seemed to gently help me to recover.

I walked through the living room to the bedroom. As I reached for the knob, my hand trembled.

"You're afraid of me, aren't you?" Eric seemed amused.

"No, I'm not frightened. Why should I be frightened?"

"Why are your hands shaking?"

"So, I'm frightened. I've just never met anyone like you before. I don't know what I'm doing, going into my bedroom with a man who I know nothing about." I wanted him. I wanted to possess him. Our conversation seemed to say he wouldn't be managed.

"You shouldn't be so skeptical."

"I'm not a skeptic by nature. It's just that there are rules to this game. You aren't playing by any of the rules. I'm confused."

"I'm not in the game." He smiled, placed the ashtray on the bureau, and stubbed out his cigarette.

"You know what I mean."

"And I think you know what *I* mean," said Eric. "Now, we can settle into a polite debate about game playing and lines and raps and bullshit, or we can make love."

"I knew it."

"Hey, relax…only testing."

"Well, you tested the wrong—"

"Shhh," he said, placing his forefinger on my lips. "Let's start over. How about I ask you for your phone number. I'll give you a call. We'll spend some time together, and then we'll make love."

I couldn't hold back the smile. My lips tingled. I marveled at his wit and his self-confidence. I wanted to take control of him. Once again, I felt his mouth cover mine. His tongue brushed my lips and parted them slightly. I was wearing a halter top and shorts, and his fingertips toyed with my bare back, found their way to my buttocks, and rested there.

"So, do you have a pen and a piece of paper?" he whispered. "And you will write down your number, and I will call you in a couple of weeks. By then you should have sorted out your confusion."

I had to catch my balance, I was so out of sorts. I then went to my desk to get a pencil and pad. Eric lit another cigarette and exhaled the smoke through his nostrils. I handed him the paper. He folded it neatly and placed it into his wallet.

"Good night, beautiful."

"You're leaving?"

"Look, I don't generally go to big parties. I'll call you." He kissed me on my lips. The sensation was electric, traveling straight to my center, making me moist. He turned and walked out of the room. I leaned on the bureau for support, breathless.

"Hey, Jewel. Who was he?"

"Huh?"

"Who was the gorgeous Negro who just walked out of here?"

"Saundra, you wouldn't believe this guy."

Camille peeked in through the doorway. "He was cute as sin, girl. That dimple in his chin. You could just eat him up."

"He's cute, and he knows it," Saundra added with an edge in her voice.

"He told me I was lovely."

"That's a good line." Saundra drew a long drag of her Salem.

"He said it wasn't a line."

"That's an even better one. Sounds to me like your nose is wide open. Let me just say this, beware of cute niggers."

"Saundra, stop saying that word. He's a student, right?" Camille was wide eyed.

"Columbia, prelaw."

"Uh oh. A smart son of a bitch."

"Saundra, you know we could all do without your negative vibes right now."

"Well, I know this, that Negro's been watching you all night long."

"She's right," said Camille. "I said to Saundra, about an hour ago, when is this man gonna make his move?"

"He said he was watching me."

"Well, he was. You were so busy running around lighting incense and changing records. And then you were dancing with Jerome."

"I had to give him some...'member, he helped me pay my rent this month," I said.

"Well, he was watching you then too. So I just said to myself, how long is it going to take this pretty man to make his move? I was checking him out. I went over to him. You know me and my bold self. I asked him to dance."

"Saundra, you're too much. You actually asked him to dance?" Camille said.

"Sure I did. So he says to me he's just mellowing out." Saundra dragged the last puff of her cigarette and stubbed it out. "I guess I just wasn't his type. I stepped back, and hey, it was clear. His eyes were all over you like white on rice. So what happened?"

"Nothing, really."

"I know he kissed you. Hell, right there on the dance floor," Saundra said.

Camille stopped asking questions. I sat down on the bed. I wished everyone would go home. I rested my head on a pillow, trying to remember everything about Eric.

"You tired? I'll take care of everything outside," Camille said.

"That's OK. I'll do it."

"She's turned on," Saundra said with a laugh.

"Saundra, let's go out and get rid of these people. Jewel, you want us to stay over? Tomorrow we'll all clean up," Camille said.

"I don't mind staying. There's not one man here who I'd want to leave with."

"You have your period coming or something, Saundra? Girl, you have been a bitch on wheels all night long," Camille said, picking out her 'fro while looking into the mirror at Saundra's reflection and then mine.

"I know. I can't help it. I thought Santos would be here. He said he was coming."

"You know that he's the most unreliable Negro in New York."

We headed into the living room. I turned on the torch lamp in the corner near the couch, and the two couples who were making out squinted and shaded their eyes.

"You guys gotta go. I have to study tomorrow."

Two guys sitting on the floor talking and gesticulating stood up and stuffed their cigarettes in their dungaree pockets and headed for the door. Camille picked up paper cups and two ashtrays and took them into the kitchen. I followed her with a stack of paper cups and some greasy paper plates with plastic forks.

"My chili got gobbled up."

"I saw this guy scraping the pot." Saundra laughed.

I emptied the cups into the sink, catching the wet cigarette butts before they floated down the drain. I pushed the plates into the already-stuffed garbage bag.

"Should I throw these plastic forks away?" Saundra asked.

"No, gimme. I'll wash them," Camille said.

I threw the red-stained plastic forks I had in my hand into the sink. After the last girl and guy came out of the bathroom and left, I locked the door behind them.

"Were they in the bathroom together all this time?" I laughed.

"Think so," said Saundra. "Camille, do you ever wonder where we'll be ten years from now?" she asked.

"I have fantasies. You know me with my little fantasies."

"No, I don't mean fantasies. I mean where we will really be."

"I guess I hope Derrick gets his act together and maybe we get married, but I don't know."

"Me either," I said.

"I know I'd like to have a baby by then, and probably teach," Camille said as she collected the ashtrays, dumped them, and stacked them in the sink. She walked back into the living room, taking off her right sandal as she sat down on the couch. Saundra was sitting on the windowsill. I was sitting on the couch, listening.

"Camille, you know I look at you and Jewel, and I know you'll both make something of your lives. Jewel will probably marry some rich guy. I know you're gonna teach or write, but sometimes I don't think I'll be here ten years from now."

"Where do you think you'll be?" I asked.

"No, I mean I don't think I'll be around at all. I feel maybe I'm going to have a short life."

"Oh girl, stop!" I said.

"No, I mean it. I don't want to be here if this is all there is."

"Saundra, you're just down because Santos didn't show up. Derrick didn't come either. You can't let him depress you like this."

"No, I've been thinking this for a long time now. I'm not cut out for college. I barely graduated high school. These classes are kicking my ass. I get headaches all the time. I only feel good when I forget about school, about my parents, about Santos, about everything. I only feel good when I'm high."

"Santos is not worth it. He's shaky...unreliable. He's got your head all mixed up. You're always depressed when he doesn't call," I said. "I try not to let these men control what I do."

"Look, it's not him. Fuck him," Saundra said, her eyes filled with tears. "Why do I love him anyway? He's shit. A real shit!"

"You need some sleep." I took the pillows off the couch and lined them up on the floor like a mattress. I went into the linen closet and got a sheet and a pillowcase. I threw it over the pillows.

"I don't understand why I love this man who deliberately tries to hurt me."

"Why do I wait around for Derrick to call? Why do I think I love him? He's with me a few weeks and then gone the next two months."

I threw a sheet over the couch. "You guys choose for who gets the couch and who gets the floor."

Camille took the floor.

"Camille, if I'm not around, you know, in ten years, you'll know it was because I just couldn't hang around. You'll know it was 'cause I just got tired."

"Saundra, you'll be here, and things will be better," Camille said.

"I know where I'll be. I'll be with that pretty man who just left here. I'm not big on kids, but if he says he wants them, I'll say, how many? I am going to bed to dream about Mr. Gorgeous."

"When I'm asleep, I forget too. You'll remember what I said, right?" Saundra said.

"What do you mean?" Camille asked.

"You'll remember if I'm not around, it's just 'cause I couldn't."

"Saundra, I would try to talk you out of this depressing mood, but I have to go put my head down. I'll see you guys in the morning." I shut the lamp.

I was the first one up. In the living room, the shades were only half drawn. Camille turned over onto her back, arching it and stretching it out. Saundra lay quietly. I didn't know whether she was awake or asleep.

Camille sat up, tilting her shoulders to the right and then to the left. She flexed her feet.

"Camille, is Saundra still asleep?" I whispered.

"No, Saundra's awake," Saundra said. "What was in that last batch of punch? My head feels like a bowling ball."

"I don't know. I didn't have any. This guy brought some kind of wine, and this girl poured in some tequila. Beats me what else was in there," I said.

"What's it doing outside? I wish it would rain and get it over with," Camille said.

"Coffee, anyone?"

"Jewel, how can you be so cheery? Oh, I forgot. Mr. Wonderful," Saundra said, lifting her head, only to rest it on the back of the couch.

"Did you have sweet dreams?" Camille said.

"Aspirin. Big aspirin," Saundra groaned.

I went into the kitchen and ran the water. "Would you rather some Darvon or Valium, if it's tension? They're stronger."

"Yes. Anything."

I got the Darvon from the bathroom. "These are stronger than aspirin. You only need one." I took out the Lipton's and the jar of Maxwell House coffee.

"What was his name?" Camille asked.

"Eric. All I remember was I kept smiling at him. I couldn't stop smiling. He was so cute. And his voice—he had this deep voice. I didn't know what to do with myself. Then he asks for my telephone number. And he says he'll call me."

"Well, girl, you want to take a trip with me to my gynecologist? She'll give you the pill," Camille said.

"I didn't say I was going to sleep with him."

"Well, that smile on your face says something."

I got up and turned off the flame under the kettle. "I'm having coffee. You want tea?"

"Yeah…you're going to try to put this guy off."

"I don't know. He might not even call. Saundra, tea or coffee?"

Saundra walked slowly into the kitchen, rubbing the sleep from her eyes, and eased herself into the third chair, which was against the wall. "Coffee. Jewel, you're crazy. That guy was beautiful. A little stuck up, maybe, but beautiful. I say enjoy him while you can. And I hate to say this, Jewel, but you're a tease."

"Hey, look," Camille said, "when Jewel wants to, she'll—"

"She'll be sixty by then and all dried up."

What Saundra said struck Camille funny. She put her hand over her mouth to hold in a giggle.

"You know what he said? He said, 'I want to make love to you.' I just stood there. I'm looking at that dimple, and I'm thinking, how can I resist?"

"So don't. You don't have your aunt and uncle breathing down your neck anymore. I may go to the other extreme, but you—"

"What do you mean, Saundra?"

"Well, we talked about it, Camille and me. We were saying you're a tease."

"So you both think that."

"Not exactly," said Camille. "What I said was that it was as if you were still obeying your aunt and uncle. Face it, they were damned strict. You shut them out just long enough to see what it feels like to have a good time. You tease the guy, doing everything but…and then…"

"What is this, your psych I class? I'm the psych major."

"All we're saying is, admit that you get turned on like the rest of us," Saundra said.

I felt exposed. Each word stung. Tears filled my eyes. "I can't help it. I get scared. I told you how scared I get."

"What are you afraid of?"

I couldn't look them in the eye. They saw me as this virgin tease. What they didn't know was that I was scared to death that once I did it, I would be just like my aunt and uncle said, just like my mother. How could I explain that to Camille? I held on to my virginity because it was the last vestige of evidence that I was not my mother's child. I was not the whore that they said she was.

"Camille, I just feel afraid that if I am not careful, someone will think the worst of me." I wanted to tell my friends all of it. But I couldn't. I was too ashamed.

"Hell, I totally get it," Saundra said. "But they can think that no matter what you do."

"We only brought it up because we care about you. I think you should get protection, just in case," Camille said, her eyes seeming to tear up.

Saundra looked as if she was starting to cry. She pulled two napkins out of the holder and handed one to me and one to Camille. "All I have to say is, he was one pretty Negro."

"Saundra, do you think he'll call?"

"Don't go pinning your hopes on it. That's one thing I've learned."

"Let's get started cleaning up this mess," Camille said, wiping her cheek with the napkin and moving into the living room. "I'll put on some music."

"No, no music." Saundra put her hand on mine. "Hey, I really am sorry."

"How did I forget this last night? It's a sticky mess," Camille said as she filled the chili pot with water and dishwashing liquid.

My mind backtracked to what Saundra had said the night before. I wondered where we would all be in ten years. There were no images. I settled in on the strength I felt when I thought of the three of us together. We could lean on one another.

I took out the vacuum cleaner from the closet. As I pushed it back and forth on my worn old carpet, Eric filled my mind. There was no space for anything else. I needed him in my life.

"Whose idea was it to go to summer school?" Camille called out from the kitchen. "Shoot, I think it was mine. I've still got that sociology paper to write."

"Two weeks left, and I'm having hell with economics, and my poly sci professor's giving a final in addition to a paper." I must have been crazy to throw this party. But if I hadn't had the party, I would never have met Eric. It was fate. I was glad I had schoolwork to do. It would keep me from thinking about him calling. It was all fated—our meeting, my finals, all of it. It would be good to look back at all of it with him years from now, if he'd just call.

11

SAUNDRA

"**G**ood afternoon, National Standard Life, can I help you?"

"Saundra, you better do something…make that man stop callin' my house."

"Mama? What are you talking…you can't call here and…suppose someone was covering for me…" I was so thrown hearing my mother's voice that I didn't know what to say to her. I looked around to be sure that no one else was listening.

"That husband of yours just called here asking me why I am messin' in his business."

"I don't…look, Ma, can I call you back? I can't…I'm heading home soo…in a half an hour." It was four thirty. I cupped the phone as my supervisor, a nosy woman in her fifties, put a memo on my desk.

"You know there are no private calls, Ms. Farrell."

"Sorry, it's my mom. A bit of an emergency with my daughter."

"You are free to use the public phone down in the lobby. You can call Gina to cover…"

"You better take care of this soon, or…" My mother went on, oblivious to the trouble she was causing.

"I'll take care of it. I have to hang up. Sorry, Mrs. Ryan."

She straightened my appointment calendar, which was on the front of my desk. She surveyed the waiting area, looking at the magazine racks, the armchairs, and the brochures on the small display rack, and said, "You keep this area well organized...so important, because it's the first thing our customers see. Good work."

"Thank you, Mrs. Ryan." I knew she was just making conversation to be sure I wasn't on the phone.

Why did she call me at my job for this? What did she expect me to do? I didn't know Santos even remembered her number. I need to call my lawyer...see what I can do about this. I straightened my desk, sorted the callback slips for the agents, and put them into their boxes. My knees felt weak. This man is poking his head into my work. I can't let him lose me this job.

I searched through my bag for my lawyer's business card. The phone rang, and I jumped. I was afraid to answer it, thinking it was Santos, that somehow he had found me. At the same moment, Gina, the girl from the office next door, peeked in to say hi. I was just staring at the phone as it rang, terrified to answer. It rang three times. I picked it up. "National Standard Life. Good afternoon. May I help you?" My voice wavered. The caller wanted one of the agents, and I put her call through to him.

"I was going to say how're you doing, but you seem a little rattled," Gina said.

"Yeah, guess I am. Just ready to get home."

"Well, I can answer for you for the last fifteen minutes."

"No, I don't want to leave early. Just thinking about what to make for dinner."

"I brought in from the pizza joint yesterday. Check on the specials when you pass Luigi's going to the subway. Sometimes it's worth it to just bring in. Get out of here...you've covered for me longer than this."

"Thanks, Gina, but I really need this job...my luck, the minute I leave, Ms. Ryan...don't want to screw up."

I took my purse out of my drawer, took out change for the phone, and got my token out.

"Who do you think is going to win? Did you vote today?"

"What?" I was trying to focus. "I don't know what you're talking about."

"The election—George Bush and Bill Clinton? I think it's time for a change…and…" She kept talking, and her words were crowding in around me. I couldn't breathe.

"I got a lot on my mind right now…you know I'm moving…"

"Girl, go home! What is it, five minutes? You went to the ladies' room if anyone asks."

"I told Ms. Ryan I had a bit of an emergency at home, so you can just say that. Thanks, Gina." I was grateful for her kindness. I grabbed the quarters and dimes I had lined up for the phone and got my jacket out of the closet. The elevator was filled with people getting a jump on the five-o'clock rush, but I squeezed myself in and rode down to the lobby. A gray-haired woman was in the phone booth, and I tried to make my presence felt, looking in at her. She finally hung up and opened the door, and as I was stepping in, she put her hand out to stop me so that she could check for change. Once in the tight space, my chest tightened. I needed to find out exactly what he had said to my mother. I wished I didn't have to talk to her. She obviously blamed me for Santos calling.

"Mama, it's me. I can talk now. What happened?"

"So, I'm making dinner for Wanda and me, and that animal calls and asks to talk to her. I say no, and he tells me he got the papers on the guardianship."

"What papers? Guardianship?"

"Well, the day after they took him and you were at the precinct or the court—I don't know—the CPS people wanted to take Wanda. I said absolutely not. The woman asked if I could take care of her in case you were not well enough. I said yes."

"When were you going to tell me this?"

"Well, you were well enough, so I didn't think anything of it anymore."

"What about the papers?"

"That day she gave me papers to sign that I would act as temporary guardian. They must have sent him a copy."

"How come I'm first hearing it now, Mama?"

She was quiet. "Maybe yours are coming."

"Thanks, Ma. It would have been great if you had told me about this weeks ago. I gotta see if I can catch my attorney."

I hung the receiver up and just sat there trying to process what she had said. I dialed the lawyer's office and glanced at my Timex, the first thing I had bought with my first paycheck. I got his voice mail. Shit. Five fifteen. He's gone already.

"This is Saundra, Ben...Saundra Farrell. I need your advice. My ex-husband has been calling my mother from Rikers. How do I get him to stop? It's an issue with my daughter, and—" There was a beep, ending the call. I put another quarter in and dialed again "Saundra Benitez again. My number is 636-3425." I hung up. "Shit, I left my old apartment number." Though the door was closed, I looked outside to see if anyone had heard me. The lobby was deserted except for the security guard, and he was seated at his desk reading a book. He didn't even seem to notice me.

As I was trying to collect the dimes I had on the shelf in the telephone booth, I realized that as tired as I was, I had to go back up to the Bronx to the apartment. It was the last place I wanted to go now, but I needed to check the mail for the papers to see what my mother was up to. I would call the lawyer back from there and leave my mother's number. Most of our stuff was over at my mother's. I had left the towels and the kitchen stuff so that Santos wouldn't find an empty place and go berserk on me.

The fall air made me breathe better, but my stomach had begun to roil. I passed Luigi's, and the special was lasagna. My stomach was so upset, the thought of it made me feel as if I would throw up.

The subway was crowded, and I had to stand all the way to the Bronx, with people jammed next to me. The odors coming from them made me nauseated, and I tried to avoid them breathing in my face. Once the crowds thinned out a bit and I got a seat, it hit me that my mother was planning to take my child right from under my nose. *Bitch.* I need my attorney to protect me from my own mother. Mama, please don't do that to me now.

It was growing dark when I trekked up the steps to the Concourse. I stopped at the bodega to grab a loaf of bread.

"Hey, Mami. How are you?" Raul said. He was a short man in his early forties with a paunch, a friend of Santos's from Cuba. I really didn't want to talk to him, but I needed something to eat. I still had peanut butter and jelly in the house, so I figured I could make a sandwich if I felt well enough to get it down.

"OK, I guess. Just this." I pushed the bread farther onto the counter. "You have any aspirin?"

"You need a good man, Mami. Who treat you good."

I put two dollars on the counter. I wanted to fold up and hide, but I couldn't let him know. "Raul, don't start. You don't want no trouble with my ex. Here." I took out another two dollars and pushed the money closer to him.

"I can take care of him. If you change your mind, you know where I am. No charge, Mamita."

"That's OK. I can't." I left the money there and walked out. Halfway down the block, I began to dry heave. I almost walked past the house because I didn't recognize the new graffiti on the heavy maroon steel door to the building. The smell of urine hit me when I opened it. I don't know how I had forgotten that odor in just a week. There were so many keys on my ring, I couldn't find the one for the mailbox. It was stuffed.

"Where's my mind…forgot the change-of-address card." Upstairs, I fumbled with my keys to find the one to the deadbolt, and then the bottom lock. All those locks, and they only locked me in there with him. After I put everything down on the table, it hit me. The place was bare. Only the table and chairs, our beat-up old sofa, and the two boxes on the floor.

Focus. Look for the papers. I opened each of the envelopes. My Con Ed bill, the telephone bill. "Shit, the hospital is billing me six hundred fifty-two dollars for the emergency room. Where the hell am I going to get that?" I noticed a large black envelope and turned it over. "Onyx" was written in silver on the back. Jewel's reception. There were no legal papers anywhere. I put the bills in a stack and opened the envelope from Jewel.

"Fancy dancy." The invitation was a black card with a silver overlay with black lettering.

Jewel Jamison, Founder
of
Onyx Management
Invites you to a champagne toast to the opening of
our Chicago Office
and
Celebrating our 10th year in the Entertainment
Industry
We will be showcasing our talented models and actors, who already have made their mark on fashion, film, television, and music videos.

November 20, 1992, at 6:30 p.m.
Tavern on the Green
Central Park West
Between 66th and 67th Streets
Hors d'oeuvres and cocktails will be served.
RSVP (212) 777-3242

I wondered if Jewel even really wanted me there. The brunch had reminded me of all of the insecurities that I had fought against in college. Not smart enough, too impulsive. I was working at feeling worthy, and after seeing Jewel and Camille, I was right back where I had started.

Except for Les. He had been the one bright light that day. Hell, he was the only bright light back then in college. As crazy as he was, as we both were, it was the one time when I felt wanted just for myself. It was so weird, just thinking about him, that a calm washed over me.

"I can't believe Camille of all people is against me seeing him." The sound of my words bounced against the walls.

The day of the brunch, when Jewel told Camille to bring Cole, I wished I could ask Les to go. It sounded like such an odd kind of happening, the models and actors. It wasn't like going on a date. It was more like going to a play or performance art back in the day. *I must be crazy. He would never want to go.* I looked through my bag and dug his number out of the pocket with the lawyer's card. If I sit and think about it, I probably won't call. I picked up the phone and dialed.

It rang three times. He's not home. I guess it's not to be. As I was about to hang up, Les's machine answered. There was some cool jazz playing and then his voice saying, "If you are calling about a gig, please leave the time and date with your number, and I will get back to you as soon as I can."

I don't know why I did it, but I laughed and said, "Les, this is Saundra, I…does that mean, if this is not about a gig, you won't…"

Before I could finish, he picked up. "Sandy. How're you doin'?"

The way he spoke made me smile. I didn't know when I had smiled that day. He spoke like a musician, stretching out his words as if he were enjoying each minute of the sound of everything.

"OK, working, packing. I'm moving by next week—the week before Thanksgiving, actually. As a matter of fact, if you hear of any vacant apartments, let me know. I'm movin' in over at my mother's for a while until I find my own place."

"I'll keep an ear out. It was good seein' you the other day. Man, you look the same. It's so far out."

"Get outta here."

"No, it's true. You know, I used to be high all the time, and sometimes people come up to me I knew then, and they insist I know them and I don't remember them at all. But you, you look the same."

"You really know how to make a girl feel good," I said, laughing. "You look pretty much the same too. Your hair is just a little shorter."

"Yeah, well, right after I saw you back then, you wouldn't have recognized me. I ended up in the army. They buzz cut my hair, and before I knew it, I was in 'Nam."

"You were in Vietnam?"

"Yeah, I got lucky and got hit in the upper chest. They let me out 'cause I was damaged goods. Maybe it was a good thing. It made me kind of funny about my lungs. Stopped smokin' cigarettes after that."

"We were so crazy back then. Do you remember how we met?"

"Sure thing. In the park. Washington Square."

"I was so crazy. If my daughter took the chances I did, I would…" Images from the day we met filled my mind.

"Yeah, but it was so different back then. It didn't feel…it just felt free."

"It's true. How did it get so turned around and screwed up?"

I wanted to tell Les about Santos, but I felt ashamed that I had spent my life secluded in an apartment with a man who beat me. I didn't know how he could say I looked the same. I felt so broken up inside. I was looking for something positive to say. "I just got a divorce. That's what I was celebratin' on Sunday."

"You cool about it?"

I didn't expect him to care. "It's the best thing I ever did for myself. So, let me tell you why I called, other than hearing your voice, which was the most important thing."

"I remember that about you. You always just came right out with what you were thinking."

"Can't help it."

"Shouldn't try."

"I don't really," I answered, enjoying the back-and-forth. "Anyway, my friend Jewel, who was at the table on Sunday, is having this thing to celebrate her new office."

"Sandy, I'm not real into parties."

"Well, it's not your typical party. It's this cocktail thing that she's giving to promote the opening of her Chicago modeling and acting agenting office. She says lots of show-business types and designers and editors are going to be there. I thought it might be sort of a goof to see how the other half lives. It's at the Tavern on the Green. Might be music people there too, 'cause her models do music videos."

"I don't know."

"Les, if you don't want to go, it's cool. I can totally understand. I was just curious about it. I've never been to the Tavern on the Green. For me it's like a 'Happening'. Remember them? I was in one once."

"Yeah. How'd you even remember that? Happenings. Shit." Les laughed. "Sandy, hey, I'm up for it."

"You sure?"

"Sure. Unless I get a gig. If I get a gig..."

"I understand. Of course. I guess that's a date."

Les laughed.

"Did I say something funny?"

"You're just funny, the way you say things. What time is this thing?"

"Six thirty. Should we meet there, or...I'm running home to change."

"Where do you live?"

"Well, I'm going up to the Bronx, where I still have most of my clothes. I'm gonna have to rush."

"I teach in the Bronx. I can pick you up there, and we can drive in."

"No. I can't have you come to my apartment…" I didn't want anyone from the building to see me with Les.

"Well, are you near the Concourse? I can pick you up on the Concourse somewhere."

"OK, what about the corner of 150th and the Concourse at six, maybe?"

"Sandy, before you go. Just curious…why didn't you call back, back then?"

"Long story for another time. I'm sure you didn't lose any sleep over me." I laughed.

"Actually, I did…wondered what happened…if you were OK." He paused. "Some other time, like you said. See you there."

It was done. I felt light as a feather for the first time in years. I couldn't believe he remembered that I didn't call and cared what happened to me. There was something accepting in him. He didn't judge me. It was easy being with him. I hoped that I could explain that to Camille. I didn't think Jewel would get it. It was hard to describe and I was not that good with words, but it was important to me that Camille understand. He just accepted me.

I looked like hell the day I met him. It was mid-September in 1967. My eyes had dark circles around them. I was sitting on the beach in Coney Island at about six in the morning, watching the seagulls feed on what was left of summer. There were no boats on the horizon, no people nearby. The ocean quietly spilled its scum on the shore. Brown weeds and blackened shells lined the water's edge, stretching out to the right and left as far as I could see. I hadn't slept in two days. Snatches of conversation whipped into my mind. My mother saying, "You have to finish college." My father offered me a secondhand car if I stayed. Camille told me to stick it out one more term. Jewel said, "You don't know how good you have it being home with your parents." Santos shouting stupid bitch at me as he tried to hide the yellow-skinned girl in his bedroom. I heard her say, "What do you care what she thinks?" The summer had been a nightmare of expectations I could not meet.

I had registered for the classes that I had failed in the spring. A counselor assigned me a tutor in history. The first week I sat in class staring at faces of professors, their mouths moving as they handed out sheets of paper covered with black ink. The tutor, a tall, skinny boy about eighteen years old, told me to read the first fifty pages and make up index cards with something written on them. I couldn't remember what. My mind was jelly. Sound went in and got lost in my head. By the second week, I felt I couldn't take it any longer. I walked around the city that day and found my way home at midnight. My parents were sleeping. I could not. The heat was oppressive. I finally wound up on the beach.

The train was almost empty when I got on, intending to go home. The conductor, a black man in his fifties, saw me as he entered the car. He muttered loud enough for me to hear, "These kids think they're so smart. Joy riding, not a care in the world. Don't need no education." I sat, taking in his scolding, thinking how wrong he was. I felt like screaming but didn't. I decided not to go home and hear more of the same.

The train stopped at West Fourth Street. I moved through the maze of ramps and staircases and came up into the light. Along Bleeker Street then up MacDougal, I saw shopkeepers sweeping and spraying down sidewalks. In Washington Square Park, small clusters of people sat, while others stood and watched men playing chess. I sat down, exhausted, and a white guy with long dark-brown hair came and sat down next to me. He seemed a little high. I was too tired to go any farther.

"You want some smoke?"

"No, I don't have any money."

He thought awhile and then said, "I meant, you want a few hits? You look like you could use some." His eyes were focused in on me. They were a blue-green with gray and gold flecks. I felt like a fuzzy creature under a microscope as he concentrated his attention on me.

"Yeah, sure."

"You got a name?"

"Saundra."

"Les."

He took out a small stash held in an emptied film canister. He tapped it into a folded piece of paper, rolled, licked, and then lit it. He took a drag and coughed and passed it to me.

"Colombian."

He stretched his arms out, one behind me and the other extended to the other end of the bench. I took a drag and then handed it back to him. I hadn't eaten, so the smoke went straight to my head.

"You a student?" He seemed uninterested.

"Sort of."

He laughed. "Me too—sort of, that is." I didn't know if he was laughing at me. He nodded his head in rhythm, as if he heard music there.

A guy in torn bellbottoms and a headband came over to him. "Les, I'm headin' upstate with Mark...want to come?"

"No...just going to mellow out. You guys coming back tonight?"

"No. We're headed up to the farm."

"Maybe I'll catch up with you there."

"Peace."

"Peace, man."

"I'll have some quiet tonight...the pad to myself. Those guys don't know when to go to sleep." He laughed. I laughed too. I didn't know why. "You hungry? I've got the munchies. I could go for some chili, but it's probably too early. Maybe eggs."

"I don't know. OK, sure."

We walked down Mac Dougal Street to Bleeker, and from a window upstairs, a girl with a mop of sandy-colored hair called out Les's name. "C'mon up."

"That's Sarah. She's always got something good to eat—vegetarian, but good. Wanna come up with me?"

It felt strange going to someone's house uninvited, but Les went in and somehow I just followed. The stairs tilted to the left, and the banister was loose. The girl opened the apartment door at the top of the landing.

"Saundra. Sarah," Les said, sitting down at the oak kitchen table.

Sarah smiled at me. She was holding a baby boy on her hip. His face and hands were dirty. He was bare from the waist down. He stared at me with a serious, almost adult expression.

"Want some zucchini bread?" Sarah reached over with her one free hand and lifted a cutting board with a brownish cake-like loaf on it. The baby swiped at it, and once she put it on the table, she swung him onto her other hip and sliced four thick pieces. Les took a slice and broke it in half, putting half in his mouth and the other half on the bare table in front of him. I reached over and broke off a small piece and, feeling awkward about having no plate, waited until no one was looking in my direction before I reached for another piece. Sarah pushed a piece into the child's mouth.

"John and I are going up to Vermont for the winter."

"He sell enough for the oil?"

"Yeah. Well, we're buying some wood for the stove."

"Got any acid?" Les asked.

"Yeah, you know where."

Les disappeared into the other room. The girl swayed with the baby.

He backtracked to the kitchen. "Hey, Saundra, want a tab?"

"Maybe a half." I had taken acid only twice, but my mind seemed clearer after.

He went back into the room and came back, handing me a tiny piece of blotter.

"I left you something in there, Sarah. Hey, we're gonna split." Les grabbed another piece of bread and handed me a slice. I held it in the palm of my hand.

We walked down the stairs and out to Bleeker Street.

"I live just up the block here."

I was spaced…and broke off pieces of the bread and ate as we went. The pot had taken away all of the pain. When he turned into the building, I brushed the crumbs from my hands and followed him in. We walked up two flights of stairs to Les's apartment.

He put on some music. "Ravi Shankar," he said, and sat down on a mattress covered with a sheet that had been tie dyed in a rainbow of colors. The dye had run together, making concentric ovals of orange, red, and yellow. The kitchen had an old sink that looked as if it might fall off the wall, filled with dirty dishes. There was also an old-fashioned tub against the wall next to the door. It was covered with a sheet of plywood and was painted red. The wooden floor seemed to sink in the center.

"A bathtub in the kitchen?" I laughed.

"Yeah," Les said, nodding.

"Weird."

"All these old buildings have them like this. I think they wanted it closer to the stove, to heat the water." He shrugged. "Think they were called cold-water flats."

"You're kidding." The acid had begun to work. The stripes on the exposed corner of the mattress became more clearly defined. I began to notice how white Les's skin was.

"You're cool, you know that?"

"What do you mean?"

"Well, a lot of people won't drop acid with folks they don't know."

I didn't quite hear Les. I was focused on the pores of his skin. The hairs on his arm were black-brown. I looked into his eyes.

"Yeah, my mom calls me reckless. I just felt you were a good guy. You have blue eyes with gray, and it looks like golden flecks in them. It's not a cold blue, though. Almost aqua. They're warm."

I looked around the room, which had a wooden table in the corner and a big, old-fashioned desk next to it. The room seemed tilted to the left, as if the furniture weighed it down.

"Is this room leaning, or am I just stoned?"

He laughed. "It's lopsided, and I'd guess you're pretty stoned too. I think the guy who built the house was stoned." He laughed again. A furry gray animal ran in from the other room. I leaped up, screaming.

"Hey, it's cool. That's Cloudy. You're just a little freaked. Come here, cat."

Les stood up slowly and put his arms around me. I needed to be held. Cloudy came and nuzzled me, rubbing her head and then arching her back against my leg. Les picked the cat up by the scruff of its neck. I ran my fingers through its fur. I could feel each individual strand, one soft strand after another moving against my fingertips. As I stroked the cat, we sat back down on the mattress, and Les just stared at my face.

"The sunlight...your hair looks golden. Can I touch your hair?" he said.

The question seemed odd at first, until I looked up into Les's eyes, which were innocently gazing at me. I said, "Sure." He stretched out one ringlet and let it spring back.

"It's like spun gold, both wavy and curly. So how come you're sort of a student?"

I laughed.

"Your eyes are light brown, and almond shaped," he said.

"Thinking of quitting college. Everybody's trying to talk me out of it. You know, 'Get an education.'"

"It's all according to what you want. I want my mind to travel free right now."

"School has always been hard for me. I try, but I just can't do it."

"Then don't."

"But everybody is leaning on me."

"Shrug." Les laughed. I laughed too. In my mind's eye, I could see the image of people falling off in all directions. They rolled and tumbled away. I stood alone.

"You're exactly the color of coffee with milk in it, the way I drink it."

I was off by myself in my mind. "But what happens if you're all alone?"

"That's what it's all about, really—being alone."

A chill ran through my body.

"You're alone, and then you meet, and then you're alone again. That's what it's all about." Les's voice was calm and soothing.

I placed my head on his shoulder. I wanted to begin to know this aloneness, safely here. He ran his fingers in my hair, then down my arm. He turned and kissed my face. My skin warmed.

My mind focused on his movements. They were slow. Gentle kisses. Stepping out of clothing, looking, touching, penetrating. My mind went inside myself. It was bright in there. I saw the jutting bulge moving slowly, coming closer, then backing away. Coming closer still. It was that simple, I thought.

The light in the room had grown yellow-orange. The sitar music leaped out and kissed my body all over. Sound crystallized into tiny forms swarming around me. The forms had arms and legs, and they touched me lightly as they swirled and danced solely for my amusement. I heard myself laughing, as if in a cave. The echo bounced on each dancing figure, and they chimed in one by one. I listened to their voices, which tinkled like tiny bells. As I looked more closely, I noticed bells around their ankles and wrists and tiny finger cymbals on their hands. They were dressed in red and violet and adorned in golden beads.

My eyes opened and saw Les above me. The tips of his hair dripped bits of gold on to my face. His eyes were closed, and his eyelashes sparkled. I felt him deep inside the center of me. Where we connected was a swirl of ruby red, rose, and copper. Then the colors burst like fireflowers.

His smile was like sunshine. The scent of fresh coconut filled the room. He leaned down to taste my eyelashes, and then my lips.

"You taste like ambrosia spilling over." He found the center and dipped his tongue into it.

My mouth opened, and I drew him in with the painted light. It flowed into my belly, filling me till it oozed out through my pores. I glistened like a shooting star with color cascading. Around me was a rich, deep, velvet-black sky. It nestled me.

I rested there a long time. Colors dropped off and dissolved until I was only a single star, shrunken to a pinpoint. Fear entered at the center of the light. I felt cold and alone. I opened my eyes, and I saw Les lying next to me, staring up at the amber ceiling.

A question intruded, what for? and I searched Les's body for the answer. I looked at my hands and then my arms. My whole body was wrinkled and shriveled and dirty. I found no answer, only my own ugliness. The sight filled me with terror. I had no words. It shook me like an earthquake that would not stop. My eyes felt as if they might squirt out of my head.

Les reached out and stroked my arm. It became rigid.

"Saundra, you OK?"

I could not answer. He seemed so far away. I was afraid to let my voice come out. It might vomit all over the room. I kept my jaws clenched.

"You bad tripping?"

I could not speak.

"Hey, just listen to me...to my voice. Concentrate."

My head jerked to the side facing away from him.

"Saundra, listen to me. You're bad tripping. I'll take you away from that place."

Gently he stroked my cheek and rested his palm across my forehead. He ran his fingers 'cross my lips.

"Have you ever walked through a grove of peach trees? The scents are luscious, like you."

I could feel my brow relax, and my mind followed through the path with trees on either side.

"The leaves are the brightest green."

I saw them.

"They allow the sunlight to filter through and rest on your face, your beautiful face."

My hand reached out for his, and I held on tightly.

"We can rest in the cool grass over there, and I can hold you while we look up at this beautiful blue sky."

He wrapped his arm around my shoulder and lifted my head onto his chest.

"Do you ever wish you could be a cloud, resting on air? We can, you know. We can do anything."

The sound of his voice lifted me up. I felt my body floating with him, drifting in blueness. Les was good. He had taken me to a safe place above everything ugly.

"Les, how did you know where this place was?"

"I searched for it."

"How come I got lost?"

"You weren't lost. You were only a thought away."

"But I was wrinkled and ugly, dirty."

"Never."

"But I saw it."

"You only thought you did. You're one of the most beautiful women I've ever seen."

"But through my eyes…"

"Look through mine."

"Suppose I forget?"

"Remember me."

I rested there, awake, sifting through the thoughts, holding on to the beauty in them. Time seemed to extend into color and sensation. A lavender haze crept into the room with a cool breeze. Les covered us both with a sheet. I watched the air lose its pink and turn to blue. The music had stopped so long ago. I wished I could remember when. Les held me loosely. The room turned charcoal brown.

I shifted away from him to see what it felt like to be on my own. It was frightening, but not terrifying.

"Les, you chose me, didn't you?"

"Yes."

"Why?"

"Something in your eyes."

"I don't choose men well."

"We all make mistakes."

"But I do it over and over again. I lose myself in wanting them to love me."

"You can never lose yourself. Hold on to yourself. You're all you have."

"My parents, my friends, but they want things from me. I can't always give them what they want."

"If they love you, what they want is secondary. You have to find happiness in what *you* want."

"I don't know what I want."

"It takes time to know." He rested his head on his hand and stared at me.

"You want something to eat? I could make you a cheese sandwich."

I don't remember eating. I just remember watching him move away. But I know he came back, because I drifted off to a restful sleep feeling protected for I don't know how long. He slept beside me, his arm still holding me to him. I feel we laughed and ate some soup that warmed me inside, or else I dreamed it. I slept and woke again.

The morning was pale blue gray. It's too safe here, I thought. I needed to be in the world and feel it as I put the pieces of my life back in place. "Les?"

"Saundra," he said almost in a question.

"Les, I need to go."

"Now?" He lifted his head and shaded his eyes.

"I have to go. I've got to think."

"You sure you can handle it?"

"Yeah."

"I could go with you if you like."

"I just need to be alone."

I stood up and pulled on my clothing. Les rolled over toward a small pad and pencil on the floor at the side of the mattress.

"Saundra, here's my number. Call me if you need me?"

I looked at Les, and a flood of his goodness washed over me. We exchanged smiles and an energy that brightened the room.

"Did you see that?" he said.

"Yeah, I thought it was just me."

We both smiled at that too.

As I walked down the stairs, I put my hand in my pocket. I felt the paper with Les's number and held it tightly. I'd call if I needed him. For now, I could stand on my own. I decided to go home, and face them all.

12

Sex changes everything. I punched the throw pillow and threw it on the couch and took our empty ice cream bowls to the kitchen. "Don't care who you are, I am not in the mood," I said out loud to myself when the phone rang. "It's late, and I am too tired."

"Camille, this is Cole. What was going on with you Sunday?"

"Nothing was going on. I am not in a good mood, so don't start—"

"Camille, we had a nice day. I thought we had a good day together," he said.

I was trying to find something to say.

"Didn't we, Camille?"

"Yes."

"So, what's wrong?"

"Nothing."

"Why did you make me leave there and not want to come back? Something is going on, right?"

"Look, Cole, you don't have to come back. OK."

"Damn it, Camille. We had a good day, and then you pull this cold shit."

"Yeah, and now my son is walking around wondering when you're coming back." I tiptoed over to the bedroom and closed the door where Shawn was sleeping.

"That's because I left without saying good-bye to him. I just didn't want—"

"Exactly. And I can't have you leave him—"

"Don't cut me off, Camille. I was trying to say this the other day, and you cut me off. I didn't want him to see me there in bed with you, until you were ready."

"Ready. Ready? I have something to say too, Cole. I don't have men in and out of my house," I whispered, cupping my hand over the phone. "I should not have let you stay."

"Is that what this is about?"

"Cole, I can't have my son get attached to you and you leave, and I am left to put the pieces together."

"This isn't about Shawn."

"It is. You know what he did this evening? All he talked about was you. 'Wasn't that the longest spaghetti I ever ate, Mom? I'm going to be an astronaut, 'cause Cole said I can be anything I want.' Looking out the window for you. 'Is Cole ever coming back?'"

"Let's get that straight, Camille. I wasn't the one who left."

"Oh, you left."

"No, you sent me out."

"Right. You see, you can afford to have sex and leave here and hope it's all right, but I shouldn't have taken that chance. It was a big mistake."

"Like I said, this isn't about Shawn. This is about you and me."

"There is no you *and* me."

"I didn't say *us*, Camille. This is about the fact that I made love to you, isn't it?"

"Don't say that." I could not speak.

"Why? That's what I did. I made love to you."

I searched the air to find the words to say how I felt. My anger turned to embarrassment and confusion. I had tried so hard not to think about what I had let happen Sunday night. "I shouldn't have done it."

"Camille, maybe it was too soon, and...not the way we would have liked it to be, but we both wanted it. I tried to make sure Shawn wouldn't know."

I remembered how I had kissed him and enjoyed his hands on me. The thoughts filled my mind, making me feel. I had tried so hard not to feel. "I don't know what I wanted." I have to stop this now. "But I can't have you here and then you leave and I have to put my son back together."

"What about you, Camille?"

"What do you mean?"

"You tell me about Shawn. What about you?"

"I don't know how I feel. I like you, but...I have my son to worry about first. When you leave, I am the one who has to put him back together. Not doing it."

"Who says I'd go?"

"You'll go."

"OK, suppose we have a great time together, and...Camille, I love being with you." Cole's words splashed in my face and made me feel warm. My hand, which held the phone, trembled.

"Cole, I'm afraid of you." The words spilled from my lips.

There was a long silence, as if he was turning over in his mind what I had said.

"I know we haven't known each other very long, Camille, but I won't hurt you. I promise."

"Why are you saying this?"

"Because I sense that you think that somehow I'm going to do something to hurt you. I wouldn't."

His words bounced away like sponge balls.

"I am not talking about me. I just don't want you to hurt Shawn."

"Why would I hurt Shawn?"

"Look, I don't know you. I don't understand what you are doing taking out a woman and her son...taking me out...just what is your story? I don't need you to push your way into our lives, and then you split. We're accustomed to being alone. There's never been anyone but us."

"What about Shawn's father?"

"He disappeared when he heard the results of the blood test, and now he's dead. He never knew Shawn."

Cole mumbled something.

"What did you say?"

"I said that's his loss."

I did not know how to react to his words. I had made the decision to have Shawn. I had had him with Victor because I thought he was bright and sensitive, and I thought I loved him. I had fantasized about him since college, dreaming of a friendship growing into love between Victor and me. Instead, there was nothing. As he put it, he had no say in Shawn's birth. I remember he said, "I cannot fulfill some storybook ending that I had no part in writing."

"You don't understand…can't understand. Shawn has no father, and he misses that."

"I do understand that." His voice seemed to crack.

"Well, you can't understand that I can't sit here and watch my child get attached to you."

There was silence. I accepted the silence as what I had expected. "See, when you leave, I have to deal with his hurt. He's had enough hurt."

"Camille, I can't promise to be here forever. We're none of us here forever."

"So next week when you meet someone else, I have to patch my son up, and—"

"Camille, stop."

"You stop! You're playing with us. We are not toys. You come in here and make him like you."

"What about you?" Cole asked.

"What do you mean?"

"I said, what about you? You talk about Shawn. I want to know how you feel."

"It doesn't matter how I feel."

"It does to me," he said in a slow, deliberate way.

"I don't know…I know I'm not…I like you, but I…" I could not put my thoughts together. I didn't know how I felt about this man. He was allowing me to talk. I hadn't talked to a man since Victor. He was allowing me to feel. I hadn't felt connected to my senses since Victor. So there he was, listening, touching, making me feel, and I wanted to run and hide, and he wouldn't allow it. He kept pushing me to feel more.

"Cole, what do you want from me?"

"I guess I want to know if…Camille, I'm forty-eight years old. I'm not an impulsive person. I don't date—you know, go out with different people every weekend. I've spent the last thirty years in the marines, moving from Vietnam to Germany, the Mideast…you name it. I don't plan too far in the future. Do you like being with me, going out, having good times? Be straight with me."

"So you want to play and have good times, and then, when it's over…"

There was a long silence, and in measured tones Cole said, "Camille, I love being with you. It's like I'm finally home, but I'm old enough to know that we *both* must feel that way." He paused, as if he were thinking or waiting for me to say something in response. I couldn't say anything, because his words seemed too real. "Camille?"

His words were delivered so slowly and thoughtfully. They seemed to climb inside my chest, and then my belly.

"You don't even know me," I said, my eyes tearing up with the thought that this man could care to love being with me. "'Member I told you my husband died when I first met you? I just told you the truth. Shawn's father never married me."

"I got that. Camille, that doesn't mean anything to me. I feel I want to get to know you better."

Why am I so frightened? I thought, noticing that I had begun to shiver, and the tears that filled my eyes were now spilling onto my cheeks.

"So, Camille, I guess it's up to you."

"Cole, where did you come from?"

"Originally, my family is from New Orleans. Most recently 110th Street," Cole said, laughing.

I heard myself giggle.

"So I want to know, will you go out with me on Saturday night?" He would not let me hide.

"Tomorrow is Saturday night."

"Yes, I know. Do you want to go out with me tomorrow night, Camille?"

"You are actually asking me out after this...whole thing..." I didn't know what to say.

"I think we just had our first argument," Cole said, laughing.

"What? What did you say?" He made me laugh right out loud. "You are persistent, aren't you?"

"I am when I want something."

"You know Shawn was angry at me when you left."

"Well, I missed saying good-bye to him."

"Cole, most men wouldn't...do you really want to go out tomorrow?"

"I do if you do."

"I know Shawn would enjoy it."

"I said, I do if you do. Do you want to go out with me, Camille— just the two of us?"

"I haven't asked my mom to sit."

"That's not what I asked," Cole said again, slowing his words and delivering them with what sounded like cool deliberation.

I sat with this strangely new sensation. I could not escape him. He would not let me. He was like no other man I had ever known. He demanded that I take part. He required that I receive him gently and willingly.

His silence pressed at me. It pressed at me and then washed over me like a warm shower.

"I would like to go out with you."

"Good," he said, as if he were receiving my hand that had been placed gently in his. We must have said good-byes or so longs. I only recalled the sensation of comfort that settled about me. It was through this warm effervescence that the sound of the phone shimmered.

I answered, though I really did not want my world invaded by sound.

"Camille?"

"Yes?" I answered from far away.

"Camille, is that you?"

"Yes. This is me."

"It's Saundra. Girl, are you all right? You sound…"

"I'm fine. I'm just…how are you?"

"I'm OK. More grief from my ex-husband, and now my mom. Don't want to talk about them. Camille, what did you make of Jewel's attitude on Sunday?"

"I don't know. Couldn't quite get a handle on what was going on. I don't know if I was premenstrual or what."

"I don't think it was you. I just think she's…are you going to her thing at Tavern on the Green? I thought it would be…I don't know…different."

"I was thinking about it, but I don't know."

"Never mind. Did you go out with that guy, Cole?"

"Yes, I went out with him. We had a good time, OK?"

"I just wondered if you wanted a babysitter sometime soon. I didn't know if I should say anything or not," she said, seeming to fish for information.

"God, Saundra, I don't know what to make of this man."

"Hey, I don't know what to make of men, period."

"No, I mean I sent him out of here early Monday morning…"

"What'd he do?"

"Nothing, not a thing. He was a perfect gentleman."

"Maybe that's what's wrong."

"What?"

"Maybe he should have…you know, tried something."

I thought for a while to decipher what Saundra was saying and then gave up. "Girl, what are you talking about?"

"Well, all I'm saying is that maybe he's too much of a gentleman. Did he make a move at all? I mean, I get turned off by these goody-goody guys."

I laughed out loud. "Saundra, you never went out with a goody-goody guy in your life."

"I know."

"Well, Cole is not like that. He's a gentleman, but he's…"

"So, tell me."

"Well, I don't…he's…Saundra?"

"Camille, now, I tell you everything."

"Saundra, hush!"

"You have to tell me if you did it!"

"No, I don't."

"Now, Camille, here I've been worried about you. Let's face it, it's been a long time. You've got to tell me."

"Would you stop! Let's just say he wants to take me out again tomorrow."

"OK, so you didn't do it? I'll bring Wanda over, and I'll sit for Shawn. My present to you."

"Well, I didn't say we didn't."

"You did? Was he good?"

"Saundra, mind your business!"

"Oh, shoot! All right, I'll take Shawn anyway, so you can do it loud."

"Saundra, you should be ashamed of yourself."

"I'm not. You know I just stay real close to the truth. So you want me to sit for Shawn? Yes or no?"

"Sure. You're too much."

"I'll bring Wanda by at about three in the afternoon, and I'll take the kids to the park. Do you want to have the apartment, or..."

"I didn't tell my mom yet. I don't know where he..."

"We'll ask your mom to come down for dinner, pizza or something. I like your mom. She's nothing like mine."

"OK, I'll call her in the morning. How is your mom?"

"A bitch. She gave me the little apartment downstairs. But I think she's trying to...never mind. I don't want to talk about her right now."

"You are really doing it this time, Saundra. I mean moving in there?"

"I think so. I been moving things in a little at a time. I have to see if it feels right. You know my mom and me. By the way, do you remember Les? I called him."

"Saundra, now *that* you should think about."

"Camille, not you too. Frankly, I was caught off guard by Jewel's reaction, her being involved in show business. But I don't believe you are going to tell me some nonsense—"

"All I'm saying is, be careful and think about what you're doing."

"This is the nineties, Camille. I bet you wouldn't have said this twenty years ago. I can't believe that we have gone so far backward in the past twenty years, almost twenty-five years."

"Don't know what I would have said, 'cause it didn't come up."

"I asked Les if he'd go as my escort to Jewel's thing at Tavern on the Green. Camille, don't judge him until you get to know him."

"Sorry I said anything." I paused. "I don't know, it's...this is going to sound real adolescent, I know, but I think Cole really likes me."

"So?"

"So, I don't remember anyone caring about me first, like this. Nobody."

"What does my mother say—'There's a first time for everything'? That sounds great to me."

"I just can't get over him being interested in me, an overweight woman with a child. And Jewel was saying I need a makeover."

"Don't listen to her. And stop with the overweight stuff. Men don't like bones."

"I don't know. It's scary."

"All I have to say is, scare me! If I had a guy who was nice to me, and nice to Wanda…shoot. And forget about what Jewel said…it's always been the same with her. It's all about her."

"Saundra, I'll see you on Saturday, tomorrow."

I hung up the phone. I wondered about this man and where time would take us. This was far different from anything I had ever known before. There was no blueprint in my mind for where it would lead. He wasn't a boy like Derrick, unpredictable, elusive. He wasn't anything like Victor. My mind didn't go off to any fantasy-like places, as it had always done with him. I was left anticipating nothing in particular, but somehow the air around me felt less dense. I breathed more freely.

I first saw Victor on the second Monday I was student teaching at PS 192, my senior year. I was having a cup of coffee, sitting in the teachers' cafeteria waiting for Ms. Silver, my cooperating teacher. I noticed a doodle of Derrick's name I had drawn in my calendar book in August. Though I thought of him as my boyfriend, Derrick hadn't called me once, all summer long. He had the habit of disappearing for weeks on end, but this was the longest time I had spent not hearing from him. I almost wished he would never call, because then I could move on with my life. He was my first love, and he just kept hanging around in my heart no matter what I did. I scribbled over his name, inking it out.

"Sure, Victor, but I did need to talk with you." I heard Pauline Silver, my cooperating teacher's voice and looked up.

"Uh…Mr. Bowen, this is Camille Warren, one of our new student teachers," she said, gesturing toward me. "Camille, this is Mr. Bowen, our assistant principal."

I had been pretending to read some notes so as not to seem to be listening to their conversation. Having been introduced, I glanced up in a perfunctory way, to say hello, but was struck by Victor's handsome, warm smile. He surveyed me with his eyes. I felt strange. I put out my hand to shake his out of nervousness. He shook it and then continued his conversation, seeming to take no further notice of me.

"Tomorrow, Pauline, during your prep, gotta get to my meeting with the superintendent," he said and strode out of the cafeteria. I stared at his back. His shoulders were broad, and his waist was tapered into a V. He had the stature of a basketball player.

"Oh damn! I forgot to ask him about the drawing paper and other supplies I need. I'll be right back." Pauline hurried away, and I was left alone with the vision of Victor Bowen vividly painted in my mind. He had mahogany-brown skin. His hair, beard a neatly trimmed goatee, and mustache were a blue-black with silver running through. I wanted to touch them. I caught myself in that thought and then admonished myself for not wearing my black turtleneck, as I had planned.

"Camille? Boy, you're deep in thought. I have to pick up the kids. Tomorrow morning, I'd like you to take Joey and Keisha and play that silent *e* game you made up. See you in the morning."

I jotted a note to myself to bring the game, packed up my things, and left the cafeteria. I headed for the exit and saw Victor Bowen come out of the main office and turn toward the door. I was several feet behind him, and I watched his back as he walked. He went through the door and must have sensed me behind him, because he held the door open.

"Hello again," he said.

"Hi! Thanks."

"Headed back to school? CCNY, right? I spoke to your professor a few weeks ago," Victor said, sounding somewhat official.

"Yes."

"If you'd like a lift, I'm going right past there to the district office."

"Yes. Thanks."

"I'm right over here," he said, gesturing toward a car parked in front of the school.

He had a long black Buick with red leather upholstery. He went around to open the passenger door for me, watching for the traffic, and after I got in, he closed it. He walked around the back and got in on the driver's side. I felt protected. I searched my mind for something to talk about.

"So, you plan to teach early childhood, or..." Victor said, filling the silence and taking control.

"Yes, early childhood, if I pass the exams and get my license."

"Oh, that shouldn't be a problem. Those tests are asinine. Graduating senior?"

"Yes, I graduate in June." When the car engine started, I felt the vibrations run through my body. I was holding my bag and books very tightly, and I felt my arms begin to tremble.

Victor looked out his window to check for oncoming cars and then pulled the car into the street. Every move he made looked sexy. His car floated, boatlike, down the thoroughfare, and I found myself relaxing into the ride.

"By the way, you should start putting your name in at various schools for upcoming positions next September."

"Already?"

"Well, yes. Schools set up the following year's roster based on who's going out on maternity, taking a sabbatical...and, basically, that's done the year before. So, while you're student teaching, that's a good time to let people know you'll be available."

"Thanks for telling me."

"Stick with me, kid, and I'll show you the world. Where's that from? Some old film, I think."

"I don't know."

Victor glanced in my direction, taking his eyes off the road. I looked at him too. For a moment, we were transfixed. I felt embarrassed, and I looked down at my hands, which had busied themselves with an empty matchbook, bending and folding it. I had begun to fantasize about this man, and I had traveled far away with him. We were driving down a country road surrounded by trees with green and amber leaves. His silver hair sparkled in the sunlight.

"This entrance good for you, Miss Warren? Which entrance would put you closest to where you're going—this one or the one up ahead?"

I pulled myself back from my daydream and glanced up at the street sign. Somehow, all of the buildings looked the same to me. I looked across the street and finally pointed to the nearest entrance. I wasn't sure I had recovered my sensibilities. Some of them were still off somewhere, meandering down a country road.

Victor pulled over to the curb and put the car in park. "Take care."

"Thanks for the lift," I said as I picked up my books and bag. I looked up into Victor's eyes.

"Don't mention it. And if you need any advice, or anything looking for a job, don't hesitate to ask."

I stepped out of the car and dropped my notebook, and then a textbook. I bent down to get them, and my bag slipped off my shoulder. My clumsiness made me want to hide. Victor got out of the car and helped me collect my things.

"You poor kid. Those books are as heavy as you are."

I looked up into his eyes again and blushed. "Don't know how I dropped...thanks for everything."

"If you've got it, I've got to get going."

He didn't look back as he walked around to his side of the car, got in, and drove off. I watched his every movement, recording it all in my mind. There was electricity between us. I felt it, and I knew he felt it too. I was disappointed in how I must have impressed him. I didn't remember saying one word over two syllables. I filed the negative thoughts away. I would wear my black turtleneck tomorrow.

13

JEWEL

Dennis's skillful hands massaged my temples and the muscles in the back of my neck. I needed to be touched.

I pressed the intercom button. "June, did you make the dinner reservations for two at the Right Bank?"

"Of course, Ms. Jamison. They were for six thirty. If you can spare a few minutes, Verta wants to talk to you."

"Jewel, I have to speak with you in private. It will be brief."

"Can't it wait until tomorrow, Verta? I have a dreadful headache."

"It will take only five minutes. I want you to look at some photos."

"OK, come in." Dennis drew his hands away. "No, keep working your magic."

Verta entered the room. Seeing Dennis, she looked away.

"Jewel, I really did want to talk with you privately."

"Verta, my head is splitting, and whatever it is, can't it wait until tomorrow?"

"Never mind. I'll see you first thing in the morning." Verta's copper-colored cheeks were now a deep crimson. She exited and shut the door.

"You know, Dennis, I should send you home right after dinner to get your beauty sleep, but maybe we can talk about some of the assignments I see you doing."

"Dinner? I…Ms. Jamison, there's a problem…"

"Call me Jewel."

"Jewel, there's a problem with tonight. I have a prior... commitment."

"And how early does Cinderella have to be home?"

Dennis straightened his shoulders and then turned my chair around so that it faced him. "How about tomorrow?" His voice deepened, and he smiled impishly.

"Tomorrow will be too late," I responded, trying to resist smiling back. I could not stop looking at his skin. He was a deep coffee color, and his cheeks were the texture of a newly opened flower. I decided to take him home.

"Ms. Jamison, I didn't realize you were making those reservations for me to join you. I didn't..."

"Well, I will have to think about tomorrow."

"Look, I need to make a few calls. Maybe I can rearrange things."

Dennis's smile was practiced. He had the kind of face all his mother's friends must have crooned at when he was a boy. He was pretty and could turn his smile on and off at will. He moved around the desk and turned his back to me and pushed his shirt into his pants. When he turned to face me, his expression was tantalizing.

"Why don't you call from here?" I said, tracing the phone console with my index finger.

"I have a few things I have to take care of in person. How about if we say tomorrow for sure, and tonight if I can put things in order?" He put his jacket on and adjusted his shirt collar. He enjoyed being watched. He adjusted his cuffs. I felt as if I were watching a magician. My eyes moved where he directed them, from his neck to his wrists. His eyes now pulled my gaze to his.

"Tomorrow for sure," he said, moving to the door.

"I told you, tomorrow will be too late," I said, trying to let him know how important it was to me for it to be tonight. Inside I was feeling twisted up. I didn't want to be alone tonight. I picked up the telephone and buzzed June.

"June. Show Mr. Howell out, please."

Dennis moved to the door and took the knob before June came in. He was not happy. As he exited the doorway, he summoned my attention. His eyes were like onyx. He had put his smile away. He moved past June and was gone.

"Cancel the Right Bank, June. I'm heading home."

"Yes, Ms. Jamison."

The room was quiet. I smoothed my hair back with both hands. The air was too still. I had to get out of there.

"Ms. Jamison, there are three contracts on your desk I was to remind you to sign."

"Remind me to give them to you first thing in the morning."

"Excuse me, Ms. Jamison, I was also asked to remind you about your appointment with Ms. Brown at nine, and lunch tomorrow at the Sign of the Dove with Ms. Krantz."

"Yes. Yes. Yes. Fine. Is that everything? I'm leaving." I put on my jacket and put the contracts in my briefcase.

The ride down from the twenty-seventh floor to the lobby was claustrophobic. Down on Broadway, the air was cool. I needed to get as much of it into my lungs as I could. It was the beginning of November, but it felt more like December. I waved down a cab and stared out the window at the moving patches of color. As the cab turned up Central Park West, I saw nothing but bare trees. I remembered how Gordon and I would walk along the park last summer when everything was green and lush and I felt so alive. I bought one of those baskets of French bread, paté, and cheese from Zabar's, and a bottle of rosé to go along with it. We walked along the path in the park and never stopped to eat. He said that I was lovely. We just turned around and headed back to my apartment.

Midthought I decided to go to Chicago. In my mind's eye, I could see Gordon's face through the crowd as I walked out into the airport. I needed to feel his arms around me. I'd call Gordon and tell him I was taking a long weekend. The business would go on without me. Everything was ready for the Tavern on the Green event. I needed to see him. If I took the weekend and Monday, everything would be fine. I needed to talk to him. Why didn't he return my calls? If something is wrong, I have to fix it.

The cab stopped with a jerk. I paid the driver too much money. He thanked me profusely and jumped out of the cab to open the door. The doorman tipped his hat and tried to make small talk about the cold as I walked past him with only one thing on my mind, calling Gordon.

When I got upstairs, the apartment was dark. Where was the white? My two newly bought plants drooped in exhaustion and thirst. I left them to their own devices.

I dialed my travel agent, looking at the clock to see if she would still be there. "Doris, I need a ticket to Chicago leaving tomorrow early evening and coming back Monday morning, afternoon."

"Ms. Jamison, I don't know if I can swing that. Let me punch in the dates."

There was silence except for the tapping of computer keys.

"I just need to take a quickie trip."

"I can get it, but only in first class. That's going to be over a thousand dollars one-way. I don't have the return yet."

"You got it, I'll take it. Doesn't matter what it costs."

"You sure, Ms. Jamison?"

"Yes. Positive."

"You know what, I'll reserve this and see what else I can get. Let me call you back. You're still at the office, I bet."

"No, actually I'm at home."

"OK. Do you want me to call you at home or at the office in the morning? I might find a cancellation later."

"If you find the return soon, call me here so that I don't think about it all night."

I hung up the receiver, and the phone rang immediately. "Ms. Jamison, this is Dennis."

Somehow, now the boy was a minor annoyance. "Yes, Mr. Howell."

"I...tried to arrange things for tonight, but I can't cancel this appointment."

"That's fine, Mr. Howell. I'll have my assistant call you to reschedule."

"But, I really do want to...I can do it tomorrow."

"As I said earlier, tomorrow is too late. This is a spontaneous business, Mr. Howell. You have to be ready for assignments at a drop of a hat." I hung up without waiting for any further comments.

I can't believe I got the flight. Now let me call him and tell him the good news. "Hello, operator? Person-to-person to Mr. Gordon Ellis from Jewel Jamison. I'm calling Ellis Associates, Chicago, at 312 555-6435."

"One moment, please."

There was silence. I thought about what I would do if he didn't answer. I'll go anyway. I'll just show up there. We have to talk.

"This is Gordon Ellis."

The deep tones of his voice were like a balm to my soul. He sounded wonderful.

"Go ahead, Miss."

"Gordon, oh God. I was so scared. When I called you last week...I know you're peeved with me. You were never in. Did what's her name give you the messages? Gordon, it's so good to hear your voice. I know it's going to take time to put things in order. I wanted to tell you, I can wait." I wanted to kiss his lips, wanted him to hold me and to tell me everything is fine, just really busy.

"Jewel, I got the messages."

Again silence.

"So, how are you? I've been thinking this long-distance romance is the pits. I'm thinking of flying in for a long weekend. How is it in Chicago? It's cold here. I've just been..."

"Jewel, I've rearranged things with Celia. We have an understanding."

"Gordon, that's wonderful. I can't believe it. So maybe you can come here. Can you take some time like we planned?" I could barely breathe.

"I'm saying that we've worked things out. We've decided to give it another shot. I told you to stop calling here. If you don't stop, I'm going to have to take some kind of legal action."

"You've worked things out. What things out?" I couldn't make sense of this. "Gordon, what things? What things?"

"Look, I have my son and my daughter to think about. About our future."

I couldn't talk. I wished I could cry, but I couldn't do that either.

"Jewel, think about it. What does Celia have?"

"What?"

"I said, I had to do it this way. All she has is...I had to do this for Gordon Jr. and Emily. This thing was tearing them apart. I had no choice. I tried to tell you over and over not to count on me. I told you when I saw you it was over."

I tried to hear him, but my ears were stopped. They couldn't take in any more sound.

There was a click, and his voice stopped. I let the phone rest in my lap. I listened to the quiet. I sat there lost in the gray of the room.

I don't understand why he keeps saying that. It's not over. I am not good at over. I don't do over. After I open my Chicago office, I will take care of this. The end of the next week, Tavern on the Green, and after that, I will have what I want.

It was Labor Day weekend, and I was lying across my bed debating with myself about cleaning up the apartment. Finals were over, and I had turned in the paper two days late. I longed for nothing to do, but I had two weeks of laundry, and I hadn't washed the dishes in five days. I couldn't even stand to walk into the kitchen.

The bedroom was cluttered with books and dirty dungarees. I closed my eyes to shut it all out. When I opened them, my gaze rested on the bureau, and memories of Eric and his kiss flooded my mind and filled my senses. I could feel him as if he were there. Three weeks had passed, and he hadn't called. Saundra had said he wouldn't. Camille, always the optimist, said he would. I struggled to drive him out of my thoughts but lost. His hands, his lips, his smile were all there, vividly etched in my mind. It felt good to think about him.

Beneath my level of consciousness, there was a droning sound. I wasn't quite sure, but I thought it was my phone. With the windows open I couldn't be certain, because the only phone that actually rang was in the kitchen. But as I focused on the sound, the ring became more distinct and insistent. I opened my eyes and reached for the receiver.

"Hello, beautiful." His deep baritone voice flowed into me, making my center quiver.

"Who is this?"

"Someone out of your confused past."

"Eric? Is that you?" I wished I could think of something clever to say.

"Your two weeks are up."

"It's a little more like three weeks." I hated myself after I said that.

"You've been counting."

"Not really. I've just finished finals. This is my first free day. I haven't had a moment to—"

"How would you like to spend your first free day with me?"

Dumbfounded, all I could muster was "Huh?"

"You said it's your first free day, and I said, would you like to spend it with me?"

"Well, I do have some laundry to do…and cleaning up this apartment, and…"

"Is that a no?"

"No, I didn't…"

"Then it's a yes?"

"Well, it's just that I was caught off guard. I was sort of going…"

"Why is it so important to you to be on guard?"

"Huh?"

"Never mind. Listen, I was planning to go to the park. Would you like to come?"

"Yes," I said, noticing that my hand was shaking, and my body felt like Jell-O.

"So, I'll be over in about an hour."

I heard myself say "OK," and then there was a click. It was so quick. He was coming over. I ran to the shower and turned on the water. Then the dishes darted into my mind. I ran to the kitchen and ran water into the sink and squeezed dishwashing liquid into it. As the suds ballooned up, I cleared the table and the counter and wiped them clean. I ran through the living room to the bathroom, grabbing a blouse and socks off the living room floor and jamming them into the too-full hamper. My body was trembling and I couldn't stand up, so I sat down on the toilet and held on to the sink. This is silly, I thought. He only asked me to go to the park. Why am I so nervous? I wanted him. I was afraid that I wouldn't want to make him stop.

I pushed my hand past the edge of the shower curtain. The water was barely warm. I took off my blouse and panties and stepped into the cascading water. As the warm water sheeted my breasts, the tightness in my chest disappeared. What is it about this man? I thought. Looking up at him made me feel weak kneed. Then I thought it might be his intelligence that attracted me. I turned around to let the water flow over my back and down the backs of my thighs.

"It's not just his mind," I said out loud. It's when he looks at me. God! When he stares at me, it's…I don't know, I thought. A luscious calm enveloped me, and I stood there, letting the water wash over me, not knowing how much time passed. As I stepped out of the shower, my body cooled even more and felt thoroughly alive.

I went into the bedroom, mentally discarding one blouse for another, trying to settle on what to wear. I pulled three different blouses out of the closet, holding each one against myself and then tossing it onto the bed in disgust. I decided on my last pair of cut-offs and my orange halter. I penciled a little around my eyes and put some mascara on, and then I picked out my 'fro and patted it neatly into place. I looked into my jewelry box and found my new beaded earrings and put them on. I stepped back from the mirror to get a better look at myself. Am I gorgeous or what?

The dishes darted back into my mind, and I headed for the kitchen. In the living room, I spotted a pool of papers and books on the couch. I pulled the books together into a neat pile. I collected the papers, and the bell startled me and the papers escaped me, the sheets floating off this way and that onto the floor.

"Just a minute," I called, cursing my clumsiness.

I took a deep breath. I shook my hands to stop them from trembling. As I opened the door, I could feel my composure seeping back. I was ready.

"Hi, beautiful!"

"Hi. Come on in," I said as coolly as I could. "The place is a mess. I was just looking through some papers and they fell, so let me just pick them up."

I busied myself bending down, collecting the papers, and carefully placing them on the couch. I felt him move to the armchair and sit down. I hadn't really looked at him fully, but when I did, he looked delicious. He was wearing a black T-shirt and cut-off dungarees. His arms were exquisitely chiseled. And his legs were lean and muscled like a swimmer. I had to make myself not stare.

"I'm ready, though."

"I've been rethinking the park idea," Eric said, unfolding the newspaper he had tucked under his arm.

"You don't want to go, right?" I said. I hated this kind of thing. Guys were always saying they wanted to go out and then always ended up trying to stay at my place just to get me into bed. I stood up out of habit, because this was when I usually asked guys to leave, though I really didn't want to do that with Eric.

"Well, it's really hot out, and..."

"And?"

"And I thought you might like to go to see a movie. It'll be air-conditioned. We could go to the park later if..." Eric stopped. There was an edge in his voice.

"I thought...never mind." I sat down on the couch.

"I know what you thought. Your eyes are very expressive, and I couldn't miss the tone." He moved onto the couch with me.

"I couldn't help it. Guys are always—"

"Jewel, let's get this out of the way right now. I am very attracted to you, but I'm not about to attack you or try to take advantage of you."

"I didn't say—"

"Let me finish. I am twenty-two years old. I'm not a kid. I don't know about the 'guys' you've gone out with...don't care to know, but I don't need to screw every woman I meet. I have women friends, and women friends who have been lovers. I don't know which you'll be, but to get the tension out of the air, why don't we make an agreement."

"Is this a lawyer thing? An agreement?"

"Yes. If I do anything you don't want me to do, say, Eric, stop, and I will."

"I feel kind of foolish."

"Don't. I didn't mean to make it heavy."

"No, I just feel silly."

"Wasted energy." He put his arm around my back, lifted my chin, and kissed me lightly on the lips.

"You want to take a sweater for the movie?"

"Um, I'll take my shawl. Eric, I'm sorry."

"Hey, no need for sorries."

I got my bag from my bedroom, and we moved out into what became a magical day. Eric held me around the waist at first and then took my hand. In the bus ride downtown, splashes of green and red and yellow, signs, stores, people, swept past. The colors were paled at the edges, softening everything into a lovely blur.

The bus wound its way downtown until we reached the Village. We walked a block to Sixth Avenue. Eric had chosen a film at the Waverly called *Black Orpheus*.

"I hope you don't mind subtitles," he whispered as we entered the theater.

I didn't think I could focus, but it was cool and dark inside, and there were only two couples and us. The film was a wonderfully romantic tale of two star-crossed lovers, Orpheus and Eurydice, but set in Brazil. Eric put his arm around my shoulder and held me close. When Eurydice died, I felt a tear fall from my eye. I didn't wipe it because I didn't want Eric to think I was childishly sentimental. My cheek felt cold.

After the movie we went across the street to see a pickup basketball game, which Eric said had some great players. The men were sweaty and played a fast game, with onlookers gasping at the passes and dunks. Then we walked to Washington Square Park and passed hippies sprawled everywhere, singing and passing joints and staring and smiling. We sat at the foot of a tree talking, and I couldn't stop staring into his eyes. I learned he was just starting law school. His parents were paying for part of it. He was getting a scholarship and working for the rest. I told him I wasn't sure what I wanted to do yet, but I was planning to work too.

By the time I slipped the key into the door of my apartment, I felt elated. All of my fears of Eric had evaporated. All that was left was a longing to be close to him.

"You want to come in and have a glass of wine or something?"

"No, I think I'll head home." Eric leaned over and kissed me, holding the door open.

"You don't have to go...I..." I whispered. "Please stay." My bottom lip quivered, and my hand moved to cover it.

Eric took my hand away and kissed me lightly. He closed the door behind him with his left hand. And he kissed me again, this time fully. His tongue toyed with my lips and met mine. When he let me go, I was dizzy, trying to recover myself, and I turned to put my shawl in the closet.

"How about some wine? I have some cheese and crackers."

"Sure." Eric followed me into the kitchen.

I bustled about, grabbing a plate and tiptoeing to reach for glasses, which he got for me. I took out the wine, and Eric poured it and handed a glass to me. I placed the cheese on a plate with crackers around the edge. I caught Eric smiling at me. "What are you smiling at?"

"You."

"Why?"

"I don't know."

I picked up the plate and carried it into the living room, talking to him over my shoulder. "You must be a good student. I mean, going to Columbia and..." I wanted Eric to kiss me again. "What law school are you going to?"

He lit a cigarette. "I was hoping NYU Law, but they didn't come up with enough...so it's Brooklyn Law," he said. "From what I hear, I'll be working my ass off the next three years."

As I sat down, my eyes met Eric's again. I felt he could see through to my soul. I wanted him so bad. He looked at me, as if he were studying me, waiting to see what I would do next. It made me hot having his eyes on me. I took a piece of cheese and put it on a cracker and put it to his lips. He put his hand up as if to say no, took a drag on his cigarette, and then stubbed it out. He picked up the glass of wine and took a few sips, and I saw resolve in his eyes. He lifted my chin, kissed me, and opened my mouth with his tongue. I enjoyed the taste of him. His fingers caressed my back.

My defenses departed, leaving me craving him, and my mind began to race. I had never gone with Camille to the doctor. I had to tell Eric I was a virgin. I had to find out if he had any protection. I froze.

"Eric, I haven't been with anyone—"

"It's OK. You are so lovely," he whispered in my ear as he caressed my neck. His fingers slipped under my halter and brushed against the undersides of my breasts, making them tingle.

"Eric, I'm a virgin."

It must have taken a few minutes for my words to enter Eric's consciousness. He pushed me away and reached over to the table for his cigarettes. The pack on top was empty. He crushed it, tossed it back onto the table, and picked up the fresh pack. He tapped it to force out the first tightly squeezed cigarette. He lit it, inhaled, and let the smoke escape through his nostrils.

"Why didn't you say anything? Let's stop right here," he said, taking a gulp from his wine glass.

"But I want to do it."

"That's cool. I just don't need any heavy trips right now."

"Eric, what's wrong? I want to do it with you. I shouldn't have said anything."

"Hey, I would have known."

"Eric, I don't understand what's wrong."

"I just don't want you counting on me for some longtime thing. I just thought we could have some fun. Let's be straight here. I don't want some girl feeling she's giving me some prize and then expecting something in return."

"Eric, I wasn't trying to make a big deal." I could feel my eyes welling up. "I don't want anything from you. Just hold me..."

"You're probably not taking the pill, are you?"

I shook my head no.

"Shit. You sure you want to do this? No strings."

I nodded.

"Don't worry. I have something." He kissed me lightly on the lips. "Let's go inside," he said, grabbing his cigarettes and his lighter and stuffing them in his pockets. He led me into the bedroom. I gathered my blouses that I had left on the bed earlier and threw them onto the chair in the corner. The room was dark except for the light from the living room.

He turned me around and said, "Ah, buttons," as he fingered my halter. He unfastened it and let it fall as he caressed my breasts with the palms of his hands.

I felt I might leap out of my skin, the sensations were so intense. Sometime today I had decided it. I had played it out in my mind, a mental game of coquettish play. But now it was real, and Eric was directing it all. My body was trembling.

"You look like you need a massage. Lie down. Turn over."

Eric's hand moved deftly down the small of my back and up again over my shoulders. He brought his hands down my sides to my waist and then up my back again. Then he traced the small of my back with his fingers.

"Your skin is so soft." His voice was throaty and deep. He straddled me and kissed my back. I could feel him resting against my buttocks. I felt warm inside. He caressed my neck and shoulders and gently turned me over, kissing my breasts and abdomen. He opened my shorts and pulled them down with my panties as he kissed my stomach. I closed my eyes and gasped for breath, too scared to think. He kissed my mouth and I felt him get up, and he took off his cutoffs. He was bare underneath. God, he was gorgeous. I could see his silhouette. He lay down next to me, and I could feel his nakedness against my thigh. He leaned over me and held my breasts in his hands and kissed them, then took them each in turn into his mouth. My back arched involuntarily. I felt myself drift into a craving for him. It happened imperceptibly at first. Then each brush against me, each stroke gave me a flush. His fingers opened me. My hand found its way to him. I feared I could not accept him, that I would tear. There was a pause. He moved away.

I could hear a crackling sound. He kissed me again. A tingling went through my body, and a thin sheet of perspiration moistened my skin. I kept my eyes closed. I felt him on top of me. I drew in a deep breath, trying to hold on to the good sensations. I felt an intrusion. I stretched and I burned.

"Oh!" I parted, I thought like the delicate flesh of a ripe peach pulled apart. For an instant I was surprised. Just simply surprised, as if I thought, "So this is how it is."

He kissed my lips. "You are so beautiful," he said, staying still there in me. And then he moved, slowly at first. I wrapped my arms around his back. I felt myself accept him. He continued, and I received him again and again and again. His power was intoxicating. I became lost in the movement; I didn't know for how long. I felt feverish and full, and then I burst inside. I felt as if I did not know where he ended and I began. He rested his weight on my chest and my middle. I held him tightly. His lips brushed against my shoulder and my neck. It tickled. I giggled.

He rose up on his elbows to caress my face. He lifted himself out of me and reached for his cigarettes and lighter and lit one. He took the ashtray and rested it on his stomach.

I rested my head on my hand and allowed myself to love him with my eyes. His skin was the color of ebony, his face like some magnificent sculpture, chiseled for my delight. His chest was smooth, and his biceps were like those of a swimmer, strong but not bulging. The muscles in his abdomen flexed and rippled each time he raised his head to dust ashes from his cigarette.

"Hey, Eric," I said, hoping to keep him close. "Eric, what were you thinking just then?" I asked, smiling because he smiled.

"Just now?"

"Yes."

"You."

"Really?"

"A lot of virgins don't seem to enjoy the first time. You seemed to. You want a towel? I want to get rid of this thing." He eased my head off his chest, sat up, and headed for the bathroom. I watched his bare back and buttocks disappear.

"A lot of virgins, Eric?"

"Well a few," he said from the other room. I heard the toilet flush and the water running in the sink. I breathed in the sounds of him. When he came back, he was holding a towel, which he handed to me. He lay down on the bed and lit another cigarette. I felt very comfortable with him. It was as if he had always been there.

"You know I was really scared before, but you're right. I loved it."

"I could tell. You OK?"

"Yeah." A sigh escaped my lips. "I'm…fine."

"Hey, Jewel, I've got to study with some people in a group tomorrow—actually later today, around twelve. It's a special course I'm taking. I could split now or in the morning."

"Stay, Eric. I'll make you breakfast."

"Well, I've got to catch some sleep or I'd make love to you again."

That thought had never occurred to me, but it made me smile.

"Do you want me to set the alarm?" I offered somewhat distractedly.

"Yeah, about nine?"

"Sure."

I leaned over toward the clock. "Do you know what time it is, Eric? It's three thirty."

"Yeah, I figured that. That's why I've got to get some sleep."

I felt truly happy for the first time. I wanted these moments to stretch into forever. I felt that they would. I had wanted him, and he was mine. We were going to sleep together.

I opened my eyes and stared at the forms in the ceiling for a moment and then remembered the night before. There was only the pillow and a gaping space in the bed where Eric had been. My thoughts raced through our last words for something I might have said, or he might have said, that would explain his absence. There was nothing. I put my head on his pillow to capture the sense of him. I looked at the clock. It was ten to nine. I pressed in the alarm button. I wanted no reminder of my disappointment. At the edge of my consciousness, I heard water running in the shower.

"Eric?"

I grabbed the towel he had used the night before and wrapped it around my breasts and tucked it in. It felt so sexy.

"Eric?"

"Hi! Do you want to join me?" His face and chest were covered with rivulets of water. "I figured I'd take a shower before you got up, but it's much better with company. By the way, you sleep cute."

I dropped the towel on the floor, and he pulled me in. "You know, you hug your pillow as if it were a lover." He held the soap and rubbed it in circles, up and down my back and behind. He turned me to him and soaped up my breasts and let the water rinse them and sucked them dry. My body was on fire.

Everything was happening so quickly, I felt faint. I held on to the wall to steady myself.

"I'm going to take you back to bed." He held his hand 'round my waist, led me into the bedroom, placed the towel on the bed, and sat me on it.

"Shit, I forgot, I don't have protection. I can pull out. Trust me?"

It was strange. I did trust him.

"Jewel? Do you trust me?"

I nodded my head, never once opening my eyes as he laid me down.

"God, you are beautiful," he said as he parted, then entered me. He reached deep inside.

"I love making love to you." The mellifluous sound of his voice flowed into me. It was a strange feeling, but I was beginning to enjoy the openness. I became overwhelmed by sensation. Lost in his power, moving with him, I convulsed.

"Jewel, I've got to come out."

I tried to hold on to him, but he pulled away from me, and I watched his seed spill on my belly.

I was absolutely motionless for some time. I had no real thoughts. There was no sense of time or space as I had known it before. I was not even sure where I ended and the rest of the world began.

I heard Eric light his cigarette, and then a deep inhale.

"Listen, it's after ten. I've got to get going."

"But I wanted to make breakfast for you."

"Next time."

"It won't take long, Eric. I can—"

"No, I want to remember you just this way," Eric smiled. I became aware of my nakedness.

He went into the bathroom and ran the water. I covered myself with the sheet. Then he came back and pulled on his cutoffs and T-shirt. He sat down on the bed and put on his sandals. When he stood up, he sucked in his stomach, squeezed his cigarettes and lighter into his pockets, and then leaned over the bed and kissed me.

"I'll give you a call." He pulled the sheet off me. "I said I wanted to remember you like this. Bye, beautiful."

By reflex, I reached for it. There was a mischievous twinkle in his eye. He turned and walked out of the bedroom. I heard the door open and then close. He was gone. But I knew he would be mine.

14

COLE

D awn always wakes me. So much of the time it is gray. Today
it was yellow. It filled the room, as we lay wrapped in sheets
and each other. She looked so beautiful there in my bed,
so many shades of cinnamon. I loved looking at her.

I had always felt secure in my aloneness. It was not that I never
wanted the encumbrances of a woman. I had had that. Women had
moved into my world; brought their plants, suitcases, and pillows;
stayed; and then moved on, leaving photos, makeup, assorted un-
dergarments, and memories in drawers where I least expected to
find them. I had loved a few, one deeply; felt sorry for some; nursed
their wounds; and sent them on. But Camille—I wanted her all the
time and into the future. My passion for her made my skin warm.

Funny, it occurred to me while walking to her house last
night. The heat did not come up in my building yesterday, odd
for November. The chill never left the apartment. I worked on the
chair I was building for Shawn, but even as I sanded and smoothed
the back, my body did not generate enough heat to take away the
cold that covered me. But as I dressed to see her, and as I got to the
street where her house was, I could feel the warmth rising in my
body. That was when I noticed it.

As she let me into the apartment, her head tilted downward,
her eyes lifted to meet mine, I had to fight the urge to grab her

and hold on. She had kept an arm's distance, carefully placed and fitted between us since we met. The only time I managed to push that arm aside was when I made love to her. Even then, I felt her draw away.

At first, I thought it was because of Shawn. He's so bright, and maybe she didn't want to have to explain anything that might make her seem less than the perfect mother that she is. I got it. But last night Shawn had stayed with Saundra. I took her out to dinner alone this time. We went to O'Henry's in the Village. The candle-light caressed her cheeks. She asked me why I was staring. I did not want to answer, but I finally said, "I love looking at you." She had searched my eyes, I thought, looking for insincerity. Not finding it, she simply fidgeted a bit and seemed uncomfortable. I wished I could hold her in my arms.

But now, as she slept, the aqua dawn filled the room around us, the light playing on Camille's nose and cheeks. I kissed her there, there, and there. She didn't startle. She sighed as if she were dream-ing. The arm was not there. I kissed her eyes. So often they were walled behind her glasses, keeping me away. I kissed her neck, and she giggled. I could not contain my pleasure. I kissed her throat and breasts and moved to kiss her belly. I became lost in her.

Dawn brightened the room so that I could see her fully. There was a scar there on the left side of her stomach. I had felt it, but now I could see it. It looked like a rosebud unfolding, resting there of-fered up to me. I opened my mouth on it with my lips, taking care not to touch her with my teeth. I devoured her, enjoying the tastes and smell and textures of her.

"Oh God," she whispered, stroking my head with her hand.

I looked up at her face, drew myself up, and covered her lips with mine. As her mouth opened, I went inside and tasted her. I was rigid and needing her. I wanted so much to feel her wrapped around me with nothing between us, and she had said nothing about it, my waking her as I had. But I wanted to keep her trust. I had had myself tested the week I met her. I knew there was nothing to concern her, but we hadn't talked about it. I could not break the trust I had worked so long to build. I stopped and took a condom from the night table and tore the wrapper open. It rolled onto me so easily. I was no longer capable of stopping myself. I had tried to enter tentatively, but I needed to be in her so badly, fitting deeply inside there. Her eyes were open now. She smiled at me and held me in her hand. So I went there. She moaned. I held on, and she let me. I felt the warmth of her as I went into her.

"I think I love you, Camille. I love you."

She tightened her eyes closed, as if she were frightened of the words that fell from my mouth onto her face.

I sought that space again, more deeply this time, wanting to climb inside of her.

"I love you so much," I said again this time softly, afraid to raise my voice. I felt as though I were in a sacred place but wanted to yell her name. I went deeper inside. Feeling her accept me over and over again excited me more than I could stand. I felt myself explode inside her.

I felt her tighten around me. She opened her eyes reflexively. She pushed my face up and held it with her hands and looked at me, studying my eyes.

"I love you so much," I said.

The water welled in her eyes and then splashed onto her cheeks, making her face sparkle. Her eyes searched mine.

"I do," I said.

She bit her lip.

"You are so very beautiful."

Slowly and imperceptibly at first, as the tears streamed down her temples and into her hair and made it glisten, her eyes smiled. I felt that my heart would burst from my chest. I had never felt like this before. Now I pulled back and raised myself up just to look at her, to see that she was real, not some illusion I had made up out of my desire. Light splashed about in the room. The veil had lifted from her eyes. I had made love to her in the morning, and she had dazzled me.

She stayed quietly in my arms after we made love and fell asleep. "Coffee?" I whispered, easing myself out of the bed and covering her with the sheet. She didn't answer. I stopped at the bathroom and cleaned myself up. Then I went into the kitchen, scooped the coffee into the basket, and filled the coffee maker with water. All I had was eggs in the refrigerator. I hadn't known she would stay over when I brought her to see Shawn's chair. I hoped, but I didn't count on it.

I took out the frying pan to make the eggs. I hadn't cooked for anyone in a year or maybe more. The sandwiches I made for my sister's kids didn't count. I heated the butter but had to deep six the bread. It was green. Having only five eggs, I just scrambled them up the way I like them. I heard footsteps.

"I knew this coffee would finally get you up."

"What time is it? I didn't look at the clock."

"A little after eleven. Some coffee?" She looked beautiful. She was wearing her blouse, but I could tell there was nothing under it.

"I should really get home."

"Do you want some eggs?"

"Sure, lightly over."

"Forgot that. Sorry, they're scrambled."

"Scrambled's good."

I put the mug of coffee in front of her. I took out the milk and sniffed it, glad it hadn't gone bad.

She had a strange look on her face that I could not quite understand. "You have a beautiful sculpture on your end table."

"I bought it from a guy who got it in Somalia."

"And I saw the photo of you in the hallway with a platoon, or whatever you call it. How old were you? You had that cute little baldy haircut." She seemed as if she were trying to have a conversation, but her voice was strained. I hoped she didn't want to talk about politics and the war again.

"Eighteen, just before we deployed to 'Nam."

"Don't you want a robe or something?" The words just burst from her mouth.

"Not really!" Now I understood her discomfort.

"Cole, I'm not accustomed to…"

I pushed the mug, turning the handle to meet her hand, and turned to pick up the spatula.

"I cannot believe you are cooking with no clothes on."

"Notice there is no bacon." I laughed. She did not. "Look, Camille, I'm in uniform a lot, and when I'm at home, I'm more comfortable without clothes."

"Well, I'd be more comfortable if you'd put on some clothes."

I reached for a plate. I scraped some eggs into it, placed it on the table, and handed her a fork and knife.

"My home is the only place I'm at ease, Camille."

"But I'm not comfortable being here with you…naked."

Something in the way she said that, and the whole idea of it, made me laugh.

"What's so funny?"

"You."

"What do you mean?"

"Don't you know?" I took my eggs and placed the pan in the sink. I was trying to think of how I could get her to see that I just wanted to be at ease with her in my home.

"No."

"Well," I said, drawing out the word, breaking into laughter again, and pouring my coffee.

"What the hell is so funny?"

"Are you sure you want me to tell you?"

"You don't have to tell me if you don't want to," she said, dropping the handle of the fork against the plate. Her eyes darted from me to the wall behind me.

"Take it easy," I said, sitting down.

"Are you going to tell me or not?" she said, this time pushing away from the table as if to get up.

"I was just thinking how ridiculous it is for you to be uncomfortable eating food in my kitchen with me naked, when I have just spent the last twelve hours lying next to you, on...well, let's just say next to you, naked."

"Don't say that! You're not supposed to say things like that."

"Why not?" I enjoyed watching her search for a reason.

"It's...it's...it's not nice."

What she said made me laugh out loud.

"I'm glad I am so amusing to you." Camille looked as if she, too, was trying to hold back a smile.

"I don't believe you said that. 'It's not nice?'"

"So."

"So?"

"So! So, I said so. So?"

"So, you are incredible. And I find you wonderful, and for you, I'm going to put something on." I headed toward the bedroom, stopped at the coat closet, grabbed my scarf, wrapped it around my neck, and pulled on my boots. In the bedroom, I dug around in a drawer, way at the bottom, pulled out what I was searching for, and walked out into the kitchen and sat in my chair.

"Very funny."

"At least I got a smile out of you. You're unbelievable. 'It's not nice'?"

"You know what I mean."

"And you know what *I* mean. Like I said, this is the only time I have to be relaxed, and I want you here with me. I love you, Camille. Now, if you're really uncomfortable, I have this little— hell, I call it a skirt—my sister bought for me. This terry-cloth thing I'm supposed to wrap around my waist...I can wear this, but I'd be so much...Camille, I want it to be comfortable between us."

"You're movin' too fast with this *us.*" Her face grew serious. "Suppose I don't love you? Suppose that?"

"So I'll love you anyway. Didn't you ever love anyone who didn't love you back? Hurts like hell, but I'm willing to take the risk. I'm almost fifty. I have maybe fifteen years left. I'm too old for bullshit."

"What do you mean fifteen years?"

"C'mon, Camille. Life expectancy. Maybe if I'm lucky I've got about fifteen good years left. My dad died in his fifties."

"That doesn't mean…"

"No, but I don't have a lot of time to waste. I feel damn lucky to have met you, and I want to see where this takes us. For the first time in my life, I feel right. Can you understand that? Everything feels right."

I searched Camille's eyes for some response. The telephone rang. I grabbed the phone on the wall.

"Your dime. Yes. Hi, Saundra. Yes, she's right here."

"Saundra? Is Shawn all right?" She was quiet, concentrating on what Saundra was saying. "Cole, do you have a TV? I didn't see a TV anywhere."

"Yeah sure, in the cabinet in the living room. Why?"

"My friend, Jewel, is on the TV."

I moved into the living room, stretching the coiled telephone cord taut, and opened the black lacquer cabinet doors, revealing my television.

"What channel?"

"Channel four."

As the image on the screen became more and more distinct, I saw her friend whom I had met at the restaurant talking.

"And in my first account, I got a model in a Johnson product ad. Then I got *Essence.* I booked a model to do the cover. From there I booked models for two ads for Clairol, but the Revlon ad got me the most attention."

"Your agency was founded here in New York, and we hear it is now expanding to Chicago."

"Well, New York is our home, our base, but now we're opening an office in Chicago."

"What's next for you?"

"I will be expanding the business to include many more actors to service the film industry and music now that videos are becoming so popular. And we are looking at possibilities down the road for an office in Los Angeles."

"Well, the Onyx modeling agency and Jewel Jamison are on the move."

"We're now Onyx Management, Inc."

"Thanks for joining us. Ms. Jewel Jamison, founder of Onyx Management, Inc., New York and Chicago, another New York woman on the move. Next week we'll be speaking with..."

"What an unhappy lady," I said out loud, not meaning to.

"What do you mean, unhappy? How could you know whether she is happy or not?" Camille said, covering the receiver. "What? No, Cole said she looks unhappy."

"Saundra said to tell you, she thinks you're right. She says she does look kind of...haggard." Camille paused and then inserted her own comment. "Well, if you were running a business in two cities, you'd be tired..."

"Why are you so defensive about her?"

She was quiet, listening. "I don't know, Saundra. Let it go. You asked Les to go? I thought...how's Shawn doing...I think so. Cole, do you think we'll be heading home soon?"

"Sure, if you want to."

Camille nodded her head and said, "Saundra, we'll be there in an hour or so, OK?" She walked the phone back into the kitchen and hung it up. She stared at the television. "Jewel did everything she said she would."

"She looks like it took its toll."

"I don't understand how you could say that. She looked terrific, and at least she didn't gain weight like I did. She still looks like she looked in college. Her figure...what are you talking about?"

"Her eyes and her mouth. Her face looks old, and her eyes look as if she is holding back tears, and her mouth looks like someone who wants to scream. The day I met her, I noticed it...just didn't say anything, 'cause I didn't see the point."

"What does that mean?"

"Look, she's your friend. It's just a guess. I usually am a good judge of character. That's what I see." I headed toward the bathroom. "I'm going to take a shower." I felt her follow me and then stop. I looked back, and she had stopped to look in the hallway mirror at her face.

"You think she looks old? You must think I look ancient."

"No, you have a light in your eyes. That will always make you look young. That lady looks as if she's given up on the world, like she's bitter. Sometimes you look sad, but never bitter."

I squeezed out shaving cream and dabbed it on my upper lip and cheeks. I held the razor under the stream of water and focused on my image in the mirror. Camille was staring at me. I pulled the razor up under my chin, and she looked transfixed. I rinsed the razor again and noticed Camille so focused on me that I had to ask her, "What're you thinking? You seem..."

"Just remembering my dad shaving. I was four when he died. So that's a memory that goes as far back as I can remember."

"You look like it was a good memory. I'll be out of here in about fifteen minutes."

"Am I bothering you?"

"No, I just thought you wanted to get in here..."

"I'm just enjoying watching you shave. Do you mind?" Camille asked, tilting her head to the side and leaning on the doorjamb.

I grabbed the towel on the rack and wiped the streaks of lather still remaining on my neck. Camille seemed mesmerized. Her mouth had fallen open as she studied my movements. I could see her, the child in her.

I touched her under the chin with my forefinger, kissing her parted lips before she closed them.

"I'm going into the shower. Want to come?"

"No, I couldn't," Camille said, folding her arms across her chest. "Maybe another time."

I watched as Camille washed her face. She seemed to glance at me through the shower door. I soaped up. She mumbled something.

"What did you say?" I pushed the shower door open.

"Nothing, just thinking."

"Sounded like you said, 'Do you care for me?'" I closed the door and put my head under the running water to rinse off, then shut it.

"I said, 'You scare me.'"

"Why? What am I…"

"You're…it's like…when I'm with you, I can't hide."

I dried my hair and face. "Good," I said, climbing out of the shower and standing behind her, looking at her image in the mirror.

"No, but that scares me. So…" She inched forward so as not to get wet.

"So?"

Camille laughed. "Don't start!"

"Why not?" I said playfully.

"I'm serious."

"I know," I said, wrapping the towel around my waist. "I'm wearing a skirt." She turned to look at me and laughed. I couldn't help kissing the nape of her neck, making her giggle.

"So stop."

"Why? I love to make you laugh."

"That's what I mean. You make me laugh, and cry, and feel scared, and…everything feels so real with you. Too real. Cole, I was fine by myself."

"I know."

"I was fine, and now I…I don't know what I'm saying. What happens when you go, Cole?"

"I'm not planning on going anywhere no time soon."

"But when you do." She looked so serious.

"Camille, let's just see how this goes. Let's not mess with it." I wanted to say that I wanted it to go on and on forever. I could see the fear in her eyes. I knew that no matter what I said, I would have to let time prove to her that I was there to stay if she let me.

"Cole, do you want to go with me to Jewel's affair at the Tavern on the Green? I wasn't going to go, but…"

"Sure. It was an evening thing, right?"

"Friday evening, cocktail hour. Saundra's going."

"I'll escort my lovely lady."

"Get out of here." Camille laughed, shaking her head.

"I'm growin' on you, huh?"

"Stop. I will not even pretend to know what to make of you, Coleman Barnes."

As I looked at her, I was grateful the arm was not there. She did not push me away. I was content with that for now.

15

"**C**ole, are you sure you want to go to this thing?" The dark circles under my eyes said it all. I had not slept well last night, up thinking about Saul's visits to the superintendent's office the past two days. Two parents had spent a half hour in my office telling me whom he was meeting with on the school board and what they thought it meant. They were looking to me for strategies to address his political connections, and I had none. It made me weary. By the end of lunch duty, the smell of the vegetable soup in the cafeteria made me sick to my stomach. I began to wonder if this was what I really wanted. I loved teaching, being close to children learning and growing. Being an assistant principal was so different, so stressful.

I left the school at three forty, rushed to Shawn's after-school, and then home. I took Shawn up to my mother's and watched him tug off his backpack and lean his head on his grandmother's chest as he hugged her hello.

"Grandma, the train took so long." My mother rubbed his back and said, "I think someone is going to have an early bath tonight." He did not protest.

Cole rang the bell the moment I got downstairs, and I didn't have a minute to just sit still.

"What do you think, Cole? Do you want to go?"

"Only if you do. I'm just here as the handsome escort. It's up to you, pretty lady." Cole adjusted his cuffs and then smoothed back the sides of his hair in a mock primp.

The movement caught my eye, and I looked up at him, catching the full-length vision of him, and he looked quite wonderful. He was wearing a black double-breasted suit, a pale aqua shirt, and a tie that had splashes of magenta and turquoise. His sideburns were trimmed. He has a handsome face, I thought, somewhat by surprise.

"You look really good, sir."

There was something about his smile, the way he was with me, that drew him closer. It was partially the fact that he asked for nothing in return. He was autonomous. He did not seem to need me. His not needing me made me try to care, so as not to feel guilty that I only took from him. I had never only received affection. It was an odd feeling. It made me feel ill at ease, but I was unable to make it different.

I didn't pretend to love him, and he still gave of himself to be with me and with my son. I asked him why he never married, and he paused awhile and then said it was the marines—always moving, most of the women he cared for unable to cope. There seemed to be much more to it than that.

I pulled out my black *peau de soie* skirt, the silk blouse with the gold-, rust-, and champagne-colored print, and the black blouse with black beading. "Which one do you like better?" I asked, holding the hangers up under my chin, one at a time so that he could judge.

"I don't know. They both look nice. Are you going to wear any jewelry?"

I drew back and looked at him.

"Hey, it comes from having a sister."

I opened the bureau drawer and took out two jewelry gift boxes, taking out the gold braid necklace and the large gold clip on earrings from one, and the black beaded necklace with matching loop earrings from the other. Then I pulled out the long rope of pearls and pearl-drop earrings.

His eyes moved between the three and back to the bed at the outfits displayed there, and he said, "I like the gold and that blouse. The bright colors and the sparkle draw attention to your face."

His comment went in and moved itself about in my psyche. There was something about the way he seemed to enjoy looking at me. It was so new to me that each time he said something like that, I would have to look at him and study his eyes closely to see if he was sincere. I ran into the bathroom to wash my face and sponge off. Then I followed his advice, putting on the outfit he had chosen. I had already stepped into the skirt and was pulling the blouse over my head when I caught sight of myself in the mirror. I liked what I saw. "How did you know that?"

"I know what I like to see."

I decided to put on a little makeup. I threw a towel over the blouse to protect it. I dug out my makeup bag and took it to the bathroom mirror. I put on some foundation and put on a little shadow under my brow and on my eyelids. I penciled my eyes and put mascara on my eyelashes. I put on a little blush and lipstick. I wondered if I used too much but decided just not to call attention to it.

"Wow! Look at you," Cole said as I walked into the living room.

He made me blush. "It's not too much, is it?"

"It's enough for me to ask if you meant it when you said we could stay home. We do have a babysitter."

"You stop. Let's go. It's too late now."

Then, as he was looking at me, his brow creased abruptly. He paused and said, "Camille, we ought to talk about Thanksgiving. I've got a week-long drill starting next weekend. I didn't want to say anything, but they're talking about sending a few units back to the Mideast, and some to Bosnia. They haven't said specifically." He followed me into the bedroom.

"What makes you think they are going to take you?"

"I haven't met my quota of recruits for a couple of months in a row."

"How come?"

"Just didn't have the stomach…anyway, I know how it works. If you miss your quota three months in a row, you could go back to a base assignment."

I was looking into the mirror at him, trying to hook the clasp of the chain. He took it from my hands and fastened it, laying it so gently on my back that I didn't know he finished except that he looked back at my reflection for some kind of response.

"What does that mean?" I asked, for the first time seeing the real man with a real life other than being there for me.

"Given the threat to move units overseas, I would be a likely candidate. I'm just guessing, but…"

"When will they tell you?"

"Don't know. I won't know until the end of the weekend probably. The reason why I'm mentioning it is that the last time we were sent to the Mideast, they told us the weekend before Thanksgiving. I was sitting there at Thanksgiving dinner knowing I was leaving the next day. I didn't want to spoil it for my mother and sister, so I didn't say anything till the evening. But I can't do that this time."

"I haven't thought so far in advance, Cole, but I usually invite my mom down." I didn't know what kind of commitment to make. All of a sudden, his presence was a pressure. "I don't know what to say. What do you want to do?"

Cole had been studying my expression. I glanced down at the clock near the bed. It was close to six fifteen.

"Can we talk about this in the car, Cole? I don't want to be late."

I could see the disappointment in his face. He began to tense his jaw. The muscle there pulsated.

He waited as I got my coat and helped me put it on, and then he followed me out into the cool evening. He pointed in the direction of the car and opened the passenger door for me, taking care of my coat as he closed it. As he drove down Central Park West, I said,

"Cole, I just don't know what you want me to say. What do you want to do for Thanksgiving? You want me to say, but you haven't told me what you did last year. You tell me. What's different this year?"

He looked at me, and an expression of complete incredulity settled on his face. "Camille, you are different; Shawn is different. If they send me, we have to deal with this. I can't just tell him I'm going away after dinner, and then the next morning I'm gone. We're adults. We have to prepare him. Hell, I might not even be here for Thanksgiving. They could send me…" The timbre of his voice changed, revealing his irritation with me.

"Cole, look. You throw this at me now. I wasn't expecting to have to make these kinds of plans. I don't know what to do."

"I just felt you ought to know, especially since I won't be here this weekend. It just came into my mind."

"It's hard to switch gears like this…heading out to a party, and you're talking about…" I stopped talking, feeling so foolish for what I had just said. Instead I let the silence grow between us, not wanting to say something that would make this man regret the tender moments he had created for me, because I cherished them.

He was quiet. The brakes squealed as he stopped short for pedestrians, who dodged cars in the middle of the block. He banged the horn. I hoped that what I said did not hurt his feelings. But I just wanted to go out, see my friends, and have a good time. I didn't know when I had last done that.

My guilt made me speak. "Cole, why don't we wait until after they tell us? This may all be for nothing. If they say you're going, we'll deal with it." I hoped that he was taking what I said at face value. I had chosen my words as carefully as I could. There was no future implied in them. There was only the respect and affection I felt for him. Nothing more.

"We'll deal with it. Don't worry."

The tension between us seemed to dissolve when I said that.

"Well, there's the Tavern on the Green," he said as he stopped at the red light the block before it.

"It's pretty, the way they have the trees lit."

"Let's do the valet parking. The whole nine yards," he said.

The valet, an energetic young man with a crisp demeanor, opened the door and then extended his hand to help me out of the car. Cole took the ticket and wrapped my arm in his.

Inside, we checked our coats, and a beautiful black woman wearing glasses who seemed to be in her thirties graciously greeted us.

"Good evening. Welcome. I am Verta Alexander, and your name is…"

"Camille. Camille Warren, a friend of Jewel's…Ms. Jamison."

"Of course. June, this is Ms. Camille Warren and her guest." She smiled at me as if she knew who I was. "Please take a press packet."

The woman seated at the table looked through her list and crossed off my name. She handed me a folder that was black and silver and directed us into the next room. It was quite crowded, with people clustered in groups, standing, holding glasses of wine and other drinks, talking, and laughing. In the background there was instrumental jazz music playing, which gave the cocktail party an easy feel. Some people were seated at small round tables along the edge of the room with their heads together, engaging in conversation. Sporadically, flurries of movement would erupt, and people would hug and kiss one another, and then the group would settle again into talking and laughing. There was an array of gold and silver lamé, black silk and glitter, all moving about the room. It seemed a curious mix of those who loved to be looked at and those who loved to be listened to, competing for the attention of the other.

Cole whispered to me, "I think the bar is over here." We worked our way through the crowd. As we walked, I noticed people who would catch my eye, seeming to think about whether or not they knew me. Once they seemed to decide that they didn't, they would smile and go back to their conversations. The bartender asked what we would like, and Cole ordered a scotch on the rocks. I ordered a rum and Coke. I was turning around when Saundra came up behind me and whispered in my ear, "Girl, did you look around this place. Look at you, you look terrific!"

"Saundra, I'm so glad you found me. I was just thinking, what the hell am I doing here?"

"Seeing how the other half lives, sweetheart. Did they give you one of those spicy shrimps yet? Hi, Cole. Very handsome! Come— Les and I have a table over here. He hates these affairs," she said to Cole. "You look great, Camille. I think it's this man," she whispered in my ear.

Saundra wove her way through the crowd in one direction and then tiptoed to see over the people and changed direction to move toward an archway to the right. I followed the path that formed as the crowd parted to let her through. As I got to the table, I made myself smile hello to Lester and introduced him to Cole. The funny thing was, it wasn't that I didn't like him. I didn't really know him. I just felt my friend always did things that were not in her best interest. And I think the way Jewel put it at the brunch was right, "You just got out of a mess."

Just as we were about to sit down, Jewel appeared. She was wearing an ivory tuxedo-type jacket with a matching skirt with an eggshell-white silk camisole. It was striking against her dark skin. She looked stunning.

"Camille, I'm so glad you could make it. Saundra." She hugged Saundra and me both in turn, holding her face away, taking care not to smudge her makeup or muss her hair. It was full and mane-like, and it seemed to sparkle as the light hit it. "Well, girls, what do you think?"

"We saw you on channel four the other day," I said, smiling at her.

"Did you get one of the press releases?" she asked. She tapped a woman who had her back to us and whispered, "Joy, where are the press releases?" The young woman stepped over to the periphery of the room and came back with a handful of sheets and cards. The leaflet had Jewel's picture on it, and I could see the words Onyx

Management, Inc. and New York and Chicago, but little else because of the dim lighting.

"It's better than I expected. People have flown in from California,
Paris, and Milan. That young man—he's mine," she said, pointing,
"and those girls are mine. A little later we're showing a brief promotional video on the agency. Stay. The ends of these things are so depressing. Maybe we can have a drink after." She turned and looked
at Lester and Cole, both standing out of politeness, even though
she had not even acknowledged them. As she looked at Cole, she
seemed transfixed for a moment. "Les, Cole, forgive me. Good to
see you again. I'm glad you could come. Have something to eat and
drink. Relax, enjoy."

A strikingly beautiful, tall young woman came over to Jewel, excused herself, and whispered something into her ear. All the while
that she was talking, Jewel did not take her eyes off Cole. She studied him from the top of his head to the tips of his toes, taking time
to peruse every inch of the length of him. He didn't notice because
he was looking at me, but Les saw it and so did Saundra. And it
wasn't lost on me.

"Certainly. Excuse me folks. I've got to go speak with my biographer. Enjoy! I'll see you a little later."

"Her biographer. Well, excuse me," Saundra said, punctuating
her comment by letting her head shake from side to side.

I was torn between pride in Jewel's accomplishment and a
strange sickly feeling in the pit of my stomach. I knew that it had
less to do with Jewel and more to do with me, but I couldn't sort it
all out.

We all tried to chat when Jewel left, but it was difficult speaking
over the music and the din of the guests. Their flamboyant gestures and howling enjoyment of one another rose over our voices
too often for us to carry on a coherent conversation. The people
serving interrupted to point out barbecued shrimp, broiled mush-
room caps, and caviar. Saundra asked me how long I was staying
and said something about Jewel asking us to stay until the end. She

shrugged. Various models came over and introduced themselves and gave a few of their credits and did a twirl and moved on.

At one point the music stopped, and the woman who had greeted us at the door got people's attention by tapping on the microphone, which had been placed midstage on a parquet dance floor. "Good evening. I'm Verta Alexander, operations manager of Onyx Management, Inc., New York and Chicago."

There was spontaneous applause punctuated by whistles of the type that young boys work at perfecting with their fingers in their mouths.

"Welcome to the celebration of the expansion of Onyx. We think of our Chicago Office as Onyx^2, or Onyx to the Second Power. Tonight we announce the opening of our Chicago office, which continues our expansion into the entertainment industry from modeling in print and runway to music, video, film, and television." She introduced the promotional video on a big screen television with images of the models, female and male, and a feature presentation of their newest female model, Nadege. A montage of head shots of actors followed, with their names and brief descriptions of their credits. As the screen images faded to black, the music came up on cue, and there was a parade of models who strode onto the dance floor as Verta announced their names. Each moved center floor, struck a pose, did a turn, and strode off. Then she read off the names of the actors, who came onto the floor and stood as others joined them, and they then arrayed themselves in an arc, catching hold of one another's hands. They then bowed and disappeared behind a black curtain.

There was more applause, and after it died down, Verta said, "And now I would like to introduce the founder and CEO of Onyx, Inc., Ms. Jewel Jamison."

The applause began again, with hooting calls and more whistles.

Jewel looked out at the group, beaming and waving at various individuals in the crowd. She paused and smiled all around before she began to speak. "Fifteen years ago, if you told me this would be happening, I would have said you must be kidding. I began this business seeing the need to represent women of color in an industry that didn't recognize their beauty. I set out to change that by cultivating and refining all the natural talent I could find and presenting it for the world to see. And from a small operation in New York's Greenwich Village, we moved to Broadway, and now also to Chicago."

Jewel seemed infused with energy, and her audience listened in complete silence. She thanked industry people for coming and called special people by name, who then bowed and waved, and the audience broke into applause. Designers, editors, hair stylists, makeup artists, casting agents, and celebrity actors all took turns being acknowledged and enjoying a bit of the limelight. Jewel then thanked her staff and the models and actors themselves and made an invitation to everyone in the room to come to the celebration in Chicago on January 15, 1993. "We'd like to leave you with a special gift, our brand-new 1993 Onyx calendars, featuring our beautiful female models—and, for the first time, a calendar devoted to our handsome and talented male models." She then had her staff and the models and actors move through the crowd, on cue, to hand out the calendars.

I couldn't help feeling some sense of dissonance as I returned to the table. I was proud of Jewel and feeling somewhat confused. "I guess this is really a big deal," I said, trying to take in the comments and applause. Cole looked at Les and said, "They sure make you think so."

Les smiled. "Public consumption. They present these models and actors with all this hype, and behind the scenes they treat them like just another commodity. Agents sell people. I know, because I actually let them sell me." He shook his head, smiling at himself.

"You need people to make the deals and do the hype," Saundra said. "I remember when I wanted to be a model, I didn't know where to begin to sell myself." She paused. "I don't know about you. Oh yes, I do. Les, be honest. Could you sell yourself?"

I was trying to sort out what troubled me about what I had just witnessed this evening, the crowd and the spectacle I had observed. I wanted some paper. I needed to write.

"You get the feeling these folks think they are real important." The deep tones of Cole's voice washed over the table.

"But you have to admit that she's accomplished a lot. This is a major business," I said.

Cole did not respond.

Soon after the presentation, the crowd quickly thinned out. The room began to get quiet, and Cole and Les continued talking about the show they had just been privy to. The conversation segued into the seemingly obvious lack of sincerity in show business.

"At least in war, the sides are clear," Cole said. "You know where people stand."

"You know where you stand, but you don't always know why. There's a lack of clarity there too," Les pointed out. His comments were offered with the same calm he always seemed to exhibit. He punctuated his statement with a bobbing head, making him seem to be in his own world.

Les looked at Cole, and they seemed to share a knowledge that we women did not get.

"Now that I think about it, the way I remember 'Nam, nobody knew where they stood. You couldn't get high enough to either figure it out or forget about it." Les laughed.

As they talked, despite their disagreement, I could tell they liked and respected each other. Cole seemed to respect the fact that Les had served, saying, "You earned the right to say that." Les seemed to respect Cole's ability to go back into the fray so many times, saying, "I don't know if I could do what you do, man. Civilians don't have a clue." As I listened to the two of them, I began to rethink the way I viewed Les.

There were still a few people in the room when Cole said, "Ready to go, babe?"

"But Jewel invited us out for drinks after," I said.

Disappointment washed over his face.

"Camille, let's go to the powder room," Saundra suggested, pulling me by the hand.

As soon as we were out of earshot, she whispered, "What is wrong with you? This man is telling you he wants to go home. Isn't your mother watching Shawn?"

"Saundra, your mind is always on sex. Where is the bathroom?"

"Not always. Did you see the jewelry on some of these people? Over this way." She pushed a swinging door and stepped into a powder room and stopped to look in the mirror. She pushed her fingers through the curls in her hair. She leaned in to look more closely at her face.

"There was so much money in this room. You know what else I noticed? These models are all so young. They're the age we were when we all met again in college."

"I noticed that too. I would see one of them and be talking and then realize that they are at the beginning of things," I said. I caught sight of myself in the mirror and confirmed my displeasure with time. "There are so many things I wanted to do, and so much time is gone."

"How do you think I feel? I wanted to be a model. But I'm making a start."

"Saundra, I don't know if I can stand this new optimistic you. I was just thinking, why do I struggle so hard for so little when I could have done something else in life and made much more money?" I said through the door of the stall.

"You've done so many wonderful things for kids. Don't compare yourself to these people," she whispered. "And what the hell is the matter with you? I think that man is in love with you."

"The matter with me? Aren't we just a little bit past this?"

"What do you mean, past this?" she said, rinsing her hands.

"Aren't we too old for this falling-in-love stuff?" I said, pushing the door open to the next room.

"I'm not."

"You're crazy."

"I may be crazy, but I'm not dead." Saundra laughed, throwing her head back, enjoying the sound of her own voice. "Girl, you better take that man home with you."

When I stepped out of the ladies' room, Cole was looking in our direction. Then I saw Jewel walk over to him, sit in the chair next to his, and take off her shoes. I couldn't hear what she was saying, but she raised her hand to call over a waiter. Cole and Les seemed to say no to her offer for them to order a drink.

"Girl, you better get over there to that man."

"If I have to…watch him…"

At that moment, Jewel leaned over and whispered something in Cole's ear.

"Not him, her."

Cole pulled away, just staring at her. As we got closer, I heard Jewel say, "Did you have a good time this evening? A little different from your area of expertise, war," she said, and then she added, "which I find fascinating." Les and Cole looked at each other and laughed. Jewel then rested her hand on Cole's thigh and said in a little-girl voice, "I don't get it."

"Nothing," Cole said, adjusting where he had his feet planted.

"Did Camille have to get home early for the baby?" she asked, taking a sip of her drink.

"No, they're in…here they are," Les said, getting up and straightening his pants.

"We're back," Saundra said.

"Everything I know about the marines says that you must find this little gathering a bit frivolous," Jewel continued, not taking notice of us.

"A little," Cole said. "But, like you said, ma'am, this is not my field."

"Ma'am? I think the last person who called me ma'am was a young man up from Georgia who wanted to break into the business." She took another sip, almost finishing the drink and then running her finger around the rim of the glass.

"It's habit," Cole said, now visibly uncomfortable. Seeing me, he stood up and said, "Camille, are you ready to go?"

"I thought you would all like to go out for something real to eat, or coffee and dessert, a nightcap? My treat."

Jewel seemed a little tipsy. "I'd like to go out for a little something," I said.

"I think I'll pass," Saundra said.

"Come on, Saundra. It'll be like old times. Hanging out." As I said these words, it hit me that it wasn't old times I was seeking. The uneasy feeling that I had had all night finally had crystallized. I had hoped that we could go out and that maybe Jewel, Saundra, and I could stay up till all hours and just talk. I had hoped that I could share how time seemed so short all of a sudden and how I felt that there was not enough of it to do any of the things we used to dream about as girls. How I always questioned whether my choices were the right ones. I needed to find out how they felt about gray hairs, sagging skin, drooping breasts, and missed periods and this gnawing sense that all that made us girls was draining away.

"I would rather head home, Camille. I've got to pack, remember," Cole said in precise measured tones. He tightened his jaw and began to crack his knuckles.

Saundra looked first at Jewel then at me, "I'm not really in the mood tonight."

"Cole, I don't know when I last did this. Saundra, are you sure you don't want to stay?"

"I'm leaving, Camille. I'd like you to come with me."

I looked at Jewel, who seemed to be amused by the chaotic dance that she had set in motion.

"What's it gonna be?" Les interjected, seeming like odd man out.

"Another time," Saundra said, grabbing his arm.

"You're all abandoning me," Jewel said as she pulled the sling back straps of her heels on. "No matter."

I could feel Jewel partition the space about her. "Are you sure you're OK, Jewel?"

"Of course I'm OK. What the hell is that supposed to mean, Camille?"

"I'm asking, do you really need someone to stay?"

"*Need* someone to stay? Give me a break."

"What's your problem, Jewel? She's just concerned about you," Saundra said.

"Would you please…this is laughable. Were you paying attention this evening? Does she really think that I need her to get me a few blocks to my house? Jonathan will call me a cab."

"Forget it," Saundra said. "Les, let's go home. Camille, I'll call you tomorrow."

"You know, Saundra, you don't grow up," Jewel said, flinging her words like stones at Saundra.

"What the hell does that mean?"

"This white man. It's not the seventies anymore. Are you really going home with this white man?"

"You don't know anything about this, Jewel."

"I know it seems ridiculous."

Saundra looked to me for support, then to Cole, who had stopped briefly to take my hand.

"I don't know what you're talking about. Most of the people in here tonight were white. You were hugging and kissing and talking with all of them," Saundra said.

"This is business."

"You know, Jewel, you shouldn't drink," I said.

"I'm not drunk. Forget it. Sorry I brought it up. Good night, folks!" Jewel turned her back on us and shut us out. She went over to one of the tables to retrieve the last of her press releases.

I watched her as she took her briefcase out from behind the now-cleared bar. She was right. It was absurd for me to think that Jewel needed anything from me.

Saundra didn't look at me. She turned and grabbed Les's hand and walked through the huge room out through the darkened foyer.

Cole now focused on the door. "I'm out of here, Camille."

"Cole, I'm coming," I said, looking over toward Jewel. I started to ask her if she was sure she didn't want me to stay, but then decided not to. We just headed for our coats.

I was torn. I wanted to talk and say out loud how I felt. Jewel had to be feeling it too. I thought it was why she didn't want to be alone. I hated feeling my body grow tired. I wanted to know if my friends felt it too. Time was taking my *womanness* away. I had the nagging sense that we were closer to the end than the beginning. I had said it with some lack of clarity in a short piece I had written, but I needed to say it out loud to my friends and to know that I was not alone. Leaving them in this silence left me feeling empty.

The air outside was cool. The valet had already brought our car over. We were the last to leave.

"Camille, why did you do that?" Cole said as soon as he closed the car door. He gripped the steering wheel, trying to contain his anger.

"Do what?" My thoughts had to be brought back to this man, who would not leave me alone.

"I asked you to go, and you started making plans to go out."

"I didn't want to go home yet. I thought it would be fun to go out. It's been so long since we'd done this kind of thing. And couldn't you see how lonely she was?"

Cole glared at me and seemed to grit his teeth.

"She said to me earlier that she hated the ends of these affairs. I told you I wanted to stay then."

"But when I said I didn't want to, you weren't listening. And didn't you hear the way that lady was talking to everyone?"

"That's Jewel, but she was also hurt because we weren't staying."

"She was rude."

"Don't try to push me into making a choice between you and my friends like that. I look at Jewel, and I think she's accomplished so much. I feel like such a waste."

"What? How can you possibly say that?"

"It's true. She's done so much with her life."

"Camille, don't do that."

Cole pulled the car over to the curb.

"Why do you put her on a pedestal like that and make so little of yourself? Your work is so much more important." He tried to caress my cheek with his fingertips.

I pushed his hand away. "Cole, take me home. You don't understand what I'm saying. You couldn't possibly understand what I'm thinking and feeling."

Cole turned the ignition off. "Camille, I'm in love with you."

I started to say something flip, and as I looked into his eyes, I saw a depth of being that reached out, grabbed my shoulders, and shook me. I could not speak at first, because I did not understand all that I felt. Once I began to speak, my center poured out all over.

"Cole, I spent a long time waiting for some knight in shining armor to come into my life and make everything right. It did not happen. I had to depend on myself. And it's funny how when you have to take care of everything for yourself, you change. There's a part of you—you know, that feminine 'I can't do this' part of me. That part of me got squeezed and pressed into a fine paste and got wiped away. It doesn't exist anymore. And now you're here, and I don't know what to do with you. I don't know how to be with you. I feel frantic when I think about it. I'm afraid it's too late for me to love." The vision of him folded and draped itself in the tears about to spill from my eyes.

I recalled the image that had filled my mind the night before. It had made me leave my bed to write it down. I captured part of it, but I knew that I did not express it as powerfully as I had felt it.

I feel like spilled milk. You know how it lies there spreading itself all in the ground. Milk with flecks of gray and brown dust floating every which way the mess would flow. That's how I feel, like spilled milk. You know how useless that is, 'cause you know what milk is about. But that's how I feel.

The thought took all available space in my mind.

"Your being here doesn't make any sense, Cole. I was ready to be here alone, all alone, and I had accepted that." This dusty, dirty milk feeling had grown familiar when you came along and tried to wipe me up.

"Camille, I don't know how you could feel like that."

"But I do. And now you are getting ready to go away, and I waited too late to tell you why I have so little space in me for you. Time has drained away the center of me where I had life."

He sat quietly and studied my words.

"You've never been married, Cole. You probably want kids. I'm past that. I'm almost forty-five years old. There's Shawn and me. This is all there is." That's why I need my friends, I thought. When I conceive of myself, they are the part of my history that fills me up, that makes me remember my innocence and my setting out.

"Camille, I can't make children. I had a vasectomy years ago. I didn't want children."

"Well, you see. There's no future for us. I have Shawn."

"I told you I never got married because of the service. I don't bother telling most women I was married unless there's any real reason to."

"You're married?"

"I said, I *was* married…for about a year…a girl I had been going with in high school, before I went into the service. I married her back in seventy. She wanted babies. We both did, and she got pregnant right away. We had a son." Cole stopped talking and seemed to draw in a breath and then expel it to give him the impetus to go on. "The baby was sick. He had respiratory problems and these wine-colored marks all over his face and body, an' he died within a few days. Then I was talking to my buddies and, you know, cryin' in my beer at the bar one night, and one guy said the same thing happened to a friend who had just come back from Vietnam. When

I told Jeannie, she cried and cried. She wanted babies more than anything. After that, she wouldn't let me touch her, hold her, nothin'. I had the vasectomy to be sure it would never happen again. No point us bein' together after that. I don't tell anyone unless it's serious enough between us to make a difference."

The silence filled in around us. I knew that what he had said required something of me, but I did not know what to say to this good man who dared to love me. I did not know whether I would ever find that light, joyous, young space in my heart again. I felt I needed to find it in order to love him back.

The traffic light changing from red to green penetrated the windshield. Hearing no response, Cole started the car and pulled out into the traffic. I searched for some place within myself from which love might spring, and I found none. I knew now that I could care for him, but to do so, I would have to let him stay and be with me. It was so much easier to be alone.

Sometimes when I think about you and how close you try to come, it makes me shake inside. I am afraid that I am dying inside, and you keep staying here, and I don't want any witnesses.

"Cole, I need time. And I don't need you to try to make me choose between you and my friends. My friends are like my family. They're like my sisters."

He shook his head and continued to drive into the night. He drove me home and walked me up to the door. He stroked my cheek and looked at me with this perplexing gaze. I didn't know what it meant. But it was striking, and it puzzled me. I wanted to ask him what he was thinking. But I had no space for his feelings. The emptiness had filled me up.

I checked my watch. It was ten to one. I had just enough time to catch Jewel before her one-o'clock class. As I darted toward the administration building, a boy pushed a flyer in my hand that said,

"Teach In: End the War." I folded it and put it in my notebook. As I looked up, there was Saundra walking out of the building. I called her just as a tall black guy was pushing another flyer into my hand. "Sister, come out this afternoon for the meeting about black studies."

"I know about it, thanks." I didn't have time to tell him I had written the petition. Saundra didn't hear me, and I almost lost sight of her.

"Saundra," I shouted. She seemed deep in thought, walking and reading a piece of paper. "Saundra!"

"Hey, Camille?" She stuffed the paper into her bag. "I've been calling you."

"I know. My aunt told me. You've got to hear about this man I met."

"Camille, I've got something important to talk to you about. Haven't told my folks yet…I wanted to tell you first."

"On my way over to catch Jewel before her one-o'clock class. I wanted to see you guys. Maybe we can go hang out at her place."

"Camille, I just wanted to tell you first—I mean, without Jewel."

There were dark circles under Saundra's eyes. Whatever was bothering her was serious.

"Do you want to go over to the cafeteria, or to the lounge or something?"

"I'd like to get away from this place, someplace quiet."

"I tell you what. I'll run over, get Jewel's keys, and tell her to meet us down at her place. She's got classes till four. We'll have time to talk, but let me run right now, or I'll miss her. Wait here for me… OK?"

I ran off. Students were milling about or sitting everywhere, but I dodged around them and got to the building where Jewel's class was and caught her as she was going in. "Jewel, glad I caught—"

"No time. I'm late, Camille."

"Just wanted to know if we can get your keys, and maybe sit and talk till you get there."

She frowned and then said, "What's the matter?"

"I don't know. Saundra's upset…needs to talk."

"OK, here." She dug her keys out of her bag. "But don't mess things up. I just cleaned."

"Of course not," I said. "See you when you get there." I walked back to where I had left Saundra and looked around till I saw her sitting on the grass staring into space. "I've got the keys. You ready?" I asked.

"Yeah. Don't mind me, I've just had a really hard week."

I did not press her. We walked in silence to the bus stop. As the bus worked its way downtown, I made small talk about clothes and needing more money. We picked up hamburgers and fries for all three of us at the luncheonette at the corner of Ninety-Sixth Street. The grease seeped through the bag. I held it away from me.

As we entered the apartment, Saundra and I couldn't help noticing how neat it was.

"Think she's expecting Eric this weekend?" Saundra said.

"I don't know, but she's sure got everything in its place. What's that saying? By the way, she said not to mess it up," I said. I headed for the kitchen and got a paper plate from the cabinet and put the paper bag down on it. I dropped my bag with my books on the floor. Saundra followed me into the kitchen, opened the refrigerator, and took out the orange-juice bottle filled with cold water.

"Camille, I did some acid the other day."

"You better be careful with that stuff, Saundra."

"Just listen, OK, before you start mothering me."

"OK…sorry."

"Anyway, I tripped, and when it was hitting me heavy, I started to see myself…" Saundra searched the air for words. Before she could find them, the doorbell rang. We looked at each other, startled.

"Class was canceled," Jewel called out.

Saundra looked disappointed.

"He's sick, or maybe all the professors are at the Teach-In this evening and are canceling. I don't know," Jewel said, dropping her bag in the foyer and putting her books on the counter. "You all right, Saundra?"

Saundra had a trapped look in her eyes.

"I was just talking about student teaching," I said, trying to cover. "Hey, I'm OK."

"I thought you were depressed. I thought you said Saundra needed to talk, Camille?"

"I couldn't wait to tell her about this man I met." I looked at Saundra as if to say I'm sorry and then continued. "You know me, it took me this long to get into the story. The assistant principal, in the school where I'm student teaching, comes over to the table where the teacher and I are having coffee, and...well, this man, I can't even describe it. He's gray at the temples—actually, silver. He's poised beyond belief. It's like he doesn't say anything or do anything that isn't totally perfect."

"Camille, give me a break," Jewel said, reaching for a glass from the cupboard. "How old is he? Sixty?"

"No. I think he's about forty or so." I blushed.

"Is he married?" Saundra asked, trying to take part in the conversation.

"I don't know." I lied. I had seen the picture of his wife and two kids on his desk.

"But Camille, this guy is old enough to be your father. What makes you think he's interested in you?" Jewel asked.

"I don't know. Just a feeling. He gave me a lift to school...and there was just this connection I felt with him. We had drinks the other day."

"He took you out for drinks?" Jewel asked.

"It was my last day at his school, and I waited till he was leaving to knock on his office door. I remembered how I had reminded him that he had said I could come to him if I needed to talk, and he suggested drinks. I tried to explain how confused I was, wanting to be a writer, but I knew I couldn't make a living doing that. And

I loved to teach. I told him how I was not ready to go out there and make money, pay bills, and help Lil.

"I remember he said, 'Wait a minute. Slow down. You are making this debt to your aunt, lifelong payback, *big time*.' I felt so lost. Then he said, 'All I'm saying is, we all feel we owe the people we love everything, but we don't owe them ourselves, our dreams. If we aren't happy inside, or at least at peace, then we have nothing to give.'"

"Deep. He said that to you?" Saundra searched my eyes to see if what I had said was real or invented for Jewel's sake.

"I am totally serious. He's such a turn-on 'cause he's so smart and so wise."

"But, Camille, you have to think he's too old for you," Jewel said as she took a French-fried potato from the mound piled on the bag Saundra had torn open.

"I can't explain it, but with him, it's like he's a man, and he knows it. He's not trying to prove anything. Unlike Derrick, who hasn't called in months...no matter what happens, I'd just like to have him as a friend—you know, someone to talk to."

"That's not how you sounded a few minutes ago," Saundra said with a lascivious smile.

"I'm attracted to him. Shit, the truth is, I wish he would make a move on me." I felt ashamed when I remembered his wife and kids. That wasn't how I saw myself. "Let's be real. I'm the good girl who would never really do that. I know it's a fantasy, but I love talking to him, and I wish I had the guts..."

"I just think you'd better be careful. He is...much too old for you," Jewel said.

"I would love to have a man a real man, not a boy, want me... love me," I said.

"Jewel, why do you do that all the time?" Saundra said.

"Do what?"

"You always pass judgment on what people do," Saundra said.

"I don't," said Jewel. "Do I, Camille?"

"Well..." I hesitated. "Saundra!"

"Camille is too nice to say it. You always act like your opinion is the law. I mean, every damn time you open your mouth, it's like whatever we think or feel is wrong, and what you say is right."

"That's not true," Jewel said.

"Sometimes it is," I said, searching Jewel's face for forgiveness.

"Jewel, I think growing up with your aunt made you a little..." I couldn't think of a word that wouldn't wound her any more than she already appeared.

"Jewel, you're a pain, with that holier-than-thou crap," Saundra continued. "Sorry if your feelings are hurt, but you do this all the time. Camille tells you she met a guy she likes, and you turn it into some moral trip...like you're so goddamned perfect."

"I didn't mean it like that..." Jewel said, her voice trailing off.

"I figured after you finally did it, you'd stop that crap. But the place looks ready for Eric to come over again, and you're still—"

"You're right," Jewel whispered. "Sometimes I just can't stop myself. I know I'm saying things that I don't even believe, but it just comes out. Like my aunt is there inside with me." She looked to Saundra and then to me.

"She always made me feel like I would turn out"—Jewel seemed to struggle for the right word—"bad."

"That doesn't give you the right to do that shit to us," Saundra said.

"I always felt they thought I was...dirty." Tears rolled down Jewel's cheeks.

This time Saundra just listened. She stared at the air as if she saw something frightening. She did not draw away. She seemed to defy it to hurt her. Her bottom lip stiffened, and so did her chin. It was at this moment that Jewel noticed it too. Jewel had always envied Saundra's beauty. We had talked about it. Her almond-shaped, light-colored eyes, fair skin, and full red lips always turned men's heads. And if that wasn't enough, Saundra's full breasts, behind, and long legs seemed to beckon attention from both men and women. She was stunning. She drew stares simply moving about her business. That was why this expression, which was now so vividly painted on her face, was so painful to observe. Jewel and I looked at each other, wondering what was wrong.

"Saundra," she called, reaching out to touch her but hesitating for fear she might push her closer to whatever she seemed to fear so much.

"'Member that man Mr. Lynch who lived upstairs in my house? We were about seven? He was friends...he used to hang out with my father sometimes?" She looked at me to see if I had traveled back in time with her so that we could view him together.

"Yeah. Sure," I answered, bewildered.

"He used to make me come to his room." Saundra paused, thinking, and then bit her lip, making a deep depression in it, almost drawing blood, and it soon turned purplish red.

"The first time, he tricked me. He...I was coming in from school, and...my parents were still at work. I was supposed to let myself in, and lock the door, and wait till they got home." She took a deep breath.

"You all right?" I said as I saw tears well up in her eyes.

"Yeah. I have to say this out loud." She swallowed the saliva in her mouth.

"I was coming in from school one day, and he told me I could wait at his house. I told him I had to go inside. And he said I should come for just a minute, he had something for me." She paused again and stared off to the left, as if she could see him. "He started talking about this kitten he had for me. I don't remember its name. When I got into his house, there it was. But when I went to look at it, he pulled me in and started touching me. He put me in his lap and took out his...he exposed himself to me." Saundra scraped the back of her palate with her tongue, as if she could wipe away the words as they came out.

"I tried to get away, but he kept hold of my arm and kept touching me, and he told me to touch him." Saundra looked up as if there were other people looking down at her. "I was scared. I did what he told me. He made me promise not to say anything to my parents. I don't know why, but I didn't tell."

I didn't know what to say. Jewel and I looked at each other, trying to read each other's thoughts and come up with something.

"He kept making me go there and making me do things." Her voice softly punctuated every syllable, quietly recounting the secret. "I kept going...never told them. I kept wishing my father would make him stop...my mother to protect me. But they never did. But that's the terrible thing in me. I saw it this week when I tripped. Inside, I could see myself. I was all shriveled and dirtied up. Why didn't *I* stop going?"

"But Saundra, you were a kid," I said.

Jewel just stared at her with tears filling her bottom lids and refusing to drop.

"I kept going there. He used to touch me and rub himself on me, and I kept going. There is something wrong with me. Part of me must have liked it. Why else would I have kept going?" Tears rained down from Saundra's eyes. She wiped them with the heels of her hands.

"And I get the same feelings with Santos. I'm scared of him, yet I keep going back to be with him. Hell, I'm scared I love the dirty feeling of being with him. There's something wrong with me."

She sat quietly for a long time and then said, "But I'm not going to see him anymore. I'm tired of this feeling scared all the time. Sometimes I feel I keep going to him to have someplace to get away from my life. I can't do it anymore. I'm quitting school," she blurted out and then looked up at both of us as if she dared us to challenge her. "I'm not a student. I'm not as smart as you two. I don't have it. I'd like to model or something, even do secretarial, but school is not for me."

"Saundra, why don't you see a counselor?"

"Camille, we've been around and back with that. I just saw a counselor. He thinks I should take a leave of absence, so that's what he gave me. The paper's in my bag, but I'm not going back." Her tears bathed her cheeks.

"You're sure about this, aren't you?" I said.

Saundra nodded and then rested her head on my shoulder.

"I can't do this anymore. I hate going to school, and I run to Santos to get high and get away. It's crazy. I'm going to find myself a job. I just don't know what my parents are going to do. They may put me out."

"Saundra, if you need to, you can come here," Jewel whispered.

Saundra seemed exhausted. She pushed her chair out and walked into the living room. Jewel and I followed her, just wanting her not to be alone. When we got in there, we arranged ourselves in a haphazard manner. Saundra sat on the couch. I sat next to her. Jewel sat cross-legged in the overstuffed armchair to Saundra's right. Between Jewel and Saundra was the window through which time escaped.

"This guy I tripped with," Saundra said, and then she paused to look at me and then at Jewel. "He said there was a beauty in me."

"There is, Saundra," I said, pleading her to believe me.

"I have to know if it's really there, Camille. This ugliness, that part of me, feels really big sometimes."

Tears pooled in the bottom lids of my eyes, and they fell, splashing on my hand, bursting, sending bits of themselves off in all directions. "Saundra," I said, letting the words spill from my lips any which way, "we're going to be OK."

"When I look at you, Camille, it's like I see sunshine. You make me smile. I just hope you're right."

At that moment it seemed we all became one. It was at that moment that I looked at Jewel and saw an aura of lavender blue. It permeated the space just around her. So often when I looked at Saundra, I saw vermilion. At times she was a hot orange-red. At other times she felt more like a dark crimson, a blood red. But today I felt more certain of what I saw, her true hue. There was a tinge of blue there, making her more a magenta than a pure red. Somehow

I felt a sense of us all being three lovely splashes of color set in a patchwork of greens.

"Nobody's stuck by me like you." Saundra laughed and cried the words out. "And Jewel, thanks. Thanks for understanding. I really appreciate..." Saundra could not force any more sound through.

I felt it first. I encircled my arms around Saundra. Jewel moved on to the couch and slipped her arm around Saundra's shoulder.

Sundrop yellow, lavender-blue, and magenta enfolded with tiny bits showing themselves in the oddest spaces. We held onto one another, knowing the closeness, loving the velvet soft touch of each other. When we finally untangled ourselves, we each seemed brighter and more brilliant than before. We had no words for the love we felt. It was quite enough to simply be.

16

SAUNDRA

Les and I walked to the car, and I don't know when it happened, but our hands were laced together. He was parked up on Seventy-Second Street near Amsterdam Avenue a few blocks from the restaurant. The anger flowed out of me once I was on the street. Jewel's words jarred my insides. I had been looking forward to the rest of the evening with Les, and now I feared her comments had ruined it. But walking with him was like a restful relief from the loud gaudiness of the affair at Tavern on the Green. When I looked at him, his peaceful face made me feel a calm that I had never known before. I wanted to tell him how ashamed I felt about the comments my friend had made, but that did not seem necessary. It was as though the comments hadn't touched him. It wasn't as if he hadn't heard them. It was as though what she had said didn't speak to him.

As we got to the corner of Amsterdam and Seventy-First, three black teens brushed by Les. One who bumped into Les turned and looked back, saying, "Watch where you're goin' man." In the instant that he said those words, he looked into my face and back again at Les, and then said, "What you doin' with him, sister?"

"You got a problem?" Les said, turning to face them and dropping my hand.

"Les, come on. Let's go," I said, trying to grab for his hand.

"I can make it my problem," the tall, light-skinned kid said as his two friends pulled him away. "You thinkin' of makin' one like me?" He stood on his toes, walking backward and gesticulating with his hands, shouting at me, "You need to get yourself a brother." He turned his back and continued talking to himself out loud, although I could not make out what he was saying.

"Saundra, if that kind of thing ever happens again, don't try to pull my hands like that. You could get us killed."

"You weren't thinking of fighting with those guys, were you?"

"Not if I didn't have to, but if I did need to defend myself, and us...you have my hands, you could slow me down and get me hurt, or killed." His voice now had an edge.

"I'm sorry," I said, uncertain what was going on in Les's mind.

"Cool," he said, his head now bobbing characteristically once again.

"By the way, I felt that my mother's neighbor who we bumped into up on the Concourse was kind of funny when she saw us."

"Yeah, I noticed it. You give a shit?"

"Not really, except my mother's been giving me a hard time lately."

It was an odd energy I had just seen in him. His blue-gray eyes seemed the color of steel. There were layers of this man that I did not know.

He opened the door to his old Volvo. Where the light from the streetlamp hit the hood and door, I could see rust spots. The passenger seat was split, letting the foam stuffing seep out, and the gaping hole in the dashboard screamed stolen radio. He told me how he had replaced it with the kind you're supposed to take out, because he liked hearing his music.

"The one time I forgot, they took it...just gave up on fixing broken windows." Les drove down the West Side Highway to the Brooklyn Bridge and into Park Slope near Fourth Avenue. When I began to notice that we had passed the same stores more than twice, I said, "Weren't we just here?"

"Park Slope. No parking spots...don't know why I live here." He finally pulled up beside a car to back park, turned off the ignition, and looked at me. "Did you ever think we'd get such hassles in the nineties?"

I had no warning about what he was thinking, so I simply shrugged. "I didn't expect it from my friends."

He nodded his head while he put the metallic locking device on his steering wheel, opened his ashtray and glove compartment, and put his No Radio sign on the dashboard.

"Got to try to keep ahead of these guys."

He got out of the car and went around to open my door, but I had already done it. He seemed happy he didn't have to make it a habit. He put his arm across my shoulder, and we walked up the block. It was a strange feeling to me. When Santos put his arm around me, it was a demonstration of ownership. I always felt like his property. He gave me an ankle bracelet when we first started going together. I wore it because it was pretty and a curiosity, him being Latin and into that kind of thing. But as I wore it, the sensation excited me. It felt like a connection to him, a belonging to him that made me feel full inside. I wanted to be owned. With Les, his touch was more like a comfortable, affectionate embrace, like being tied up with brightly colored ribbon.

"Your friend, the heavier one—she doesn't seem like an assistant principal. She seems more like an artist type."

"Why do you say that? She does write poetry."

"I don't know. She seems kind of sensitive. At first I was thinking a master sergeant and an assistant principal—perfect together, except when they both give orders." He laughed as he opened a wrought-iron gate to a brownstone building.

"They seem good together, don't they?" I followed him into the dimly lit hallway into a big kitchen.

"Seems so. He's in the wrong field. You could tell he's unhappy with the service. She doesn't seem too happy either. But they look like they might be happy together." He turned on the light to illuminate a brick-walled kitchen with an old Tiffany-style lamp above an oak table that leaned precariously to the right.

"Is this room sort of crooked, or is it me?"

"No, you're right. Old brownstone; what can I say."

"Am I remembering it right, but wasn't your old apartment…"

"Lopsided too? Yup."

We laughed.

"Your other friend is a trip." This time he laughed to himself, as if to his own private joke.

"I guess I should apologize for her, but I didn't expect any of that."

"Hey." Les put up his hands as if to say, "What could you do?" And then he said, "The three of you are close?"

"We used to be." I searched for the words that might describe what we were now.

"Gimme your jacket…in here," Les said as he went into the adjoining room. He took off his leather bomber jacket and hung it on a wood clothing rack that held a suede gaucho-type hat and quilted vest. He put on a tape and looked at me.

"You were laughing when you started to say something about Jewel."

"Hey, it's none of my business."

"You noticed it too?"

"Couldn't miss it."

"We're talking about the same thing…her throwing herself at Cole? I have to tell Camille."

"It's amazing. You haven't changed in twenty-some-odd years," Les said out of the blue, now looking at me fully.

"You're crazy," I said, feeling a blush fill my cheeks. "I'm about twenty-five pounds heavier, all in my hips." My mind immediately went to all the scars on my body from the blows by Santos. I could feel my expression change, so I tried to force myself to smile again.

He brushed my hair back from my face. It felt as though he had done it before, and he was looking at me too closely.

"Except for that mark right there," he said, pointing to the corner of my eye.

I pulled my hair down on my face. "That's a scar where I fell against a sink. How could you remember that that wasn't there?"

"I remember your face. I spent a lot of time studying it."

"We were together, what—a couple of hours?"

"More like a few days. And one whole day, all I did was study your face. I remember wishing I were a painter."

"Get out of here."

"Serious business. I can't be the first man who told you how beautiful you are."

I turned away from him. It was too uncomfortable to face him, feeling that for so long all I had heard was how ugly I was.

Les moved in behind me and pointed to the mirror on the wall. "Look at that face," he said, seeming to be enjoying the vision of me. As I caught sight of our reflection, I was struck by how pale his skin was. I hadn't noticed his coloring until I saw his face next to mine, or maybe it was all the comments tonight. His hair was dark brown and long, covering his ears and almost reaching his shoulders. His eyes were light blue-gray and he had long dark-brown lashes, but his skin was cream colored. Next to him, though my skin was fair, it was a warm almond brown.

"How come you never called?" he said, pulling my gaze to meet his eyes.

"I don't know. Life."

"I remember you were having a hard time with your folks."

"Yeah. I left home. Went to live with a guy. Got married."

Les seemed to look right through me to my soul. "Same guy you just divorced?"

"Yeah. He was bad news. I can't believe you thought about me more than five seconds after that day."

"Not true."

"So what about you? What have you been doing for twenty-five years?" I laughed.

"Been here and there, 'Nam, Vermont, in Mexico for a year. Lived on a commune in New Mexico awhile…back to New York in '86. Finished my degree, started teaching music."

"We look good together," I said, now studying his face.

"Seems like we turned a few heads." Les laughed, turning me around to face him and touching my nose with his fingertip.

"I can't believe what happened tonight. I really didn't expect it from Jewel."

"Don't sweat it. Not a big deal. It doesn't much matter to me."

He kissed my nose and then my eyes and rubbed my arms with his fingertips. The gentleness of his touch warmed me. But as my body relaxed, my mind became more vigilant in case he should change. I had grown mistrustful of maleness. It was my memories of when I had last been with him that helped me to rest in his arms. I wanted to touch his serenity and have it flow all over me. I wondered what I might have been like had I stayed with him.

"So why did you stay with him?" The question seemed to be plucked from my thoughts. It wrenched me away from my comfortable place.

"What did you say?"

"You said it was a bad marriage. Why did you stay?"

"I guess I thought that he loved me. Maybe I thought that I was strong enough to take it, and I had nowhere else to go. I had my daughter..." It was strange, I thought, how large a presence Santos was in my world. Before he started calling the house from jail, there were times I forgot that he existed. Now that he was coming out soon, his presence was so large, I rarely escaped it. I hoped Les could make him go away.

"You want to come upstairs? I've got a piano room up there." Les moved out to the hallway and up the darkened staircase. He flipped a switch at the top of the stairs and looked down at me. I noticed how easily I seemed to follow him, although I felt uncertain about where he would lead.

"Did you ever get married?"

"Nah. Living together is as close as I got. Lived with a woman in Vermont for a few years, and moved down to Mexico with her. Lived with a woman here in New York for about four years."

As I moved into the second floor, I saw a darkened bedroom with a four-poster bed and an old antique wooden armoire. The living room had the piano, an upright, and a wall full of bookshelves filled with albums, a dingy old overstuffed armchair, and nothing else. There were sheets up at the window. No sign of a woman anywhere. I wondered why.

"You're not living with anyone now?"

"Not for a while."

"How come?"

Les laughed. "You do that so well—say just what's on your mind. The last woman I was living with still had some of the nomad in her. Couldn't stay put too long. I've kind of carved out a place here. Not into travelin' around anymore."

He sat at the piano and began to play. I sat down beside him on the bench. The tune seemed quite regular and melodic at first, and then it seemed to take flight in jazzlike variations up and down the keyboard. He played with it. I enjoyed how his mind could move it about. His creativity made me smile. He looked at my face and then began at another place on the keyboard and played across the keys, creating a slight cry in the tune. I looked off to the right, letting the sounds take me away.

He stopped for a moment and then picked up the notes again, repeating them with chords this time. He opened the tape recorder on top of the piano. "Sandy, can you look over on that shelf and see if I have a blank tape there." He continued to play with his right hand, taking the tape out of the machine with his left hand.

I found a pack of three cassettes held together with cellophane. "Do you want me to open this?" I said, holding it up for him to see.

He nodded. "Do you like this?" he asked, this time playing both hands together letting the full range of sound from the piano fill up the room. The tune had a blues feel to it.

"It's beautiful. What's it called?"

"I don't know. 'Saundra's Melody.' No, 'Sandy's Tune.'"

"Get out of here. Did you just make that up?"

"I just put it all together. Some of it's been rolling around in my head since that Sunday when I saw you at the restaurant. And some of it I remembered from years ago when I had written this little melody for you."

"Stop!"

"I'm serious. Just sort of thinking about you, I played with the tune, and it came back to me when I was foolin' around on the piano Sunday night."

"I can't believe you thought about me once after that day. As stoned as we were."

"I had a big fight over you. All those people who were in my pad that night that you called, I put 'em out. The woman who was kind of holdin' on to me, I told her I was tired of her, to get rid of her. I figured you'd call back."

"That's weird, 'cause I wanted to call back real bad, but I felt I couldn't get my head together with all those people there."

"Figured that, but I guess it was too late, 'cause you didn't call."

"Funny how things…" Memories of that time filled my mind, filling me with sadness.

"Got my papers right after that. Was on my way to Georgia, to boot camp, three weeks later. After basic, they shipped us off to 'Nam. Digging bunkers. Shit! This is so fucking unreal. I thought about you a lot."

He put the tape into the machine, pressed the record buttons, and said, "Sandy's Tune." His fingers moved over the keys, and his brow creased in places where the melody seemed to take on the moan that punctuated it in places. The music took off in another direction, sounding more playful, making me smile. Then he would return to the bluesy refrain that would make my hips move while making my mind feel close to the tears in my chest. He had somehow woven together the desire to dance and to cry, which seemed so incompatible.

The music touched me; I felt uncomfortable. I got up from the piano bench, and went over to the window and stared out into the darkness. The street below was deserted. I rested my forehead on the cold windowpane.

Now the music went off into an improvisation of the melodic phrases he had played at first. Les's head seemed to anticipate and then move with the rise and fall of the music. He had transported himself.

I had to get away from the music, which was too close to me. I struggled against it, but somehow it found its way back into my consciousness. As it did, it played itself into a melodic conclusion. Les sat for a while, as if he were still hearing the notes at the end of the piece play over in his head.

He pressed the button to stop the recorder.

I felt exposed. The music had taken down the structure that I had so carefully built over the past few months. I had struggled so hard to regain my sense of who I was before I felt trapped and afraid all the time. I had forced myself to laugh and to feel. But behind the facade, I held back the sensation that I might cry out loud at any moment. *What happens when he comes back?*

Les made it all surface. The music revealed the pain I felt and had not shared with Camille, Jewel, or my mother. Although I had planned to go to my mother's, my fear was that he would find me there, bring his craziness to her home, and she would ask me to leave.

"You don't like it, do you?"

"It makes me feel like I'm going to cry. I don't let myself cry."

Les looked out the window behind me. He didn't say anything. He wrapped his arms around my shoulders, letting me rest back into his embrace.

This music scares me, I thought. I had spent so much energy trying to pretend that I was fine, and as I listened to Les's music, I realized I was not. The time that I had was growing shorter. In a few weeks, he would be out. I wanted to stay in this peaceful space Les had created for as long as I could.

He kissed my neck. My mind became alert. He kissed my back and my cheek. I turned my head to reach his lips with mine. He led

me to his bed. Though I held on to him as tightly as I could, I began
to tremble. It was cold in the room, but it wasn't the chill that made
it happen. The shaking came from deep, deep inside. I hoped he
wouldn't notice it. I tried to hold still to make it stop, but I couldn't.
He stroked the length of my back as if he sensed the tremor. As he
kissed my face, he pulled my body closer to him to steady me.

"Do you want me to stop?" he whispered.

I shook my head no.

As he kissed my shoulders, I took off my clothes. He kissed my
neck and then my arms. As I began to trust his touch, my mind
relaxed. He peeled off his shirt and jeans. He pulled back the com-
forter and made his way closer to me. I held on to him, for fear I
might lose the sense of peace that I was seeking. As he touched
my center, stroking the tender space that I had allowed to him, I
began to accept the pleasure that he made me feel. I remembered
the taking in of him. My eyes were closed, and I wanted to see this
man who touched me so gently. I imagined that he watched me as
he poured his love into me. When I opened my eyes, I saw that I was
right. He was looking down at me.

For so long, sex with Santos was an assault. The animal in him
needed to dominate me, force me and then pound me, pushing
into me before I was ready. There were times my insides hurt.

But now, waves of pleasure washed into me, around me, and
swallowed me up. Moving with him felt like a dance that I never
wanted to end. I lost control, and my body spasmed, pulling, drawing him into me. I wanted to stop. He did not. He moved past my
pleasure to pain. My body shut closed. I needed to be by myself, no
intrusion. He did not stop. He wanted more of me, and I had nothing more to give.

I closed my eyes, and losing sight of him, I began to feel the fear
swell in my chest. I covered my mouth so that the cry there would
not escape my lips. Santos's presence lurked nearby, searching for
me. *He is going to find me.*

"What's the matter?"

I shook my head, so lost in my thoughts that I was amazed that he knew I was hurting, though he was looking straight at me. *Where can I hide if he wants to find me?*

"What can I do?" he said. His manhood shriveled.

Who am I kidding? I thought. You can't do anything. No one can help me. *He would kill you if you tried to help me.*

"Saundra, where are you? I feel like it's déjà vu all over again."

"I've got to get more things out of the apartment over to my mom's. I still have things to fix." I pushed him off me and sat up to go.

He fell back on the bed. "Now? Wait till morning. I'll drive you."

"It's too easy and comfortable here, Les."

"What does that mean?"

"If I stay here, I won't want to leave. I have to get the things out of the apartment this week. They're letting him out a week or so after Thanksgiving."

"So stay. I'll drive you tomorrow. What is it? The nineteenth or twentieth? I'll drive you tomorrow, and you can bring your things here."

"No...don't want you to come to my apartment. The neighbors..."

"Do you give a shit? What do you still have there?"

"A few boxes of odds and ends. My work clothes. A couple of my jackets and skirts, Wanda's and my heavy winter coats. I have to fix stuff."

"Who's Wanda?"

"My daughter. 'Member, I told you about her that Sunday."

"Forgot. How old is she?"

I watched Les become visibly tense. I knew that the complications of my life pushed people away. "My mom has temporary custody...a guardianship. She's twelve, and I'm beginning to think it's better for her with my mother, the school, and the neighborhood... waiting till I get on my feet."

"So I'll take you tomorrow. Cool out awhile. Why are you so jumpy all of a sudden?"

"I need to finish up packing, clean it up, and leave the keys with the super."

"What are you afraid of? He's not there. I'd be with you. Just relax."

I couldn't describe my fear. It was too all-consuming. I could not explain the indignities that Santos had subjected me to. I had never told anyone, not even the women in the support group, how many ways he had found to hurt me. When I traveled to those places in my mind, I felt I might get lost there alone and find Santos waiting for me.

"Les, you don't get it. My ex-husband is a violent man. I am scared to death of him."

"I really don't like talking about things like this, but if I have to, I can take care of him." There was something in the way that Les said those words that made me feel that he could keep that promise or threat.

"I don't want you to have anything to do with him." I knew I couldn't let Santos muck him up.

"OK, then let me drive you. Just give me a little time for a cat-nap. I'll be fresh, and I'll take you. I'm wiped...wasn't counting on going out again tonight." Les closed his eyes and seemed to drop off asleep in a matter of minutes.

I loved watching him sleep, but I had to get my things. I eased myself out of the bed, picked up my clothing from where it had fallen, and tiptoed out of the room.

"Sandy?" Les whispered, "I'll be up in a few minutes." I did not answer.

I have to go now. I dressed in silence, trying to avoid placing my weight on the floorboards that creaked. The tape Les had made was on the piano. I started to take it, to keep with me for luck. As I held it in my hand, I felt that I might cry from the beauty of it. No one had ever done anything like that for me. I put it back. It is safer here. I wouldn't want Santos to touch it. I looked around Les's place, wishing I could simply hide there forever. I remembered wanting to hide with him before. I left knowing that I could not.

It was absolutely quiet when I opened the door to my parents' home that Saturday morning. At first, I thought there was no one at home, but the second lock was undone. There was a light on in the kitchen, but no sound. I was prepared to face my parents. I needed to put it behind me. The quiet was filling up my ears. Through the crack in the door in my parents' bedroom, I saw bedclothes piled on the side of the bed. As I moved closer and pushed the door open, I saw what I thought was a crumpled blanket. It was my mother, turned on her side, reading her religious tract, the *Daily Word*, which she said gave her strength. She wasn't an overly religious woman, but she turned to her faith in times of stress.

I swallowed the saliva that had collected in my mouth and said, "Hi, Mom. I'm sorry I didn't come home last night…I've…I…"

"Your father wants to talk to you."

"Where is Daddy?" I asked, taking a deep breath. It felt good to say that. I had roamed the city so long, drifting without any sense of belonging, it felt good being at home.

"He went out. I don't know when he will be back." My mother pushed her feet into her slippers and moved past me to the kitchen.

"Mom, I know I've been hard to live with, but—" I said to my mother's back.

"Saundra, talk to your father."

"You mean you don't…won't speak to me?"

"I mean I have nothing to say."

My mother was a talkative woman who enjoyed sitting around the kitchen table with a pot of tea and home-baked bread with butter swirled through it, which she sliced and served but hardly ever ate. When she wasn't talking about her garden, or women at the dress shop where she did alterations, she was talking back to the radio as if it could respond. That was why her silence was so disturbing.

"I'm sorry, Mama. I know I've been a pain in the ass. I know it. I can deal with things better…"

"Saundra," she said, not looking at me, "you will have to talk to your father. He said he would handle this."

"All right. I deserve this, but Mama, I want to tell you that I am sorry."

My mother turned and looked into my face. I felt she knew saying that was not easy for me. I remembered how once she had held me by the arm saying to me, "Say you're sorry." I wouldn't. I would cry before I would apologize, and it took a lot to make me cry.

"Saundra, why do you do these things?"

"Mama, I've had so many decisions to make. I've been so mixed up…"

"So you stay out till all hours, even days now…three days…don't know where you are, if you're alive or dead."

"I know." I accepted my mother's words, wishing they were more pointed and less pained. She had cut herself off from me. I didn't know I had been gone so long.

I wanted to explain. "Mama, remember how it was always hard for me in school."

"I don't want to hear it. You have something to say, tell it to your father," she said, turning her back and filling up the teakettle.

I sat down at the kitchen table, hoping for the chance to resume the conversation. It never came. My mother moved out of the kitchen and went into the living room. The kettle wailed. I called out that the water had boiled, but she didn't answer. I made the tea and called out again, but still she did not utter a word. I brought the cup to her, and she went into her bedroom, leaving it behind, and closed the door.

Hours passed. I straightened up my room, putting my books into neat stacks on my desk. I cleaned out my desk drawer and tied up the stack of pictures of Santos with a scrap of wool I found in the dresser. I put them in a shoebox of photographs I had kept since I was a child. It contained mostly school pictures that I had collected from classmates in exchange for my own. There were photos of Camille when we were in junior high and high school. I looked through some of the pictures of the old block. I couldn't help smiling at the one of Jewel and me. We were sitting on a stoop with our legs crossed like bathing beauties. We were about seven at the time and were wearing sneakers with lacings that crisscrossed up the leg and tied under the knee. We sat on the stoop with our sundress skirts pulled tightly above our knees, smiling at the camera. I couldn't quite believe that so much time had passed. But it cemented in my mind the idea that Santos would also become just an old photograph with some memories. I closed the box and put it up in my closet. I felt lighter.

While I waited for my father to get home, I straightened the clothing in my drawers, took the sheets off my bed, and put all my soiled things in my pillowcase. I opened the window, and a fresh, cool breeze blew in, filling even the corners with a sense of newness. As I opened the door to my room and went to the linen closet for fresh sheets, my mother's door was now open, and I heard her moving about in the kitchen. Despite my mother's anger, the sounds of her footsteps were comforting.

A rush of feelings surfaced. I felt ashamed and sorry and happy to be home and anxious to try to make my parents proud of me all at once. I wished I could tell them how much I loved them for just being. My eyes filled with tears and I wiped them with the back of my hands. The sun began to set behind the building across the street. There was now a chill in the room. I lowered the window and then decided to close it altogether. My feelings were becoming overwhelming. My chest felt so full that it might burst if some of what I was feeling did not come out.

I called Camille. As soon as I heard her voice, a flood of emotion poured out, splashing all around me.

"Camille, I have to talk to someone. My mom's not speaking to me, but I'm sure I can make it right. I'm so lucky. I was looking through old pictures and thinking I'm so lucky. I've got good friends and great parents. Shit. I could have gotten myself killed with the kind of stupid things I've done. But I'm here. I have people who love me." I just stopped to hear Camille's voice again. "Camille, are you there?"

"Yeah, sure."

"I know it sounds crazy, but I'm feelin' really good about bein' home."

"So your folks took it OK? I knew they would."

"No, I haven't told them yet. My dad isn't here. My mom is peeved, but it's all going to be all right." I wiped my eyes with the heels of my hands.

"What did your mom say?"

"Not much…said to talk to my dad. She's mad. Hey, she's got a right to be…if I had a kid like me…I'm going to make this up to them. Maybe I won't be a doctor or a lawyer, but I'll make them proud."

"I know you will. Hang in there. Sounds like your dad may be pretty angry."

"I know, and I'm prepared. I'm not the kid who ran out of here three days ago."

"Three days ago? You haven't been there since…"

"You're right. I haven't had any consideration for how they feel. Starting tonight, I change. I already have. They just don't know it yet. Camille, I think I hear my father. I better go. I'll talk to you later or tomorrow. Who knows if they'll let me use the phone."

I stood up and wiped my eyes again and looked into the mirror over my dresser. I couldn't tell if the redness was from my crying or from lack of sleep. I pulled my hair up and back into a ponytail and brushed it to get out the tangles. I could hear some talking in the kitchen, and I heard my mother say something, and then the words, "…her room."

"Saundra, where have you been?" my father asked as he stood in the doorway. He hadn't even actually looked at me yet.

"Daddy, I know you're angry at me. You have every right to be."

"I said, where have you been?" My dad was a man in his fifties. He was muscular, with a belly from drinking stout. He was brown-skinned and his beard was pitted and pimply, but he had a broad, warm expression on his face that always made people smile. Now his face was an angry mask of disappointment.

"Daddy, I've been at Jewel's and just roaming around the city thinking. I've been…"

"Roaming around the city?"

"Daddy, I've had so much to think about. I'm not able to do college work. I don't think I'm cut out for college. I don't have the brain for it."

"No, because you're roaming the city."

"You have every reason to be mad. I didn't call."

"Who were you with?"

"I was by myself most of the time. The other night I was with Jewel and Camille."

"And the other nights?"

"I was with a friend." I couldn't lie to my father.

"Yeah, that's what I thought. The same *friend* who gave you the black eye."

"No, Daddy. A different friend."

"Right. How many friends do you have, Saundra?" he said with disgust, turning away from me.

"Daddy, I'm trying to tell you that I'm going to get a job. I'm going to make you proud of me, Daddy. I promise."

As I looked at him, there was something I had seen earlier in my mother's expression—distance. He had stepped back from me, only further than my mother had.

"Daddy, listen to me. Anything you want me to do, I'll do. I'll do anything you say to make this up to you. Please."

He was deaf, or was stopping up his ears.

"Saundra, you have hurt your mother very deeply."

"I know. I'm sorry. I told Mom how sorry I was. You don't have to worry about anything like this happening again."

"I know it won't happen again. We will not let it happen again, because you are packing your things."

"Daddy…" Before I could say anything more, the words my father spoke sliced through the air and stabbed me in the chest. I could not think of what I might say to him. There was no vestige of the caring man who I knew as my father, who had always forgiven me. He was not there. I thought it was ironic that now that I wanted to set everything straight, my chances had run out. I thought about pleading and begging my father to let me stay, but I could not find him. The man who stood before me was hollow.

"I'm sorry," I managed to say.

The man turned and walked away. Dazed, I sat on my bed. My mind was a blank. Night had fallen behind me while I was looking for my father. I could feel my eyes blink. My eyeballs were dry, and my eyelids seem to scrape over them. I could hear my eyes close with each blink. I wished I could rest. I tried to think of what I would do come morning.

Then I heard a sound at my door.

"Here's your suitcase," my father said.

"Can't I stay till tomorrow morning? I have nowhere to go."

"You found a place last night, and the night before that."

There was no longer any room for me here. I needed to see my mother's face to see if there was any reason to hope that I was wrong. I walked into the kitchen. My mother was sitting at the table twisting a paper napkin.

"Mama, I tried to tell you this before, and I tried to tell Daddy, that if you would give me a chance, I will make up for…the pain I have caused you."

"Saundra, you are twenty years old. You are a woman. You act like a woman. You are out being a woman outside in the street."

My throat was dry. I tried to swallow, to take in my mother's words and let them go down and digest. I walked back to my room, and as I tried to swallow, my stomach spasmed. I covered my mouth with my hand and went for the toilet. I dry heaved, making an animal-like sound, which made me feel ashamed. I felt someone behind me. As I turned I saw a glimmer of my parents standing in the doorway. As I studied their faces, seeing their concern created a longing for the way things used to be.

"She's OK," I heard my father say as he turned to leave.

I'm not OK, I thought as loudly as I could, hoping they might hear. They didn't. I packed.

It was strange. Maybe it was because I had been so hopeful earlier in the day. Perhaps it was the impact of being told that the only home I had ever known was no longer mine, but there was a split that happened inside me. I stepped back outside myself and observed. I watched myself pack all the socks in my second drawer. A pair of bobby socks had been stuck in the roof of the drawer space. I paused and felt the socks and the time that was my youth. I felt connected to who I was for a brief moment, and then I watched myself pack my blouses, bellbottoms, and skirts from my closet. The box of pictures caught my eye. I clutched it and the frozen images of my past and kissed them good-bye.

Somehow, I found myself on the street walking toward the subway, and then on the Broadway/Seventh Avenue train. I have no place to go, I thought. Staring straight ahead, I went inside some space that I perceived as being in front of myself and watched. I didn't know how long I had stayed there, but at some point I heard someone softly say, "If you need to, come here." It was Jewel's voice from the conversation we had had. It guided me.

"Thank you, Jewel," I whispered.

I took the train to Ninety-Sixth Street. I walked up the block and stood in front of the building. I turned around and went back to the corner and dug into my pockets for a dime. The numbers blurred and danced around in front of me. I had to grab at them to make my finger connect and dial. There was a wailing busy signal screaming in my ear. I waited and then dialed again. I stared into the glass wall of the telephone booth and stood there inside the strange reflection until I heard the busy sound again. So I parted the space before me with the suitcase, and then my body, and followed myself to Jewel's house. The front door to the building was open, so I began climbing the stairs. My shoulder hurt from the weight of the suitcase. I watched the landings, checking the numbers painted in gray next to the apartments in Jewel's line. When I finally reached the fifth floor, I stood there, my mouth open and my lungs sucking in the stale hallway air. I saw my fist fly up and bang on the door, almost at the same time that I heard a voice come from deep inside my belly say, "Jewel. It's me, Saundra." Then I saw my fist come up again and pound this time.

"Jewel, are you there?"

"Who is that?"

"Jewel, it's me. I'm sorry to just—"

The door unlocked, and Jewel peeked through a narrow opening. "Saundra, Eric is here!"

"Jewel, can I just come in? My parents put me out."

"Eric's here," she repeated. "Can't you come back tomorrow?"

"Jewel, I have no place to go. Please let me stay in the living room. I won't bother you. Please."

"Saundra, you should have called. How can I...look, I'm sorry. What the hell would I tell Eric? Did you call Camille?"

"You said I could come...I called...it's busy. Forget it!"

"Oh, I took it off the hook. I'm sorry. Call me tomorrow. OK?"

I turned around and walked down the stairs, which wound down into the night. I thought about calling Camille, but Lil had a two-room apartment. Camille slept on the pull-out bed in the living room. There was hardly enough room for the two of them. I stuffed my hands down into my pockets to see how much change I had. There in my pocket was the slip of paper with Les's address and telephone number. My left arm ached with the weight of my suitcase. I shifted it to my right hand and walked back to the telephone booth on the corner. I fumbled through my pocket, feeling for change, and dialed. The phone rang about six times before anyone answered, and there was a woman's voice on the other end. I wanted to hang up, but after thinking about spending another night in the subways, I decided to speak. "Is Lester there?"

The voice said, "Who's this?"

"Tell him it's Saundra! Sandy."

"Saundra, Sandy...Les, Saundra Sandy is on the phone," she said in a mocking tone.

"Who?" Les said. "Oh, Sandy."

I could hear music in the background, and lots of voices. "Sandy. What's doin'?"

It felt good to hear a voice that welcomed me.

"I just got kicked out of my house. I was wonderin'..."

"There's a whole slew of people here, but come on over."

"I just have nowhere to go."

"I can dig it. Come on over, but you'll have to pull up a piece of floor like all the rest of us."

I thought about being with so many strangers.

"Les, can I have a hit?" I heard a girl say. "You keepin' it all for yourself."

I said, "I don't know if that's a good idea. Thanks Lester."

"Look, come over. I'll see what I can do tonight, but it should be less hectic here on Monday. They're all headin' south to Mexico."

"I'll...thanks."

I hung up. In desperation, I dialed Camille's number. If I could only stay there for the night, maybe I could go to Jewel's house tomorrow. A droning busy signal whined in my ear. I dialed again. The blaring tones now screamed at me, making me draw my head back away from the receiver.

"Where am I going to go?" I picked up my suitcase and walked back down into the subway. The train became a huge outstretched palm that moved me about its dirty tunnels while I searched for the darkest spot in which to hide. An old woman sat hunched over like a sack of potatoes in the corner, her head leaning against the window. A man in his thirties immaculately dressed stood near the door reading the *New York Times*, his attaché case between his feet. He folded and unfolded the paper, glancing up from time to time to check the station. I had no idea where the train was heading. I checked too. The train pulled into 145th Street, and the man folded his paper under his arm and got out. It hit me. The train was turning toward the Bronx. Without trying, I was headed to Santos's.

"Oh, God. I'm going back there." I followed the glimmer of light through the tunnels to the 177th street station. My arm ached under the weight of my suitcase. I walked two blocks. My hand was numb. I knocked on the door that led to his basement apartment.

"Knew you'd be back." His oily hair hung in his face. He left the door to the apartment open. I closed myself in, locking all the locks, and sat on my suitcase. I leaned on the door, seeing myself on the other side of it, walking, then running away. I could hear myself screaming "No."

Then I heard him. "Saundra, get in this bed. I got someplace to be in the morning."

"Yes." I heard my voice breaking. "Yes."

I took off my jacket and went into the bedroom where the yellow-skinned girl had been. I smelled her there. I sat on the edge of the bed in my clothes.

"Set that clock over there for eight. I got someplace I gotta be at nine thirty. Make sure I'm up…hear me?"

Santos was a small man with a big voice. It commanded you to listen to him.

"I hear," I answered, feeling his words hit me on the back of the head.

"Fix me some coffee in the mornin'."

My teeth clenched. I went deep inside myself and stared out through the tunnels that were my eyes. I'm not going to stay here, I thought. I'm scared here. I closed my eyes to block out the light that filtered in from the streetlight outside. My mind remained alert. It found a dark space in which to sit. It waited, watchful, vigilant. It did not dare rest.

17

CAMILLE

"I'm almost done here, Camille. This part of my life is over. I can't believe it."

Shawn had run to catch the phone in the kitchen as we got in and handed it to me. We had had dinner at the coffee shop because I was exhausted. I would have told Saundra I was too tired talk, but she sounded so excited. Shawn dragged his backpack into the bedroom.

"Glad you really did it this time." I pulled the telephone cord into the bedroom to gesture to Shawn to do his homework. He was sitting on the floor with his action figures, still wearing his jacket, mouthing the words, "Five more minutes. Please, Ma."

Saundra said something, but I didn't quite hear it. "Give me a minute, Saundra. OK, but just five. It's almost seven. What did you say?"

"Just saying that it felt like I would never finish. The super came up twice, telling me he wouldn't give me my deposit if I didn't clean the stove better and fix the knob that Santos broke on the bedroom door. He's getting out of Riker's in about a week or so. If he wants the place, he can talk to the super. But they're both Cuban, so you know how that goes."

"So are you going to your mom's, like you said, or..." Holding the phone in the crook of my neck, I put up water to boil for tea.

"Or am I movin' in with Les? You know, Camille, I expected you to say something to Jewel the other night. And just because I went home with him…never mind."

"What was I supposed to say? You know Jewel. Anything I said would have just made her say something even worse. And I think you're kind of jumping into this thing with Les, not taking into consideration the consequences."

"The consequences seem to keep slapping us in the face…don't seem to have much choice. I don't remember her, or you, for that matter, having those kinds of feelings."

"What kinds of feelings?"

"Camille, are you saying that you think Les and I shouldn't go out together because he's white?"

"No. I'm not saying that. I just think you do always seem to go looking for trouble. He seems like a nice guy, but Saundra, this is America. I know there are places in the West Indies and South America where this is not a problem, but we're in America, 1992. This is still a problem here."

"I can't believe this. You're my friend. I thought you'd see that he's good to me. I thought you'd say if he's good to you, that's all that matters. That's what I think when I see you with someone. I hope he treats you good."

"Nothing against Les. I take people as they come…just saying that you have to be aware that people are going to give you a hard time. I like Les, and I think…you should do what makes you happy."

"Forget it…never said I was moving in with him anyway. But girl, I think that man is in love with you. Girl, girl, girl," Saundra said in almost musical tones that first rose and then descended the scale. "I would keep him away from Jewel if I was you."

"What do you mean?" I dunked the tea bag and spooned in some honey.

"Camille, this man is fine. The way he looks at you…how old did you say he was? His body is like a wall of muscle."

"Saundra!"

"Well, it's true. Did you see his body?"

"Yes, I happen to have seen his body."

"What is wrong with you? Back in the day, you'd be on cloud nine."

"It's just that he's not the type I usually go for, and he's movin' too fast."

"When is usually lately, Miss Thing? Is he good in bed?"

"Saundra!"

"Camille, please. I don't care how long it's been, you should be able to tell."

"Saundra!"

"He looks like he's good, and he seems like he's sensitive. You know, like he's gonna talk to you after, and hold you, and all that nice stuff."

"You know, the first time we made love, he just sat and waited for me to wake up. He didn't want me to wake up by myself, and he didn't want Shawn to see him in bed with me, so he got dressed and just sat there and waited. I still can't get over that. I thought he was weird or something, but that's just how he is." As I said these words out loud, I breathed in a sense of acceptance of this man who dared to love me.

"I hope you marry this nigger."

"You know, Saundra, I told you I wish you wouldn't say that. I really don't like that word...never did, really. Now with Shawn, I really don't like him hearing—"

"Hey, I can dig it. With me...just habit...the circles I run in sometimes. Speaking of school, guess who I ran into yesterday at the supermarket when I was buying oven cleaner."

"Who?"

"Derrick. He looked fine as ever. A little heavier, but fine. He says he's got a couple of kids. He asked about you and about Jewel."

"Talk about the past. Derrick? He's got two kids?"

"They're big already. He said one is twelve and one is seventeen."

"Seventeen?"

"And she's a girl too. He says it's real hard trying to…I think he said 'guide her,' 'cause he remembers all the shit he used to do. So I told him it was good for him. He laughed."

"So what did he ask about me?"

"Just how you're doin' and how's Jewel doin'."

"How did he remember Jewel? He met her…what, one or two times."

There was silence on the other end of the line. It clogged up my ears.

"Saundra? You there?"

"I'm here. I guess Jewel never told you? Shit, what does it matter now? Jewel slept with him."

The words flew through the earpiece and raced 'round my head and slammed me in the mind, taking my breath away. I almost dropped the cup of tea I was sipping.

"I thought…all these years she had told you."

"When did she do this?"

"I didn't say anything, 'cause…well, it was during one of the times when you and Derrick weren't seeing each other. And you remember how fucked up I was at that time. I was back with Santos, doin' acid and smokin' all day long. Hey, I…"

"Never mind. I just can't believe she did that. Was this while… was it during or after college?"

"I can't remember exactly, but I think it was when you were seniors, just about to graduate. I think, no…yeah, during college for sure. I remember it was after she and Eric broke up at the end of her senior year…after the time when the students took over the college and shut it down."

"I still saw him on and off until a few months after graduation. You mean she was sleeping with him while…I don't fucking believe this."

"I wouldn't have said anything if I thought it would hurt you. You know how shaky Derrick was."

"I know, but I didn't expect my best friend to sleep with my boyfriend."

"Did he sleep with you too?"

"Girl, I was very messed up back then, but there are certain things I did not do. Do not do. I always went after my own men. You know that. Remember when we'd stake out a party. I'd tell you when we walked in which one was mine."

I did not have words for why I felt the way I did, but the betrayal of my friend reached out like a powerful fist and grabbed my heart, squeezed, and wrung it out. I did not feel like talking.

"Camille? You know Jewel. She was always more involved in herself. I'm sure, at the time, she didn't even think about you. She just was, you know, getting back at Eric, enjoying not being a virgin. Remember how after making such a big deal of it, she just went wild for a while. Anyway, you have this wonderful man who would do anything for you, and you're thinking about Derrick. He's as shaky as ever...doesn't have a job. He's fooling around talking about deejaying. Please. Derrick is forty-eight years old. Give me a break. Speaking of which, be careful with Jewel around Cole."

I had nothing to say. I pushed the tea away and stared at the air in front of me as images of Jewel and Derrick filled my mind.

"Camille, I'm sorry I said anything. Who's there? Someone's at the door."

"Saundra, I've got to go. I've got to bathe Shawn. I've got to go."

"I'm sorry, Camille. I really didn't think...I'm coming! I don't know who the hell that could be."

"Forget it, Saundra. I don't know why I even let it bother me. Hell, Derrick and I were always on the outs...wouldn't see him for months. Gotta go." I hung up. That bastard, I thought. Where was my head? The phone rang, and my anger at Saundra grew. How come she didn't tell me?

"Saundra, I have no time—"

"Camille, it's me, Cole. Are you all right?"

"Cole, I'm fine. Just a few things on my mind."

"I just called to tell you, I have to report early. I'm running the drill next weekend, so I'm going to be away all week. Maybe longer."

I searched my mind for a reason he was telling me this and came up blank.

"Yes…"

"Well, I'm leaving tomorrow, and I just wanted to tell you."

"So?"

"What do you mean, 'so'?" Cole asked. "Camille, I'm telling you that I'll be away for two weeks. I thought you'd want to know how you could reach me."

"Not really. Why are you making such a big deal?"

"No big deal. I just figured I won't be here for Thanksgiving, and I wanted to tell you where I'd be. Shit…Camille, what the hell is it with you? Why do you go hot and cold with me? I don't know where the hell I am with you."

"Look, I just found out that a boyfriend I had a long time ago was sleeping with my best friend. Frankly, I'm feeling like he's a shit, and you called right when Saundra told me, OK? And about where we are, we are no place in particular. Don't make this any more than it is. We spent a few nights together. It was nice. We like each other. That's it."

"A few nights together? Is that what this is to you?"

"I didn't mean it like that. What I mean is, I think you're getting too serious too fast. I don't like the fact that Shawn can end up depending on you. I feel…you know, I don't understand why this thing between Derrick and Jewel has me so upset."

"With Jewel? When was this?"

"When I was in college."

"Was this guy important to you?"

"He was my first boyfriend…my first love."

"That's why you're upset."

"What do you mean?"

"It's obvious. You can't understand how your best friend could betray your trust and sleep with your first love."

"I just feel…how stupid I was that I didn't know."

"You just feel that because you can't deal with your anger at your friend for being in bed screwing your boyfriend."

"Don't say it that way."

"Why? That's what she did. And when you don't sugarcoat it, you begin to feel the anger. Don't you?"

"What are you doing? Jewel is my friend. She was a little…I don't know…flighty back then. I…this isn't a big thing." Saundra's conversation replayed itself in my mind. "I don't even know why I'm making such a big thing out of it. Hey, forget it. But Cole, Saundra said something…I should watch Jewel around you? Do you know what she was talking about?"

"Camille, I guess she noticed what I was trying to tell you about her when you told me not to step between you and your friends. She came on to me at Tavern on the Green."

"She was drunk that night."

"Look, you asked. It doesn't mean anything to me. I'm not a teenager. Anyway, just because you choose to be angry at your old boyfriend instead of Jewel, that doesn't mean you have to take it out on me."

"What the hell does that mean?"

"I mean I called you to tell you that if you don't hear from me, I didn't fall off the face of the earth, and you give me this cold shit. Maybe it's a good thing the drill is coming up. Maybe you ought to figure out what the hell you want in this relationship. I know what I want. I need to know what *you* want."

"I don't want anything. OK? Thanks for caring. I thank you for being nice to Shawn. That's it. Leave me…I told you I was fine without you, Cole."

"Camille, don't do this. All I'm saying is…you know how I feel about you. I think I love you."

"And that's another thing. How can you love me? You've only known me a couple of months. Do you run around loving every woman that you meet?"

"I told you I've seen you. I've watched you with Shawn. Once I got to know you—"

"Every time you say you've watched me, it makes me feel weird."

"Camille, I've seen you from time to time. I've been attracted to you, but I never had the opportunity to speak to you. It just all fell into place that Sunday. I guess I feel as if I've known you so long."

"You mean you've watched me and watched Shawn—"

"Camille. I'm not saying I stared at you or followed you. Nothing sinister here. I just saw a woman who I wished I might meet, and the fates obliged. Anyway, maybe it's a product of my age, but at forty-eight, you cherish time. So yeah, I know what I want. I want this…I know you don't love me. I just figure maybe in time you will. So, there it is. That's what I want."

"And if I don't?"

"I think you will. I'm willing to bet on it."

"I'm saying, what if I don't?"

"If you don't, I'll manage," Cole said. "Camille, I would never force myself on you. I would never hurt you. If you say it's over, it's over. That's why I think you need to use this time to think about what you want. I'm not a masochist. I don't want to go on with this if there is no chance at all. So just tell me."

His words were so direct, I could not duck or hide from them. They sliced through my mind to a place that would not open. There was a dead end there.

Shawn walked into the kitchen. He climbed up on my lap and rested his head on my chest. No man had ever talked to me like this man. It was so foreign to me that it was as if he spoke another language. No one ever cared like him. No one had ever been so real. It was as if my entire life before him had been some childish fantasy.

"I don't know. I just don't know." I whispered so as not to wake Shawn, who was now falling asleep on my lap.

"I'm not pressuring you, Camille. I'm just saying think about it."

"I don't know what to think."

"Just leave it there, the idea of us. See how you feel next week and the week after. That's all. Don't work at it. Let it be; see what happens."

"OK," I said. My insides were jarred.

"Sorry about Thanksgiving."

"Oh, Thanksgiving. That's right."

"I'll talk to you in a couple of weeks."

I put the phone on the table and lifted Shawn up with two hands. He was getting so heavy. I hung the phone up on the wall and looked down at Shawn's face. His head was rested peacefully on my breast, and his mouth had fallen open. I carried him into the bedroom, and put him into bed. I groped around in my mind for some answer to how this would all go. For the first time, I had no fantasy in which to dance about. I felt the muscles in my neck tighten. What is wrong with me? Then I heard his words, just let it be. I closed my eyes and tried to summon a vision of Cole. I had always been good at daydreaming. I could draw in images as I pleased. I could not draw him. I opened my eyes and then closed them again. I could not see him, but somehow I felt him. It was odd at first. I fought the sensation because it was not what I had wanted it to be. Then, somehow, I grew tired of the struggle and could not push it away no matter how I willed it to go. I let it sit there inside me, the sense of him. There was peace about that spot where he rested. It felt good that it was there. I felt I would travel there again as I pleased, just to know that this space existed.

"Cammy, where were you last night? I waited up till two in the morning, and you still weren't home. All the cookin' I have to do for Thanksgiving, and you weren't even here to help me cut up my onions, peppers, and celery for the stuffing, and the potato salad."

"I was with a friend." I didn't want to tell her I spent it with Victor.

"You know you could invite your friends to come over here sometimes."

I smiled to myself.

"By that look on your face, I bet it's a boy," Aunt Lil said.

"Not a boy, Aunt Lil."

"Well, a young man. You know what I mean. You should invite him over. You know young men respect you better when they know you have a family that looks out for you."

I was always amazed at how uncluttered a view of the world my aunt had. Sometimes it was better to appease her than to argue with her. "OK, Aunt Lil," I said, wondering how the old woman would react to meeting Victor, who was twenty years older than I was and hearing about his wife and children. I didn't know about them when I first met him. But by the time we had drinks together, I so loved being with him that I made all sorts of excuses for keeping contact with him.

I filled the kettle with water and yawned. Then, surveying the kitchen filled with a good-sized turkey on the counter and a bowl of potatoes on the table, I said, "How much food are you making for the two of us, or are you inviting some of the church ladies over or something?"

"I invited your mother to have Thanksgiving with us," Lil said in an off-handed way, seeming to invite no conversation on the matter.

"Why did you do that? And without telling me."

"Last time I checked, this is my house and I can invite anyone I want to my table."

"I'm just saying, it would have been nice not have this sprung on me. And, Aunt Lil, the last time I saw her, we had nothing in common. You were right. I was glad you made me meet her, but that was it. I didn't see any reason to call her back."

"That's why you need to break bread together—to get to know each other better. It's more than a year, and you haven't called her or anything. I'm not getting any younger, you know." Aunt Lil's hair was white. She held onto the counter and then the table as she moved the mayonnaise jar from the refrigerator. She was heavy and her back was bent and all of her movements took effort.

"Aunt Lil...never mind. What do you need my help with?"

"You can put that bird in the oven. You see how I rubbed the butter all over the skin, and then I sprinkled it with the onion powder, black pepper, and paprika. That gives it its color."

Aunt Lil always gave me cooking lessons each time I cooked alongside her. I couldn't tell her the advice she gave had now been given so many times it was almost irritating to hear. I just did as she said.

"And you can finish cutting those potatoes and put the peppers and onions and celery into that glass bowl over there so I can mix up my potato salad. Ellie hasn't had it since…I don't know when."

"What am I going to talk to her about? I have nothing in common with her."

"Talk about college and your friends, and that you are graduating in June."

"I hope."

"You better not just be hopin'."

"I don't know if you saw it on the news, but there are students boycotting, and the school suspended classes for a couple of days."

"I heard, and I told your mother, it's good you have a head on your shoulders and aren't causing any trouble over at that school."

"I did sign the petition to get a black history course." I didn't want to tell her that I had rewritten it, because the students asked me to read it over. I finished cutting the potatoes and peeling the eggs she had placed on the table in front of me.

"Camille Warren, what in God's name is wrong with you?"

"Nothing. I just think it's about time there is a black history course. Do you know that all of the history we are taught in school doesn't even mention our contributions or our fight against slavery?" I pushed the bowl over to her.

"Girl, I don't want to hear all this nonsense. You better hope that that school…oh my God. You got what…seven more months, and you go puttin' your name on some piece of paper, givin' them the chance to kick you out. You think I worked hard, your father worked, and your mother worked for you to throw it all away?"

"Aunt Lil, I felt it was important...I don't want to argue with you. I don't think they can kick us all out. There are a lot of us who signed that paper."

"You don't know what they can do. They can do anything they want to do. It's their school." She banged the wooden spoon on the bowl too hard as she spooned in the mayonnaise.

The room got quiet save Aunt Lil sucking her teeth and then shaking her head every now and then. "Take the folding table out of the closet and set it up in the living room. Use my two good table-cloths. Put the lace one over the damask one and set the table. And take out the good silverware and the good glasses."

"Why are you making such a big deal?"

"I don't know how much time I have left. I feel I should use my good things. And I'm glad Ellie is coming."

Aunt Lil insisted I dust the tables and make her bed. I set the table and washed all of the bowls and spoons she had thrown into the sink. Then I finally took a shower and changed clothes. It was barely 4:00 p.m. when the doorbell rang. Eleanor stood at the door holding a big paper shopping bag. "I brought my sweet-potato pud-ding, like you asked, Lil." She smiled at me and said, "You used to like it when you were little."

"Come on in, Ellie. Take off your coat. You hungry?" Lil asked, and then added, "I made my potato salad, just for you."

"I could eat now or wait, whatever you prefer," Ellie said, looking at me, seeming to try to gauge if she had said the right thing. "You all hungry?"

Eleanor was thin, and though her body was trim, her shoulders hunched, and she seemed to have to force a smile on to her face, as if smiles were uncomfortable there.

"It doesn't matter to me," I said.

"Well, then, get that bird out of the oven. I'm just keeping it warm anyway. I put everything else on the table, while you were in-side. Cammy, take out some ice and put it in the glasses. You know what I made for you, Ellie? Some sorrel. I remember you liked that.

You didn't care much for ginger beer, but you said you like sorrel." Aunt Lil had always tried to introduce Ellie to the food and drink of the Islands, since she was from the South.

"I did. It tasted fruity. Can I help with anything?"

"Just come over here and sit down," Lil said, tapping the chair she had chosen for her.

I helped Lil put the turkey on the platter, and then I carried it to the table. Eleanor moved the glass so that I had room. Aunt Lil carried in the gravy bowl and her rolls, and we finally sat down. Lil smiled at my mother and at me in turn and said, "I will say grace. Oh Lord, thank you for these blessings we have at our table, that we were strong enough to make one more Thanksgiving dinner, that my grandniece is graduating college in just a few months, and that her mother is here to celebrate Thanksgiving with us. Bless our table and this family, and bring it together again as it should be. Amen." Aunt Lil nodded as if she had said everything she wanted to get off her chest before the meal.

She smiled at me and Ellie again and immediately began telling me, "Now pass Ellie the potato salad. You'll want some of these turnips, and Ellie, you don't have any of my stuffing. You know, Cammy helped make the potato salad."

It was so irritating watching Aunt Lil treat Eleanor like a queen. And my mother seemed to try so hard to include me in every comment. "Camille loved mashed turnips with butter when she was little...I'd have to pick out the onions and the celery from Ma's potato salad so Cammy would eat it when she was small."

"So tell you mother how you're doing in school," Lil said, trying to nudge me into the conversation.

"I'm doing fine."

"They have her on a dean's list, and that's a good list for the students with the highest grades. And tell her how they have you teaching already."

"I've been student teaching this semester."

Aunt Lil shot me a look as if to say, I know what you are doing.

"I knew you would become a teacher from the time you were two. You would sit your baby doll and teddy bear down and read them the story *Color Kittens*. You remember that story? It was your favorite. And you would turn the pages and tell them the story just like I read it, never missing a word."

"All kids do that."

"No, not like you. You were the perfect little teacher." When I looked up at her, there was genuine pride in her eyes. "I remember telling your father that, and he said he thought so too. We both knew it."

I wanted to enjoy my mother's comment, but I couldn't help feeling a mix of loss and then anger after digesting what she said.

"Then I guess it's too bad he won't get to see me graduate."

The room got quiet. Eleanor looked down at her plate.

"Cammy!" my aunt said.

"I just think that if you—the two of you—were so concerned about me…you should've thought before you went out driving drunk that night. Maybe if you didn't kill him, we'd all be sitting around this table."

"I ought to go. Lil, I told you this was a bad idea."

"No, you stay. I'll go," I said before I could stop myself.

"No, you aren't going anywhere. I did not help raise you, nor did my sister, to be rude to your mother like that."

"Ma didn't like her. She felt the same way," I said, looking at Lil, my back to Eleanor.

"My sister grieved the loss of her son until she died. She needed someone to blame, and she blamed your mother. Ellie, you need to tell this girl what happened that night."

"It's OK, Lil. I accept whatever blame Winifred dished out, because maybe I should have…I don't know."

"Your father, Johnny, was drunk that night. He drank overproof rum. Ellie didn't feed it to him."

"I told him it was going to hurt his stomach, but he and his friends were being men, showing off how they could hold their liquor. He could hold his liquor, but that stuff was too strong," Eleanor said.

"So when he started to drive, he was banging into the car in front of him," Lil said.

"I had my license, but I hardly ever drove. I had a drink of rum and Coke earlier, and I expected that he would be driving. When I saw he couldn't drive, I looked for some of our friends, but everyone had left already. It was deserted up there near the armory, so I drove..." She stopped and seemed to see the scene played out in the air in front of her. "And a few blocks later, this car sped by, and I ran into a lamppost trying not to hit him. There weren't seat belts back then, like now, and he went through the windshield. The ambulance took him, and I begged them to let me go with him, but they said they smelled alcohol, and they took me to the precinct."

"I know all this, and he's dead. So like I said, he won't see me graduate."

"You know, Camille, I loved your father more than anything. Winnie was angry with me, and I was angry with myself. It took me years to accept what I had done. I guess what's wrong between us is I haven't told you. I am so sorry, so very sorry. I wished so many times that it could have been me instead of him. I wish I had yelled louder that he not drink that rum, that I couldn't drive well enough to get us home. But I can't make it turn out right. Lil asked me to bring these...I had them for you when I saw you last time. These are the last photos I have of your father and you and me together, that night. You were dancing on his feet in one, and the other he lifted you up. And the other one, a neighbor took of all three of us. I wanted you to have them. I am sorry. I just can't fix this."

Eleanor got up and went to the closet and took out her coat. I looked at the broken spirit that was the woman in the photo I now held in my hand. Her face was like sunshine there in the picture, as she looked at her husband. And in the photo where she held me in her arms, she looked as if her heart would burst.

I looked at the photos of my father dancing with me and smiling, and I was so grateful for these images. "Thank you for these," I said, tears filling my eyes. I felt embarrassed and ashamed of what I had said to this woman whom I could not love but who seemed to care so much for me. "Don't go."

"It's all right. I understand. I've caused so much pain." She pulled on her coat.

"Ellie, come sit down," Aunt Lil said. "God knows I loved Johnny, and I know my sister would not want to hear this, but I said this then. Johnny played a part in this. It is not all your fault. This child has to learn that things in life aren't just black and white."

"I want you to stay," I said, the tears now spilling from my eyes.

"No, it's OK. I just came to bring Camille the pictures."

"Maybe we can have some of your sweet potato pudding. Anyone want tea?" I said, wiping my eyes with the napkin, trying to make things right.

"I think that is a good idea," Aunt Lil said. "Ellie, please don't go."

Eleanor sat down at the table, her coat still on. I took away the dinner plates and made tea for all of us. It was so quiet as my mother cut the pudding and served it. She didn't speak.

"Ellie, you're gonna get warm with that coat on," Aunt Lil said.

She took her arms out and left it on the chair behind her. I felt she was keeping her words pushed down in her throat.

"What do you put in it, Ellie? I think I taste nutmeg," Aunt Lil said, trying to make conversation.

"Yes, a little." She didn't look up.

The taste of the spices in it seemed familiar to me, somehow. I could not believe it was a memory from so long ago, though my mother said I liked it as a child. I glanced down at the photo of me dancing with my father and laughing, and his broad smile. And for a second I felt I had gotten him back.

The evening ended with Aunt Lil taking out her box of photos and telling stories about my father—her nephew, as she put it—when he was a boy visiting her house. "He would bring over the seventy-eights and play them on my Victrola and swing me around and dance. He did that at my place but wouldn't dare do it at his mother's. My sister was such a prude. She was always quoting her Bible, and all that nonsense."

I looked down at the photos of my parents again and saw the playfulness and happiness that was on their faces. I wondered how different I would be had life not frozen our joy on that night. I wondered how I would fit this sad woman into my life.

18

CAMILLE

November 30, 1992
Indian summer was like a last passionate embrace. The trees had been ablaze in a red-hot blush for weeks and then had shed their leaves, with a few hardy patches of color holding fast. Then it turned windy and cold, and the trees disrobed completely and shivered in the night like naked children caught at something naughty.

I wrote that the week after Thanksgiving. The chill caught everyone by surprise. People hugged themselves and walked at an angle, some with their heads burrowed into the wind, with collars upturned, trudging like soldiers into battle. I had spent the afternoon at a school-based planning meeting. Now, late getting home, I pulled Shawn behind me as he tried to hide from the cold wind. Having fallen asleep on the train, he was struggling to keep up. It was that time when darkness seemed to fold in on itself.

"Shawn, we're going up to Grandma's for dinner tonight. She said she had enough left over turkey for us. When we get back downstairs, bath and straight to bed."

"Aw, Mom," he said. "Mommy, when is Cole getting back?"

"Next week sometime, I think. I have to look at the calendar." Every day since Cole had gone to Camp Lejeune, I listened for reports on the television about sending troops back to the Mideast. There were none.

I had become closer to my mother during the last few weeks. I tried to put aside all the old hurts. I made efforts at seeking her out to say hi and talk about Thanksgiving. She said she wanted to make her sweet potato pudding with Shawn. He loved it. It was funny how Eleanor would always work a question about Cole into the conversation. Sometimes it would be right away, and sometimes it would be after we were sitting together, eating something, or having a cup of tea, but at some point she would say, "How is that young man?".

The first time she said it, I said, "He's not so young, Ma. I'm not so young either."

"Well, you're both young to me," she'd say, her voice now so thin.

There was this strange sensation I had watching this woman, who had seemed so huge a figure to me because of how my grandmother had painted her. Now I watched her shrink and shrivel into a sallow birdlike form. There were times when Shawn would jump up on her, happy to see her, and her frail body seemed as if it would break. There were moments when I was caught between stopping him and watching as he leaped on her, waiting to see how this brittle woman would look shattered to bits. My thoughts made me feel guilty, so I tried harder to make my kindnesses seem as genuine as they were becoming. Time and something about remembering Cole's gentleness while we were together focused me on the small kindnesses unconditionally given by my mother. I was grateful to him for helping me discover her.

Despite my efforts, there was still this bitter taste in my mouth sometimes when I spoke to her. It rose up in my throat when I least expected it and gave what I said an edge even though I did not want it to. My mother knew it, because at those times she would look at me and then look down as if she deserved it.

The heavy metal door to the building was left ajar. I cursed the thoughtless person who had left it unlocked. I pushed it closed and made sure the latch snapped. Letting go of Shawn's hand, I fished through the keys for the one for my mailbox.

"Bills, bills, more bills," I said to myself as I then opened my mother's mailbox and pulled out her Con Ed and telephone bills. I gently pushed Shawn ahead of me up the stairs. He struggled to keep far enough ahead of me, saying, "I'm going, Ma."

As I opened the apartment door, I noticed all the lights were off. "Mama, we're here. Mama? Damn!" The hallway and the kitchen were dark. "She probably forgot about us, Shawn."

"Grandma's not here," Shawn said, stumbling behind me, dragging his backpack on the floor. The sound of our footsteps reverberated in the long hallway, breaking the complete stillness.

"Mama?" I called, now expecting no answer but feeling uneasy. "I wonder if she went to the beauty parlor or something." At the end of the hallway, a faint light from the bedroom painted a golden glow on the wooden flooring just outside the room.

"Mama, are you sick in bed? Shawn, stay here."

"Why, Mommy?"

"Because I said so." Something wasn't right.

Deliberately and slowly, I pushed the door open and glanced around the room from the bureau to the chest of drawers. The chenille spread was thrown haphazardly on the bed, but everything in the room was in its place, from what I could see from the door. On the chair near the window was Ellie's floral bedspread, neatly folded. Everything on the dresser was arranged as it always was. A big photo of Shawn was in a frame facing the bed. I walked to the side of the bed, and on the floor was my mother's rumpled rose-pink chenille robe and a sheet lying crumpled around it. I bent down to pick it up. It took a few seconds for me to register the weight of it and to notice my mother's hand hanging from the sleeve. "Mama?" I said, this time softly, disbelieving.

"Mommy, it's dark in here," Shawn said from in the living room.

I slumped to my knees and tried to lift and nestle my mother's head onto my lap. Her hand was ice cold. Her yellow-brown skin had a blue cast to it, and her head dangled to the right, a heavy weight, as I tried to turn her. Her eyes stared off, as if she were sadly contemplating the tattered dust ruffle around her bed.

"Mommy? Please, can I come out of the dark?" Shawn's voice quivered as if he were going to cry. I had to let him come in. I had to tell him.

"Shawn?" I said as I put my fingers over my mother's eyes and closed out the light, "Grandma's…" The words stuck in my throat. I put my mother down and walked into the living room where Shawn stood, right where I had left him. He looked up to me, putting his arms up. I pulled him to me and squeezed him tight. We sat on the couch, and I rocked him. He tried to draw away, but I held him so tightly that he succumbed.

In the darkened living room, I reached up and turned on the lamp, which cast a dim glow on the end table. There was an ashtray with one cigarette butt ringed with my mother's rose-colored lipstick.

"Shawn, Grandma's dead," I said softly, still rocking, not knowing whether it was he or myself I was comforting. On the end table was a photograph of Shawn standing beside my mother's spindly Christmas tree from the year before.

"Grandma's not dead," Shawn said, and then he broke away from me and ran to look into the bedroom.

"Don't go in there, Shawn."

"Why, ma? My grandma."

The little boy knelt next to his grandmother and smoothed her hair and stroked her cheek as he had so many times before. "Grandma's cold," he said. He pulled the chenille spread off the bed and tried to spread it on her and pulled it up to her neck. "Don't worry, Mom," he said. He turned and went into the living room and sat on the couch. I took him onto my lap. He had taken in all that he could absorb.

Across the room was a picture of me in my cap and gown from my high school graduation. And next to it was a photo of me at my college graduation. Aunt Lil had insisted that I get those pictures, and she sent each one to Ellie. I found them beside her bed in her old apartment when I helped her move. Once she unpacked here, she kept them on the mantle in a gold-toned frame she bought that first week at the Woolworth's on Broadway. It struck me, as I looked around this room, that Ellie's only treasured mementos were the pictures of Shawn and me. Ellie didn't have much else. The room was sparsely furnished, with just an end table, coffee table, couch, chair, television, pictures of Shawn and me, and nothing more.

As I rocked Shawn and myself, I heard his heavy sleeping breaths. He had escaped this sadness. He was a wondrous little being who tried to do and be everything I wanted. I knew I was too hard on him and promised myself that I'd try harder to let him have his childhood.

As I hugged Shawn closer, it struck me that there were things to be done. I'd have to call someone about my mother. I put Shawn down on the couch and walked across the room to the phone. I was face to face with my college photo. That young, scared, hopeful kid that I was, caught frozen in an awkward smile, seemed so far away in time. I could feel that time had stretched and sagged my face, and my body was heavy with disappointment and unfulfilled dreams. I felt no grief yet. I didn't know if I could cry for this mother who had shown up so late in my need of her. But standing there in her room of few things, I felt the sadness of loss.

I picked up the telephone and dialed 911. "Yes, hello, this isn't an emergency, but I just got home and found my mother dead." I heard the word "dead" as it tumbled from my lips. It had come out without my trying. The person on the other end of the line was talking, but I had not focused enough to hear her. The word had to make its way into my consciousness.

"Excuse me, what did you say?"

"Ma'am, I think you should call your precinct, and they'll tell you what to do."

I put my finger on the button and dialed. I knew the number by heart from having called it on account of Monroe and Claudette always fighting up on the third floor.

"Hello. I don't know what I should do. My mother has died. I just came home and found her."

"Any reason to believe her death is the result of foul play?"

"No, I think she just died…maybe, old age," I said.

"OK, ma'am, we'll send someone over. Where do you live?" the male voice said in a monotone.

I gave them my address and hung up the receiver and sat awhile in the quiet. It hit me that I didn't know anyone whom I could call to tell of my mother's death. She had no real friends. There were people in the building I could tell tomorrow, but there was no one whose closeness required a call now. My mother had no one except Shawn and me. "Oh God, I've got to talk to somebody," I thought aloud. I picked up the receiver and dialed Jewel's number. I hadn't heard from her since the affair at Tavern on the Green.

"Hello." Jewel's voice sounded cheery.

"Jewel…" I found that my words were trapped in my chest.

"Who's this?"

"It's me, Camille." I was trying to sort out my feelings as I spoke.

"Oh, Camille. Can't talk. I've got a hot date. Gordon's in town," she said. "He called me this afternoon. He's—"

I had to cut in. I didn't want to listen to this chatter now. I felt I was beginning to cry for my mother. I began to hurt in places I didn't know existed. I ached to tell my mother that I hated her and loved her and missed her.

"Jewel, I just lost my mother." I realized when the words came out that what I had said sounded ridiculous. I had not misplaced her somewhere.

"Camille, what did you say? I'm getting dressed, and—"

"I said, I just found her dead on the floor here." As the words flowed out, so did the tears. There was a rushing out of emotion that I could not put into words. I held myself and then placed my hand over my mouth to push back the flood.

"Camille, get a hold of yourself. Calm down. Your mother was never a well woman."

"I know, but...look, I don't know where that came from. God, she's really dead."

"I don't know what to say, Camille."

"There's nothing to say."

There was a long silence. I was lost in a rush of images of my mother. There was a sepia-tone photo, where my mother was wearing platform shoes with the strap around the ankle. There was the picture of her holding me as a baby and smiling at the camera. And there was the mental image of a woman driving down Atlantic Avenue and crashing into a lamppost.

"Someone's knocking." I lied. No one was at the door, but I had to get away from the phone. I went to the kitchen to get the Yellow Pages. It felt oddly jarring to search for a funeral parlor there, but I couldn't think straight, and I didn't know where else to begin. For some reason I could not find the word *funeral*, or even the letters I was searching for. My eyes began to blur, and I stared through the semidarkness at the bedroom. I picked up the phone and dialed Saundra's number. The phone rang and rang until I was just about to hang it up. A thin, weak voice answered.

At first, I thought I had the wrong number. Then, as if I recalled that voice from long ago, I said, "Saundra, is that you?"

There was a long silence. The person drew a breath and then said, "Yes?"

"Saundra, I'm so glad I got you. I just found my mother lying here dead. I'm sitting here waiting for the police to come, and I'm just so lost. I called Jewel, and she tells me she has a date. She's unbelievable. Saundra? You there?"

There was a long silence again. "Not really." Saundra seemed to struggle to get her words out.

"What's the matter? Do you have the flu or something?" As the words left my lips, it hit me. I knew what had happened.

"I just got in from the hospital. Santos came home two nights ago. 'Member the other day when I was talking to you? That day. They said he was coming next week…guess it's this week now…but they let him out on early release. Nobody told me." Her voice was muffled, as if she was crying, trying to stuff the tears and swallow the wail in her mouth.

"What did he do to you?"

She could not speak.

"Saundra, I can't come there; I've got my mother here. I've got Shawn."

"I'm OK. I'm so sorry about your mother, Camille." She began to weep. "Camille, you probably need help, but they gave me these painkillers, and I don't think I can stand up. They wrapped my arm in this sling, because of my shoulder, and my head hurts me…"

"Don't worry about me. What the hell is the matter with that man? Where is he?"

"He barricaded me in the apartment. He heard from someone in my mother's neighborhood that I went out with a white man, Les. He kept hitting me in the face and asking me did I think the white man would want me now. Camille, he hurt me bad. I can't see out of my left eye."

Her voice seemed to be fading away.

"Saundra, are you in bed?"

"Yes. I had to put my head down."

"Why don't you go to sleep? Can you sleep?"

"I don't know. I hurt so bad."

"Did you call your mother?"

"No. I can't bring any of this into her home. She'd never let me see Wanda if I brought any of this over there."

"Saundra, I can't leave here. Are you sure you are all right?"

"I'll be...just feel groggy. You..." Her voice trailed off again.

"Saundra, hang up and rest." I called her name again. There was a click.

The phone rang, and I thought it was Saundra calling back.

"Camille?" Cole's voice was deep and warm and welcome.

"Cole, how did you know to call me here?"

"I can't believe I'm hearing your voice. I called you all yesterday afternoon, but I get these odd times when I'm free. I was calling your mom because I was worried, and I found out today that I'm going to be here another week."

In that brief few minutes, I felt I needed him. I wanted to tell him about my mother, but suddenly he felt so far away.

Cole heard the silence. "I'm sorry, Camille, I've got to stay for special training...something to do with where they are sending us. Looks like we ship out some time around Christmas. I know this is bad news."

I felt numb. There were no resting places.

"Camille, I promise you, someday I'll make this up to you. Are you all right?"

"My mother died tonight, Cole."

"Oh baby, no."

"There's no one here. I called Jewel, and she's...forget her. I called Saundra, and Santos got out of jail and beat her up real bad."

"Camille, I'll get a hardship, and I'll take the first plane out that I can."

"Cole, you can't just do that, can you?"

His presence became so large that for a few minutes, I wanted him to hold me and protect me from everything I had to face. I knew at that moment that I could lose myself in this man.

"If they don't give it to me...shit, now I know how guys just lose their minds and go AWOL."

"Cole. Don't you dare do that. I can handle this. I just needed to talk to you."

"Are you sure? Where's Shawn?"

"He's here. He fell asleep."

"What happened?"

"I don't know. I came up after work. Actually, I got in late, and I just found her lying on the floor. I'm waiting for the police, and I think the coroner's office."

"She's still there with you. I'm so sorry. I can't believe I've spent twenty-nine years of my life in the service, and I can't even come and take care of you without permission. I'm not a man in this fucking uniform. I feel like a fucking eunuch."

"Don't say that, Cole. And please don't do anything stupid like going AWOL. I can handle this."

"But why should you have to?"

"Because I can. Please don't take away my ability to do for myself." I said those words almost before I thought them completely through. I loved him for wanting to be there, but I needed to do this on my own.

"I'm sorry, baby. I just feel so bad that I can't be there. I won't do anything crazy…I have less than a year to put in…just frustrated… just feel bad. I'll call tomorrow."

"I may be at the funeral parlor."

"Maybe I can call my sister to come by—you know, just to watch Shawn so that he doesn't have to go there?"

"No, he'll be with me, and we will be OK. I can do this."

"You sure?"

"I am."

"I'll call anyway to see how you are."

I hung up the phone and looked around my mother's dimly lit living room. I picked up her two ashtrays and her cup from the coffee table. I went into her bedroom and put her slippers in the closet. With the broom, I swept along the baseboards, pushing the bits of dust and hair to the door. In the kitchen, I got my mother's pale-pink, dented old dustpan and pushed the dirt up into it. I didn't want the room to be a mess when they finally came to take my mother away.

The doorbell rang. The task of taking care of my mother began to unfold. I'd take each step as I went along. I could do this. I wanted to curse Jewel for her insensitivity, but that would wait. First I would bury my mother.

For two days I moved through the details of choosing a dress, a casket, and a final resting place for my mother. I had contacted Saundra and told her where they were burying her. She cried when she heard. "Camille, I want to come, but my face. I can't make it look right." She said her left eye was closed, and he had loosened one of the teeth in the right side of her jaw and pounded her right eye purple and blue. The white was now red from the blood that collected there.

I heard sobs on the other end of the line until the click. The air around me grew thick those next days. The emptiness had a substance, which I took in with every breath. Shawn grew quiet and sullen. He just sat and sometimes said, "It's very quiet here, isn't it, Mommy?" I tended to his needs for food, and on the weekend, he would nap at odd times in the day. I let him sleep. I just inhaled the nothingness that surrounded me.

The following week the super helped me clean out the apartment. He said someone in the building had a friend who wanted it and would give him some money if he could get it ready by the end of the first week of December. Midweek, a fat woman with two noisy children came to look at Ellie's place and made plans to move in.

19

JEWEL

I pushed the hangers about in my closet, trying to find something to wear, but Gordon hadn't said where we were going. The buzzer whined from the next room, and looking down at my half-slip and black push-up bra, I pushed the hangers back to reach the back of the rail and pulled out my short Chinese red silk kimono. I did not belt it. I fastened the latch of my pearls and knotted them so that they fell between my breasts. Maybe we'll stay in tonight, I thought. I moved to the intercom, dimming the lights as I went.

"Mr. Gordon Ellis here to see you, Ms. Jamison," Bob announced in his typical gossipy tone.

"Send him up." I ran back to the bedroom for the bottle of Opium, spritzed my wrists with it, and then my cleavage. My excitement overwhelmed me for a moment, and I had to sit on the arm of the sofa so I wouldn't faint. It had been almost four months since I had seen him. I had to force the air into my lungs by taking it in through my nose and my mouth. I'd missed him so much.

The doorbell rang, and I walked to the door, trying to breathe as deeply as I could. When I opened it, there he was. He was wearing a black wool coat and black silk scarf. His glasses had a brown tint, which made it difficult for me to see his eyes. He was so tall, with me in my bare feet. He had this beautiful five-o'clock shadow that turned me on so much. He stood close to the doorframe and seemed to have a strange expression on his face, as if he were annoyed at something. A bad mood, I thought. I know how to fix that.

"Gordon, you look like you could use a drink. Why don't you take off your coat, loosen your tie, and let me fix you one? Better yet, let me open some champagne. We can toast my new office. I missed you at the Tavern on the Green party, but you'll be there in Chicago, won't you?" He had always needed an hour or so to wind down, especially when he was in New York. His schedule here was always so tight. I reached for his coat, and he shrugged it away from my grasp, which I took at first as his rush to get inside.

"Jewel, you cut me off earlier. I told you I wanted to meet you somewhere." He took off his scarf and put his attaché case down in the foyer before he entered the living room.

"This is somewhere. It's central to every restaurant in the city."

"I told you I wanted to talk."

"We can talk here. It's quiet. It's private. Gordon, what's the matter? I called you, I don't know how many times. I told you about the opening event that I wanted you to come to. I open Chicago soon." I moved into the living room toward the bar to take out two glasses.

"Jewel, I keep telling you not to call my office. You've got to stop calling there. My secretary suspects. She knows my wife, my family."

I went from the bar to the kitchen and filled the glasses with ice. I enjoyed moving about in the silk kimono as it opened and revealed my thighs and breasts.

"Look, I came here before the Chicago opening because I want to make something really clear to you," he said, getting to the doorway just as I was coming out carrying the ice-filled glasses. He couldn't take his eyes off my breasts as I moved and they jiggled, inviting his touch.

"What do you care what she thinks? Fire her." I opened the Johnny Walker Black, his favorite, and poured it over the ice.

"It's not that simple," he said, coming in behind me.

I loved making him follow me about. I was putting on a show for him, and he had to run behind me to see it. I made a quickie sloe gin fizz for myself, standing with my back to him, and then turned to hand him his drink.

"Stop! Stand still. I'm trying to talk to you. " He sat on the arm of the sofa.

His mouth and the pout made me kiss him. I held the glasses behind his head. "I know you're angry with me, but I needed to taste you. It's been too long."

He gave in to the kiss and then tried to pull away, taking care not to spill the glasses. "It's not a matter of being mad with you… angry. This is my goddamned life you are playing with."

"This is my life too, Gordon. Do you think I like calling you long distance, wondering what you're doing, when I'm going to see you?"

"I keep telling you, don't call. Don't call me at my office. I came here to tell you face to face. I am working things out with my… Celia. I've been avoiding doing this, but you just don't let up. I…"

"I heard you. I love you. When you don't call, I think maybe you're back with your wife. Is that it? Are you moved back in with her?"

"Not exactly. But I don't want any more complications. I'm dealing with enough. Every day there's a call from you, and I know when you come out there, you think it will be…you're going to expect more from me…you made me feel…"

"I know how I made you feel." There was an opportunity to topple him and take him back. I pulled his coat off with his jacket. He put the drink up on the bar, afraid to spill it, so he did not resist. I ran my fingers over the embroidered initials of his name on his shirt pocket. I opened the top buttons of his shirt and loosened his tie and kissed his neck at his Adam's apple.

"Don't do this. I can't…"

He sounded like a woman who wanted to play hard to get. It was amusing.

"What are you smiling at? My wife saw your messages."

"The messages you didn't answer?" I took a sip from my drink.

"You know what I mean, Jewel. Don't play with me."

"No, I don't."

"My wife came to my office two days ago and brought in my messages and saw that so many were from you. She said, 'This Jewel must have a thing for you.'"

"She's right."

"You know what her reaction was?"

"I could care less."

"She did not yell or scream. Looked like I punched her in the chest."

"Sorry, Gordon, but it's about time she knew." I took another sip of my drink.

"She said, 'I guess this is how it feels to lose your best friend.'"

"So? That has nothing to do with me."

He just looked at me silently with an expression I could not decipher.

"Put things in order, Gordon, so we can move on." I sat on the sofa right where he had made passionate love to me the second time we were together.

He sat down beside me, looking at the air in front of him as if he were trying to collect his thoughts. I felt so full and resolute. It was as if I might simply take him, pluck him from where he was, and have him for myself. I knelt down in front of him and ran my forefinger over his chest, letting my fingernail trace around his nipple. His stomach was flat. He had lost weight since we were last together. I opened his shirt and pulled it out of his pants and kissed his abdomen and then his stomach. He began to lose himself, and I took control of him. I pulled his head toward me and kissed him, tasting his lips and then his tongue, drawing it into me. "I don't understand how you can do this to me. Stay away from me so long. All I want is to make you feel good. You know how I hurt for you," I said as I kissed his face and pulled his belt back through the loop of his pants.

His surrender was delicious. It was always that way between us, since the evening we met. He had always seemed to hide his passion, making me have to look for it, like a child searching her father's pockets for the gift he had brought her. I loved the game and wouldn't stop until I found it. It was a familiar starting point, and as he responded to my touch, I unclasped his pants. He seemed poised to allow me my way. He leaned back and breathed in deeply as I tasted him. "You are luscious. I missed you," I said, looking up at him, his eyes closed as he enjoyed the pleasure I was giving. So I enjoyed holding him and tasting him again. I could tell he had missed me too. His hand toyed with my breast and lifted it out of the cup that offered it up. "Come inside, Gordon." I stood up, taking his hand and trying to lead him to the bedroom. He was mine.

He followed. I took off my kimono and let it fall at the foot of the bed, and I unfastened my bra and freed my breasts. He smothered his face in them, kissing and taking them into his mouth. "Gordon, you are so good to me." His shirt was off already, and he stopped briefly to pull his pants off. His body was in silhouette because of the light from the living room that was behind him. He pulled my panties off, and when he climbed on top of me, I could feel his desire for me fully.

"Why do you do this to me?" he said, now fitting tightly where I wanted him.

"Because I love to make you feel good."

And then I did. I took him into me over and over again until the muscles inside me pulsated. Then I rolled him over and took control. I knew how to take him in and pull away just enough so that he hungered for me. It was so easy to have him, take him, bring him to the point of such pleasure, that he lost himself to me. I let myself quiver all over him. He was so easy. And there he was, my deflated poor baby. It made me laugh inside. I leaned down to kiss his lips.

Without warning he pushed me back, making me fall backward onto the bed. "Stop that! You make me sick." He pulled away from me and sat on the side of the bed. "You don't listen."

He grabbed his pants and walked out to the living room. I heard him then in the bathroom.

"You think that you can use sex to control me," he said, pulling on his trousers and looking in through the doorway.

"That's not what you were saying a few minutes ago." I sat up and looked for my kimono and walked over to it.

"Shut up. You sicken me. You're like a whore who is never satisfied. I can't believe I came here again. I let you do this again." The force of his words threw me back on to the bed and then suffocated me.

"Why are you saying that?"

"You don't stop. I came here to talk to you. Don't call me at my office again. Do you hear me?"

I sat in a place in my mind on a tiny stool all alone.

"You love me. Why did you say that to me?"

"I never loved you. I never ever said I loved you. I told you being with you was a mistake. I have tried not to hurt you, because you seem so needy."

"What does that mean?"

"Forget it. I can't explain it. You are relentless. I am not going to carry on an affair. I came here to tell you that. Don't call me anymore."

"You don't mean that."

"I do. I love my wife." He buttoned his shirt and pushed it into his pants.

"Well, what was this? What were you doing here?"

"This was lust. You think that screwing someone—*getting some,* as you put it—is love. You don't have a clue what love is. This was just sex."

His words punched me in the belly.

Gordon grabbed his coat, walked to the door of the apartment, picked up his briefcase and left.

I sat with the quiet and retreated in my mind far to the back where I could be by myself, where no one could see me.

That's not nice, what you said to me. I am not a whore. I am not needy. I just wanted you to love me. I don't understand why they just won't love me like I want them to.

෧

The last weeks in October, the weather grew cold. I went out only to do my laundry and bring in some food, because I dreaded being away from home too long in case Eric called. I hadn't heard from him since September. Camille called me and asked me to go to a meeting of the Black Student Union once, and then to a teach-in on the war, and I had said no both times. Camille and Saundra came over and spent the night. We all stayed up till dawn talking about how shaky men were.

I spent the weeks reliving a kaleidoscope of emotions. I wanted Eric to call more than anything. I hated him for being able to hurt me so much. I expected too much. Because I needed him to be, I just expected that he would be there. Life isn't like that, I said to myself. So I killed him, took two Darvon, and lay on my bed waiting for sleep. It finally came.

The phone rang, startling me.

"Hello." His voice was deep.

I didn't know what to say to him. He was a ghost.

"So, how have you been?" Eric filled in the space. It was untidy.

"Fine. And you?" I wished that I could say what I wanted to say.

"I got through the first round of exams. Law school pressure…a little awesome."

I didn't want to talk to him.

"I'm running a bath, Eric. I was about to get in. I have to go shut the water, so…"

"So, can I join you?"

"I was going to say I have to go."

"Go shut the water. I'll wait."

I wanted to hang up. I lay there covering the mouthpiece of the phone, pretending to have gone inside.

"Look, Eric, I'm very busy, and—"

"Fine. I just thought before I got heavy into the books for finals, I could see you. If not, hey, that's fine too."

Eric's icy statement poked holes in my facade. "You know, Eric, you are very cool, calling here after six weeks—or is it seven, eight—acting as if nothing has happened. You go to bed with me. You knew how scary that was for me. It was the first time for me. The very first time for me, and you don't even call me."

I had said too much. I had exposed myself again. "Look, don't call here anymore. OK?"

"I don't believe this. Me, me, me! I went to bed with you. I don't even call you. It was scary for you. You seemed to enjoy it. You looked damned content when I left. You think because I went to bed with you, as you put it, that my whole goddamned life revolves around you. Listen, when I finished up at Columbia, I had arrangements to make at Brooklyn Law, because of the screw-up at NYU. I had things to do that were important to my future." He spat out the words in a staccato fashion. "You see things from a damned self-centered place. Fuck it!"

"Eric, wait a minute."

"What the hell for?"

"I didn't realize that. I felt lost when you didn't call."

"Hey, don't pin that on me."

"I'm just saying that I wanted to see...be with you, and you weren't there."

"I was busy. I'm not going to apologize for—"

"I'm not asking for apologies. I'm only trying to tell you how I felt."

The floodgate opened, and the hurt spilled out all over the place. I was crying, and I was embarrassed.

"Look, Jewel, I've got a lot of things I have to do in the next few years. You seem to want some kind of involved relationship. I thought maybe we could have some fun together from time to time. My mistake. No hard feelings."

"I've got things to do too. I don't know why I laid this whole thing on you. I only want to see you again. It doesn't have to be anything heavy. I just didn't know. I thought I'd never see you again."

"That's what I'm saying. I could see you today, have papers and exams, and be tied up the rest of the term. I can't give you any timetable."

"I know. Eric, I just want to see you."

"You know how I feel about games. I'm being as straight as I can with you. I like spending time with you, but that's it. No strings."

"I just want to see you, that's all."

"Are you sure?"

"Yes."

"You said you were busy with something. When will you be free?"

"You can come over anytime. I was just angry when I said that."

"Well, I'll be over in an hour or so."

There was a click, and the line was dead. I put the phone down. The tears flowed from my eyes. My thoughts wandered aimlessly, lost in a maze of desire and fear. I looked around my bedroom as if there were an answer somewhere in the walls, ceiling, floors, furniture. There was none. Through my tears, the room looked wrinkled. There was only one small space of clarity in my mind: I would never have him as I hoped. I searched for a way of being at ease with that. It did not come.

Two hours later, he still had not arrived. By then, I figured he wasn't coming. I had a glass of wine. It was midnight when he rang the bell. I hated him for doing this to me, but when I saw him, I needed him to touch me. There was tension between us. It was as if the air connecting us was filled with silky thin fiber that vibrated with each word spoken. I served the wine I had bought six weeks earlier in the now not-so-new wine glasses.

Once I had a few glasses of wine, I was able to suppress any thought of tomorrow. I drew pleasure from the moment, and it was sufficient. I lit the candle in the bedroom. We made love twice. The first time, I simply studied him. There was no orgasm. The second time, pleasure and pain sliced deep in my abdomen. There was a schism. My mind and body were two separate entities. I observed myself from the inside. There was a quaking there, as if my body were trying desperately to close the wound.

His dead weight pressed all air from my chest, and I contemplated dying there. It was a toy thought, as light as a brightly colored beach ball. I tossed it off. For just a moment, he took on the same significance for me. He was a plaything that had outlived its pleasantness, so I flung him off.

"Eric, I can't breathe." I pushed him off my chest. I got up and went to the bathroom to pee. I went into the kitchen to find the cigarettes I had bought the day before. They were half gone. I lit one, inhaled as deeply as I could, and expelled the smoke. It made me feel a little dizzy. In the living room, I poured another glass of wine and then emptied the bottle into Eric's glass. I carried them both into the bedroom. He lay on the bed, motionless, deflated. After placing his glass on the night table, I walked around the bed, propped up the pillows, and sat up with my outstretched legs crossed at the ankles. I was waiting to watch him leave. The stage was set. I had had the finale. Applause was inappropriate. Certainly the curtain had come down. It was the play after the play. I read the line I had written in my mind.

"Eric, it's two thirty. Didn't you say you had reading to do tomorrow?"

There was no response. I pushed him.

"Eric, you said you wanted to get home early tonight."

"Huh? I must've dozed off."

"Well, if you want to get home..."

"I could stay and leave in the morning."

"No, I have reading to do tomorrow too. So it probably would be better if you left now."

A gust of cool air swept into the room, as if on cue. I felt the chill, but my body welcomed it.

"Are you up, Eric?" This line was not planned. I said it without thinking.

He sat up and walked into the bathroom. "Are you putting me out?" he asked as he reentered the room. He pulled on his jeans.

"What do you mean?"

"I mean you woke me up. You are very insistent that I leave all of sudden. Your voice has an edge in it, sharp enough to disembowel me." He then buttoned his shirt, sat on the bed, and put on his shoes.

"I think you're imagining things, Eric. You said you wanted to go home tonight. I was only reminding you. I do have about two hundred pages of reading to do tomorrow."

"I'm going. I'll call you."

"OK. Good luck with law school."

"I'll call before I'm finished."

"Whenever."

I got up and walked over to him, and he took a step back. I initiated a kiss, which seemed to surprise him. He walked to the door, and, I guess because I was close behind him, he turned and kissed me deeply. I stifled a choking sensation and replaced it with a smile on my lips and in my eyes.

Slightly off balance, he exited. I locked the door and put on the chain. As I walked into the bedroom, I turned out the lights. The candle cast a warm glow on the bedroom. The flame reflected in the half-filled wine glass on the side of the bed where Eric had been. I reached over for it, positioned myself in the middle of the bed, and drank it down. I felt a magnificent surge of self-possession. The smile on my face was now real. I blew out the candle. Sleep came like a welcome lover. I wrapped my arms 'round him, and he lifted me up and took me off.

20

CAMILLE

I t was a midnight-blue suede vest that caught my eye. The mannequin wearing it was posed with his jacket open and pulled back at the waist. It was the kind of blue in which one becomes lost, like in a velvet summer-night sky. Cole would look great in that, I thought. I had already bought him a Christmas present, a sweater, rugged looking. But the vest was something special. When I saw it, I wanted it for him. It was impulsive, something I hadn't remembered ever doing for a man. It was strange.

Two stores down, in the window, I saw the X-Men action figures Shawn wanted. For days I had searched for them. I turned into the toy store and pushed past two women to get the counterman's attention. He pointed down the aisle, where I found stacks of the cellophane-wrapped packages ready for sale.

Walking up Broadway, I enjoyed the colored lights and strains of Christmas music that spilled out onto the sidewalks. As I got to my building and unlocked the heavy metal door, I felt someone coming up behind me. Quickly, I slammed the door shut. I ignored the knocking and went to the mailbox. Do they think I'm fool enough to open that door? I thought. I pulled out the bright red and green envelopes, feeling guilty about not having sent out my own Christmas cards yet this year. I wondered if I could send the box of stamped, addressed, and sealed cards from last year sitting in the closet, or if I had written something timely in one. I never really was any good at getting Christmas cards out. Sitting down and calling folk during the week after Christmas to talk was more my style. The muffled call of my name at the door filtered into my consciousness. I cautiously peeked around the corner of the darkened hallway wall to see Cole wiping away the mist from the diamond-shaped windowpane.

"Cole, is that you? I don't believe it." I struggled to hold the pieces of mail and turn the knob to open the door. Before I thought about it, my arms were around his neck, hugging him close to me, packages and all.

"I missed you so much," he said.

"Where's Shawn? I have so many things for him for Christmas."

"A sleepover. And it's not Christmas yet."

Cole was silent.

He tried to take my packages as I unlocked the apartment door and reached back to turn on the kitchen light. Once inside, Cole craned his neck to see into the living room.

"Where's the tree?"

"I didn't set it up yet. I haven't been in the mood. Today is really the first day I even felt like shopping. Cole, you're worse than Shawn." I turned to enjoy his laughter and then noticed he was wearing his dress uniform. "Well, look at you. Blue is your color, isn't it?"

"My schedule was crazy. We got in, then I had to go to an award ceremony earlier. No time to change. They have me in the office for the next few days familiarizing the replacement officer with follow-ups he has to do."

I was taken with the dark-blue uniform, his blue pants with the blood-red stripe down the sides. With his white gloves and his white hat resting gently in his hands, he looked beautiful to me. I couldn't help but smile at him for no reason other than the pleasure of taking in his image. What is happening to me? I thought.

We put down the packages, and I looked down at the envelopes that I had mechanically placed on the kitchen table.

"Sorentz Associates? Cole, this is the agent I sent my poetry and short stories to. I ended that with a preposition," I added, laughing nervously. As I stuck my index finger under the flap and opened the envelope, I accidentally tore the entire back of it trying to get the letter out.

"Cole they're interested, especially in the short stories. They say they want to discuss representation. They want to meet with me at my earliest convenience." I sat staring at the letter.

"I told you they would be interested," Cole said. "I think we should celebrate."

"Do you think that it might really get published? I've got to tell Saundra. I'm pissed as hell at Jewel, but I should call her too." I got up and took the telephone off the wall cradle and began to dial.

Cole watched me, waiting till I called. He looked impatient, as if he had something on his mind. I pointed to the phone and nodded, letting him know she had picked up.

"Saundra? I got you. I can't believe it. I didn't know whether to call you there or at your mother's. What are you doing tonight, right now? You want to come out to celebrate with Cole and me?"

"Camille, I don't know. My face is still...well, the area around my eye is still a little yellow-green. You know how funny my skin is."

"Girl, put some makeup on your eye and come on out with us."

"What is it? Camille, are you getting married?"

I looked over at Cole, smiling and shaking my head. "Just come out with us, and I'll tell you. Where should we go, Cole?"

"Why don't we go downtown to B. Smith's? I could go for some soul food before I go away. Down on Forty-Sixth and Broadway."

"B. Smith's. I've never been. Cole says it has good soul food. So, Saundra, come on. Just come, girl. Don't worry about money. Just come on. Is eight good?" I said to Cole. He nodded. "Saundra, about eight."

I deliberated about calling Jewel. I had not heard from her since the night my mother died. She had sent flowers four days later, but that was not what I needed. I felt as if they had been sent as a polite afterthought. I swallowed the hurt and thought, someday, when we are old and gray, I'll bless her out for that one.

"What's the matter, babe?"

I picked up the phone. It seemed to ring forever. "Jewel? No, it's me, Camille. Just wondering…I got some good news and was wondering if you could come out with us to celebrate tonight. Why don't you come down to B. Smith's?"

"What're you celebrating? Who's coming? You got the principalship?"

"Saundra and Cole and you. It's a secret. We're thinking eight."

"I can't believe I got them both. They are so funny." I laughed. "Saundra guessed that were getting married, and Jewel asked if I got the principal's position."

"I love to hear you laugh," Cole said. "It's like you filled the room with confetti and toy balloons." He began to laugh too.

"Camille, do you think you can hold still a few minutes? I've been sitting out in that car waiting to talk to you. I need to ask you something."

It was interesting how the authority in his voice had commanded my attention at first, and then, when I looked up at him, his voice cracked a bit.

"You look all mushy faced. I don't know if I want to hear this."

"I have something for you…" He started to take something out of his shopping bag.

I felt sideswiped. I had wanted to see and hold him. I missed his loving presence, which seemed to effervesce about me when he was near. The sound of his voice had strengthened me the night my mother died. The past two weeks, I had filled the void created by his leaving with the anticipation of his return. Without realizing it, my thoughts gently took him in here and there and allowed him to be with me. I had taken him in at the department store and placed him in that vest. But I was scared to death of what he might say.

"Cole, I didn't wrap yours yet, but why don't I give it to you first," I said.

"No, just open it, Camille," he said, and he took out a scarf-sized box wrapped in gold foil paper. I felt more at ease seeing the shape of the gift. I carefully peeled the tape, and the white box top seemed to give way to the pressure of the contents that stuffed the box to capacity. It was filled with red tissue, and when I pulled it back, a pair of long black leather gloves was nestled there.

"They are absolutely beautiful, and so soft," I whispered, touching them ever so lightly with my fingertips.

"Aren't you going to try them on?"

"These are just too beautiful. I'm usually out with Shawn and with the kids at school. Where would I wear these?"

"You'll wear them anywhere you go. See if they fit. You can wear them tonight."

As I put my hand into the left glove, I felt tissue paper stuffed in the finger and opened the glove to look inside. I pulled it out and noticed it had a tiny gold ribbon tied around it. I pressed it and felt the outline of a ring. "Cole, you..." the words got caught in my throat. His trusting face told me I had to sort through my feelings and my words very carefully.

"Cole, I think we should think this through a little. This is not something you do impulsively. We should take our time with something like this. If we wait until you come back and we spend more time together and we know if this is right..."

His eyes flashed cold.

"Thinking about leaving is probably what's getting to you. You could wake up a week from now and say, what am I doing?"

"I don't ever do something without being dead sure, Camille. I want to marry you. I'd like to do it before I leave. If I don't come back, I want to leave some things in place for you and Shawn. I've thought this through."

He searched my eyes. For some reason, I did not avoid his gaze. I looked into his eyes, trying to understand this man who seemed to love me.

"What happened when you were away? And how could you even consider going AWOL?"

"Nothing but the same old stuff, babe. I'm a master sergeant in the US Marines. The AWOL thing was just my frustration...not being able to be here when your mother died. Sometimes it binds me. Did you read that book, *Beloved*?"

"Toni Morrison's book? You read that book, Cole?"

"Why do you say it like that? A woman friend I knew was reading it, and I picked it up...to see what it was about."

"I just never thought of you..."

"Anyway, she was describing this man. I can't remember the character's name, but he lived back in the days of slavery, and she described how they took him and put a *bit* in his mouth. And I remembered going over and over that passage 'cause I couldn't believe what I was reading. I couldn't believe they would put a *bit* like they put in a horse's mouth in a man's mouth. But so many times, I feel like I have a bit in my mouth." He paused to draw breath.

"I have to finish this, 'cause I set it out for myself, but every so often, lately, especially since you and Shawn, I've been thinking this is no life for a black man. There are things I want to say, and I can't say them. There are things I want to do, and I can't do them."

"That's what I mean. Maybe it's not us. Maybe it's just the marines and going away."

"Camille, I've gone away more times than I care to remember. I've always gotten a kind of high from it. Can't explain it. It's an adrenaline kind of thing. Packing your gear. And sometimes it's not like the civilians think. This woman once told me she thought it was like being in a romantic movie. It's not like that at all. It's as if all of a sudden you're real. Everything is real. It's like your senses are going wild. It's like you're more alive when you go away to fight than when you're at home. And then, sometimes, it's as if you just wish you could turn it all off, and you can't. You just pray that when it's over, you're in one piece with all the parts you went away with."

He paused, seeming to assess where he was going with his thoughts, and said, "Look, they're sending us somewhere to keep one army of guys from killing some other army of guys. They say I should give a damn about them, when I see them come to my country and step in front of me and mine. Now, you see, I've got a bit in my mouth. I can't say that out loud. I'm just supposed to say 'Yes, sir' and salute." Cole's nostrils flared as he drew in air. "Well, I'm having a real hard time with that. Now, I feel I can justify in myself to go, because I don't like hearing about women getting raped and babies bein' killed, but I sure as hell would have more reason to be protecting some kind of something in America if I was doing it for you and Shawn. Maybe that's not a good enough reason to get married, besides the fact that I love you, but, hey."

There was a silence in the room that filled up all available space and pasted itself onto the flesh. It felt cold and still. A crease had etched itself into Cole's brow. It was slanted and looked a bit like a gash that needed mending. I wanted to rub and smooth it away, pressing it out, so that the pain would be erased. There had been so much more to this man that I had not known. The writer in me wanted to push aside any obstructions and poke about inside him and have him inform my soul. The woman in me wanted to hide from him, finding his words to be too real and his world too raw.

"Cole, I need to think about this."

"I know. Let me just tell you, if we're gonna do it, we have only three days to decide so that we can get the license. I'll be shipping out on the twenty-third."

"The twenty-third? Why the twenty-third? They're making you leave before Christmas?"

"The orders say the twenty-third, babe. Welcome to the service. They want us there by Christmas. I've got to help set up administrative quarters in one of the sectors."

"That doesn't make any sense. Just based on morale, it's stupid."

"This is about war and peacekeeping. I'm a marine. I better have good morale. This is my last tour. If I come back from this, I'll have my thirty years in." He shook his head. There was the gravest sense of loss in his eyes. He avoided looking at me. I looked away because he seemed as if he might cry and that it was something he would not wish to share.

"So…" he said, trying to regain a semblance of happiness, "will you marry me this week is on the back burner cookin'. Do you want to get engaged?"

"You are funny. You are the straightest guy I ever met."

"Is that a yes?"

"Suppose you meet someone else and fall head over heels in love."

"Camille, I've been there, done that. And here I am. I'm the one who knows what I want. It's you who doesn't."

I could tell he would not back away from the confrontation. That was what I liked about him. His perseverance. I understood it viscerally. Persistence was also a part of who I was. "Sometimes I worry that we're too alike. You don't give up, do you?"

"Not without a struggle."

"Me too."

"I know."

"You really think we should do this."

"I think we should go the whole nine yards and get married. Camille, I want to take care of you."

"That's what I mean. I don't need taking care of."

"Everyone needs to be taken care of sometimes. Are you going to open that tissue and look at that ring? See if you like it."

I can't believe I'm really considering this. *He's good to you,* I heard Saundra say. It felt so strange to have this man want to give me a ring and ask me to marry him. It was so totally outside of anything I expected to happen to me that it was not real. I untied the gold ribbon and opened the tissue. The ring was so lovely sitting there on the red tissue. It sparkled so. I could feel a tear in my eye resting on my eyelash.

"Cole, it is just so very beautiful." The tear fell and ran down my cheek. He kissed my cheek where it first fell.

"Can I place it on, Camille?"

I put my hand in his, and it began to shake. The trueness in his eyes that seemed to reverberate through his being was what drew me. He was good, and he loved me. He cloaked me in a velvety caring that felt warm and cozy. It was as if I could rest a bit. He placed the ring on my finger and kissed me. I held him.

It was curious having him needing me. It was a new sensation. I had never felt that Victor needed me. Derrick certainly didn't need me. But Cole wanted me, and he needed me to be. There was something beautiful about that. Something wonderfully lovely and painful all mingled together where it could not be separated out ever again.

Cole seemed so taken with me not saying no that he disappeared into me saying yes. He held on to it and to me as tightly as he could. "So do you want to celebrate?"

"Aren't you wonderful."

It began as a tiny wisp of thought as I looked at him. His back was to me as he was filling a glass with cold water. The thought was so delicate and slight that I feared I might rend it if I said it aloud. I think I can love this man. His shoulders were so broad and his back so straight that I wished I could drape myself about him and rest there forever. I don't know how I feel about this dandelion fluff of an idea of love, I thought. I am afraid to breathe, or I might blow it away.

He turned around to face me, and I guess since he had no words to express how he felt, a smile inside of him spread all over his face. "Let's celebrate. Let's go out and eat some ribs, and some corn bread, and some potato salad…"

"And some greens," I added, picking up his cadence.

"Sure thing. Some greens, and some peach cobbler. A good dinner. I'm hungry just talkin' about it."

"Me too." I laughed, enjoying the lightness in the room.

"Go change or whatever you want to do. Let's go celebrate us for a while."

21

FUGUE

1a: a musical composition in which one or two themes are repeated
or imitated by successively entering voices
2: a disturbed state of consciousness

Jewel

What is that buzzing sound? It pierced my ear, or was it already there? The room was charcoal gray except for the red digital numbers that glowed six ten. The shade and the drapes were closed so I wouldn't see any light. I knew it was evening because Verta had just awakened me to tell me about the day.

"Jewel? You all right?"

"Yes, fine."

"Just to let you know, the travel agent called, said she got you on the flight to Chicago for the date you want, but it's an early one... you there?"

"Yes. I said yes."

"Everything's set for the reception in Chicago."

Why is she bothering me with all this? Can't she just do this? I wanted to shut my eyes.

"Jewel..."

"Yes, yes. Something else?"

"Tonio called back and said he'd like to use Nadege in the show."

"Is that all, Verta?"

"Look, I just wanted to catch you up. Oh, and I wanted to talk to you about the Christmas gifts."

"Some other time, Verta. I can't concentrate." I wish they would just leave me alone. I hung up.

Have to pull myself together to face being in Chicago without him. There's that buzzing again. The phone again? Didn't I tell her to leave me alone?

"Verta, can you please just—"

"Jewel…it's me, Camille. Just wondering, I got some good news and was wondering if you could come out with us to celebrate tonight."

They keep talking in my head. She's got a new job. Good for her. I'll go. Maybe it will take my mind off Gordon.

"B. Smith's at eight? Sure."

I hate going there by myself. And Camille will have her boyfriend there. He has a thing for me. Last time he undressed me with his eyes. I know I undressed him. Maybe later.

Perhaps Dennis. He won't come. I need him to come, so he won't. I don't want to go there with no one. Well, he won't get any work, either. This is your second chance, Dennis. I don't believe in three strikes. I turned on the light and pulled my telephone book out and dialed his number.

"I'd like to chat with you about the direction of your career, before I leave for Chicago, but it has to be this evening."

"This evening?" He paused.

Don't do this, Dennis.

"OK. Sure…I can make it."

"My apartment, 7 West Seventy-Second Street, in an hour or so?"

I expected to hear him say no. There was no struggle. He seemed excited when he said, "I can be there by seven thirty."

"Wear something casual chic—in case we go out for a bite, that is…"

I sat up in bed to head for the bathroom to wash my face. The picture of Gordon and me at the Grammys was on the night table. I turned it face down. Didn't want to see his face…big mistake to stay home with my memories of him. Pictures of him, mementos of his trips, the pressed flowers, and his love notes were everywhere. There were photos on the wall in the foyer so that he would be there as I entered the apartment and there as I left to face the day.

The city glowed through the sheers in the living room. On the end table was the photo I had asked a stranger to take of us at Central Park. My knees felt weak. I had to sit. Alone with him for days, I could not bear to tear his images from the wall. The day he left, I conjured up the image of ripping his pictures down, tearing them into pieces, and throwing them off the terrace. When I saw the scene played out in my mind, I could only weep wanting to hold on to him so, seeing myself floating down after the tiny bits of paper, desperately trying to pluck them from the air. I could not stop myself. I dialed his private line.

"Hello."

His voice filled my ear, my mind, and I felt it fill my soul.

"Gordon, I'm so glad you answered. I know you're peeved with me. After you left here, I thought I'd kill myself. I can wait. I know it's going to take time to…" I wanted to kiss his lips. I wanted him to hold me and to tell me everything was fine, just real busy.

There was silence.

"So, how are you? I'm thinking of flying in so that we can talk. How is it in Chicago? It's getting really cold here. I've just been—"

"When I was in New York I explained things to you. I've rearranged things with Celia, and it's working out. I told you to stop calling here. If you don't stop, I'm going to have to take some kind of legal action."

"Legal action?"

"You heard me."

I couldn't talk. I wished I could cry, but I couldn't do that either.

"You've got to stop, because it's done. Neither one of us needs any bad publicity."

"What?"

"I said it's done. If you make me go the legal route, it will get ugly."

There was a click, and then silence.

I don't understand why he keeps saying that. It's not done. You need some time. Everything will be fine. I just need to get out of here. I'll go see Camille, celebrate her new job.

I needed to feel strong and powerful again. I shouldn't have called him. *Dennis'll take me. Gordon thinks he'll be happy without me. I am perfect for him. We are perfect together. He said so. Or did I say so? You're dead, Gordon.*

There was that buzzing sound in my head again. I searched for where it came from as I walked into the bathroom. The noise came from over there and stuffed itself into my ear.

The water running on my wrists helped. I cupped my hands and held the pools of it up to my face and let my eyes rest there in the coolness. The mirror didn't lie. My eyes were puffy and red. Where are my drops? I opened the medicine cabinet and pulled the bottle out. I held my eye open and squeezed in the solution. It ran down my cheek. Did my best to make up my face, and I put on a black silk blouse and a pair of black slacks. The Merry Widow, I thought as I painted my lips and made myself laugh.

"Yes, I am perfect for him," I said as I looked at myself in the full-length mirror.

As I started to feel like myself, I decided to call B. Smith's and ask them to make up a platter of appetizers like they usually prepared for the office. By the time I hung up the phone, the intercom was sounding. B. Smith's will be a good place to cater my engagement party when he comes to his senses, I thought.

"Ms. Jamison. This is James. There's a Mr. Dennis Howell here to see you."

"Who?"

"A Mr. Dennis Howell? He says you are expecting him."

"James, could you let Mr. Howell make himself comfortable in the lobby and send him up in five minutes." Howell? Thought we changed that. Won't work for acting.

Time to put thoughts about Gordon away for the time being. Gordon, you do realize we have to straighten all this out soon, so I can be a June bride.

The intercom hummed. He was on his way up. I wanted so much to rest. "Where are my pills?" The kitchen...where are they...shelf over the sink. Just one, to make my hands stop shaking.

The doorbell rang. I waited a minute or so, took a deep breath, put on a smile, and pulled the door open. Dennis was wearing a camel-hair coat over a toffee-colored suit with a cream shirt. His dark skin framed by the smoky-brown glass in the hallway gave him the appearance of a cherished sepia-toned photograph. For a minute he reminded me of Eric. Boy, where did he come from? He was a vision.

I stared at his face for a full minute or two before realizing that I should allow him to enter. As he stepped into the living room, it seemed to brighten. His hand, which had been behind his back, was now outstretched.

Flowers. I took them, still not speaking, and he then produced the other package as if by magic. This boy-man, who had walked out of an old picture to bring me gifts, delighted me.

I began to tear at the paper that concealed the flowers, and when I saw the roses, I lifted them, paper and all, to take in the scent.

"How lovely. I must get these into water," I said in a breathless exhale, moving into the kitchen as Dennis followed.

"I needed these. I don't know how you could have known, but I really needed these today."

He didn't seem to understand or to focus too closely on what I said. Instead, he leaned comfortably against the doorjamb, holding the other package and watching me arrange the roses.

"Would you like some white wine?" he asked.

The tension in my chest seemed to disappear. It was the boy. Then, without wanting to, I could hear Gordon's voice. "It's done."

It's not done. I know it's not done.

"Hello there" came a voice from just outside my private thoughts. "Ms. Jamison?"

"I...I'm sorry. Where was I? Call me Jewel, please." My right hand started to tremble again. I rested it in my left to hold it steady.

The boy's neatly manicured fingers moved so nimbly as he opened the bottle that I could not take my eyes off them. He seemed so at ease with himself that I leaned back against the counter and became his audience as he poured the wine into the glasses.

"You do that so well, it's as though you've been doing it forever. How old are you? Sometimes I look at you, and you're so poised, it's as though you're forty."

"My mother says I'm an old soul. I'm twenty-three."

He handed me a glass, took the other for himself, and lifted it toward me. I sat down on a barstool near the center island to collect myself.

"Sorry I asked." I thought about becoming forty-five in June, closer to fifty than I could bear.

Dennis twisted the cork off the corkscrew, gently placed it on the mouth of the bottle, and then eased it back in. Shit, he's turning me on. He rinsed the corkscrew and placed it in the drainer. I sipped a bit more of the wine and enjoyed the sight of him. Wet hot. I decided it was time to take him out and show him off.

"Dennis, what time is it?"

He looked at the inside of his wrist, checking the time. The gesture pulled my eyes to his hands again. Long fingers.

"It's seven thirty-five."

"A few old college friends called me a little while ago and asked me to go out to dinner. You want to run downtown with me for a short stop, an obligation?"

"Of course," he said without pausing.

I finished the glass of wine, moved to the foyer, and opened the closet door. "Should I wear my mink coat? It's a little chilly out, isn't it?" I loved wearing my mink. It was the one gift I had bought for myself that I loved having on when I was out with a man. I saw it as a play within a play. As I put it on and felt it on my body, it said that I could buy whatever I wanted for myself. I didn't need a man to do it for me. To the public, it was this magical garment that turned heads, especially of women, other black women and white women. Invariably they would look at the man on my arm. I watched them calculating about whether or not it was a gift. When I was out with Gordon, sometimes I would catch their eye and participate fully in the play, trying to make them wonder further by stroking it, and then his arm.

"I guess," said Dennis.

"You guess what?" I asked, having lost myself for a minute or two. I handed Dennis the coat and put my arms into the sleeves, looking at him over my shoulder.

"The coat...never mind."

His voice made me turn my head to look at his mouth. His lips were crowned by this wisp of a mustache. "We've got to get you lots and lots of work. You're just too beautiful to behold." I made him blush.

I called the doorman to get us a cab. It was waiting when we got downstairs.

"This is some sort of celebration for my friend Camille...B. Smith's Restaurant, Forty-Sixth and Broadway," I said to the driver. "She's getting a promotion to principal or something. You may remember them from the restaurant..."

"Do they know I'm coming?"

"No, but we're not staying long. I know the owner there. They cater parties for me, so I'll just have them make up a platter of goodies. We'll go, maybe make a toast, and then split. I don't have much in common with them anymore."

As I entered the restaurant, I tiptoed to see over the line of people waiting to be seated and then moved past them. There was a beautiful Christmas tree in the anteroom. "Lovely tree, Randy. Is Bea in town?"

"Not tonight, Ms. Jamison."

"Can you secure my coat, please?" I said, taking my arm out of the sleeve.

"Of course," he said, taking it. "And you can come right this way. We have your table waiting."

As I turned back to survey the crowd, my eyes met Camille's. "Camille, come. I called ahead and had them set aside my table." I leaned over to offer my cheek to her. "I know what kind of wait there can be here on a Friday night. I've been so busy. I've had you on my mind for weeks. Hi, Cole. Don't you look wonderful?" I winked at him and waved them to follow me behind the maître d'.

As usual, B. Smith's had a warm buzz and chatter that said people out enjoying one another. Dishes and glasses clinked, and conversations and laughter flowed together and bubbled about and seemed to glisten in the glow of the colorful décor. Jazz renditions of Christmas music were playing in the background. It felt good to be out.

Camille

We followed Jewel into a room that was very beautiful and a little quieter than the previous one. Once we were seated, Cole seemed uneasy. He called the waiter and whispered something in his ear. I looked down at the ring on my finger and marveled at how it picked up the light and tossed it about. I thought about how much had changed since September. Ruby's death had made me think about who I was, separate and apart from my work at school, and had made me value time. That event had made me seek out and find my friends, who were my connections to my childhood. My thoughts traveled back to Hancock Street and where I first remembered myself. From the day I had found them, I felt grounded, as if

I had roots that had settled in and anchored me. I had finally sent out my manuscript. The sense of calm I felt flowed back in time and somehow seemed to stretch forward into the future.

It felt so peaceful to know that my friends were all coming together to celebrate my book, my engagement, and what seemed like a whole new beginning. The coming together of all those thoughts filled me with emotion, and before I could stop myself, my eyes began to tear. I wondered where Saundra was. I hoped that she wasn't letting her bruises stop her from being here.

Cole looked so handsome. He had his hand in his vest pocket. It looked as if he needed a watch with a gold chain to play with there. He made me smile. I had given him the vest just before I changed clothes. When he opened the box, he brushed the vest with his hand and looked at me as if to say, I didn't think you would do this. Then he said he was going out to the car to get his turtleneck and his sports jacket to change into it. I laughed at his impatience, saying he was just like Shawn. He playfully shook his finger at me and said, "No time like the present. Think about it." He then kissed my ring finger and then my nose.

"I think I see Saundra," he said.

I turned and looked at the entranceway to the room and waved in Saundra's direction. Her movement toward the table seemed strained, and she held her head tilted downward as if she did not want anyone to look directly at her. I got up and hugged her, holding her and telling her I was so glad she had come. Her embrace felt as if she were clutching at something that was eluding her.

"Hey, Jewel. How you been?" She seemed to wince from the pain in her shoulder when she hugged Jewel. "How're you doin', Cole? Been thinkin' about you, hearin' what was on the news."

"Headed out in ten days. Tryin' to get this lovely lady to marry me before I go."

"Get out of here. I knew it. I said that. Didn't I?" Saundra said, hugging Cole around the neck and then sitting down and squeezing my right hand. "I told her to marry you."

"Saundra, stop," I said, shaking my head and laughing.

"When was this?" Cole asked.

"Months ago, when she first told me about you. I said marry him. Didn't I, Camille?" Saundra reflexively looked down at my left hand and burst into a big smile. "Oh my, Camille, your ring is beautiful."

Jewel looked from Cole to me and then down at the ring. "You didn't tell me."

"Jewel, I haven't heard from you," I said, realizing that it was something I needed to say. "And this just happened tonight anyway."

"Glad to know you were in my corner. I'm still working on her," Cole said to Saundra but smiling at me.

Saundra's eyes grew misty. "I'm so happy for you."

"Saundra, don't you start crying and getting sentimental on me. I was just starting to do that before. That's all I need."

"It's just been such a long road." Saundra's gaze seemed to take in so much more than she could share.

"Time for some champagne," Cole suggested, raising his hand to call the waiter.

"How are you?" I asked Saundra, breaking the silence.

"All right. Just haven't figured out where to go from here. I don't think I can stay in New York."

"Where's Les?" Cole asked. "I was sort of expecting to see him here tonight."

I shot Cole a look, trying to tell him not to pry.

"He called a couple of times a couple of weeks ago, but I...I've been trying to put things in place with this...little setback." Saundra swallowed her words.

The strangest quiet settled at the table, as if someone had shared a secret that we all should not have heard. When I finally looked around at everyone, I noticed the young man seated at the table fidgeting. I didn't realize he was with Jewel as we walked through the crowd. She hadn't said anything. He stood up and stretched, as if he were straightening the length of his spine. "Excuse me, I'll be right back."

Jewel

Looking at Camille's ring made me lose myself in thoughts about Gordon. It should have been me. I had forgotten Dennis for some reason and caught his hand and held it so that he had to lean in toward the table. "Oh, I'm so sorry. Saundra, Camille, this is Dennis Howell, a friend." Camille and Saundra looked at each other. They recognized him.

As Dennis moved away from the table, Saundra leaned in and whispered, "That was who I thought he was, right? Ow, Camille did you kick…seriously, Jewel, is that the boy from the restaurant?"

"Saundra!" Camille said.

"Camille, we go way the hell back. She's got to tell us."

"I told you he was cute then." I smiled. "He joined the agency last week, and I had plans to meet with him tonight, and then you called."

"Well, go on, girl!" Saundra said.

"What is your point?" I placed my gloves on the ledge next to me.

"Hey, no point. I'm no expert, but they say older women and younger men are more compatible in many ways." Saundra laughed.

"He's one of my models, Saundra. He happens to be very mature for his age." I shifted in my chair, feeling exposed. Every time I'm around them, I feel as if there's something wrong with me.

"Perrier-Jouet Fleur, as you requested, sir. Shall I open it now?" He took the bottle out of the bucket, held it in the white cloth napkin, and let Cole look at it.

"Good. Yes, please do."

"The bottle is beautiful—painted flowers, Cole…so lovely," Camille said.

"Excellent taste, Cole," I said.

The waiter then popped the cork and poured the champagne. Then, turning to me, he asked, "Would you like me to bring out the platter of appetizers now, Ms. Jamison?"

"I called ahead and had them make up a platter I usually get when they cater for me, affairs at the office—some crab cakes, barbecued shrimp. I bring clients here who have never had soul food," I said, taking control. "If that's all right with everyone?"

"Thanks, but I know what I want," Cole said. "I'll have the ribs with greens, potato salad on the side, and some corn bread."

"I think I know what I want too," Saundra said. "Fried chicken and a side order of greens and biscuits."

"I'd like the shrimp, with macaroni and cheese and greens," Camille said.

"OK. Well then, forget the platter. I'll just have an order of the greens."

"Is that all you're having?" Camille asked.

"I really can't stay too long. I have to discuss a few things with Dennis."

Almost as if on cue, Dennis came back to the table and asked for a Perrier water and handed the menu back to the waiter.

"Well, to you and your engagement, Camille," I said, lifting my glass.

Cole lifted his glass, looked at Camille, and said, "To us, and to you, babe, and the success of your book."

"Camille, they're interested in your book?" Saundra said.

"What book?" I asked.

"Remember, I was telling you about my short stories? An agent is interested in—"

"When did you tell me anything about any stories?"

"At the brunch, I think. I told you how I was writing stories set on Hancock Street."

"Jewel, you know Camille has been writing since we were kids."

"Well, you have just about everything you've ever wanted, now, don't you?" She's writing about Hancock Street? "You damn well better not be writing about me." My thoughts squirted out.

"What do you mean by that?"

"Just what I said." I got up. Had to get away from that table.

"What is your problem, Jewel?" Saundra said.

Camille

My words stuck in my throat. I tried to sort through the words that had been spat at me.

"Babe, don't…" Cole said something, but I had to keep sight of Jewel.

I followed to catch up with her and saw her enter the ladies' room. As I went in, she was sitting and staring into the mirror, throwing a tube of lipstick into her bag, pressing her lips together.

"Jewel, how could you say that to Camille?" I didn't know Saundra was behind me. She spoke to Jewel's image in the mirror.

I could feel my mind turn blank. It had always been so difficult for me to deal with confrontations. I had even forgotten why I had come into the room.

Our gaze met in the mirror before I could dredge up any words that might begin to say how I felt.

"Jewel, why did you say that back there? What do you mean write about you? I am not writing about you. I made up characters…I have always been happy for you; why can't you be happy for me?"

"Happy for me? Cut the crap."

"Why are you reacting like this? We've been friends since we were children."

"Let's be real. When we were children, all you guys did was let me know how much you had that I didn't."

"That's not true," Saundra said.

"I just don't want you using me anymore."

"Using you?" Saundra said.

"Yes. Using me. You both were always using me."

"We were always using you?" I asked.

"Yes. For a place to hang out, for parties to meet men."

"We were friends. We weren't using you. How could you say that?" I said.

"Because that's how I felt."

"I'm the one who asked to stay over and you said no, because Eric was there. You told me I could come. Then you wouldn't even let me in," Saundra said.

"Don't look so hurt, Saundra. What was that, more than twenty years ago? And you didn't call; you just showed up. What was I supposed to tell Eric?"

"Jewel, I don't understand how you think sometimes. You just did that to me. The night I called you when my mother died, you told me you had a date." Her face seemed so strange, reversed as her image was in the mirror. She would not face us.

"I did have a date." She opened her compact and powdered her nose and blushed her cheeks.

"I tell you my mother died, and you tell me you have a *date*?" A woman pushed past me and went into the restroom. I lowered my voice to a whisper. "You didn't even call back."

"I've been busy. My business keeps me busy…I sent flowers."

"But Jewel, my mother had died, and you said you had a *date*."

"You say it as though he was just some guy. Gordon and I are getting married in June."

"Jewel, that's not the point."

"Camille, this is getting very tedious." She glossed her lips.

"You know, Jewel, whatever guy was the flavor of the month always came first," Saundra said. "Then, when they'd dump you…"

"We'd be up with you until three in the morning," I said.

"Don't you even talk," Jewel said to Saundra.

"Never even called back to see if I was OK. Nothing."

"You were always OK, Camille. No matter what happened, you were always OK. It was always me who made the mistakes."

"Don't change the subject. Why are you so angry? In college we were very close. At least I thought so. I understand you slept with Derrick." The words vomited from my lips. A woman came out of the rest room, looked at us, and then looked away.

Jewel swiveled around on the stool to face me. An odd smile painted itself upon her lips. "So?"

Time became a funnel, focused on the many times Derrick was unfaithful to me. I had known some of the girls he was with in high school. But by the time we were in college, the women had become phantoms who simply occupied the space in time that he was away from me. I could not make it right that one of the phantoms was my friend with whom I spoke, and laughed, and whom I loved all these years.

"What did you s…" There was a fish bone caught in my throat.

"I said 'so,' as in 'so what?' He wasn't that good. Never understood why you made such a big deal over him—or, for that matter, what he saw in you."

"He was the first guy…you know how I felt about him. How could you betray me like that?" I felt as if I would choke.

"I figured you'd get over him. Like you said to me after Eric, 'You'll get over him.' Remember that? Always made me feel like I was stupid or crazy."

"I didn't do that."

"You both did. You and Saundra had so much more, knew so much more. Saundra's so streetwise she's got some man beating the shit out of her." Her upper lip was drawn tightly across her teeth, and her jaw hardly moved.

"I loved you. We went through so much together. I was there for you. And Saundra? She took her last pennies to give to you when you needed."

"Let's be real. I had the apartment, so you used me to have a place to go. And for the last few weeks, I didn't know what you wanted, how you wanted to use me this time, but I knew I'd figure it out. Did you know Saundra called the office a week ago, asking me about getting her a job in my Chicago office?"

"I know her ex-husband got out of jail, and he hurt her. She didn't tell me she called you."

Saundra

"Jewel, I was…" I saw the events of that day unfold, and I got trapped in the images of Santos pounding my face, and the room blurred. He pulled me by my arm. I felt it pop. I could not lift it. When I got home from the hospital, I hurt everywhere. I think I talked to Camille. I needed to hide. When he gets out the next time, he will kill me.

I thought I could hide there, Jewel. Maybe in Chicago he wouldn't find me. I could hear Jewel and Camille talking about me somewhere outside my thoughts.

"That's what I mean being used," Jewel said.

"She probably was looking for someplace far away from him. Don't you have any compassion for her? You know Saundra gave me her last little bit of money for you when you needed it," Camille said.

"Give me a break."

"She did for you when she could. You act like you don't give a damn about her. Remember Washington."

That was so long ago. I had forgotten how I had done that. I always felt that it was them always helping me.

Jewel

"You have the nerve to bring that up," I said, looking around the bathroom to see if anyone was there. "The two of you ruined my life by talking me into that. If I hadn't done it, Eric and I would be together right now. I don't have time for this. Like I said, she used me and you used me. Maybe you think writing about me will help sell your book." I threw the powder and the lip gloss into my bag.

"You are delusional. Eric didn't even call to see how you were. And it's like you never gave a damn…still don't. You tried to put the make on Cole, too, didn't you?"

"That's what this is about," I said, smiling. "He told you it was *me* who put the make on *him*?"

"What?"

I could see Camille begin to doubt him. You finally stopped talking, didn't you? Yes, do think about that, Camille. I loved the chaos I had created and couldn't help laughing out loud.

"Jewel, this isn't funny to me. I always thought of you and Saundra as my family, my sisters. I felt closer to you than to my own mother."

"Spare me the theatrics. I have no family…have no sisters… been alone for as long as I can remember. You didn't do shit for me. Everything—and I mean everything—I have, I got for myself. Me, all by myself. And you better not try to use me or capitalize on me. So you think hard and long about writing anything that even remotely—and I mean *remotely*—resembles my life. And, by the way, I didn't just put the make on Cole, as you put it. I slept with him too. That night at Tavern on the Green, he came back to my place after he left you, and I fucked him. He wasn't that good either." I got up and pushed the door open and left. Let her think about that.

Camille

There was a tapping at the door. Cole's voice seeped in under the door. "Babe, are you all right?"

As I opened the door, he peeked in hesitantly. He seemed ill at ease in this woman's place.

The tear in my belly was becoming a burning, searing wound.

"Are you OK, babe?" Cole asked again.

"Camille, don't believe her. She just wants to hurt you."

"Believe what?" Cole asked.

"She said you slept with her the night of the Tavern on the Green when you left me. Did you?" I searched his eyes for betrayal.

I felt that I might take comfort in it at last. It was much more what I expected than this love he always professed.

"Camille, you are not really asking me that, are you?"

Saundra said, "Camille, please don't believe her. Don't let her ruin this night."

"Well, I need to know if you fucked her like she said." The words came out in a spurt, and the sound seemed to come from somewhere deep in my gut.

Cole just looked at me and then moved in to put his arms around me. I shrugged and looked up at him, pushing his hand away, unsure of his touch. I felt unsure of everything.

"This is the ladies' room," a woman said, pushing past him.

Cole ignored her, shaking his head no. He looked as if I had punched him in the chest.

"She's hateful, Camille," Saundra said.

"Camille, I only tolerated being in her presence because of you."

"It's like she destroyed all of my memories," I said to no one in particular. I felt my body grow cold. There was a palpable gaping space in my consciousness. "I thought of her as my sister."

We went out to the table and tried to eat, but everything was spoiled. I hurt where my memories had been ripped away. I searched Cole's eyes, trying to see into his soul, looking for the betrayal I feared. There was not a trace. I wanted to bellow at Jewel to tell her that she could not rewrite my memories like that, could not intrude and tear away my happiness like that.

The waiter came over to the table. "Excuse me, Ms....Jamison..."

"She left," Saundra said, with her expression taking on the air of good riddance.

"Ms. Jamison asked me to get these things for her." He began to reach for the pair of long brown leather gloves she had been wearing. I hadn't even noticed them on the shelf next to her seat.

"Where is she?" I asked.

"She's outside. She came back for them," he said as he picked the things up.

"I'll take them to her," I said, grabbing the gloves and finding the small pillbox wrapped up in them.

"She asked me to do it," the waiter said.

"No, *I* will take them to her."

"Do you want me to come with you?" Cole said.

"No, this is something I need to do myself," I said, now standing.

As I worked my way through the restaurant, my mind raced through the hurts that I had felt from the words Jewel had hurled at me. I saw Cole's face and the sadness in his eyes when I told him what she had said. I remembered the many times we had just laughed and cried together. Then a strange sense of clarity began to form in my mind. It was as if I could see the puzzlement in white light. It was more of a clear view of the confusion. Time had not been the same for me as it had been for her. The feelings had not been the same.

When I got outside, there she was, smiling up at Dennis and then laughing. There was something so vacuous in her eyes. She didn't care what she had just done.

"Jewel, I need to say something to you." I clenched my fist, squeezing my thumb to contain the anger that was building in my chest.

"And just what is that, Camille?"

"You may not have the same memories as I do of our friendship—"

"Friendship?" She smirked at me.

I searched my mind for the words that I could use that would not betray my own sense of myself. The anger I felt was so huge that it squirted filth all over me. I could not believe that my thoughts of love for her and shared memories could be so wrong. "No, you cannot do that. No."

She looked at me in such a disdainful way and turned her back to walk away.

"No, no, no. You will not just walk away from me." I reached out and grabbed her by the arm. "Jewel, don't you turn your back on me. Don't you turn your back on everything we were to each other, everything I remember."

"I know you are not touching me."

"I am trying to get you to stop. You cannot let our friendship end like this."

I grabbed her shoulder and spun her around to face me.

"Don't touch my coat," she said through clenched teeth.

"Your coat? Is that what's important to you at this moment?" My thoughts ran together. "Look at me, Jewel. I just got engaged. I am happy for the first time in I don't know how long. I wanted you to be part of it. You are not just going to walk away."

"Watch me! Watch me walk away. I couldn't care less about you… never cared that much back then. I could certainly care less now. You're probably pissed because you're afraid Cole will leave you for me, just like Derrick did." Her voice now lowered to a guttural whisper. "Do you really believe any man would choose you over me?"

Her words took my breath away. I just stood and stared at her for a minute, her face a distorted venomous image.

"What is wrong with me? I keep looking for who I thought you were. But you were just the whore who betrayed me with my boyfriend, and the whore who tried to do it again with my fiancé." My words vomited out with the bile that I tasted.

"What did you call me?"

"You heard me." I covered my mouth. I shouldn't have said that. I wanted to take it back.

Jewel

"Did you see…hear what she said?" I turned to Dennis. I know I never told her about my mother. How did she know about my mother?

"Let's just go," he said, his hand up, waving down a cab.

"I'll have my lawyers contact you."

"For what? I am not afraid of you, Jewel."

"For writing about me, telling my secrets."

"Nobody is writing about you."

"You'll see. You'll take back what you said about me."

Camille

"Jewel, you hurt…pushed me…you're going to wish you had friends like us back. Here are your pills. Go get screwed. Forget who you were."

"You think I care what you say to me. You've hated me since we were kids, plotted against me and tried to manipulate me all through college." Her voice became shrill as she got into the cab. People on the sidewalk now began to stop and look at us.

"Trust me, Jewel, you will end up all by yourself."

She slammed the cab door and was gone.

"Jewel's crazy. I hope you don't believe her, Camille," Saundra said, shaking her head.

"You OK, babe?" Cole asked, pushing the door open behind her.

"I had to get that off my chest. I kept looking the other way. It's been a long time coming. But my hands are shaking. Saundra, do you believe…"

"She's crazy. Did you see her eyes? The things she said…"

I felt Cole's hand cover mine. I looked up at Saundra.

"Let it go, Camille. Don't you let her ruin this night for you." But the night was spoiled.

As we sat back down at the table, I looked at Cole, and I saw such pain in his eyes. I had caused it. I don't know how I let Jewel make me mistrust him. There was a bitter taste left in my mouth. I had said things I hadn't wanted to say, at least not the way I had said them. But they were true. She had betrayed me not once, but twice. I didn't want to look at it because it was too ugly, but I believe she would have tried to rip us apart if I had let her.

She was right about one thing. She didn't care. She didn't care to remember what had really happened. I knew that my memories of the past were closer to the truth.

Camille

"As the president of City College, I strongly urge the students who disrupted this institution this past week to return to classes on Monday morning. I have asked the city's police commissioner to provide us with protection for the administration building, which will be open Monday morning. If there is a repeat of this blatant disregard for both the law and the rules of this institution, we will have no recourse but to use expulsion and criminal charges against any student who engages in acts of anarchy at this college. Any faculty member who is found to be engaging in unlawful acts against this institution will face dismissal and criminal charges as well."

"Shit!" I was putting away Aunt Lil's good silver and glasses when the message came on the radio. I had cramps and was wondering whether there would be class Monday morning. The last few weeks had been crazy. Autumn of 1967 had exploded all over the City College campus. I had written that the oaks and sycamores erupted like volcanoes, spewing bits of crimson, gold, and amber onto the yellowed grass of summer. The days had cooled at first and then reheated with a blaze, bringing students out of their homes the last two weeks. They were scattered across the campus on blankets of russet and ochre leaves, sitting in clusters, talking and arguing about the Vietnam War, thousands of miles away but witnessed on the nightly news in our living rooms.

The black students finally put up games of spades for debates on civil rights, apartheid in South Africa, and the absence of black history in the schools. We questioned why we should die in some far-off land when we didn't have equality here in our own country.

Images of dogs drawing blood of students in the South were imprinted on our minds, giving us our sense of urgency.

Collectively, the students woke up to the notion that the world was not the idyllic place we had thought when we were children. The most immediate enemy was the school's administration, a monolithic wall much like the building that bore its name. Students petitioned, protested, boycotted, and finally clogged the doors of the administration building with their very bodies the week before Thanksgiving.

I called Saundra twice during that week, and she wasn't home. I needed to talk to someone now. I dialed her again.

"Yes?"

"Saundra, is that you?"

"Yeah. Camille? Thought it was…"

"Are you crying?"

"Not feeling so well."

"Did you hear the news?"

"What news?"

"The president of the college is going to kick people out who protested and fire professors."

"What d'ya mean?"

"Were you on campus last week?"

"No, not since my leave…"

"Well, we boycotted classes, and some students blocked the administration building."

"You're kidding."

"No. And now he says he's going to expel people."

"Shit. I missed it." She mumbled something about Santos. "Like walking on hot coals. Never know when he's gonna get angry."

"Why don't you go back home?"

"They won't let me come back. I'm saving, though. I have almost two hundred dollars," she whispered, "hidden all around the house in my socks and empty juice cans."

"Is he there?"

"No, but I never know when he's going to come in. There he is. Gotta go."

I felt so bad for Saundra, but I was also scared for myself. I kept hearing the president's words over and over again in my mind. I had signed the petition and helped write it.

I went into the linen closet to put away the tablecloths and napkins Aunt Lil had washed and ironed. I wondered if he would punish all the students who had signed the petitions. He couldn't expel all of us who boycotted classes. There were too many. It felt as if it were some kind of bad joke. The telephone rang, but I was so deep in thought I wasn't sure I heard it. The ring was persistent. I ran to pick up the phone in the kitchen.

"Camille, you're not going to believe what I just heard."

"I know. Do you believe this?"

"I think he means it," Jewel said.

"The thing is, if he wants to punish us for demonstrating, where the hell do we go? Shit, I stayed out of classes. I sat in on the steps of the administration building."

"You sat in, Camille?"

"Yeah. We took the petition for the black history class in to him. We had about five hundred signatures on it. The SDS guys went in with a petition for him to take a stand against the war in Vietnam. That was on Tuesday, and then on Wednesday morning, we sat in."

"Well, I didn't go to class on Tuesday or Wednesday. I called you a couple of times, but you were out."

"I've been at a lot of meetings this week."

"Camille, do you think he'll punish the students who boycotted class?"

"I doubt it. He'd have to punish the whole damn school. I hear there was hardly anyone in class on Tuesday, and Wednesday the campus was deserted except for those of us at the demonstration. That's why he canceled classes."

"You think he's just bluffing?"

"Frankly, I think this bastard wants to make an example of a few students, and then everyone else will fall in line."

"You don't think...you don't mean you, Camille? Do you?"

"I don't know. There are many more vocal students than me. I was just there at the demonstration. But shit, they took our pictures. They could do anything."

"Who took your pictures?"

"Well, the press was there, but the administration had people there too. They took pictures of all of us."

"What are you going to do?"

"What can I do? Just wait and see what they do. I can tell you one thing. Lil is going to be mad as hell with me if I get kicked out of school. Jewel, I'm so close. In June I get out, and in September I start teaching."

There was a long silence.

"Camille, you all right?"

"I guess so. I just can't believe this."

"Look, don't worry. I'm sure...shit! I can't believe it either."

"Yeah, and on top of everything else, I've got cramps. I've been in bed all morning long, taking Midol. Now trying to get done some of the stuff Lil asked me to do and listening to the radio...my cramps get worse every month. Anyway, how are you?"

I heard only silence.

"Jewel...you there?"

"Yes." Jewel's voice was weak. It had lost its energy.

"So, how're things with you? Haven't heard from you. Seeing Eric, I bet?"

There was silence again. I heard her swallow.

"Jewel? Is there something wrong? Something between you and Eric?"

"Camille, what's today's date?"

"I don't know. The twenty-seventh or twenty-eighth. I'm not sure. You want me to go look at the calendar?"

"Camille, I haven't gotten my period in almost two months. When you just said you had cramps, it hit me."

"What?"

"I don't remember having it at all this month. Let me go look at my calendar."

I could hear footsteps, then silence.

"Camille? Last time I got it was in September."

"OK, look, don't panic. Did you ever go to the gyno—"

"No."

"You'll go to my doctor. Call her as soon as you get off the phone."

"Camille, I'm scared. My period comes like clockwork."

"Don't worry, but you've got to call now. I'm not even sure she's there this late on Friday. If she's not, tell her service you need an emergency appointment for whenever her office opens on Monday."

"What if she won't see me?"

"Call right now. She's Dr. Ruth Sasseen. Her number is 555-3036."

"What's she going to do to me?"

"She'll give you a test and examine you. Jewel, you've got to call now. Did you write down the number?"

"Huh? No."

"Jewel, get a pen and write it down, and call right now. It's almost five."

"Yes."

"Do you have a pen?"

"Uh, yes."

"It's 555-3036. Call me back after you get her, OK? Jewel?"

"Yes."

Jewel

The receiver felt heavy. It fell into its cradle. I looked down at the number on the paper and realized I didn't remember the doctor's name. I started to dial Camille, and then I broke the connection and dialed the doctor's number.

"Drs. Perry, Engle, and Sasseen's office; please hold," a voice said.

Dr. Sasseen—that was it. I had no idea what to say.

"Hello, doctor's office. May I help you?"

"Yes. I'd like to make an emergency appointment with Dr. Sasseen."

"Ma'am, the doctors just left for the day, we were just closing up, and Dr. Sasseen will not be in next week."

"Is there anyone I can see on Monday?"

"For Dr. Perry, you will have to call back on Monday to see if he will squeeze you in. Dr. Engle is in on Monday and has a few openings from three till seven…ma'am?"

I couldn't think straight.

"Are you there, ma'am?"

"Yes. I'm sorry. I'm…with Dr. Engel."

"He has an opening at five thirty."

"I'll take it. My name is Jewel Jamison."

There was a click. I sat staring at the phone and my hand, which rested on top of it as if they were permanently attached. I felt numb. My mind was blank. I stared out the window into the window shaft, which was now charcoal gray except for the rectangular blocks of gold luminescence, the apartments of so many strangers.

I had no real thoughts. No pictures. No words. My head began to ache. Ringing rattled inside my head. My hand picked up the phone.

"Jewel? Did you get her? You didn't call me back."

"The doctor wasn't there…"

"So, you didn't make an appointment?"

"The nurse or whoever…not…with another…doctor."

"What do you mean? Jewel?"

"A man doctor is seeing me on Monday. I don't know what I'm going to do."

"Just go on and see what he says. Then, if you're pregnant…"

"It's the wrong time for this. I've got so much I need to do. I've got a paper due before Christmas. I've got...I haven't got a lot of money in the bank."

"Saundra might have somebody who can do something. Don't worry. Jewel...don't worry. Just go to him on Monday. Have you got twenty-five dollars for the visit?"

"I can take it out of the bank."

"OK. After you hear what he says, we'll go from there. Let me call Saundra, see if she's got any cash. I could lend you a hundred fifty, if you need it."

"I don't even have Eric's home number." I don't know how to reach him, I thought.

"Don't worry. If you need more money, I'll ask Lil. I'm going to call Saundra to...I'll get back to you, OK?"

My hand rested the phone down, clenched itself into a fist, lifted up, and pounded my belly. A wail escaped from my lips and then thinned into a moan.

Camille

I sat for a moment, picked up the phone, and dialed.

"Hello...oh, hello Santos. Is Saundra there? This is Camille."

He never even seemed to acknowledge my presence. He was gone and yelling, "Saundra, pick up."

"Hey, Camille."

"Saundra, I think Jewel's pregnant."

"What?"

"Yeah, girl. She hasn't got her period since September."

"Did she go to your doctor?"

"Not yet."

"What's she waiting for?"

"She didn't know she was late till today. She's going on Monday."

"What's going on with her? Her head's so turned around since she met this guy."

"Saundra, you remember the lady you went to?"

"Oh, you mean that nurse?"

"How much do you think she will charge?"

"I don't know. When I did it, it was two hundred fifty. I don't know. Three, I guess. Did she try those pills?"

"Which ones?"

"Oh, shit! What were they called? You get them from the Botanica store. Damn it. I can't remember the name of them. They didn't work for me anyway, but if I think of the name, I'll call you."

"You know if my doctor can't do anything for her, she may need some money."

"Camille"—Saundra's voice changed to a whisper—"you know what I'm savin' for. I can loan her the money, but I really would like her to try to get it back to me."

"I understand. You think you can find her someone?"

"Hell, I don't even care about the money as much, but I really don't want to be the one who gets her somebody. I can just see if something goes wrong..."

"I'll tell her I got the person. No sweat."

"Hey, Camille, understand me. I just don't want her sending the cops up to my parents if anything goes wrong. You know Jewel. She goes through this self-righteous thing."

"Hey, you don't have to explain. I'll tell her I found the person. If she wants to go, fine. If not, hey!"

"OK. Like I said, I'll call you back. Hey, it just hit me. How's her head? I mean, I dealt with it, and I know you handled it, but it's heavy."

"She's real fucked up. She's scared. I had to tell her—step by step, you know—to call and get an appointment. She's real scared."

"Camille, I can't call Jewel yet. I think you know how I feel. She hurt me very badly. But I want to be there for her."

"I know."

"Look, I'll make a few calls. Some girl on my job was talking about a doctor who does it. Maybe he's better than the lady who did it for me. I'll get back to you. Camille, when you talk to her, tell her you do get over it, sort of. It takes time, but…"

"I'll tell her. I better call her, or go over, or something. You'll call me Monday?"

"Yeah, Monday night."

"Thanks. I know Jewel would thank you too."

"Hey, we're friends."

I dialed Jewel's number. The phone rang and rang. Finally, it stopped ringing, but no one spoke.

"Jewel? Jewel…"

"Yes."

"Look, I called Saundra, and she has some money, so don't worry."

"Why'd you tell her?"

"You said you needed money. She's gonna help."

"I don't want her to go telling anybody about this."

"Who's she gonna tell? Look, you're upset, so don't say anything you'll regret."

"Camille, what's going to happen to me? I don't want anybody to cut me up."

"Cut you up?"

"I don't want some butcher…but I can't have a kid right now…"

"Look, we'll find someone good. Stop worrying."

"I'm going to go to Brooklyn Law School tomorrow to see if I can find Eric."

"There's no classes tomorrow."

"Well, Monday, then."

"Monday you've got to go to the doctor."

"I'm so confused. My head's splitting."

"Take some aspirin. Do you think you can sleep? You want me to come over?"

"No, I just want to be by myself."

"Take some aspirin for your headache. It'll probably help you sleep too."

"Camille, would you come with me on Monday? To the doctor, I mean."

"I can meet you after, but if there are classes, I have an exam in bio, and I can't miss it."

There was silence.

"I'll call you right after my class, OK? Jewel?"

"It's just that I'm all alone in this."

"Look, Jewel, I just can't miss this exam, especially with this mess with the protest. I gotta take some more Midol. I'll call you on Monday."

"Camille, this is happening to me, not you or Saundra. It's my body."

"Yeah, I know, but...I'll call you on Monday."

Jewel

Camille hung up. I listened to the silence and finally put down the receiver. I am all alone. I listened for footsteps in the apartment above me. There were none. It was just five thirty, yet the city was gray-black. What little light there was in the apartments across the way stopped at the windowsills and stayed inside. I turned on the lamp next to my bed. The room devoured the rays, sucking them into the dark corners and swallowing them up.

"I hate the dark."

22

"**W**hat did Camille ever do for me? I did for myself. And she's going to write about Hancock Street?" This evening was an assault on my sensibilities. I shut it out. I have plans for this boy.

And she calls me a whore? A whore. I don't think I told her about my mother. Talked about a lot of things...never told her what they called my mother. It was a secret.

"I want you to make love to me when we get upstairs." The taxi driver, a heavy-set black man in his forties, watched me in the rear-view mirror. Loved having his eyes on me.

"Did you know that I'm planning on getting married by the end of this year?" I said, tracing circles in the palm of Dennis's hand.

"Why are you telling me this now?"

"Don't know. Sort of a turn-on."

"Not really."

"It doesn't turn you on? No matter. It turns me on." I wanted to manipulate the boy. Twist him 'round and watch him dance. Time had spun me about. No more. By the end of the year, Camille and Saundra will read about my wedding in the newspapers and magazines. Gordon will call, and things will be fixed. *It is not done.*

I ran my fingers along the edge of Dennis's belt.

"My fiancé is in Chicago right now. Have you ever been to Chicago?"

"No."

"You'll come with me. You'll meet him."

He drew his hand away.

The cab driver pulled up to the curb, and the doorman ran to the car door for me.

"That will be seven fifty."

Dennis reached for his wallet, but I handed the driver a twenty-dollar bill and patted Dennis's hand.

"Just give me back ten."

"Thank ya, ma'am," he said, resting his arm on the seat back. He handed me the bill and eyed my legs as I parted them to step out of the car.

The brisk wind outside stung my face and made my bosom tingle. Dennis stepped out of the cab behind me, and I linked arms with him and stared up into his eyes, letting the heat from my body pour out at him. The lobby was deserted. I so wanted an audience. When the elevator door closed behind us, I pulled his face to me and explored his mouth with my tongue.

"You taste delicious."

"So do you." His voice was deeper now than I remembered.

"Would you take me for the same age as those people we were with? I don't know why I still see them...nothing in common. Can't believe she'd try to move into my world like this."

He didn't answer. He seemed tongue-tied. As I drew the boy along, I could feel the dead place in my center ignite. I handed him the key over my shoulder, leaned against the wall, and watched as he pushed it into the lock.

"You did that very well." He smiled at me. I flipped the foyer light switch and led him into the living room, letting my coat drop on the couch. The living room was charcoal brown. "Have you seen the view from this window? It's stunning at night." I doubled back to turn off the light. Only the golden light from the city entered. The skyline crowned with jeweled spires sparkled and glittered with the lights of so many spaces of life.

"I want to do it here in front of the whole city," I whispered.

Dennis was behind me and took my cue, placing his arms around my waist and brushing his fingers against my breasts. He turned me around and kissed me and began to unbutton my blouse. I couldn't wait to feel his skin, so I returned the favor. Then he unclasped my bra, and I felt the heat rise in me and fill me up.

"Let me help with that." I pulled his belt out of the loop, and he unclasped his pants. I ran my nails gently down his back as he stepped out of his trousers. His legs were long and lean. His body was so perfect and so pure. I unclasped and then pulled off my slacks. He kissed my stomach and pulled my black lace panties down and off. I wanted to climb atop him and stay until I could feel calm inside, so I did. I placed him down where I wanted him on the floor. The window was open. The cool air flowed in and bathed my bare breasts. A brown glow that warmed the room made his body glisten.

I so needed to feel him that I hated the helpless hunger that drove me to hold him and keep him locked beneath me. He tried to touch my breast with his fingertips, but I held his wrists to control the sensations entering my body. He would only be there as I permitted. I reached behind me and took him in my hands and felt him grow. I rose up then took him in. Before I began to move, I just enjoyed the fullness of him. His stride excited me. I lost myself in the awareness of his presence.

"It's been so long," I said before I could stop myself. He was so beautifully strong and rhythmic that as I bore down on him, I felt myself almost fill and then empty.

I opened my eyes. The city sparkled. The gaping hole that was my center was endless. I had to close it. Shut it. Dam it up. I had the sensation of falling—just a feeling, as though I might swoon. My hand covered my mouth. There is no one there to catch me.

"Oh, oh no!" My passion closed me up.

I felt him hold my hips to steady me.

"You are so beautiful."

I had begun to tumble onto him.

He held my shoulders and drew me to him.

The sound entered, and I began to vibrate. My body began to shake. He stroked the length of my back. *Why are you pretending?*

"You are so beautiful."

"You are lying." I wanted to pull the words from his mouth and rip them to shreds and throw them out the window. "Don't you say that to me."

As I reached for his face to claw his mouth off, he grabbed my wrists.

"What's the matter? I just said—"

"I know what you said. I'm sick of hearing you say that. You don't mean it."

"What did I say?"

"You call me beautiful and then call me needy. What about your wife? Is she needy?"

"What are you talking about?" Gordon got up and started to put on his pants.

"Where are you going? Back to her?" I lunged for him to make him stop.

He stuffed his right foot into the pants leg, staring at me.

"Look, Ms. Jamison, I don't know what's wrong here, but I think I'd better go."

"Ms. Jamison?" Wait, the boy.

He put on his shirt, backing away from me, and bent down to pick up his shoes.

"None of this matters. The date is set. June first. I'll be the first June bride."

"What?" he asked.

"Oh, nothing." I watched him pull on his loafers and look for his jacket, which was on the couch.

"When should I expect you, Gordon? Will you call first?"

He didn't answer. He walked to the apartment door and left.

"I love you." It will be beautiful, I thought. The bodice will be lace, with a high neck and a pinched waist. A full skirt. No, a low cut off the shoulder with a mermaid look to show off my figure. Gordon will have to get a morning coat. I started to call after him, but he was already gone. Oh, and I'll invite Camille. Why not? I'll have white roses for my bouquet. And it will be beautiful. I'll call Saundra and Camille. I'll invite all the models. It'll be a media event.

The clouds were high and white and feathery. They were the kind that let you know that they could not be reached or touched. I positioned myself to the right of the doorway of the law school building so that I could see everyone who entered. It was eight thirty. I had gotten there at ten to eight. My toes were burning cold. The bustle of students and professors darting in and out of the building seemed to accelerate. I couldn't scan all the faces. Students clustered in twos and threes and then moved up to the entrance. I craned my neck to see over group after group. A thought intruded. Suppose I had already missed Eric? He might have arrived early. I pushed the thought out of my mind, seeing visions of him running up to me. My mind mixed the real scenes with my imagined ones, and I focused again on the strange faces moving, stopping, conversing, and moving again. A block away, I could see a tall, dark figure coming toward me. I studied his gait and squinted to refine the details in his face, but his features ran together and blurred. I rechecked all the new faces collecting nearby, hoping I hadn't missed any, and then looked back toward him. He was much closer now, and I could see clearly that he was not Eric.

A short, stocky African student in full Ghanaian garb passed by, nodding and saying "Good morning" in melodious tones. I tried to smile back, but my face was frozen, and my cheeks refused to move.

He must have taken the lack of expression as a rude rebuff, because he frowned as he moved past me.

I glanced at my watch. Eight-fifty. I tried to think ahead to nine o'clock and what I would do if I could not find him. My thoughts were muddled.

Now people began to converge on the building in larger groups from right and left and across the street. I couldn't see all the faces. They moved too quickly. The men bounded into the entrance with long strides. The few women I saw seemed to scurry mouselike into the building. I tried to sweep my eyes over the crowd to take in each of them, but I saw only blurs of movement. There was Eric. He passed me.

I called out his name as he moved into the building.

"Eric!" I called, louder this time. Two students turned around and looked in my direction. I ran up to the entrance, pushing past people. As I reached the doors, I realized that I had lost the sensation in my feet. In the main lobby, I saw him rounding a corner. I yelled his name. My voice echoed, bouncing back and slapping me in the face. A group of students turned and frowned disapprovingly at me. As I reached the corridor where Eric was walking, I pushed past people and was hit by elbows and briefcases, but I dared not yell again. When I was close enough to touch him, I reached out and clutched his wool pea coat. My hands ached from the cold. The tips of my fingers burned from the cold.

Eric lurched around in a combative gesture. There was nothing of the welcoming smile I had imagined.

"What are you doing here?"

"I…I…" My throat hurt. I could not catch my breath. He pulled me toward the wall.

"Jewel, I've got class in two minutes. What the hell are you doing here?"

"I have to talk to you, and I didn't have your number."

"What is this? Some kind of romantic bullshit? I've got an exam in this class. I'm not going to miss it. I'll be out by twelve. You want to wait, fine."

"Eric. I have to wait. We need to talk. It's important."

"There's a coffee shop across the street. I'll meet you there after class." His teeth were clenched, and the muscle in his jaw pulsed.

Eric strode across the hall and into the classroom. A short, squat girl pushed past me as the door closed behind him. She pushed it open, and I turned to leave, noticing that the corridor was now deserted. His anger had startled me. I didn't want to tell him with his eyes piercing and slicing away at me.

I walked outside and up the block, trying to warm my feet. I felt so confused. I walked down Fulton Street and passed A&S and Martin's, then turned around and came back again. I sat on the granite bench in front of one of the buildings and lost my sense of time. When I walked back toward the law school, I found the coffee shop Eric had mentioned. The students were collecting around the entrance again. I was afraid to leave the front of the building in case he forgot, but I was freezing and my nose was running. I walked across the street and into the coffee shop, and I asked for a booth. "Only three or more in the big booths, miss. It's lunchtime."

"Then the small one, over there?"

She frowned at me. Just as I sat down, Eric came in and pushed past the people waiting for takeout.

"OK, now what the hell is going on?" he said, putting his case down, sitting but not removing his jacket.

"Eric, I think I'm pregnant."

He looked stunned.

"I went to the doctor yesterday, and he took a blood test. I didn't get the results yet, but he says…he examined me and says he's sure that I am."

"Shit. This is shit!"

"I know this is the wrong time. It's the wrong time for me too."

"How long? Do you know how long?"

"He thinks from when...eight weeks, or nine weeks, he said."

"I've got to talk to a friend. I know this guy, he has a doctor." The muscle in his jaw rippled. His brow bunched together. "Shit!"

"Eric, I'm scared too...my girlfriend said she knows a nurse who can do it, but—"

"Look, give me a day. This guy knows a doctor. He got him for his girlfriend a few weeks ago. I know he's expensive. He's in Washington, DC. Just let me call him."

"And what will you have, sir?" the waitress said.

"Nothing for me. Just coffee."

"And you ma'am?"

"Tea, please, with lemon."

"There's a dollar minimum per person at the booth here...people waiting for lunch," she said disapprovingly, but she moved away before we could respond.

"Look, I've got some calls to make. I'll handle this, but I need some time."

"Eric, I'm so scared."

"How much can you come up with?"

"Huh?"

"If I get this contact, how much money can you come up with?"

"I don't know. My friends are saying they can loan me two hundred. I have a couple of hundred in the bank."

"I'll call tomorrow." He took out his wallet and threw three dollars down on the table. He picked up his briefcase, turned, and left. His shoulders looked as if they were weighted down, but he moved past the crowd and disappeared through the door.

Two days passed. When the phone rang, I thought it was Eric. The thick German-sounding accent was jarring, and my memories of the doctor who had examined me came flooding back into my mind.

"Miss Jamison, I called with the results of the test. I take it you do not get your period. The results indicate that you are pregnant.

If you would like prenatal care, you can call my office on Monday for an appointment."

I had known what he would say, but it still took my breath away. I would have to go with Eric, as we had planned, to get the abortion. He had found the doctor in DC. We would take the train, have it done, and come back. I was supposed to call him once I heard from the doctor.

I picked up the phone and dialed his number. A woman with very refined speech answered the phone. "Eric, there is a young lady on the phone."

"Thanks, Ma. Hello, Jewel? Let me pick up inside."

I waited, listening to the silence on the line. "Hang the phone up, Ma." There was a click. "OK, look, I got the number, the address, and I got some money. You need to call and make the appointment."

"Eric, why do I have to call? Can't you call? I don't know what to say."

"Jewel, look. I'm…hey, never mind. I'll call. What day can you do this?"

"I don't know. Any day."

"I'll make it for the earliest day they give me. Let me call right now, while only my mom is here. I don't want a lot of calls when my father gets home."

"You'll call back as soon as you find out?"

"Yes."

There was a click. Eric seemed so capable one minute and so afraid of his father the next that I wanted to vomit.

The phone rang. When I picked it up, I expected to hear Eric's voice. It was Camille.

"Jewel, how are you feeling? Did you get any news?"

"Yes, I'm pregnant, and I'm going to get an abortion. Eric is making the arrangements."

"He is?"

"A doctor in Washington, DC."

"That's good. He's a doctor. We only know nurses who could do it."

"I have to get off the phone. He's calling back to tell me when the appointment is."

"Are you OK?"

"No, I'm not OK. I'm pregnant."

"I'll call you back later. Saundra said to hang in there."

"Yeah, sure."

I had barely put the phone in the cradle when it rang again.

"Jewel, I got the appointment. D'ya have some paper?"

"Yes."

"It's set for Thursday morning at ten o'clock. There's a five-o'clock train out of New York. You can catch that, or, to be on the safe side, you can go earlier. That would put you in Washington at about nine. Or go the night before and stay in a motel or something. They say it's a thousand. My father gave me five hundred, and I took two fifty out of my account. You might need more than a thousand. My friend said when he got there, they raised the price from a thousand to twelve hundred. Write down the address."

"Wait a minute. Aren't you coming with me? You keep saying you can go, you can...and my father this and my father that. When are you going to grow up, Eric?"

"You want this money or not?"

He gave me the address and I wrote it down, but I was on automatic. I was furious.

"Look, I have an exam that day. If I miss an exam, I fail a course. If I fail a course, I get kicked out of school. I get kicked out of school, I'm out on my ass, and I get drafted. Are you following me? When are you going to grow up? You couldn't even call the fucking doctor. Ask one of your girlfriends to go with you. I'll drop the money off tonight. But don't fuck with my head and make this a bigger hassle than it already is."

"Fuck you, Eric!"

"Fuck you too, Jewel."

I called Camille, but before I even heard her voice, I began to cry. Thinking about going to Washington by myself seemed like a dark tunnel.

"Jewel, is that you?" Camille asked.

"Eric won't come with me. He says he has some fucking exam."

"When is it?"

"Thursday. This Thursday."

"I'll go with you. I don't know if Saundra can come, but I'll ask her."

"I don't even know if he's going to come through with the money anymore because we had this big fight."

"How much is he giving you?"

"About seven hundred and fifty, but he says it could cost a little over a thousand, but he says I should bring more just in case."

"At least he's supporting you."

"He's not coming with me."

"I had to do this myself and put the money together myself. And Saundra did too. And like I said, at least he's supporting you."

"You, Camille?"

"Yeah, when I thought I was in love with Derrick, and I let him do it with no protection. Anyway, do you want to go in the morning or the night before?"

"I'll go in the morning…don't have extra money for a hotel."

"Saundra said that she can loan you the money she's got. I think it's about two hundred or so. She's saving to get away from Santos, so that means a lot."

"Camille…can't talk anymore. I'll call you tomorrow?"

I put the phone down and sat on the edge of the bed. This is happening to me. They say they want to help. Well, it's not happening to you. It's happening to me. I felt as if I would throw up. I hated this thing growing inside me. I would have it cut out and be rid of it.

23

SAUNDRA

"That white man called here looking for you." She didn't even say hello. When I got out of the restaurant, I looked for a telephone booth and called my mother to find out how Wanda was doing. "Thought that's where you were when you didn't come back here."

"No, still at the apartment. Doing some fixing." I never told her what Santos did. Just stalled, saying I was working on the apartment.

"Thought you said you'd be moved in here by now."

"The super gave me a hard time about fixing stuff Santos broke. How's Wanda?"

"She likes her teacher, and he said she's a good student."

"OK, I'll call back a little later this week." It was a little noisy on Broadway. Lester had called after the thing with Santos, but I couldn't talk, and I couldn't tell him the details, and I was so drugged up from the painkillers. He called later that week, and I didn't answer the phone. I could hear his voice on the answering machine. I wanted to keep him away from my mess. I figured once I moved in with my mother and my face was getting back to normal, then I would call him. I pressed my ear to the phone to block out the sounds on the street and dialed his number. The phone rang once and then a second time, and my mind was too jumbled to come up with a message. He answered.

"Les, it's me, Sandy. So much has happened. I know I should have called."

"Where are you? How are you? What happened?"

"I'm sort of living at my mother's. I'm headed there now."

"Did this have to do with your ex-husband?"

"Yes."

"Be straight with me. Are you back with him? Is that why you haven't called? I'm a big boy. If that's the story, just let me know."

"No, no, no."

"Look, by this afternoon, I was thinking maybe this meant more to me than you."

"No, no, I don't want to talk about all this on the phone. I just left Camille and Cole. Can I come over?"

"Sure."

Heading to Brooklyn, I was thinking about how much of this sordid story I should share with Les. I felt such shame at staying and accepting what Santos had done to me. As the train rumbled through the stations one by one, I remembered how the detectives looked at me the night they took him away again. They were the same two cops who had come months before. There was pity in their eyes that time. This time, when they looked at me, there was disgust. I didn't think I could bear seeing it in Lester's eyes.

As I walked down the block from the subway station and rang the bell, I worried about what he would say. As I entered, I could not read his expression. He had a mug of coffee in his hand, and he asked if I would like some. I said yes, and, without thinking, forgetting the bruises on my eye, I took off my scarf and coat and hat that I had pulled down over my eyes. As I sat down at the kitchen table, his stare fixated on my eye and then moved down to my jaw. As I looked into his eyes, I could not read the complex mix of emotions registered there. There was such sadness mixed with something else I could not decipher that it made me reflexively cover my eye with my hand. He gently moved my hand down and then cupping my face in his hands, he kissed each of my bruises ever so lightly. He then opened my hands and kissed their centers. Seeing his pain, I found myself crying, not certain whether it was for myself or for him. I still had not wept for myself.

"What happened?"

"He got out early. I was there, just sweeping the apartment clean so the super couldn't charge me anything against my security. When Santos came in, I was shocked. He asked me where the hell I thought I was going. I told him I knew he had gotten the divorce papers."

Lester's eyes seem to register the pain and surprise I felt being caught off guard as I was. He shook his head. I searched his eyes for disapproval, and seeing none, I continued. I heard my own words echo in my head as the scene came back to me.

"He told me to take my clothes off and go into the bedroom. And I told him I wasn't going to let him hurt me anymore. He twisted my arm behind my back and said, 'I know you are not disrespecting me.' I told him it didn't matter what he did to me I wasn't going to stay. And that's when he hit me in my eye. Then he twisted my arm so hard, I heard a pop." The scene played itself out in front of me. The smell of him filled the air. As I watched and felt him tear my vagina, I heard him say, "I heard you got in some white man's car down on the Concourse." I didn't want to say his words aloud, so I looked at Lester and said, "Lester, he knew about you." I, once again, watched the images in front of me. I recited the events as I saw them in my mind. "I was scream-ing, and there was a banging on the door. The guy from upstairs was yelling at him to stop, and he didn't. He kept saying that I would always belong to him. Then there was a loud sound at the door. The police rammed it open. They took him away, and they took me to the hospital."

Lester's face contorted in pain with each new detail. When I fin-ished and the tears bathed my cheeks, he took me in his arms and kissed the tears, and then he held me against his chest.

"I only wish you could have called me."

There were no more words. I began to shiver. I rested my head and let the images leave my mind. "Les, this is my mess. The last thing I want is for you to be drawn into it. And what could you have done?"

"Nothing the way it happened, because he surprised you there. But had I known in advance, I could have stopped it."

I looked into his blue eyes, which now seemed to take on an aqua hue like the sea, and smiled. "No offense," I said, "but I knew a lot of sweet Jewish boys when I was in elementary and junior high school, and none of them knew how to fight." I laughed.

He smiled, and as he wiped the tears from my face with his thumb, he said, "You never ran into a Jewish boy like me. I grew up in Brownsville. They used to say I was just a little bit crazy. Nobody messed with me."

"Santos is a thug…"

"A thug who beats up on a woman. What's the story? Arrested… where is he?"

"He's at Riker's till the trial, but knowing him, he'll have his lawyer delay, hopin' the DA will lose interest."

"What charges did they bring?"

"Assault, and assault and battery. And assault with a deadly weapon."

"What do you mean assault with a deadly weapon?"

Then I revisited the part of the horror I had avoided earlier. I had kept the worst from him. I did not want him to see me as the person who had allowed this to happen. I pulled away from Les and put my head down, hiding my face from his gaze. "When he said he found out about you, he asked me if I was fucking some white dick. And then he pulled his knife out as he unfastened his pants, and he made me…" My tongue scraped my palate, as if I might scrape away the filth he had deposited there. "And then he held the knife on me while he made me…"

"Shhh, shhh," he said. "Don't have to say any more."

At that moment Lester's visage changed. There was a look on his face that I could not discern. His eyes were now the color of steel. It was puzzling. I was exhausted, and he asked if I was hungry and if I wanted to crash.

"Sandy, I feel that we lost all of those years together. Had things only turned out different way back then. I need to know where your head is this time."

"I know I love being with you."

He laughed. "That's what I love about you. You are just so wonderfully up front. You have to trust me. You can't lock me out. Why did it take so long for you to call me?"

"I kept wanting to have my face get better, and to have a job again, and to be a whole person. Not this broken-up punching bag."

"Don't say that."

"That's how I feel. You have your music and your teaching. I can't just be some liability and bring some crap into your world and muck it up."

"Saundra, when I started teaching, I made a conscious decision to put down roots here. I was done with traveling around. When I saw you at the restaurant a few months ago and you told me what happened back then, I thought, 'Could this be our second chance?' I felt maybe this time we were lucky. This is our chance. Take it with me this time."

I looked into his eyes, and the sincerity there was so profound that I could not contain my love for him, and the tears filled my eyes and squirted out.

"Why are you crying?"

"I just love you."

"So, I've never asked anyone to marry me. New territory for me. But since you say your divorce papers are final, will you marry me?"

"But what if…if Santos…"

"Shhh. You have to trust me. I will not let anything happen to you ever again. I promise."

Later, as we lay together in Lester's bed, I felt the strength of his embrace. I could feel my shoulders begin to relax into his arms. They had been hunched in fear so long that the feeling of calm was strange. I couldn't remember when it was that I had last felt this way, or if I ever had.

24

CAMILLE

The next two days were a strange mix of shifting perceptions and changed realities for me. It was as if nothing was familiar or predictable. For so long, I had felt that Jewel and Sandra and I were a threesome, with our lives so intertwined that their beginnings and ends might never be sorted out. Even when we didn't see one another, I felt that way. That conception unraveled.

It wasn't a conscious pulling apart, but that kind of easing away each part of my braids would engage in when I was little. Each of the three parts of hair that Ma had so carefully plaited together would seem to secretly agree to part, and without provocation they would dislodge themselves and move and shift until they first became a soft twist and then a frayed section of hair, each strand finding its own way.

It was disconcerting not feeling a part of some lovely braided pattern. It meant feeling alone. It meant reassessing the past. Saundra said that Jewel was always that way. "Always for herself," she said. I knew I had not remembered that and that my memories were real. This understanding did not come all at once. First there was the gaping hole in my consciousness. I wanted to fill it in, reconstructing my perceptions. I had no time for mourning my lost illusions of my childhood, because Shawn needed me to help him say good-bye to Cole. I resolved that I would not bring any more of Jewel's chaos into their lives.

Cole was quiet as he drove me to get Shawn from his friend's house. When Shawn came to the door and saw Cole behind me, he leaped up into his arms and hugged him around his neck so tightly that I thought that he might choke. We knew we needed to take Shawn home to tell him about Cole's leaving so that he could ask questions, or cry or do whatever little boys do when they hear such a thing.

"How about if we go get a Christmas tree. You can pick it out," Cole said as he put Shawn down. The boy reached for his duffel bag and stuffed in his sleeping bag, which he was dragging behind him.

"Do you have all your toys?"

"My action figures are in the bag," he said, handing Cole a plastic bag filled with toys that he had looped on his arm.

"I think that's everything," Jordan's mother, a thin woman with curly hair, said.

"Jordan, this is Cole, my friend," Shawn said, waving in the little boy's direction.

Jordan, a spectacled little boy with full cheeks and freckles, waved back.

Cole tucked his belongings in securely while I tied the hood on Shawn's jacket and admonished him for taking too many things. Cole then wiped away the frown on his face by taking his hand as he lifted the duffel and slung it over his shoulder.

"Mom has our tree in the closet."

"What about a real tree this year? What do you think?"

Shawn looked at me as if asking permission. When I nodded, his face lit up, and his steps took on a bounce that I had never before seen. We spent the whole morning riding around looking at trees, with Cole pulling out tall ones, full ones, and squat ones, giving Shawn the ultimate say. The child finally chose one. "I like that one. It's cute."

"This little tree? What do you like about this one?" Cole asked, a baffled look on his face.

"It's like the one we have at home in the box," he said.

"My child is very conservative. He doesn't like change." I laughed and then locked eyes with Cole. When I thought about his leaving and the truth that I had just uttered, I turned my head away to hide the tears that were beginning to well up in my eyes.

At home, I made some tea for myself and some hot chocolate for Shawn and Cole, trying to keep my hands busy. Cole stared out the window, deep in thought. The quiet in the kitchen felt as if someone had died and no one dared speak about the terrible sadness. Each in turn seemed to come to the table and sit down, and Cole took the lead after looking at me. I looked at Shawn and could not find the words to begin. Cole asked Shawn if he knew why he had gone away. The little boy nodded. "You had to go to the army." The look in his eyes revealed a depth of understanding that seemed to transcend his years, but then he said nothing more.

"Close enough," Cole said. "Shawn, I have to go away again for a long while."

"Are you ever coming back?" Shawn asked in a straightforward way that made me look at him and then at Cole. It felt as if he were asking him to peer into the future to tell him that it would be so.

"I'm coming back, but it's gonna be a long time." Cole straightened Shawn's collar and brushed his head with his hand, trying not to look into his eyes as he gave his answer.

"When?" Shawn asked immediately, not giving Cole a chance to think past the previous question.

For a minute Cole looked at me for help. He saw the tears collected in my eyes, and he said, "The way it looks right now, June."

"For my birthday," Shawn said, putting things together, as children often do, in terms they understand.

Caught by surprise I said, "Yes."

And with a serious expression on his face, Shawn said, "Good." Without saying anything more about it, he walked into his room.

The abrupt end of the conversation left Cole and me feeling out of sorts, but when I tiptoed in to check on Shawn, he had begun to play with his action figures and seemed to be fine.

We sat awhile and made conversation about the tree and where to put it. I dug out the tree stand and a box of ornaments from the bottom of the coat closet. The silence and the anticipation of Shawn's reaction had been stifling, so Cole put on the radio. The time filled up with hanging bulbs, draping garland and tinsel, and singing along with tunes from the seventies and Christmas songs.

As Nat King Cole sang "Chestnuts roasting on an open fire..." I began to absorb the notion of Cole's leaving. It began as a tiny slit, as if you snipped a piece of paper with a scissor. As the song came to an end and I realized that Cole would not be there on Christmas Day, there was a cleaving away of a part of me. At first it made me angry. I kept feeling that he had just gotten there and that his leaving was premature. Then I wanted to cry and to strike him and ask him why he made me feel.

I could not continue, and I went into the bathroom to be alone, so that neither Cole nor Shawn would know. I cried for Shawn and what he was feeling or trying so hard not to feel. I cried for Cole, who cared enough to face the child's tears no matter where they led.

Cole stayed with us the next two days, and we felt like a family. We went down to Central Park, where we had gone the first day we met. Cole was pushing Shawn on the swings, and he was laughing and yelling, "Higher, higher."

I said, "Aren't you cold, Shawn? I think we should get going soon."

He protested, as he always had. "Aw, c'mon, Ma." And then he was quiet.

I thought for a minute or so that he was enjoying the sensation of soaring through the air, but Cole must have sensed something was wrong, because he moved around the periphery of the swing area to look into Shawn's face. I heard him say, "Don't cry, son. I'll get you down." But as he reached for the swing, it escaped his grasp. As I moved to face the swing, I could see my child's face contort in pain or fear, I could not tell which. Tears bathed his cheeks in a stream and dripped from his chin, yet he clutched the chain links of the swing.

"Just hold tight; we'll get you down," I said, but he did not seem to hear me. His eyes were fixed on the air in front of him, as if he saw something there that was terrifying.

Once Cole snatched the swing from midair and pulled it toward him, the boy seemed to heave in breaths, sucking in the frosted air, and making it disappear. When Cole finally stilled the swinging metal seat, he had to pry Shawn's small fingers back from the iron links in order to take him into his arms.

"I don't want you to go there. My friend Jordan said they got mines that can blow your feet off." The child took in short breaths and finally said, "It's not fair. I want you to stay here with me."

Cole tried to hold him, but he pushed himself away, as if to stand on his own feet.

"I know it isn't fair. Life isn't fair sometimes." Cole seemed to search for something more comforting to say. There was silence. "But you'll see. When I come back, we're gonna have more good times."

I pulled my son from him, needing to protect him from those promises.

"Camille, don't do that. Please. Don't do that now," Cole said. He was not imposing. He was simply steadfast. I let Shawn go and watched as my son allowed his rigid body to collapse into Cole's arms and settle there. He moaned and tried to catch his breath and shivered slightly, but in time he relaxed with his head on Cole's shoulder.

At that moment, I wanted to marry Cole just to give Shawn this daddy. It was as if they belonged together.

When we got back to the apartment, Cole took me aside in the bedroom and said, "Come on, Camille, let's get married. It'll be so much easier. Communications and everything in the service is geared to the family unit. The armed forces will take care of the family unit."

"Cole, I just feel we should wait."

"Camille, wait for what?"

"I don't know. For everything to be right."

"Camille, I don't know about right. It's as right as it's ever gonna be for me. I promise you I'll do everything I can to make it right for you too."

His words climbed inside my belly and jarred and twisted my insides. My head hurt. You're the best thing that has ever happened to my son and me, but I don't know if I love you. I cannot have you for our convenience. You deserve it to be right, I thought.

Two days passed, and my body grew calm. Somehow I felt that I would be all right, that I could handle what I had to do despite my uncertainty. The tightness in my chest dissipated. My shoulders, which had tensed into a hunch, relaxed.

The next afternoon, Cole went to his apartment to close it up and to talk to the super of the building to make sure that he would look out for everything. He seemed to have made some kind of peace with our fate. While he was gone, Saundra called and said she had closed her apartment and was planning on moving in with Les. She said he was good to her, which always seemed to surprise her for some reason. When I told her that Cole was leaving that night, she told me to hug him and kiss him for her. "Let me get off this phone," she said, seeming not to want to encroach on any of the time we still had remaining.

When Cole came back, he was pensive. He was dressed in his fatigues with the olive-green-and-brown camouflage pattern. He lifted his duffel bag off his shoulder and let it drop onto the kitchen floor just inside the door. I told him about Saundra's call, and he said, "I have a good feelin' about those two."

I studied his face to remember this time before he left.

He unzipped his duffel bag and took an envelope from inside and handed it to me. "It has my division and the temporary address they give us till we get wherever they are sending us. I put down my sister's number in Jersey. They will notify her as next of kin if anything happens, and she knows to call you immediately. There is an insurance policy in here for Shawn for college."

"Cole, you can't do this."

"I want to, Camille. Don't deny me this too."

I wanted to hold him and tell him that my not loving him was about me, not him. He was the best thing that had ever happened to me.

His dark eyes were fixed on me.

"I hope to come back. I expect to come back, but I have to be realistic about this. By the way, mail is very slow, so even if I write, it may not get here for weeks. There's a group of wives in Camp Lejeune who will try to circulate information to everyone based on any letters that they get. My buddy's wife said if you don't hear for a long time, call her and tell her who you are. She will tell you anything they know. Her number's in there too." Cole stopped talking and searched the air to see if there was anything that he had forgotten to say.

From his chest pocket he took two gold wedding bands and opened my hand and placed them in my palm. With a sense of calm resignation, he said, "It's too late now, so hold on to these until I get back."

Cole went over to the sink and ran the water and filled a glass and drank it all with his back to me. When he turned off the faucet, the room fell silent until his words sliced the air. "I know that you don't love me," he said.

"I feel I might."

"I know that too," he said, smiling to himself. "I want to ask you a favor, Camille. If you should decide that you don't want this, don't write it in a letter. Scratch that. You can write it, but don't mail it. I promise you I will accept your wishes when I get back, if that's what you want, no questions asked. I just don't know what I'm going to have to deal with over there. I don't know how I'd deal with a Dear

John letter from you." He paused. "Forget I said that." Cole studied the air in front of him and then said, "That's not right...shouldn't have said that." He looked away as if he were trying to keep back tears.

"Cole, we're going to get past this. It's gonna be OK. We're gonna be OK." My heart began to break.

"I hope so, babe."

Cole caressed my cheeks with the backs of his hands, as if he were afraid to hold me. He had tried to make love to me twice during the last few days, but he couldn't. He had held me and said he was sorry, as if I cared about the sex, except that he did. I had held him as tightly as I could those nights, hoping he could feel how close I felt to him. I remembered that embrace now, as we stood just lightly holding each other.

He kissed my lips, so gently at first that it was as if he were simply studying the sensation in order to take it away with him. Then he called Shawn, who had been so quiet in the bedroom that I thought he might have fallen asleep. He came out carrying a book. Cole lifted him up and hugged him tightly. Shawn rested his head on Cole's shoulder and then said, "I'm gonna write to you, and you write to me, OK?"

"You bet," Cole said. "And you take care of Mommy until I get back, and maybe then she'll let me help take care of her too. Work on her for me while I'm gone, OK?"

"Okeydokey."

"Hey, that's not fair, enlisting Shawn to help you," I said, trying to hold on and not let the tears I felt forming fall from my eyes.

"I'm a marine. Marines don't fight fair. We take every advantage." Cole laughed in that deep baritone voice that filled the room. "This little guy's my buddy, right?"

"Yup," Shawn said again, and though I was afraid that my child might cry, he did not. He must have been all cried out, because when Cole put him down, he just went to the bedroom and climbed into bed and went to sleep.

And then Cole left. It was not how I had pictured his leaving. He looked at me, shook his head as if he were saying no, and said, "Now I know how the guys who leave wives and kids home feel. God, this is tough." His eyes welled up.

He kissed my lips again, and then my nose as he had so many times before. He stopped to search my face a minute, picked up his bag, and threw it over his shoulder. He then opened the door, moved through the doorway, and went out.

I went to the window to watch him leave. The sky was a dark slate. He put the bag in the trunk of the rental car and then looked up toward the window. He saw me there and waved. I blew him a kiss, and then it began to happen. I felt my chin tense, and I held my thumb and forefinger over my eyelids to keep back the tears that struggled to squeeze out. I watched him drive away, not knowing if I would ever see him or touch him again. In my mind's eye, I saw his face and knew how much he loved me. It was like seeing beyond now, through both the past and the future. I felt that I had been shoring myself up, not allowing myself to attend to my feelings until he left. Now I lost my footing. I could not contain the flood of emotions that squirted every which way. They rushed about like the tide moving in to fill all available space, churning up the weeds from the ocean floor and spinning them all about and then placing them haphazardly anywhere it wished. Tears draped my eyes and made everything look crooked. Since there was nothing I needed to do, I let the sea of sadness cover me up, trusting that I could find my way through it in time.

I looked at the wedding rings I had put down on the table. I shut the light in the kitchen, unplugged the Christmas tree, and went into the bathroom. Forcing myself to look at my image in the mirror, I tried to filter out the insecurities I felt about the dark circles under my eyes and the tiny wrinkles that had formed there. Looking into my own eyes, I tried to understand the swirl of feelings. And though there was so much that I did not understand, there was one thing that I knew. I loved him, and I knew that it hurt because I knew what losing him meant. That pain was buried deep in my soul. I had felt it so early on that I had no words for it. They were gone, my father and my mother. Their loss had hollowed out the place where I had first felt love. I tried to protect my heart from that hurt again.

In the living room, I rifled through the drawer to find my box of writing paper. I pulled it out, sat down on the couch, rested the box on my lap, and wrote.

December 23, 1992

Dear Cole,

I miss you already. It is only a little more than a half hour that you have been gone. My heart is breaking.

Take care of yourself. I want you to come back to us. I never thought I could need someone so much. You have become a part of me.

When you come home, if you still want to, maybe we can take care of each other.

I love you.

Camille

Once the letter was written, it was as if I was complete. What took me by surprise was how I could feel strong and whole and distinct and still long for him so much that I ached inside.

25

JEWEL

I s that Verta I hear?

"Jewel? You're in early. What are you working on?"

She's moving past June's desk in the reception area, and I hear her footsteps coming toward my office. She's distracting me. I can't choose between these two photos.

"Jewel? Hope you're feeling a little better. We've got so much happening next week."

I have to get this done before I forget. "Ask June to come in. I need to dictate a notice."

"June's not in yet. It's barely eight o'clock."

"I know. I need to get this out first thing today."

"No problem. I'll take it down. Let me get my pad." Verta went back to her desk. I can hear her, even though her office is way down the hall.

I turned my chair around to look out the window. Gray. "I need one of my press pictures attached to it, and I'll say something about my book, my autobiography. I should call Gordon and find out his parents' names." *No, it'll be a surprise.*

"By the way, Jewel, there have been rumblings about Christmas. I don't know what you planned, but at the Christmas party today, I think—"

"Is that today? Go to Bloomingdale's. Pick up some things, scarves or something. You're sidetracking me." I have to do this now so it will be in the *New York Times* for the first of the year. They keep trying to make me forget.

"I'm kind of glad you didn't buy anything, because what I was saying is that the bookkeeper, Christina, and June would probably appreciate money, a Christmas bonus. Remember, we talked about that last year."

"Money is so...it seems too impersonal. I like the gifts. Choose something that I would choose. I can't do it this year. Just do it, Verta. Don't distract me."

"You OK, Jewel?"

"Yes!" She is making me raise my voice. "Stop distracting me. I want it to say, 'Jewel Jamison of Onyx Management, New York and Chicago, announces her wedding to Gordon Ellis of the Chicago law firm Ellis, Watkins, and Glenn. Ms. Jamison plans an early June wedding. The two will wed in New York City. Ms. Jamison, having built the largest black-owned entertainment agency, is currently working on her autobiography, which is to be published before the wedding. After the honeymoon at an undisclosed location, Ms. Jamison will do some touring to promote the book.' What do you think?"

Verta, continued writing, and when the pencil stopped, she looked up at me. Her expression was priceless. She was speechless.

"You shouldn't be surprised, Verta. Call the *New York Times*, and tell them I want it in the paper for the first of the year. It has to be in the first of the year."

"I don't think...but I'll try. Did you decide this last night? When did this happen?"

"It was a *fait accompli*. Get my file of press pictures. I don't like these. I have to choose a photo." When Verta went to retrieve the file, I opened the top desk drawer and reached to the back and to the right and pulled the pillbox out and took two of my blue pills. My hands had begun to shake again. I hate it when she questions me like a child. I need to get this done, and I need to get out of here. I can't breathe in here.

Verta put two photos on the desk. One of mine fell on the floor. I tried to catch it.

"What are you doing? Why are you so clumsy?"

"I'm showing you the ones I think you'll like. What's the matter?"

The others are falling. They are all slipping away. *I need these. I have to be the first June bride*

"Jewel, does Gordon, Mr. Ellis know about this? Leave them. I'll get them."

"Of course he does. He said, 'It's done.' But it wasn't done. Now it's done."

In the background, I heard a voice. It sounded like a bird chattering.

"What is that?"

"That's June. She said good morning and that she has only five more presents to get. Jewel, maybe you should freshen up."

I looked at the doorway, afraid that someone would enter. I smoothed my hair back.

"Jewel, did you sleep here last night? Go freshen up. People are starting to arrive."

Verta had this strange look on her face.

"Would you like me to order some breakfast for you? Some orange juice, maybe those croissants with the boysenberry preserves that you like, some coffee?"

"Boysenberries. Boysenberries. Such a funny word. No, I just want to go home. I'm going to go home. You'll take care of this for me."

"What about the Christmas party? You also had a telephone conference call meeting with George and Elena about using Nadege in the new fragrance ads."

"You take care of it. I can't do it today. This is all I came in to do."

I stood up and moved toward the coat closet, but I lost my balance.

"Jewel. Your feet are dirty. Where are your shoes?"

"My shoes? I don't know where my shoes are. I lost my shoes."

"We're going to call you a car," Verta said.

Why is she talking so slowly? "I don't want a car...need to put my head down." *Want to go home, but at home I'm alone. Nobody knows I'm there.*

"Lie down over here."

"I don't want to go home. I want to stay here. I have work to do."

"June?" Verta mumbled something. I couldn't understand her.

"What's going on?"

"We're calling Dr. Toland."

Why? I'm not sick.

"Verta, did you notice how low this ceiling is? It's pressing down on me."

I don't see what is so wrong. I just like being close to him. That's why I like to have him make love to me. Then I feel really close to him. I don't know why he called me needy. I'm not needy. Needy is when you're poor. I am not poor anymore.

"Jewel, are there any people in your family who I might talk to?"

"My family are all dead, or they should be. They don't give a damn. Did I ever tell you how they died? My mother drank and was a whore. My father said I was dead, but really he is dead."

"What about close friends?"

"No, I'm not their friend anymore. I need to get out of here."

"No, Jewel. You have to lie down. The ones at the event?"

"You remember my friends, Camille and Saundra."

"Are their numbers here in your Rolodex?"

"No. I told you, I'm not their friend."

"What happened?"

"Camille used to think she was so much better than me. Then I find out she was writing about me, telling the things she knows about me. All my secrets I told her. And all Saundra wanted was a job."

"Never mind. Dr. Toland wants us to meet him at the hospital. June, call a cab."

"I don't want to go to the hospital. I'm just tired. I just need to rest. Let's call Gordon. He will come and be with me." I just need him to come and be with me. Someone to come, and be with me.

"June, get a pair of Jewel's shoes out of her closet and put them on her feet."

"Yes, June, on my feet...and my appointment book..." Verta put on my coat. "Is it cold out? Smart girl; you got my mink."

"June, cancel the Christmas party."

"Yes. Cancel the Christmas party...I won't be coming."

26

CAMILLE

When the ball dropped, I missed it. I went to sleep at ten-thirty, because I couldn't bear to see everyone kissing and saying Happy New Year not knowing where Cole was and if he was all right. When I woke at five-thirty, the incandescent light of the street lamps still struggled to brighten the street below my kitchen window. As I watched the new day emerge out of the inked darkness, I wondered where the New Year would lead. Folding and putting away the laundry helped to pass the time. I did some writing but crumpled it and threw it away, knowing that the thoughts were forced. The now white-gray sky cloaked the building in cold, and though I could hear the steam coming up for some time, it barely warmed the space a foot from the radiator. As I stirred my second cup of tea, the phone rang. For a brief moment I thought it might be Cole and longed for the sound of his voice. I tried to snatch the thought out of the air and put it away, not wanting disappointment to drape itself about the phone each time it rang.

"Hey, lady, Happy New Year 1993." Saundra's voice was a welcome sound. "I can't believe I made it to this point. 'Member when I thought I wouldn't live this long?"

"I just can't get over how much has changed in my life. By the way, I have an appointment about my book next week. The school was a little crazy before the holidays, but I turned down the principalship. The superintendent actually called me in."

"You're kidding."

"No, it seems parents went to him, and he called me in asking my intentions, but I had just told a group of them I thought I couldn't do it because I have a young child. They understood. So I told him the same thing. He seemed relieved and said to come to him whenever I was ready."

"You're sure. Aren't you?"

"Yeah. I told you I didn't want my whole life consumed by that. Such a weight lifted off my shoulders once I did it. It blew Saul Elliott's mind. He keeps trying to figure out what the catch is. A mutual friend told me that he keeps saying to him, 'I can't figure out what she's up to!'"

"What's his story?"

"Our friend said, 'Some white folks think everybody is as involved with power as they are.' He can't understand that I liked teaching, and I like being an assistant principal. I don't need to be the boss. And right now I have other things in my life. I enjoy being with my son, and with Cole gone, he needs me. Looking forward to spending time with Cole. I need time to write...just too many other things I want to do."

"I can dig it. Speaking of jobs, I got my job back."

"What happened?"

"When Santos hurt me, I called the job and told them I had been injured by my ex-husband and that I could send them the note from the hospital emergency, but I couldn't come in. They told me to call after Christmas, and I figured, chalk it up to start again. But when I called, they said come in. They said I was one of the best receptionists they ever had and that people were asking for me. Blew my mind, girl.

And guess who called me again. Les. He asks me why I didn't call him back. I tell him how I was in the ER and about my eye, and he asks me again, so why didn't you call me?"

"He said that?"

"Yeah, so I tell him I don't want him messed up in all this crap with Santos, then I said to him, hey you don't need to be in a fight with someone like Santos. So he laughs. I say, well, to be honest, little white Jewish boys don't fight too well. He laughs again and says in Brownsville, where he grew up, he didn't take any shit or something like that. And if we are going to be together, I got to trust him to take care of us.'"

"Cole said that he's a good guy."

Saundra was quiet like she was thinking about what I said. "Yeah. I know. Then he asks me where Santos is."

"So you told him."

"I told him he was up on charges and at Rikers again. Anyway it felt better to know he still wanted me despite all that mess."

"I've been thinking about him, Saundra. I think he's a good guy too. Cole likes him a whole lot, and I trust his judgment on people. He actually reminds me of Cole."

"Camille, please. They are so different. Les is a musician, artsy, and Cole is in the military. Les is white, and Cole is black."

"I don't mean the superficial stuff. They are both steadfast. He doesn't give up on you and him. That's how Cole was. He just didn't give up, no matter what I said or did."

"Hey, Camille, I heard something on the TV last night, and I almost called you, but I decided against it."

My thoughts went to Cole. I couldn't breathe. I hoped Saundra hadn't heard that a marine unit had been hit. Before I could get my words out, Saundra went on. "On that black news show, they were doing this look back at 1992, and they said that Jewel was hospitalized last week, just before Christmas, for exhaustion. Then, you know, the gossip lady, she comes on and says, 'Sources close to Onyx management say that Jewel was hospitalized for drug and alcohol rehabilitation, while others say it was a breakdown caused by the pressure of the expansion of the business.'"

It was curious how the news affected me. It was as if I were hearing about someone I used to know but hadn't seen in years.

"Funny, I feel for her. But if I'm honest, it feels like it's my memory of her that I worry for."

"I know what you mean."

"I bet it was a breakdown. I felt she was talking out of her head," I said.

"Well, it could have been the drugs talking too. You remember the pillbox. Maybe it was the drugs."

"Wonder if she's got anybody—you know, just to be there, to bring a toothbrush and her own slippers instead of those foam-rubber hospital things. You know."

"Camille, you heard her. She doesn't need anybody."

"We all feel that way sometimes. Girl, we go way the hell back. I can't forget all those times and focus only on the falling out, now that we know she wasn't well."

"I don't know, Camille. I don't like being insulted."

"Maybe it was the breakdown. Maybe she didn't really know what she was saying. Hell, I said some things I wish I—"

"Are you forgetting everything she said? She seemed totally aware. She could remember way back to my coming to her house back in college. Did she remember what kind of shape I was in? Did she care?"

"No, I remember. That's what I mean. Her memories were so distorted."

"Right. She just remembered what was convenient. And she was always like that. She could call fast enough if she needed something, but she never remembers that."

"Saundra, if she needs my help, I can't say no. For old times' sake."

"Camille, you are too good. All I know is she really hurt me. I know I've spent time messed up, not taking your advice about school and not listening to Jewel's advice about Santos. We all made stupid mistakes with men, but she made it seem like I tried to move in on her apartment. I didn't do that, did I?"

"No, that's what I mean. I think it was the breakdown or drugs, like you said. Saundra, I just want to see her one more time."

"I don't think I want to. Whenever I see her, it reminds me of every goddamned thing I ever did wrong. And I don't know how you can want to see her, after what she said about your book. You better not write about her. You're using her."

"That's what I mean. You're using her. I'm using her. She's been in that world that we saw at Tavern on the Green so long, she thinks it's the only reality. Remember how she asked us to stay. She had nobody else. I kept saying that there was something about that night I didn't like, and I didn't like it about her either. Everyone was calculating, when they met you, what they could get out of the conversation. Everybody had a card, selling something. Buying something. No wonder she thinks we're using her. 'Member how she said those models were hers, like property. That's what her world is about. I'm sure that causes breakdowns."

"Well, you don't have to kick me twice. She seemed real happy in that world."

"It may be...if she did have a breakdown, she might see things differently."

I tried to put into words how I had tried to piece together my pictures of the past. I had sorted through many of the snapshots my memory held of the days on Hancock Street and City College and the recollections of telephone conversations when I visualized my friends as they were, never being changed by time. I was missing only this last photo of Jewel. I needed to know if she was the person I remembered, or if she was the person she seemed to be the last time I had seen her. "I just need to see her one more time."

"I've got my own troubles right now anyway. My mom says she's not gonna let me have Wanda if I move in with Les."

"Maybe she's just thinking that you should see if this is working before you bring Wanda into it."

"No. I told her that I thought it was a good idea to see if this was real."

"That makes sense."

"I know that. But she said she didn't care how it worked. She wasn't sending her grandchild to live with some white man and me. She said I still hadn't grown up, that I was living in some 'hippy-dippy' land. That's what she said. I tried to tell her to meet him and get to know him, but she said that she didn't want me to bring him to the house and have her neighbors talking about her daughter and her white men."

"What does she mean, white men? Have you gone out with any other white men?"

"No…that's my mother…always exaggerating. She's holding on to Wanda."

Her words made me remember my grandmother and the things she said about my mother. "So what are you going to do?"

"I don't know. I just feel like Les is so good for me. I'm calm when I'm with him. Just calm. But I can't lose my daughter. My life is never easy."

"I didn't know your mother was into this black-white thing."

"I don't remember her ever making any big deal about it either. But know what I learned? You don't know who's gonna make a big thing about it till they see you together. I think she just wants to keep Wanda there with her."

"Where are you now? Where are you calling from?"

"I'm at Les's. He played a New Year's Eve gig and then came home about four. I wanted to start my New Year here. You really want to go to see Jewel? She's at a hospital upstate, just out of the city. At least that's what they said on that show. They said the name of the hospital. It must be well known or something."

"Saundra, will you go with me?"

"Camille, you're the goodest one of the three of us."

"Get out of here. I'm not…I don't know…so perfect. I don't think I treated Cole as well as I should have. Or my mother, for that matter."

"Hey, I'm not callin' you a saint. I wouldn't be running buddies with a saint." Saundra laughed out loud.

"You know, Camille, no matter how long it's been that we haven't spoken—to each other, I mean—it's like it was yesterday. Maybe we can put this aside, this thing with Jewel, but I don't think so."

"I need to go, just to see if the picture of Jewel I have in my head was real or not."

"I don't know. I need to think about it." She paused, and the quiet filled my ear. Then she spoke again. "I take it you haven't heard from Cole."

"No. He said it might be a while." Without thinking about why, I said, "I'm going to marry him, if he still wants to, when he gets back."

"All I have to say is, it's about time. I like him a whole lot. He's real. And you could tell he loves the hell out of you. He was telling Les about some conversation you had with someone from school, and he was saying how you won them over with logic and charm. And then he said, with this big smile on his face, 'My lady can talk that talk.'"

I felt a blush fill my cheeks, and I couldn't help smiling. Cole always made me feel that what I did was somehow extraordinary. That was so new to me that I had to grow into enjoying it.

"He's like you said. He's good to me and to Shawn. And I almost can't believe it, 'cause I think maybe something terrible will happen and he won't come back. He kept asking me what I was waiting for. Why I wouldn't marry him. I just hope I didn't wait too long."

"Don't think that way."

"I try not to."

"At least you told him you would marry him before he left."

"I didn't. I didn't know until he left. I wrote it in a letter to him."

We were both quiet again. The stillness seemed to grow between us. I wished that time had permitted me to know myself sooner. Then I thought about how foolish that wish was.

I thought about my decision to go to see Jewel in the hospital, and I hoped Saundra would go with me. I needed to go. I needed to know that my memories of the three of us, like old photographs so neatly tucked away, were real.

✆

Saundra and I picked up Jewel at four in the morning, and we cabbed it downtown to the railroad station. We had spoken on the phone the day before. Saundra said how she had told Santos that her mother was sick and she had to go be with her in Brooklyn. She distracted him, pretending to clean the apartment, putting things away and at the same time finding the dollars and coins she had hidden, and stuffed them into her bra and her dungarees.

"If he finds out I'm lying, he'll kill me, Camille."

"Maybe you shouldn't..."

"I want to be there for Jewel. Shit, I know what it's like to do this by yourself."

Jewel looked exhausted once we could actually see her face in the light of Penn Station. She had dark circles under her eyes. She seemed confused. I used the money Lil had given me to buy the tickets to Washington. The three of us slept most of the way to DC. It was as if we were going to a funeral.

When we got to Washington, we got a cab to the address, which looked like a regular row house. "You sure this is it?" I asked Jewel.

"This is the address Eric gave me."

"Can you wait a few minutes?" Saundra asked the driver.

"Gonna have to charge for the wait."

"Never mind."

The address on the paper and the white painted numbers above the door matched, although there was no indication that it was a doctor's office. A woman with curly gray hair peeped through the curtains at us and opened the door. "Can I help you?"

Saundra whispered, "Dr. Simms's office?"

The woman—short, heavyset, white, in her fifties or sixties—looked out onto the street after us and let us in. She directed us toward the end of the hall. "Who's here to see the doctor?" she asked, stopping midpoint. Saundra and I pointed at Jewel, who had walked ahead of us. "Then you two will have to leave and come back in three hours."

"We have to wait with her," Saundra said.

"We've come from New York, and she's all alone," I added.

"You'll have to wait elsewhere. We don't have room for..." She shook her head in annoyance. "Be back at twelve thirty."

"Jewel, will you be OK?" Saundra said.

"We'll be right outside, down the block...that coffee shop," I said.

Jewel turned and looked at us. Her eyes had been lifeless all day. Now she seemed trapped in fear.

"Think she'll be all right?" Saundra asked. She lit up a Salem, and we crossed the street toward the diner.

"I hope so." I dug out my pack and lit one too, stopping and cupping my hand around the match to protect the flame.

"She's so messed up...hardly said a word all the way here."

"Wonder if Eric gave her the money."

In the coffee shop, the counter was almost full with people laughing and talking. The cash register keys made that cha-ching sound as the drawer flew open and then closed as folks paid their bills and grabbed their coffees to go. The place was warm and smelled of coffee and bacon and cigarette smoke. A heavyset black woman with a full face, her bangs pomaded flat on her forehead, wearing a white waitress's paper crown, came over to us. "Counter or booth?"

"Booth," Saundra said.

She grabbed two menus and walked down the aisle. As we passed the first one, two women were looking at the back page of newspaper, and one broke into a laugh. "Just hit 225 for a dollar and not tellin' my husband one thing 'bout it."

"You don't want Ray to know, you shouldn't be talkin' so loud," a big, dark-skinned man with a mustache at the next table said, turning around and laughing.

"You know what's good for you, Buster Lightfoot, you'll keep your big mouth shut," she said right back, not missing a beat.

"Coffee?" The waitress handed us the plastic-covered, one-page menus.

"Yes, please. Two eggs over easy with bacon," I said handing, it back without looking.

"Grits or home fries? Juice comes with that at no extra, on the special."

"Home fries, and I guess orange juice, please."

"I'll have scrambled eggs with sausage and grits. Orange juice for me too," Saundra said.

"Where y'all from?" the waitress asked in a bit of a Southern drawl, jotting our order on her green pad.

"New York."

She laughed and put her pencil behind her ear. "Thought so. Be back with your juice and coffee."

"You know Jewel didn't mention Eric at all. I wonder if he showed," I said.

"He must've, or we wouldn't be...I counted it up. I had about two hundred ten and spent about twenty on cabs. I still have about a hundred-eighty something. But we need cab money," Saundra said.

"You're right. If she didn't have the money, she wouldn't have gone in there like that."

"She must have it, 'cause they usually get their money up front."

The waitress brought the juice and then the coffee. "Eggs are coming up."

"Thanks. Yeah, they would've sent her right out if she didn't have it," she added.

We sat quietly while the reality of where we were set in. The waitress brought us two huge platters of food, mine with thick bacon and a mound of home fries and toast. Saundra's half plate of grits had a big pat of butter that melted into pools of yellow.

"We won't need to eat till tonight sometime," Saundra said, laughing.

We took our time eating and ordered another cup of coffee. Saundra told me how when she got the money back from Jewel, she was saving toward this modeling school she had seen in the paper. "I need two hundred forty-nine dollars, the ad says. They say they get you jobs in print and runway. I don't know if I'm tall enough though…five eight. Not tall enough, right?"

"With print, height doesn't matter," I said, trying to encourage her.

"I guess. You know, I don't think I ever saw a black model in a magazine 'cept *Ebony* and *Jet*."

The morning crowd thinned out. The waitress said, "You waitin' for somebody, right?"

I felt she was telling us she knew why we were there.

"Yeah," Saundra said, before I could answer.

"Figured. The owner's not here this mornin', so I'll keep the coffee comin'. I'll take care of you. You take care of me, OK, honey?"

"You got it. Thanks," Saundra said.

"Yeah, thank you so much." I leaned in to whisper to Saundra, "She knows."

"I hope Jewel's OK after this."

"Whatever it is, at least we're here."

"Yeah, when I did it, I was all alone. And 'member, you were afraid to tell me till a coupla days before," Saundra said as if it were yesterday.

The images of the apartment up on 129th Street in Harlem, with its blood-red painted door and the old mattress with its stuffing spilling out on the floor, filled my mind. The woman—they called her Nurse Mary, I didn't know if that was her real name—had a metal speculum on the kitchen table with those metal instruments. "D'you take the pain killers I gave you, and that other pill?"

I nodded.

"Where's the rest of the money?"

I dug the $300 out of my dungarees pocket. She counted it and put it in her bra. Once the images started, I couldn't stop them.

"Take off the pants and your panties." She made me climb onto the table, and she pushed in the speculum. It was cold, and it hurt. She screwed it open, put on the rubber gloves, and pushed my knees apart with her elbow. Then came the pain, the clawing pain. I began to scream and reached up to cover my mouth.

"Don't you make no sounds, you hear me," she said. "Don't want nobody callin' the police up in here."

I closed my eyes and bit my hand. A moan escaped my lips.

I looked up at Saundra so as not to see the things that I remembered. She was staring at the air too.

"Can I get another coffee?" I lifted my hand to get the waitress's attention.

"Yeah. Me too," Saundra said.

"Sure, here you go," she said, filling both our cups.

As Saundra's eyes met mine, I said, "Just had some bad memories."

"So did I."

I twisted the napkin, then the empty matchbook. We smoked about five cigarettes and drank another cup of coffee. The restroom was clean the first time I went in. By the second time, people had left pieces of toilet paper on the floor and paper towels next to the wastebasket. We left the waitress a five-dollar tip. She smiled, thanked us, and said, "Good luck."

We then decided to walk around the block to waste some more time. And by the time we got back, it was twelve thirty. A white girl who looked to be in her twenties left the house with a woman in her forties. The gray-haired woman gestured for us to wait and disappeared. A few minutes later, Jewel came out. Her eyes looked dead.

We tried to tell her that we knew how she felt. Saundra said she had done it last year, and it really messed up her head for a long time. I told her we would stay with her the night, and not to worry. We went back to New York on the railroad. We all had the feeling that people knew what we had done. When we got back to Jewel's apartment, we asked her if she had cramps. She lay in her bed and stared at the ceiling. We sent her to check if she was bleeding a lot. She did as she was told, but her voice had been taken away. We tried to rub her arms, but she flinched when we touched her. So we sat with her and watched the silent tears, gave her tissues to wipe them away, and waited until she would come back.

27

CAMILLE

T he cold had a color. It stuck its gray self all over everything. As the train left Grand Central Station and emerged from the tunnel, the city's red-gray buildings arrayed themselves against the white-gray sky. Outside the city, the black-gray trees etched themselves into the brown-gray soil on the edge of the slate-gray river. The cold then pushed itself in through the windows, hung in the air, and pasted itself everywhere.

My eyes diverted from the moving gray palette to take in the bouquet of flowers I had bought for Jewel at the Korean market on Sixth Avenue. I had asked them to mix the ones I pointed to—first the cobalt-blue ones, then the yellow ones, and then the crimson-painted daisies. It had not been the exact mix I would have made had I grown them myself, but they were colorful and fragrant, and they warmed the area just around them.

I can't wait for June. Cole once told me that he wants his own place with some land around it, because he had moved around so much. He wanted a workshop room in which to build things. I thought that if I were to live there with him, I would grow wildflowers on the land. I wanted to see them everywhere. I wanted to know them all by name so that I might speak of them more personally.

It was a strange feeling going to the hospital to see Jewel, not knowing how she was. Saundra was supposed to meet me at the

125th Street station, but when the train pulled in, she wasn't there. I figured that she must have changed her mind about going. She and Jewel had always been like oil and water. I had tried to hold them together for so long. Today it felt as if I could finally give that up.

There was a finality about this trip. The train traveled north, and the river collected floes of ice until it froze over and became a white-gray mass. The river of ice separated the land upon which the train traveled and the dark-gray hilly mounds across the river, which held up the sky. As we pulled into Croton, I adjusted my scarf, wrapping it tighter 'round my neck, and pulled on my gloves, pushing them down into the Vs of my fingers. In front of the station, I looked for a taxicab. None was there, so I backtracked to the ticket window and asked the man for the number to call one. He pointed out the public phone in the corner of the waiting room and said the number was scratched into the wall. When I told the dispatcher I needed a cab at Croton on the Hudson Station, she laughed. "We got no other. Be there...five minutes."

I doubled back to the ticket window. "Excuse me, is this where I get the six p.m. train back to the city?"

"What city?" he said.

For a moment I didn't understand why he was asking, and I said, "New York City."

"Thought that's what you meant," he said, looking at me as if he had made a point. He then said, with a veiled smirk, "There are other cities in the state, you know. Albany, Rochester, Buffalo." And then he looked back down at his tickets and slips of paper that he seemed to be playing at sorting. "Yep. The six-o'clock leaves from here."

The cold air penetrated my cloth coat and made the bones in my hands hurt as I waited for the cab. Moving from side to side trying to keep my feet from freezing, I could not stop the images of Jewel and Saundra and myself from appearing in my mind. I remembered the times when we had hung out in the cafeteria, or went down to the Village and drank coffee in big mugs at the

Figaro, or had drinks in the Ninth Circle and ate peanuts. Artists drew us, and young men tried to pick us up. We were like wonderful natural adornments on the face of the earth, to attract attention and to be enjoyed. I recalled the times at Jewel's apartment when we shared secrets and discovered the nuances of our own beauty. Then the last night at B. Smith's replayed itself, and it seemed so out of place. I could see Jewel's face as she said "You used me," and it struck me in the chest again. That comment did not fit my understanding of what we had experienced together. I hoped that I might better understand it once I saw her today.

An old, dirty, maroon-colored station wagon pulled up to the station, and the driver, an elderly white man with craggy skin, opened up the passenger-side window and asked, "You call a cab?" I told him the name of the hospital, and he said, "That will be seven dollars." He looked at me as if he were challenging me to say different. I nodded, and he said in an off-handed way, "Door's open." His car seemed to strain and groan its way up the slopes, and it struggled not to get away as he shifted gears when it went downhill. He occasionally took surreptitious sidewise glances at me in the rearview mirror. He did not speak, and he seemed to view me with mistrust. I didn't attempt to engage him in conversation. I left him to his furtive glances and fantasies while I studied the creased, thick, reddened skin on the back of his neck and the tired manner he manipulated the wheel and the stick as he shifted gears.

The bare trees laced the air and patterned themselves against the sturdy evergreens. The birches seemed at home, bending alternately to the right and to the left, the branches disappearing themselves in the white-gray sky. He finally pulled alongside a wall of poplars that stood tall and straight, lined up next to a gate that swung open onto wooded grounds. We pulled up to a rather stately looking building with a huge bare weeping willow just in front of it.

This place is certainly secluded, I thought as I handed the driver ten dollars and told him to keep the change.

"Do you have a card? So I can call."

He handed me a small card stamped with his number. As I got out of the cab, Saundra came out of the front door and whispered in my ear, "I thought you'd never get here. Do you see this place?"

"What happened to you?"

"I got a call from the prosecutor."

"What happened?"

"It seems that Santos accepted the charges, no plea or anything. He got beat up real bad by someone in Rikers, and they messed up his face, and his left arm was dislocated and broken, and his back is messed up. So anyway, he's going upstate for the duration. He got twenty-five years."

"You're kidding."

"Nope."

"Saundra, I am so happy this is over, finally over."

"I can't believe it myself. Anyway, I was late, so Les drove me. I'm a little numb from hearing this news about Santos. And we got lost, but I guess we did better than you did with the train and all. For a while there, I thought you weren't coming."

"When you didn't show, I figured you decided not to come."

"I think that's why I was so late. I just couldn't get myself out of the house. But I wouldn't let you come alone. Let's get inside."

We pushed open the door. "Did you ask about her condition? And where's Les?"

"No, I didn't ask. Les just dropped me off a little while ago and went back home. He has a gig later. I told them I was waiting for another visitor, waiting for you. I don't even know if they will let us see her."

"Why do you say that?"

"Just look at this place. I haven't seen many visitors, and they don't look as if they get many black folks visiting here."

"Did they say something to you?"

"No, just a vibe, Camille. You'll see."

"Well, here goes. We're here to see Jewel Jamison, please," I said, resting my hands on the immaculate powder-blue counter.

The nurse, a white woman in her fifties with blond hair that was combed back into a French roll, asked, "Is Ms. Jamison expecting you?"

"Not really. We're old friends, and we heard she was ill and thought we'd visit."

"Your names, please."

"Camille Warren and Saundra Farrell."

"Would you have a seat over there, please?" The woman sat down at the desk and dialed a number as she looked over at us. She nodded, glanced at us again, and hung up the phone.

"Ms. Jamison said she *will* see you. She is here to rest, but you may go up for a short visit. Here is your visitor's pass. Please return it to this desk when you are leaving. She is in room 254. Please use the elevator just over there."

"Well, excuse me!"

"Saundra, stop."

"You were worried that she shouldn't be wearing hospital slippers. Let's ask her to let us move in. I'll have a breakdown right here, right now."

"Saundra, you stop it right this minute."

"Hey, am I gonna say anything? She'll accuse me of trying to live in her hospital room. Poor you—you were probably envisioning... what was that movie with that woman in the insane asylum? *Snake Pit* or *One Flew Over the Cuckoo's Nest* or something. I'm telling you, Jewel is all right. She always lands on her feet."

Upstairs there was another desk, and a nurse in shoulder-length black hair combed into a pageboy, wearing a starched white uniform. She looked at us over the tops of lenses shaped like half moons. "Ms. Jamison is expecting you," she said, pointing down the carpeted corridor, which appeared to be more of a plush hotel than a hospital.

We walked down the hallway and tapped on the door. Hearing Jewel's voice say "Come in," I pushed the door open. The room was spacious, like a large sitting room in a hotel suite. There was a hospital bed, which was adjusted with the head in an upright position. Jewel was seated in an armchair wearing a silky turquoise kimono-type robe over a matching nightgown. Her hair was lightly curled and resting on her shoulders. Her makeup was faint but perfectly applied.

Saundra looked around and then at me. I did my best to indicate with my eyes that this was not the time for her to make one of her comments.

"Jewel, what are you doing in the hospital? You look terrific," I said, trying to speak quickly before Saundra got a word out.

"I was just thinking that I want whatever it is that you've got," Saundra said shamelessly.

"Saundra, you are incorrigible," I said, shooting a look in her direction and handing Jewel the flowers.

"I was just tired," Jewel said. "I just needed a rest."

"I feel so much better, now," I said as I sat down on the love-seat-sized couch. "I was worried about how you were. Whether you had, you know, all your own little toiletries and stuff."

"Yes, old Camille thought you had to wear those foam-rubber hospital slippers," Saundra added.

"I'm fine. My assistant brought me some things a week or so ago, and I had them send over more things when I transferred here. My beautician came and did my hair." Jewel was distant. There was an air of unreality to her demeanor that suggested that she was not quite herself.

"I should have known you would have been able to get whatever you needed," I said.

"But what happened?" Saundra asked.

"Working fifteen-hour days, flying to Chicago, and having my clock all screwed up."

"You know they're saying you're in rehab for drugs."

"Saundra…"

"No, Camille," Saundra said. "She should know it, so that she can protect herself once she comes out of the hospital."

"I know. I heard. I *was* taking Valium sometimes to relax, so they did give me something for that."

Jewel's eyes seemed to travel off to some strange place. There seemed to be thoughts that she was concealing. I looked at Saundra and could tell she noticed it too.

"A woman in my group told me that it was real hard to get off Valium," Saundra said. "She was having anxiety attacks and then feeling depressed as hell. Are they giving you anything, any therapy? It helped me a lot."

Saundra always had a way of being so direct that it made me feel uncomfortable. But as I studied Jewel's face, I couldn't tell what, if any, effect Saundra's attempts at conversation were having.

"How do you feel? Do you feel better?" I asked.

"They gave me Prozac, and it helps. Like I said, I'm fine. I'm going to stay put for another week. My assistant is handling virtually everything. The business is fine. How are you two?"

"I'm back at work," Saundra said.

"I'm working too. Decided not to pursue the principalship right now. So I know money's gonna be tight, but what else is new. Hope to be getting married when Cole comes back in June."

"Money is always tight with you guys," Jewel said, as if she were citing a character flaw. "I think I'm going to have to cancel my wedding plans. A few tiny snags." She paused for effect. "His wife and two kids."

"Get outta here." Saundra laughed.

"Serious business." Jewel chuckled.

"Isn't he the one you were talking about that night you called me? I told you that then," I said.

"Well, I'm not as smart as you, Camille." There was a slight edge in Jewel's voice. "It took me sitting here alone a week or two to figure that out. I called him and had my secretaries call to tell him I was in the hospital, and guess what? Nothing. No flowers, no nothing."

There was silence. I didn't know what to say.

"But not to worry. You have got to see the doctor I met in New York Hospital when I was transferring here. About six foot two, dark skinned, gorgeous as can be, a cardiologist. I already found out from the nurses that he's divorced, or in the process, and God knows my heart is broken. I need a cardiologist."

"I don't believe you. How did you find out all of that so fast?" Saundra laughed.

"Jewel, give yourself a break. Just wait until you're better and you feel strong."

"I'm strong, Camille. I'll be heading out of here in about a week. My beautician's promised me he'll come back and do me again before I leave, and my manicurist is coming in to do my nails. I'm fine and dandy."

"Is the bathroom in here?" Saundra asked, looking at me as if to say leave well enough alone.

I thought for a few minutes and then said, "Jewel, do you remember the night at B. Smith's?"

"Yes. What of it?" Jewel sat up, and her visage reflected the recollection, and her eyes took on a harder stare.

"Did you really think Saundra and I have been using you, or that I would use you like you said?"

Jewel smiled. "Camille, I always think about that. When the phone rang and the nurse downstairs said you were here, I thought, what do they want?"

"What makes you think that?"

"Experience. My whole life, my whole world has been someone using me. My aunt and uncle used me for the Social Security money they got to keep me. In my business, when someone calls me, I know they want something, and I'm thinking what can I get in return. They use me. I use them. You can't open up *Vogue* or *Mademoiselle*— or a JCPenney catalog, for that matter—and see black women, yourself, if it weren't for a deal. What do I want, and what do they want. I use them. They use me. That's all it is."

"You know, Jewel, I've told you this before, but I'll say it again. I'm real proud of you, that you've put black women in the media. But those women, those images, are not me. And they're not a lot of black women and other women of color that I know. Forget black, white. They're not the women I see every day working and struggling to get their kids educated and keep a roof over their heads and, and food in the fridge. When I open those books and magazines, I do not see me, or them. We're not glamorous enough. We have to be made over to even fit your image of what a woman is. And you know what? Those deals—what you want and what they want—have nothing to do with what I was talking about. I wasn't talking about business. I was talking about *friendship*."

"Friendship?" Jewel laughed out loud.

"Don't laugh. I'm serious. You know, I kept trying to understand how you could sleep with Derrick. Hearing that hurt me so much, and I tried to put it aside, thinking we were kids when it happened. Those were different times. Then I started thinking that I couldn't trust you with Cole, and it scared me, but I still set it aside because in my mind, this was thirty years of friendship. You might have had too much to drink. You were unhappy that night. But for you, the last thirty years was just a series of transactions, wasn't it? Just so you know, sometimes people give *without* expecting or wanting anything in return."

"Well, you couldn't tell by me," Jewel said.

"I can't believe that a lifetime of friendship gets distorted that way for you."

Saundra was now standing at the bathroom door listening.

"Jewel, you wasted so much time."

"What do you mean by that, Saundra?"

"I mean we didn't want anything. Hey, let me speak for myself. *I* didn't want anything. When I came over to your house, I figured you were a friend and your house was where we could talk, where we could just be ourselves."

I felt the need to try to reach for Jewel one more time. "Last time I said this, you didn't seem to hear it. Jewel, I thought of you as my sister."

"I find this so tedious. Let's remember the first time I met you, Camille, you attacked me. I never really trusted you, Saundra, from day one. You instigated trouble. And Camille, in my mind, you were the little girl who gave my aunt your old clothes for me to wear."

Thirty years telescoped, and I remembered the dress she was wearing the day of the fight, the dress my grandmother had folded up and placed in a box. I had never mentioned it.

"Well, Camille, I don't need anything from you, or from you, Saundra. As you can clearly see, I am fine without you."

"I told you," Saundra said, loud enough for Jewel to hear.

"I don't know how you can think the way you do."

Jewel looked at me and said, "That's why you are where you are, and I am where I am."

The comment struck me and made me smile inside at the irony.

The nurse came in with a tray holding two small paper cups, one for medication and one for water. "Ms. Jamison, your afternoon medication." I watched Jewel place the pills on the back of her tongue and swallow. The nurse then took her wrist and monitored her pulse, studying her wristwatch. "I think it's time for you to get some rest," she said, looking over at Saundra and me in a clear indication that we should go. She turned down the covers on the bed.

"They were just leaving," Jewel said, seizing the authority.

There was no need for good-byes. I walked to the elevator, with Saundra following. We called the cab from the phone booth in the lobby and waited for it to arrive. The same driver pulled up to the hospital doors. We got into the taxi and sat in silence. It was the same at the station, and on the long train ride home. We didn't talk much or laugh on the way back. We both knew that something died that day, and our mourning required quiet reflection.

At the 125th Street station, we parted. We hugged. But it was different without Jewel somewhere in our arms. Saundra headed for the train to Les's. I decided to leave Shawn at his friend's house for a little while longer and walked from 125th down to 110th Street to enjoy the quiet in my apartment. The sun had broken through the clouds and was now resting somewhere beneath the horizon, having left a peach-colored blush in the lavender-blue sky. I stopped on my way in and reflexively opened the mailbox, taking out the envelopes I had not retrieved on Saturday. I opened the apartment door, flipped the switch on the kitchen light, and rested the envelopes on the table. The airmail envelope, with its red-and-blue chevron-shaped design, stood out from the rest. Seeing Cole's handwriting, I wanted to grab it and rip it open, but I feared tearing important bits of it away. So I sat down and carefully tore off the edge along the right-hand side to take out the letter.

January 8

Dear Camille,

I just got your letter. I can't wait to get home. You've made me so happy. I'm walking around here, and the guys say I'm just smiling back. I couldn't believe how fast it got to me. They must be trying real hard to get communications up and running because of morale around here during the holidays.

It's cold here at night. I wear the sweater you got me. We're real busy setting up the administrative compound. It's kind of lonely, especially for the young fellas. Met one kid from Brooklyn, 17, I recruited. He tells me he never had a girlfriend. Of course, he didn't say it that way. So I told him we were going to have to set him up on a date when we get home. I'm not gonna feel right till that kid gets home safe.

The civilians seem glad for us to be here. Maybe we can do some good. It looks like they want us to help stop the fighting, and there are a lot of women who are looking for their children and their husbands. They carry pictures and show them to us. After a while they all are beginning to look almost alike. Of course they all also need food, and we've been doing our best to get it out to them. It's kind of sad seeing families like this.

I'm counting the days till June. Kiss Shawn for me.

I love you and miss you.

Love,

Cole

I thought about how long it had taken me to let Cole love me. I remembered what I had told Jewel, "Sometimes people give without expecting or wanting anything in return." I had always seen myself as the one who gave, maybe being a teacher and all. It felt safe and easy to give. What was harder for me was to receive. Cole had taught me to accept goodness given to me, and I loved him for it. The lesson deepened the meaning of giving for me.

For a moment, I felt as if my whole body was sensitive, as if I could feel all of the clothing resting on each pore. I was no longer lost in a blur. My sense of myself as part of a threesome had dissolved away into a memory. Neither Jewel nor Saundra felt as I did about those times together so long ago. I embraced the past even as I let go of the illusions that those images were shared. My memories were mine alone. And then I looked down at Cole's letter. It felt odd to stand alone yet feel connected to someone else. But the more I thought about it, the more I knew it felt right.

WILDFLOWERS

Some people cultivate wild wildflowers.
No incongruity.
To splash magenta, maize, and lavender blue in a ver-
dant field.
Placing painted faces with delicate silken petals
Unfolding, exposing velvet amber centers to the cool
pale light of dawn.
Wildflowers dance, you know.
Their stems sway in the breeze like hips sashaying.
Unmolested loveliness,
Placed for your delight.
No inconsistency.
Put, place, plant them everywhere there is a slit of
soil,
So that we might drink their color, quench our thirst,
and watch them dance.
Rampant, rapturous beauty.

The End

ABOUT THE AUTHOR

Delores Lowe Friedman was born in Brooklyn, New York and attended the New York City public schools. She earned her bachelor's and master's degrees from Hunter College of the City University of New York. She holds a doctorate from Teachers College, Columbia University. She has taught in New York City public schools and as a full professor at the City University of New York. An advocate for parental involvement, she authored an education column for *Essence* magazine called "Education by Degrees" and a book titled *Education Handbook for Black Families, published by Doubleday.* Her academic and scholarly writings are centered on an interest in equity in science education for girls and children of color.

Now retired, Delores has returned to her first love: writing fiction. She and her husband of forty-four years live in New York City, and the two have a son who is a software engineer.

Made in the USA
Columbia, SC
06 April 2022

58602473R00226